I, Destiny

Alessandro Abate

Copyright © 2012 Alessandro Abate
Image on cover © 2012 Alessandro Abate

All rights reserved. No part of this publication may be reproduced in any form or by any means without the prior permission of the author.

This is a work of fiction. Names, characters, corporations, institutions, organizations, events or locales in this novel are either the product of the author's imagination or, if real, used fictitiously. Any resemblance to actual person (living or dead) is entirely coincidental.

ISBN-13: 978-1475101768
ISBN-10: 1475101767

DEDICATION

This novel is dedicated to my father, my mother and my nieces Gina, Guia and Sara

ACKNOWLEDGMENTS

Daniela and Linda, thank you so much for your encouragement

ONE

'The happening is concealed, unobserved, in the perfect harmony of things'

Alex bowed, shut his eyes and convinced himself that he could hear the applause. Then the door opened, breaking the spell and ending his reverie.

"Wake up, Alex! We need to lock up," Joe Hammond said. He was the owner of the theatre, a somewhat introverted man of mid-fifties, slightly overweight, with a round face, and a thinning crop of hair that had once been almost black. He was standing in Alex's line of vision for a moment, backlit by the lights from the hallway. He had rounded shoulders, making him look hunched over or perhaps frustrated with Alex's presence; Alex couldn't tell which.

Joe turned the lights off and Alex left the room.

"Is there anyone left downstairs?" Alex asked.

Joe shook his head and went back into his office. The door stayed half open, and Alex was able to glimpse inside without being noticed. Joe was sitting in front of the computer, overwhelmed by hundreds of papers, in a room about a metre wide by two metres long lit up by a flickering light.

"Are you still here?" Joe didn't even turn around. He simply sensed Alex's presence.

Alex gathered up his courage and pushed open the door. He was not nearly as imposing as Joe, as he stood in Joe's office. He was in his late twenties, somewhat athletic of frame. He sported a head of dark, curly hair, with intense brown eyes and thick eyebrows. He had a beautiful smile, framed by full lips and slightly dark complexion, inheritance of his Italian mother.

"Can I help you Joe?" he asked.

"I need three things right now," Joe said, trying to be definite and forceful. "I need a son, a proper theatre, and a ton of money to maintain them all. You decide where to start."

Joe was the owner of the *Etcetera*, a small theatre that occupied the same building as *The Oxford Arms,* the pub where Alex worked, ten minutes exactly from the Camden tube stop. One could enter directly from the pub or from a door to the outside, and then by going through a twisted staircase, one reached the acting space that could hold at most forty people, arranged on five rows of raised benches. It was often hired out to young actor workshops and was much the same as other places like it in the city. The people called them *'Fringe Theatres,'* off the West End, outside of the main circuit, where one could experiment with one's acting, hoping that sooner or later some important theatre manager would take notice and buy the show.

Camden was a special place. It was at the centre of everything, from the wealthy to the poor, from the splendid townhouses that ran between Regent's Park to Primrose Hill, to the grey, anonymous buildings of King's Cross Saint Pancras. The *Etcetera* was situated on Chalk Farm Road, which filtered out this tension and liberated it with the energy of its colourful houses redolent of the hippy/punk scenes of years past and the little markets in which one found everything. Certainly, there were places that were much more beautiful, but for Alex, Camden's slightly Bohemian art-deco style was like a perfect sketch.

He walked out the door and was struck by the cold. He could sense that snow was in the air.

"Hey, Alex!"

It was Joel, whom everybody called Sketch because he designed cartoons. He was thin, with sandy, curly hair and light blue eyes. He had freckles on his face, and he loved to wear clothes slightly larger than his size.

"Sorry I didn't make it. How did it go?"

Alex hesitated, making Joel even more curious.

"Do you feel like getting a drink?" Joel asked.

"I'm a little tired but maybe tomorrow," Alex answered. He didn't say anything more and continued on his way.

"A man on his own walks a long way," Joel said, "trying to find some answers to his deepest thoughts. So will you audition with Joe?"

He almost let himself be persuaded, but Joel's laughter made him withdraw once more.

* * *

Alex Marler's flat was small and old with wooden floorboards that squeaked every time his feet made contact with them. It had one window with a view that looked out on the wall of the building opposite, giving just a hint of light to a space that otherwise would be just like a closet. But he was happy because entering that room meant the end of his eight-hour shift at the pub. He took off his jacket, removed a file from a shelf, which was in a fissure concealed in the wall, and sat down on the sofa. There was nothing better than moments like these when he finally found time to himself to read the scripts that Joe gave him every time the *Etcetera* put on a production. Acting was his passion, the only thing that kept him on his feet at night and the only reason he worked in a pub for four pounds, fifty an hour. He took out some sheets of paper and started to read, but a few minutes later, overcome with exhaustion, he fell asleep.

* * *

The following day he again caught up with Joel, his only friend, whose sometimes strange ways and weird behaviour made him seem like a cartoon character. They met up in Regent's Park, which was west of Camden at the foot of Primrose Hill. They walked around the park's Inner Circle, which ran alongside Queen Mary's Garden, and stopped by the entrance of the Open Air Theatre.

"Are you tired of walking?" Joel asked.

"Give me five minutes. I want to take a look," Alex said, already casting his eyes towards the theatre.

The gate was closed, but Alex rested against the bars, as if he wanted to push his soul beyond the barrier.

"They put on Shakespeare comedies here," he said.

"And we are going to die here if we don't go," Joel added, with a pleading tone. "It is absolutely freezing."

It was definitely time to go. It was not only cold but it had also become dark.

"I would sell my soul to act in this theatre," Alex said.

"Why don't you start by speaking to Joe?"

He turned and walked with Joel towards the park exit.

* * *

At precisely eleven o'clock the following morning, Alex started his shift at *The Oxford Arms* and began to serve the morning regulars, as well as casual passers-by, taking a moment's respite from the freezing cold. The door that led to the floor above opened, and Joe entered the pub followed by three others.

"Hey, Joe! Can I get you something?" Alex said, going up to the men.

"Four pints."

Nothing else, just 'four pints' without even saying good morning, Alex thought as he went back behind the bar to fill the glasses. Joe meanwhile spoke with his three guests, and it was clear that he was negotiating a price: one hundred pounds for the lights, ten for the smoke generator, but a discount if they hired the space for the entire week.

Alex had witnessed the scene dozens of times; he had read scripts and helped out at many rehearsals, and nobody would have noticed any difference if he had had this conversation instead of Joe. He and Joe were very close, even if neither of them showed much affection for the other. Alex was the son that Joe had always wanted; Joe was the father that Alex had never had. It was for this reason that Joe made him come up and give a glance in the theatre when nobody was rehearsing.

Alex put the four pints on a tray and took them to the table. He served Joe, then the dark-skinned guy with a marine-style haircut that sat beside him, the read-headed girl with sparkling blue eyes that sat in front of him, and finally the girl by the window. His heart stopped, for the girl by the window was the most beautiful woman he had ever seen. Her eyes were green like emeralds; she had ash-blonde hair, and her lips were so perfect they seemed almost as if Michelangelo had sculpted them. In a few seconds Lisa Ashton had entered Alex's thoughts, without even talking to him.

"Put everything on my tab," Joe said, barely glancing up at Alex.

Joe's words broke the spell, and Alex came back to reality. "Okay."

Meanwhile Joel had come in and sat on a stool near the bar.

"Who is that girl there?" he asked when Alex passed by.

Alex didn't reply but continued to stare at Joe's table.

"Another of Joe's contacts?" Joel persisted.

"No idea," said Alex.

* * *

"Yes, Judie, it will be better like this. Lisa, can you move the speaker please?" Scott, who was assembling the scene, got down from the stepladder and went into Joe's office. "Can you come and look at the mixer? One of the speakers isn't working," he said.

Joe got up to follow, but after only a few seconds, his mobile rang, which he immediately brought to his ear, devoting all his attention to it.

"Yes, sure…I'll be there in ten minutes…" Joe hung up and turned to Lisa, who was standing nearby. Her beauty was natural, delicate, refined, and it was a pity he was too old for her. Then he thought about

Alex and realised that he had never seen him deeply interested in any woman since he knew him. Lisa would have been just perfect for him. "I have to go and sign for a delivery next door, but you can ask Alex about the speaker, the guy from the pub. He's smart and knows about these kinds of things."

* * *

Alex was serving a customer when Lisa approached him. He didn't think it was still possible at age thirty to feel his heart beat so strongly and his blood rush to his face at the sight of a beautiful woman.

"Hi, Alex, I'm Lisa, and I'm in the group that has rented Joe's theatre. He told me to come get you because we have a problem with the mixer. Can you come and take a look upstairs?"

"I'll be there in a minute," Alex said, his heart still racing, as he tried to act casually.

"Thanks." Lisa smiled at Alex and turned back towards the stairs.

"Cover me, okay?" Alex said to the girl at the bar.

He took the duster from the back pocket of his jeans and tossed it to the girl. Then he went downstairs to the bathroom, washed his face and hands, looked at himself in the mirror, and made his way back up, his stomach churning with tension.

* * *

"Okay, so what's not working?" Alex asked as he entered the room.

"The speaker there at the back," Lisa said.

They walked over to the speaker and Alex knelt down. He dismantled the speaker and followed the wire that connected it to the audio system. After ten minutes, he stood back up, satisfied.

"It short circuited with a cable from another electric circuit. Now everything should be fixed," he said making the issue appear more complex than it actually was.

Scott tested the mixer. "One, two, three, go."

It worked perfectly.

"Thanks, Alex, maybe when we come down we can all have a drink," Scott said.

* * *

Scott kept his word, and at ten o'clock in the evening, he came into the pub with Judie.

"Have a drink with us?" Scott asked.

"Sure," Alex said, removing his apron and sitting down with them. Scott was a nice guy, taller than him, whilst Judie, with her freckles and wavy reddish hair, exuded a cheerfulness that always brightened up the bar whenever she entered. They were all more or less the same age.

"We start tomorrow, and if all goes well we should be here a week," Scott said to Alex about the play "You should come find us when you have time. That is, if you like theatre."

Scott could not have made Alex a more desirable offer. From the moment Alex had started working in the pub, he had wanted nothing more than to act in the theatre above. A moment or two later, Scott and Judie were on their way, so Alex closed the pub and went upstairs. There was nobody there, so he went into the theatre, turned on the lights, and stood still in the centre of the stage, pretending to be in front of the audience at the Open Air Theatre…

'The curtain falls on the actors.
A forced smile, a furtive look, a tear on
a delicate face, the expectations of a lifetime
destroyed in a single moment, in a timeless
illusion.
I scrutinize from up above the people present
there, hoping in my heart to catch a smile.
Waiting and hoping—both always ever present
in my life.
I now await the night, to share with it the
lights of that stage, which have ceased to shine.
It is over. I'm off the stage.
Another act awaits me in this unending comedy.
It is my life and it will have no reply.'

Alex bowed, shut his eyes, and once again imagined the applause. Lisa, who had been off stage and out of sight, kept silent as she listened to his words. She took one last sidelong glance through the door without being seen, then she went into Joe's office, took the notes she had left behind that afternoon, and went on her way.

* * *

South Bank was divided into two parts, which were completely different from each other. The East End, which included everything from Blackfriars to London Bridge, had been completely restructured at the end of the twentieth century, with ruins developed into offices and an art gallery, the Tate Modern, converted from an old power station into a showcase for modern arts.

The West End stretched from Waterloo Bridge to Westminster Bridge and had been revamped after the Second World War, with the opening of the Royal Festival Hall to celebrate the centenary of the Great Exhibition, the industrial fair that Queen Victoria had so much wished to take place. Grey soon became a dominant colour, as modernism in form and style asserted itself through the use of concrete, the key element for the construction of the National Film Theatre, Hayward Gallery, Queen Elizabeth Hall, and Purcell Room. This was how the South Bank Centre had been born.

Alex came out of the tube, crossed Westminster Bridge, and walked along the Thames. He passed the Dali museum, the Saatchi Gallery, and the London Aquarium and arrived at the foot of the London Eye, a steel wheel one hundred metres high that had become an obligatory destination for every tourist who wanted to take in London from a height. It was cold like winter; its colour blended perfectly with that of the river, with the stone pavement, with the benches, and with the bare trees planted along the path. There was really nothing of London in that place, nothing of its buildings in red brick or neo-classical white, nothing of its narrow streets that mingled with each other, nothing except for the Thames.

He continued his walk, navigating in full sail in the sea of his fantasy when, suddenly, an old man passing close to him, brushed his arm and interrupted his dream. Alex glimpsed the old man's face for just a moment, and he was struck, and hesitated whilst the man continued on his way. He was a strange figure, wholly out of keeping with the surroundings, as if time had decided to catapult him there as a joke.

The old man had a long, white beard, and his shiny silver hair fell all the way down to his back. He could have been a magician from another century; he could have been an angel that had fallen from the sky; he could have been many things. But he left no trace of himself as he passed, perhaps because he was a ghost, and as such, it was not possible to get a hold on him. A moment or two later, the old man turned round and smiled at Alex, almost inviting Alex to follow him, but as Alex approached him, the old man moved farther away without giving any impression of moving at all. After a few moments of this strange pursuit, the old man stopped at the book market under Waterloo Bridge. It was a small, cold place, but something about it was magical. In those few square metres sheltered by the bridge, there were wooden stalls that held books of every type and from every era. Anything and everything was available, from new to second-hand, from tragic to philosophic, and every example held a secret. The secret of the life of the author, of the interest shown by those who had thumbed through the pages, and of the person who, never having read it, had decided to sell to make some money. And the old man was there, not far away at all, hypnotizing Alex with his deep gaze and charming him with his playful smile. With just a few steps, Alex would have been able to confront him, ask him who he was, and what he wanted, but he carelessly knocked into one of the stalls, causing something to fall to the ground. He turned and picked up an old and tattered book that had lost its cover. He turned it around in his hands and opened it at random.

'The happening is concealed, unobserved, in the perfect harmony of things…to recognize it is difficult, to catch it…almost impossible…'

How strange, he thought, because besides that small phrase, there was nothing else on the pages of the book. He put it back in its place and looked around for the old man. He looked left, then right, and then into the distance, but there was no trace of him. He kept walking for a while, and then he stopped and sat on a bench along the river. A man walked by, then he stopped and turned towards him. Alex noticed his presence and looked at him. It was the same old man he had looked for beforehand who now stared at him. His expression was sweet but strong, like the one of a very, very old but charismatic grandfather. Alex felt intimidated by his presence, while trying to find the words to talk to him. Embarrassed, Alex lowered his eyes, and when he eventually found the strength to talk to him, it was too late. The old man had disappeared again.

* * *

It was afternoon when Alex started work, and his first customer was Scott.

"Does the play open tomorrow?" Alex asked.

"Yes, Alex, around eight at night. What time do you finish?" Scott's expression betrayed his nervousness.

"Is something wrong?" Alex asked.

Scott took a sip of his beer, dried his mouth with the back of his hand, and then looked at Alex. "The boy who was meant to start with us tomorrow evening has had an accident."

"Nothing serious I hope?"

"Unfortunately, he has broken a leg and I don't know what to do."

It wasn't that Alex could read Scott's mind at this point, but his intuition told him that something was about to happen.

"Is there nobody who can take his place?" Alex asked.

"No, Alex, unless you know somebody who can."

Maybe it was just his imagination, but Alex felt that Scott continued to stare at him. "Can you come upstairs quickly?" Scott finally said.

"Problems with the speaker?"

"No, there are no problems with the speaker."

"Give me five minutes," Alex said.

Later, Alex made his way to the theatre. Scott, Judie, and Lisa were all in the room, the scene was ready for a last rehearsal, and there was tension in the air.

"Hey, Alex!" Lisa greeted him, and Alex almost tripped over one of the cables.

"Will you recite some of your poetry for us?" Scott asked.

"What?"

"What you did last night by yourself in here," Lisa added.

Alex stood still, clearly embarrassed. "How did you know about that?" Alex asked, taking in Lisa's smile and feeling his heart racing.

"I came to get some notes. I saw you, but I didn't want to interrupt you."

Scott got up from the bench and went towards him. "Lisa told me everything. This is the script, Scott said, handing Alex a tattered play script. Read it and let me know what you think about it."

He had been waiting for this moment for a long time, long before Scott had called him upstairs.

* * *

The next night, the show started, and Alex finally made his debut before a dozen or so spectators.

He was direct, spontaneous, and natural. He was simply…surprising. There was no better word than that, because nobody would ever have imagined seeing such talent in a boy who served beers in the pub. Alex didn't restrict himself to merely learning the part. He really acted it, giving it all his soul and giving life to words that would otherwise have been nothing more than phrases on a piece of paper.

They finished late and everyone stayed in the room; Judie sat on the bench, Scott sat on the stairway, and Lisa crouched on the ground with her shoulders against the wall at the end of the hall. Alex was standing, leaning against a wall near the door.

"Where did you learn to act?" Scott asked him.

"From the scripts that Joe passed to me."

"I can't believe it…and this is your first time!"

Alex nodded.

"Do you want to stay on in the group?" Lisa asked, and Alex accepted without giving it further thought.

* * *

Without Joe's help, Alex would never have had this opportunity. The group convinced him to invest in the theatre company rather than limit himself to renting a room. Alex served beers part-time and spent more and more time with the group upstairs. He had never been so happy in all his thirty years.

A week later, Joe convened a lunch meeting at *Jamon Jamon*, a chilled Spanish Tapas Bar, on Park Way, off Camden High Street and not far from *The Oxford Arms*.

"I intend to expand the theatre," he said to the small group.

"I don't think there is space for a single extra seat," Scott said.

"I'm going to buy the space next door, knock down the wall, and enlarge the room."

"It's going to cost you a lot of money to do that," Scott said.

Joe passed some papers around the group. "I've given a percentage in exchange for the work being financed. The theatre will be three times the size."

"This is amazing news," Judie said.

"But what is this clause here?" Alex asked.

"Every production staged by all of you in the next year will belong to the theatre, but in exchange, I will not charge any expenses for the hire of the room, lights, or equipment."

"That's very kind, Joe, but we also have to eat. What are we going to make out of it?" Scott asked.

Joe explained that the money received would be distributed in proportion to everybody's shareholding. It was a good idea. At least this way they would not have problems finding a theatre and would make a profit much higher than the average.

"So are we all good to go?" Joe asked.

Everybody signed within five minutes, and the meeting was concluded. It took Alex exactly two days to win over the group. That was as long as it took for him to overcome his shyness.

"You were born for the stage," Lisa said to him.

Alex blushed, as he did every time Lisa spoke to him. "Thanks, Lisa."

"But why did you wait this long?"

"Because I didn't have any money, and I only began studying scripts a year ago."

"Better late than never," Scott added.

Everybody adored him, because Alex was able to make everybody love him. He never spoke a word more than necessary and was available anytime someone needed him. He was shy, sure, but his shyness disappeared as soon as he was on stage, where his introversion gave space to his passion.

* * *

"Hi, Joe," the guys said.

"Good morning." Joe returned the greeting as he sat down.

The acting troupe met at the pub, sitting around the table, whilst Alex served customers at the bar.

"We only have a month," Joe said, getting straight to the point.

"A month for what?" Scott asked.

"Our first show."

Lisa beckoned to Alex and he went over to her.

"Take ten minutes and join us. We're discussing our first show."

"My partner would like us to put something on stage quickly to get the theatre to gain momentum," Joe said, continuing his answer to Scott.

"What is this about?" Judie asked.

Joe dropped the email on the table that he had printed out earlier. "A play. It needs to be new, original, and different. I suggest you get to work right now."

Joe got up and left the pub. An hour later, everybody gathered in the room upstairs.

"One month? But we don't even have a script!" Judie said.

"It will come," Scott said. "For the moment we had better think about what we need to do."

"I agree with Scott, best not to lose time," Lisa said. "Alex, your ideas are welcome," Lisa said, including Alex in the discussion.

Lisa, always her. Alex looked at her and blushed. Scott and Judie spoke for a few minutes, and Alex and Lisa were left alone.

"You have an incredible talent," Lisa said to Alex. "I'm convinced that you'll come up with an idea."

Alex was distracted. He wasn't able to look at her for more than a minute without thinking about her.

Scott and Judie turned round and broke the spell.

"Okay, let's meet here tomorrow to try and put plot to paper," Scott said, by way of concluding their hurried meeting.

* * *

It was the longest night of his life. Alex had the story ready and only needed the right moment to give his dream a chance to come true. He had really worked on this, after reading dozens of books and scripts and serving thousands of beers in the pub. All he needed was an opportunity, like the broken leg of the actor he had never met, to help his dream materialize.

The group started without him, as he was stuck serving customers downstairs. After half an hour he went up with a little yellow file.

"Take a look at this, Scott," Alex said, handing the script to him.

"*The Black and the White*…is it a script?" Scott asked.

"Just an idea for one," Alex explained.

There was nothing left for Scott to do but to take the papers and sit down to read them.

"How many characters are there?" Lisa asked Alex.

"Three…four at the most," Alex said.

"Is it something dramatic?" Judie asked.

"Yes. The audience will be holding its breath for fear of ruining the show."

There it was. Alex was transformed from his former self. The shyness had disappeared, replaced by the force of his conviction, and Lisa could have listened to him for hours.

Meanwhile, Scott, who had almost finished reading, had got up and was now standing before him.

"Did you write this yourself?" he asked.

Alex nodded, and Scott passed the file over to the girls.

"*The Black and the White*…it's unbelievable," was all Scott said.

TWO

'This is the story of a choice. Destiny gave me just two cards and I will play them blindfolded'

Joe stood behind the curtain, watching the last of the audience take their seats in the theatre. He was holding his breath. The future of his theatre rested on the story that Alex had created. He thought back over the years and remembered when he was a child and used to follow his parents from one street to another. The street and not the theatre was Joe's only stage and hope to survive. It was hard to be a child at that time; it was difficult to make people smile, and it was even harder to raise money to buy food at the end of the day. He closed his eyes, breathed deeply, and pulled the curtain aside, stepping into the spotlight on the stage. He couldn't see the faces of the audience, but he knew they were there. He'd watched as all forty seats filled up.

"Ladies and gentlemen, good evening. We are about to live a special moment, one that represents the end of a story and the beginning of a dream we want to share with you. I am pleased to let the show, *The Black and the White*, begin. On behalf of everyone, I wish you a pleasant evening."

The lights dimmed. The glow faded with the echo of Joe's last words, and the stage fell into darkness. The only sound was the whispering of a few audience members, and then the music rose.

The show began with Scott's footsteps onto the stage, stopping when he hit his mark. Scott stood still. The only light came from above the stage giving a touch of colour to his forehead and purposely making barely visible his pronounced cheekbones. A growing tension overwhelmed the hall.

"There's music in my head," Scott said to the audience, casting his voice effortlessly to the back of the hall. "It is silent around me, no sound, yet I can hear the music. It vibrates. It doesn't need notes but fills the space that's all around it. Now it takes over my mind. I feel bad; I am just so afraid I can feel it in my heart, in my soul, inside my body. It is here now and overcomes me. It leaps on me, holds me tight, makes me suffer…"

* * *

It was a great beginning. The words overtook the music, and Scott wanted to count the open eyes, observe the wonder on the faces of the spectators, and listen to their heartbeats. He lowered his head, as if he needed some time to meditate, and then he resumed.

"I close my eyes, trying to resist. I am in terrible pain. I feel the moisture of a flowing tear, taste the pain in my mouth. I would love to stop time to let my destiny die. Before it happens, after it has happened."

It was over. Those words caressed the soul of the audience without knowing that the play was a challenge that Alex had launched against Destiny, the implacable enemy of mankind. There was no doubt at all. This night, through this play, Alex would finally seize the event that would change his life.

It was his turn now, after Scott had exited the stage. He waited for the lights to fade, and then he took to the stage wearing blue trousers and a tight, light-blue T-shirt. He stood still, with his eyes shut, waiting for the attention of the audience to be focused on him. His heartbeat accelerated, and the adrenaline began to flow. Then he breathed deeply, slowly opened his eyes, and felt ready to speak.

"I am Soul," Alex announced to the audience. "I am light, and I am transparent, and you'll never know anything of me unless the story is over, unless you read the words that started it and those that will be ending it. I will start my story now, without knowing where it will take me. And I will finish it without remembering where I started…

"This is the story of a choice. Destiny gave me just two cards, and I will play them blindfolded. Right or wrong, it doesn't matter. At any moment I will decide my future, live my present time, or write about my past. Destiny will wait and see, giving me the illusion of a path that I can choose, or he will act and show me the one he has already determined. These are the only rules, the one thing I am not allowed to change."

Alex remained motionless waiting for Lisa to come on stage from the left. She was wearing a tight, light-green body suit, highlighting her perfect silhouette. Her hair was pulled back, and the white makeup gave more power to the vivid green of her eyes, something that immediately grabbed the attention of the audience.

"Who are you?" Soul asked.

"I am Imagination. That part of yourself you don't even know."

"Might you be helpful to my story?"

"If you wish, Soul, I will be glad to write with you. But now," she added, "I need to know something I am missing."

Lisa's voice was sweet and delicate, just as Alex always dreamt it would be. He had written the play with all his heart, and in the scene Lisa was a part of it.

"It's a story I dreamt about," Soul said. "It's so different from all the others I have heard. It shines with a glow that sometimes belongs to me, one I can feel, and it lights up a path. Yet sometimes, that light becomes dark; it doesn't want to shine, and I feel all its detachment, but I can't run away from it. That glow is like a pain, and I am afraid it will come again. Imagination, can you explain this to me?"

"Your story is written by what is Black and what is White. Sometimes they hate each other; they might even turn their backs on each other, but they can't live without each other. They are the cards Destiny has dealt you, before you existed and until you could live," Imagination said.

The music changed, and its sound became dramatic. Then a narrow laser drew a line leading to the back of the stage.

"That's your path," Imagination said, pointing along the beam of light. "From now on, you'll play your cards at any moment. Destiny is not certain. The Black and the White are the possible futures that you will determine."

The laser ended next to a crystal as big as Alex, and a cloud of coloured gas filled it in a second. The music became almost a whisper, and the lights went down, leaving the audience viewing a crystal full of colours.

"What's going on, Imagination? Why is it all getting dark, even though I can see the crystal and its colours? What's happening to me?"

Music was on again highlighting Soul's anxiety with a slow crescendo.

"Close your eyes and tell me what appears. Try to tell me without fear," Imagination said.

The play was engaging and the expression on Alex and Lisa's faces revealed an almost unfair competition between the two of them. Soul was trying to steal the attention of the audience with the intensity of his words while Imagination had already succeeded and seduced the spectators with the sensuous moves of her spectacular body.

"I cannot see what's inside my confused mind," Soul said. "What appears to me right now is transformed a second after. I look at things that I can't see. I am cold. I hear sounds. Imagination! Help me understand…"

Imagination looked at him, and then she stepped forward. "You are about to enter your own story, and I am not a part of it. Once you decide, I may not help you."

Joe was watching quietly backstage. He observed the reaction of the audience, completely hooked by Alex's play. Light disappeared, and the noise of the wind became stronger. The scenery was changing. As the music began again, anxiety took possession of the hall. Soul was looking at the crystal.

"If I could know…if I could do…Time went cruelly by, and I can see its traces on my face. I have been a dreamer and I have never noticed that the things I tried to achieve were just illusions that gave me pain and left wrinkles on my skin. Never-ending hopes. I'd like to live within the beauty of my thoughts, and I wish Time would stop."

Imagination drew closer, moving slowly, while Soul was watching the back of the stage, expressionless.

"You cannot stop Time," Imagination said. "You can only run with it. Imagination is a gift you have received to colour your dreams. Whether those dreams smile or whether they are sad it will depend on you."

"Life is unfair; it hampers my path and makes it difficult to walk," Soul said. Soul's eyes were shining, like those of someone who had lost all his strength. He wanted comfort from the one who could do anything he couldn't. "Can you stop Time?" Soul asked.

"Why do you want Time to stop?" Imagination asked.

"I want to go back and change my choices, to make these wrinkles disappear."

Imagination stepped back, lowered her head, thoughtful, and then she looked at Soul again. "You ask me to do something I cannot. Your life is the gift Destiny has given you but you were not given the chance to go back in time. I cannot change the first chapter of your story."

Soul lowered his head, despondent. He dragged on, tired, the prisoner of a body he never dreamt about, made heavy by something that would never change.

"Tell me then, what can you do?" Soul asked.

"I can teach you how to imagine."

"Is that all? I don't need you then!"

The lights dimmed on Lisa and lit up Alex. He was alone on his knees in the middle of the stage, covering his face with his hands.

"Why don't you come and take me?" Soul cried out despondently. "I am waiting for you, Death. I want to avoid writing other words that make me suffer and leave wrinkles on my face."

Footsteps sounded on the stage, and they belonged to Death. She was there, covered by a long black mantel.

"You have called me, Soul, and I am here to take you away from the choices that cause you pain and from the future that you fear. No more wrinkles on your face and no more Imagination. Dream the things you wish. The dream will stay the moment I touch you."

Death knelt down next to Soul.

"Why are you looking at me that way? Are you deaf to my plea?" Soul asked.

"Death does not listen."

"I can feel your icy hand, but…you quiver! You are trembling!"

Death stayed still then she stepped back, as if something unexpected had just happened.

"Your heart keeps beating strongly. It's your conscience trying to stop you. You don't want to die at all."

"I beg you, take me, and I will ask my heart to stop and hide my secret until the end."

"What is the secret you are trying to hide?" Death asked.

"To have loved you more than Life," Soul answered.

The light dimmed.

"Why are you trying to leave me?" A new and unexpected disembodied voice asked. It was intense and vibrating, full of a power that Soul could never have imagined.

"Who are you?" Soul asked. "Why are you talking now that I have found the energy to die?"

"I am your Life!" The disembodied voice sounded like thunder.

"Life? How dare you say this word? You made me full of your illusions; you took me into the river I didn't want to cross, to paths I couldn't walk. Why do you speak now when you didn't speak then?"

"Because this is the moment when anything can change. You choose me or you choose Death," Life said.

"I have already paid for the dreams I chased. You cannot give me anything I haven't already tried to find."

"Perhaps Death can give you all these things?"

"Yes, it can."

The noise of the wind was much stronger, like fury, until Life descended on Soul with all its power.

"You think you'll find peace, dreams, and joy with Death…But you don't know what Death's about until you meet it! It changes your deep anxieties into nightmares forever, leaving you in suspense on a wire of terror between fiction and reality. It takes you, it hurts you, it doesn't listen to your pleas, and it will never open your eyes but will wait for you to drown while it steals your last breath. Death, Soul, is the end. The end of a story. The end of your story. Broken with words different from those you have imagined, with wrinkles that just mean pain, with no chance for them to heal. On the contrary, they get worse, and you suffer; while they wrap around your body, they steal your deepest thoughts; they enter your soul until you wish you were not there. Until you are lost in the darkness. Until you are dust."

The wind calmed down. The only sound that filled the hall was the heartbeat of a man who, with no energy, was lying on the stage, a body in which Soul was still vibrating, a thin wire that divided his story from the end.

"Now tell me, Soul, do you really wish to die?" Life asked.

* * *

There was magic in the air. The play was by far more powerful than anything the spectators in the little theatre could ever wish to watch, and it strove to achieve a *New Age* dimension before an audience not yet ready to face it. But despites this, no one looked away from the stage. Alex performed with extraordinary energy and his every move, expression, and word was so intense as to almost put his troupe and the same play into shade. But the spectators were not looking at him. They were looking at Lisa. Her beauty was beyond anything Imagination could ever be able to produce. Lisa's body was perfection, an undeniable object of sexual desire, and her interaction with Alex seemed to be more than just acting, something the audience was close to perceiving and unconsciously wishing for it to happen. Alex and Lisa were discovering each other, acting on the fine line between interaction with each other and physical attraction for each other. Lisa's body was unveiling her sensuality to Alex, while Alex's intensity was trying to communicate with Lisa in a way his shyness could not. She was intrigued rather than seduced by Alex and he was seduced rather than intrigued by Lisa, while the audience was figuring out what kind of relationship the two of them could have had in the real world considering the energy coming out from their acting together. The play kept going after a pause that seemed to last an eternity. Soul had to decide what card to play.

* * *

Lights slowly dissolved, and the shining crystal lit the stage absorbing the darkness all around it. Again, the scenery was changing. First the wind came accompanied by the roar of the waves. Then the silhouette of a little sail boat entered the stage, held by Soul and Imagination. The music started playing. Scott and Judie were playing the roles of the Black and the White. Destiny gave Soul the two cards. Alex, Lisa, Judie, and Scott were all on the stage, and they appeared in turn from the darkness, lit by a pale spotlight as the play went on. Soul was in the middle of the stage, and Imagination was close but slightly behind him. The Black and the White were on the left and right ends of the stage.

Judie impersonated the White, wearing a white body suit and an expressionless white mask that completely hid her face. Scott played the role of the Black, wearing the same outfit as Judie but in black. The White was tempting Soul with the promise of never-ending peace, without fear of a life that wasn't worth discovering. The Black challenged Soul, however, inviting him to move away from a motionless dimension to face Destiny and not to waste Time. Soul was struggling to decide which card to play, and anytime he played the Black he wrote another chapter of his story. The more he accepted Life's challenges, the stronger and more fearless he felt, and the more difficult it was for the White to hold him back from living.

The play was about to enter its final act. The Black and the White disappeared into the darkness, leaving Alex lying in the middle of the stage.

"Where am I now? Imagination, are you still with me?" Soul said, opening his eyes again.

Imagination didn't answer, but the stage lights were no longer white. They were slowly changing colour, as if they anticipated a discovery that Soul was about to make. Then Lisa appeared in all her beauty in the spotlight from the left side of the stage. She had her hair down and wore vivid makeup.

"Who are you?" asked Soul.

"Can't you imagine who I am?" she asked. "I am the story you have written. I am the destiny you chose, once you decided you weren't afraid of me. I am Reality."

Soul stepped back, bewildered, paused for a few moments, then moved towards her and finally embraced her.

The lights lowered, and a soft reflection from the base of the stage lit up Alex and Lisa. The audience began to applaud, but soon the music started, and silence filled the theatre again. The light moved onto Scott, back on the stage.

"I am Destiny, and this is the end of the story, written by a Soul that wasn't afraid of me."

It was a surprise as everyone thought the show was over. But it was even more surprising for Alex who remained bewildered while looking at Scott and his astonishing resemblance to the old man he had met in South Bank just a few weeks back.

"You think you are not afraid of me, and yet you prefer not to look at me. You think you can stop me if you imagine. But I am like Time. I will never die. If I am not the one who's writing your story, I will let you be a little part of mine, a little part of something I wrote long before you existed. And I will deny myself. I won't let you pursue me. I won't stop, not to give any past or future, to let you be born and die blindfolded, while I continue to play with another one like you. Someone who believed he could stop me and make me die. Someone, like you, who has imagined."

He continued talking with a slow crescendo.

"The story you have witnessed has existed beyond your fears, within your fantasies. And you could only imagine it watching actors on a stage.

It's the pretence, your imagination that lets you smile and watch a drama without being afraid. But the cruel reality is beyond the stage. Time passes and turns the pages of a story I wrote for any one of you that sits before me. And now you feel the fear. It's the terror that you have for the mistakes that you may make. Between the cards I gave you, time flows, and you must make your own decisions.

But don't ever try to challenge me or throw the cards away, as I could become angry. And when you are on that famous path, where the wall before you puts an end to your own story, there is not much that you can do."

* * *

The audience remained seated after the curtain fell, dumbfounded and silent. The power of the message left them paralyzed and unable to speak or even clap. After nearly a minute, an audience member stood up and clapped. Soon, the entire theatre followed suit with a standing ovation.

THREE

Before the end of the nineteenth century and the building of the massive bank in the quarter of Chelsea, Cheyne Walk was a beautiful walk along the River Thames.

Alex enjoyed the walk, admiring the beautiful architecture of the seventeenth century houses, and although almost two hundred years had gone by, he felt that charm almost intact. He walked past the blue plaques posted on the walls and fantasized about the extraordinary personalities who had lived there. Yes, Cheyne Walk was the road of the intellectuals, the street where *George Eliot, Henry James,* and *Dante Gabriel Rossetti,* the founder of the *'Pre-Raphaelite Brotherhood'*, had spent part of their lives.

There was no better place for his first date with Lisa, so Alex booked a table at *Cheyne Walk Brasserie*, a French restaurant with a good view of the Albert Bridge. He arrived there a few minutes early and ordered a glass of wine.

"I'll be perfectly on time next time round," Lisa said as she arrived. She was slightly late, but it did not matter. She was there. He took her hand and guided her to the table.

"How nice!" Lisa looked around and seemed to appreciate the place. It was refined and immersed in a silent atmosphere that seemed to be created just for the two of them.

"Champagne?"

Lisa nodded, and the waitress came back shortly afterwards to serve them.

"It is so nice to meet each other off the stage, don't you think?"

"I agree," Lisa said. "You get the chance to know someone as he really is."

"I propose a toast to this evening, to the success of the play and to our future."

Lisa smiled and probably thought about and appreciated the same things Alex did: a few words, a toast to the event that had brought them together and one that, he hoped, would give them the chance to know each other better.

"What are you thinking about?" he asked.

"Just about all the time we've spent acting together."

"I will never forget."

"Alex…it's our first date."

She just wanted to say that. He was silly not to understand it.

"There is always a right time for things to happen," he said.

She seemed to appreciate his answer. "It is strange to see you here and not on the stage acting or behind the bar serving beers."

"Free interpretation tonight," he said. "I leave the rest to your imagination."

"Who knows what would have happened if we had not put the show on the stage," she said, still smiling. "Have you ever thought about it?" Her words and her smile began to break down the wall around Alex's feelings.

"Not a night has gone by when I haven't thought about it."

This time it was Lisa's turn to blush. She lifted the glass and brought it to her lips, trying to hide her embarrassment. "Are you going to act again?"

"Never been so serious in my life." Alex wasn't the bartender of *The Oxford Arms* that night. His passion shone in his eyes like fire and slowly overwhelmed Lisa's mind.

"I only date celebrities." She could not find any better words. She was trapped in a corner, and she realized she was losing her defences.

"You are as I thought you were," Alex said.

"Have I disappointed you?"

How could she have? "I always thought you were a person worth discovering."

"Do you still think that?"

"I do," he said without hesitation.

"And tell me, Alex, how far do you think you are from the discovery?"

They looked into each other's eyes.

"I would think that I could discover in a second what an entire life would not give me the chance to."

She smiled again. "Time doesn't matter."

It was a wonderful night, but it ended too soon for the two of them. They said goodbye with sadness in their eyes, yet with a memory that would keep them company until the next time. Alex waited for the cab to disappear with Lisa in it, and Lisa waited for the night to swallow Alex's eyes.

She got home with the snow falling on the roofs of the houses and on the streets. She removed her makeup, and the image of her face reflected in the mirror was even more beautiful. She had beautiful eyes, of a leaf-green colour and she smiled, whilst thinking of Alex's words: *"A person worth discovering…"*

It was freezing outside, and the only things worth doing were reading and going to bed, waiting for the cold to end. She closed the door and noticed the blinking light on the answering machine. She listened, smiled, and called.

* * *

He was surprised to hear her voice in the only moment he wasn't thinking about her. He would have never expected Lisa's call just a half hour after their first date, let alone her invitation for a walk in the park the next day.

* * *

London woke up sleepy, covered by a mantle of white snow. Alex wore a heavy trench coat, took the tube, and got off at Hyde Park Corner. He could see the blanket of snow stretching far beyond the Queen Elizabeth Gate and the wrought iron of its bars…and that white silence, barely broken by the noise of two trotting horses, took him back to the sixteenth century.

Hyde Park was part of Westminster Abbey; yet, after being repossessed by Henry VIII, it became part of his shooting estate. It joined Kensington Gardens to form the so-called *'lung of London'*, a green rectangle within the areas of South Kensington, Bayswater and Kensington, and Mayfair. It had a lake in the middle, called the Serpentine, as it traced the shape of a snake.

Lisa was waiting for him in the restaurant that overlooked the lake. She wore a green coat and a hat of the same colour. She saw him and waved.

When he came up to her, he kissed her cheek. Her perfume reminded him of the emotions of the night before.

"Fancy a walk?" she asked.

Alex nodded.

"I come here often alone," she said, "anytime that my fancy takes me."
She looked at him and her eyes shone.

"I went to the South Bank last Sunday and walked without knowing where I was heading. I stopped, leant on the railing, and stared at the water. I saw it flowing, and I tried to count the lights coming from the other side of the river. Have you ever done that?"

"No, I never have," Alex admitted. He did not have the time.

"When I was little, I enjoyed putting my foot in the footprints left on the snow. You know, Alex…things may be different from what they seem to be; a footprint in the snow could stay there forever and never have a soul until a girl puts her foot on it thinking that someone left it there for her."

He saw her walking ahead, putting her foot on a footprint in the snow and turning again.

"Can you see, Alex? This footprint now has a soul and a story that one day she would like to tell. It could belong to anyone. Maybe someone left it here for me to stomp on it, or maybe it belongs to you. A footprint you forgot that the snow brought back to us."

"You're right. It could belong to me. Let me see…It's just a bit smaller. Maybe I left it here a few years ago. It probably belonged to a different self."

"Do you mean you are another person now?" she asked. "And tell me… what was Alex like before he changed? The shy person I feel for or the actor that I admire, because he can hide his own emotions?"

It was a game, and passion wrote the words the two of them were playing.

"I am the one you see. The rest does not matter."

Lisa stopped and looked at him intensely. "I like what I see, Alex."

He sensed the change. The tone of her voice was different, tender, almost betraying her emotions. He put his arm around her shoulders and she put hers around his waist. They kept walking in the silence, wishing that moment would never end. Alex caressed her cheek with his lips, and she felt shivers.

"Why don't we just stay friends?"

There was no answer to her question. She lifted her eyes, trying to reach his, until finally she did. They were dark, intense, and they were looking at her, hoping she could read his desire. She looked down and stared at his lips. That was the moment they were both waiting for. Alex lifted her chin and kissed her.

***

He woke up all of a sudden, with his heart beating; he was sweating and breathing heavily. There had been no meeting at the Brasserie, there had been no snow, there was no park, and there was no Lisa. He was alone in his bed and that beautiful kiss was just another dream.

***

Success came. *The Black and the White* soon became a hit. Joe received lots of offers and met with agents and art directors trying to get the most out of the show. He was in no rush at all, since he knew that the longer he waited the higher the price would go.

The guys were dreaming of the West End and each of them was thinking about Piccadilly, Leicester Square, or Covent Garden's theatres, because each of them would have loved to become famous. So, between fantasies and bills to pay, their chance seemed to arrive just a week later, when Yaron Rubinstein entered Joe's office.

"Good morning, Mr Rubinstein," Joe said, smiling and waving his hand. "Please, take a seat."

Rubinstein was slightly over fifty. He was one of the most powerful entrepreneurs in London show business. He was not tall, yet anyone could feel his presence. Joe felt uneasy and ashamed of his little office, definitely not adequate to welcome such a powerful man.

"I am pleased to meet you, and I would like to congratulate you for the courage you had to bet on those guys," Rubinstein said.

His words made Joe feel proud again. He forgot his little office and felt as powerful as Rubinstein.

"Thank you. I would have liked to welcome you in a nicer office, but the work will start soon. We will triple our seating, we will have a newly refurbished office, and we will put down a schedule for the new programs in the next few weeks."

These were too many words for Rubinstein. He was there for only one reason.

"I know you open only at the weekend," he said.

"Yes, cost issues, limited management, and the guys are so busy…"

It was Tuesday, not a big day for Joe. But a Tuesday on Rubinstein's calendar was worth more than Joe's dreams.

"Tell me how it all started," Rubinstein said.

Joe let himself fall back in the chair. He had answered this question so many times, and each time he gave a different answer.

"Emotions, Mr Rubinstein, they came up whenever I talked to my guys. We used to wonder how to change our lives. We decided the only thing to do was to imagine, to create something special, to achieve something new, even if we had to put at risk all we have."

Rubinstein wasn't paying attention.

"Where are the guys?"

"Why?" Joe asked.

"I want to meet them."

* * *

They all arrived in less than half hour and were glad to organize a rehearsal for Rubinstein.

"I like it," he said when the show ended. "I want it."

The guys were still on the stage, and Joe and Rubinstein were looking at them. Alex was nervous and waiting for whatever was about to happen, like the others. Joe waived to him, and Alex joined them.

"I would like to introduce you to Mr Rubinstein. Mr Rubinstein, this is Alex."

Rubinstein nodded and took a little block of notes from his jacket.

"Well done, my boy. The play was good. I liked it."

It was a polite dismissal.

"He has an incredible talent," Joe said.

"Sure." Rubinstein barely listened to what Joe was saying. His eyes were on Lisa.

"Who's the actress?" he asked.

"Lisa."

"She would be perfect."

"I beg your pardon?"

"I want the girl."

"She is okay, but Alex is the mind behind the show."

Rubinstein turned towards him. It was clear that Joe did not get the message.

"I want the girl and the show. Those are the only things that I want and the only things I will buy."

"Mr Rubinstein, Alex has the role of Soul; he is the mastermind...the main character..."

"I am not interested."

He did not say anything else, nor did he allow Joe to continue. He had made up his mind.

The effect of those words was worse than a stab in the heart for Alex. He took his bag and left the stage. He passed by the office where

Joe and Rubinstein were talking, and their words confirmed his fears.

He had waited all his life for such a moment to arrive, and now he realized that all of his efforts would be for someone else's benefit. He felt miserable and, for a moment, he thought about the guy who had broken his leg, whose place he had taken, and he could not complain. He had been lucky stealing someone else's chance, and now it was someone else's turn to steal his chance.

He began walking without knowing where he was going. It began to snow. He took the tube and got off at Waterloo. It was about midnight, and he never imagined he would be walking in the snow with a broken heart, the same day he thought his life had changed forever.

He arrived at the South Bank and walked along the Thames towards the book market. The stalls looked like skeletons. They were empty, without soul. He leaned against the railing, looked down at the Thames, and thought about the book he had seen some time ago. He had not seized the moment or, perhaps the moment had arrived but not for him. *Life is strange*, he thought. *Sometimes it smiles at you, often it deceives you, sometimes it follows you, yet more often it runs away from you.*

Cruel Destiny. He was playing with Alex. He should not have dared to write that drama. He had been arrogant, and now Destiny had taken his revenge. The air got colder. The wind grew stronger, and the snow hit his skin like needles in his face. He raised the collar of his coat and walked back to Waterloo. A man lay on a bench, one of many on the South Bank, wrapped in a plastic bag.

The dream was over. He was not on the stage, and he was not writing any play. He had to move on and forget. He did not want to die alone one night like that old man on the bench.

FOUR

"Just here…sign," Yaron Rubinstein said. He had the contract for Lisa's part in *The Black and the White* before him on his polished cherry wood desk, in his elegant office, but Lisa was not herself that day.

"Anything wrong?" Rubinstein asked, feeling a bit frustrated with his new 'star', since he was a driven and practical man and didn't like irrelevant delays.

"Just silly thoughts," Lisa said.

"Why don't you take a couple of days to think it over and then call us back?"

* * *

Lisa and Angela crossed the street. It was cold but it was pleasant to feel the sun on her skin in the early afternoon in the middle of Soho. Angela was Lisa's agent, and she could not be more different than her. She had black hair, full lips, big blue eyes, and she was a curvy woman in her mid thirties. She was sexy because of her body, not because of her attitude. She rarely smiled. Lisa, on the other hand, besides having blonde hair and being slender, was emotional. She could feel the world at her feet one day and against her the next. Angela was greedy; money drove her life. Lisa was not greedy and that's why she hadn't yet managed to get what she wanted. Lisa liked the appearance because, deep inside, she was naive; Angela liked substance because, deep inside, she wasn't naive at all. Lisa was strong among the weak ones and weak among the strong ones as she felt the pressure of power; Angela was friendly with the weak ones and assertive with the strong ones. Lisa wanted to know who she was. Angela just knew.

"I don't think you have grasped it, yet," Angela said. Do you know what the contract means?"

"I can imagine," Lisa said. She felt as if she were betraying her friends. That wasn't in the contract, but that's what it was—betrayal.

"I don't think so," Angela said. Sign and your life will change forever. They will look after you."

Her smile would have melted what was left of the snow on the street. Lisa's expression however made Angela feel the cold of the snow of the night before. Angela put her hand on Lisa's arm and turned her towards her.

"I consider myself more your friend than your agent. You are about to sign something that would make half the world happy, and I can't understand your sad expression. Are you hiding something?"

Lisa was thinking about Alex, about the invitation he had finally made and about the evening he was organizing for her. A tear rolled down her cheek and she tried to stop it before others followed.

"I am stealing the contract from Alex."

Angela sighed with relief, because she had feared something much worse. "They chose you. Had it happened to him, he would not think twice. Forget him," Angela advised.

* * *

The bell rang at nine sharp. Alex took off his apron, dried his forehead with a towel, and went to the door. Lisa looked wonderful. She was wearing a black dress that ended just above her knees. She did not wear any jewellery, just two little diamond earrings that framed her face. She greeted Alex with a beautiful smile.

"Should I stay or should I go?" she asked. But there was no happiness in her voice. She knew she was about to betray Alex, steal his contract and kill his feelings.

Alex took her hand and guided her to the living room. He turned on the stereo and handed her a glass of red wine. She looked different, and she was visibly uncomfortable. She was not the Lisa he knew the other night.

"To our first date."

They drank it all at once, and Lisa did not stop looking at him for a moment. Then she invited him to stand, left her empty glass on the table, and kissed him with all the passion she had. She grabbed his waist and caressed his face with her slender fingers, until the surprise turned Alex's hesitation into uncontrollable passion.

"Weren't we supposed to go out tonight?" he asked her, his voice broken by the excitement.

"Forget it, Alex, forget all that."

They hugged each other again, tighter and more intensely than ever. Alex's hands held Lisa's face, brushed her lips, and gradually the caresses became more intimate. Lisa began to undress him; she could not wait for that moment to happen.

"Take your clothes off," Alex said. "I want to watch you do it."

She stepped back and slowly removed her dress. They were standing before each other, half naked. Alex came closer, unclasped her bra and kissed her.

Their breath mingled. Lisa moaned, finally free from her sense of guilt, as she could never have imagined making love so intensely. They could not wait any longer; their thoughts were subsumed by their passion. Alex entered Lisa and Lisa melted with him.

* * *

She sat with half a cigarette in her hand, looking at the world outside the window, with her hair framing her face. She had never made love on the first date, and she had never made love the night before leaving someone. Remorse and passion fought inside her and doubts overwhelmed her again.

"Is there anything you would avoid in your life if you had the chance?" Lisa asked. While her question might have sounded innocent, for her it bore all the weight of what she had done, what she was planning to do.

"Everyone would avoid some things if they could," Alex replied, obviously not attaching more than a trifle to the subject of Lisa's question.

Alex moved closer to her, smiling. He was happy she was there. Lisa looked at him as she sipped her coffee. They were on the sofa, beside each other and Alex was caressing her legs.

"I would not like to be forced to choose between something and someone," she said breaking the silence.

Alex turned to face her, curiosity evident on his face, almost as if a different person had spoken her words.

"What about you, Alex?"

He hesitated, looked at the world outside the window, and then turned back to her. "I would not like you to be forced to choose between something and someone."

Here it was, he understood. She lit another cigarette, nervously. It was more difficult than she thought it would be.

"I am about to accept an offer," Lisa said, "and I do not know how it will affect my life."

"Rubinstein?"

She looked surprised. "How did you know?"

"Joe."

"I haven't signed anything yet," Lisa said. She didn't know whether she had been expecting Alex to talk her out of it, build against the arguments that Angela had made, saying that Alex would have signed, or urge her to sign, just as Angela had done.

"It doesn't make any difference, you know," Alex said simply.

She inhaled deeply, trying to escape his eyes.

"I know everything, Lisa. You don't have to hide anything."

Why do I love her so much? Alex wondered. They barely knew each other…so why? Because of love…Yes, love, the most dangerous virus of all, which unstoppably spreads, overwhelming your body, entering your soul, and tweaking your mind…And now that she was taking an offer that should have been made to him, Alex felt his love for her grow even stronger.

"How long have we known each other, Alex?" Lisa asked, still unable to fully meet his eyes.

"Have you already consigned me to your memories?" Alex asked gently. He knew their love story was over after just one night, for the price of her betrayal.

"I didn't mean that," Lisa said. "I just wanted to know to what extent we belong to each other."

"I belonged to you from the moment I saw you," Alex said. He wouldn't let her off so easily. Had he really been deceived by her beautiful smile, by her enchanting eyes and her silky hair? Was it enough for him to be in love? No, it wasn't. Yet there was something in her…It was difficult to grasp. He understood it all. "And you, Lisa? Since when have you belonged to me? Or should I say…have you ever been mine?"

And that is where she left it when she left his apartment, his final question hanging in the air between them.

* * *

"Congratulations, Lisa, and welcome to our family." Yaron Rubinstein was all smiles for her. He was the kind of man who liked to close his deals quickly, but he made an exception for Lisa, since she was beautiful, more beautiful than any other woman he had ever signed.

Lisa, Yaron, and Lisa's agent Angela were once again in Yaron's office. The smell of the leather chairs and the sofa were mixed with the wood of the library that filled an entire wall of his studio. There were no novels in Yaron's library but, rather, volumes with the smell of history. They were rare, in a few cases unique and, as such, very expensive. Rubinstein was a collector of arts and beautiful objects, and this was reflected by the paintings on the wall where a *De Chirico* stood out, the large globe a couple of centuries old, the rare pear-shaped copper-red *Ming Dynasty* vase on top of a marble pedestal, and the legendary *Muramasa* Japanese sword of the sixteenth century hung on the wall above the chimney. A few moments later the deal was closed.

The door opened and a man of about thirty stepped in. "Good morning, Mr Rubinstein."

Lisa and Angela were speechless. The beauty and sensuality of the man was beyond human imagination. His skin was the colour of amber, while the light in his hazelnut eyes called to mind the confidence of a lion before a lamb. Tall and elegant, he wore a dark double-breasted jacket that highlighted a perfect posture and extraordinary class.

"This is Klaus, my assistant. He will look after you," Rubinstein said, while Angela looked at Lisa, smiling maliciously. Maybe she was feeling a bit envious, but she was definitely malicious. One did not miss an opportunity to be with a man that beautiful. And Lisa did not intend to miss it.

* * *

She was ready. A last glance in the mirror for a boost of confidence, a drop of Chanel to feel sexy, and then she went to the door to open it onto a future she would discover. She shut the door behind her, almost as if she were shutting it on a past she needed to forget. Klaus was in the car, waiting for her. He got out when he saw her and opened the passenger door for her like a perfect gentleman. He took her hands and kissed them.

"I was told you were beautiful, but I couldn't have imagined how beautiful. You are stunning."

Lisa blushed, and she could not help smiling. Klaus was so natural, so confident. He was perfect.

"Do you mind if we stop by my place for a moment?" Klaus asked. "Five minutes."

"Fine by me," she said. She couldn't refuse.

Klaus drove the car across the gate, entered the park, and stopped by the stairs near the entrance to his house. The soft lights near the door seemed to invite her to enter a dream, and emotion overwhelmed her. Klaus was incredibly charming. His style, his cologne, his smile, his hands, his eyes, his skin—she liked everything about him. Klaus's house was the celebration of open space, as he managed to eliminate all the divisional walls, leaving only the structural pillars. The ground floor was a huge seamless area that included the lobby, the dining room, and a series of sofas and coloured pillows laid out to give a hint of the people who likely enjoyed Klaus's invitations. Beautifully cold and white Carrara marble decorated the floor, while a large aquarium stood in the middle of the hall, almost as if it aimed to separate his guests' from Klaus's intimate life consumed between the sofas and the beautifully coloured pillows.

"This is where I live. Make yourself comfortable. I will be back in a few minutes."

Klaus lived in Hampstead, a village famous in the eighteenth century for its thermal springs. It had developed on a hill, and its architecture was more reminiscent of a little town in the Swiss Alps than of a suburb of London. It was small, bisected by Hampstead High Street and characterized by the little roads that led off the main thoroughfare. One such was Flask Walk, a road so-called that led to the Flask pub, where the thermal water used to be bottled in flasks and sold to the tourists; or like the picturesque Back Lane, whose deliciously colourful houses were a good example of the historical centre.

Klaus owned a house in Winnington Road, a quiet and isolated street, just off Bishops Avenue, which was better known as 'millionaires' row'. None of the houses had fewer than ten rooms, and they were all mansions like the one where Rubinstein lived.

Lisa moved over to the window and saw the dimmed lights shining from the grass in the park. A fountain of white marble stood in the centre, and the spray of water created a pleasant effect. Then, like magic, she heard music, and the living room became warmer and cosier, while the paintings seemed to reflect different colours. Klaus held two glasses of champagne, and he smiled at her to put her at ease.

"A simple way to welcome you to my home," he said, flashing her a dazzling smile.

Lisa took the glass and sipped a little.

"I want to show you something," he said.

They entered another room, and when the lights came on, Lisa was speechless. Hanging on the wall was a picture of a woman on a stage. It was Lisa.

"Do you recognize it?" he asked.

"Yes," she said smiling. "It's me at the theatre. *The Black and the White*."

Klaus turned towards her and tenderly caressed her face.

"But why do you have it?" Lisa asked, feeling the warm sensation of both his caress and the fact that her picture was hanging so prominently in the room.

"Because you are special, and you have a gift for acting."

She felt as if she were dreaming. First the contract, then Klaus, now this.

"Fancy a drink?" Klaus asked.

"I thought I just had one."

"That was not a drink. I want you to try something special. Just like you."

Klaus moved towards her and grabbed her waist. He slowly pulled her to him until their faces were close enough to touch. Lisa trembled and did not offer any resistance; she had been unconsciously waiting for something like this to happen. Something emotional enough to erase the night of passion she had spent with Alex. Klaus came closer, and she could hear him breathing. She closed her eyes and waited. But a second before they kissed, a sense of guilt overwhelmed her.

She pulled abruptly away. "We had better have that drink."

The spell was broken. Klaus loosened his grasp, caressed her hand, and went to the bar. "I hope you like it."

"What is it?"

"You need something to make you forget," Klaus said.

"I don't understand," Lisa said, feeling confused and hesitant.

"Drink this," Klaus said, his voice suddenly hardened as he handed her the drink in a short glass.

It was an order and she had no choice. She drank and the glass fell to the floor a few moments later.

"Something wrong?" he asked her.

"My head…is spinning."

* * *

When Lisa came round she was naked, in a bed she had never slept in before, in a room she had never seen, with a blanket that barely covered her. Bewildered, she tried to focus on the night before. She remembered Klaus, the drink, her head spinning, and now a violent headache. Klaus stepped out of the bathroom with a towel around his waist.

"Good morning, Lisa." He came closer and Lisa instinctively tried to cover herself.

"What am I doing here?" she asked. Her voice trembled, and she was sickened by fear at the thought of the answer.

"We just fucked," he said, smiling.

He leaned down to face her. His arms were straight, and his hands were on the pillow where her head was resting. She admired the definition of his muscles and the incredible sensuality of his eyes. The desire grew stronger, and she felt her head become heavy again. She fell into an endless vortex, and her emotions intensified. Again she felt anguish, but this time, her body did not reject him. Klaus's hands were all over her; shivers ran all over her skin… she wanted him. Again.

FIVE

"I don't think it's a drama," Joel said. "There are plenty of beautiful girls in the world. Theoretically, we should have ten available girls each."

"Exciting statistics," Alex said. "Did you do the survey?"

"I was just trying to cheer you up," Joel countered.

Joel was eating nuts while lying on the black and blue striped sofa in Alex's living room flat, flicking through the pages of *FHM* magazine. Alex's flat was a mix of black and white pictures hung on the walls, representing portraits of actors on stage. There was a pile of *Time Out* magazines on the right side of the sofa, a tenor sax on its tripod stand in one corner, a copy of the screenplay of *The Usual Suspect* on the floor, and a bunch of handwritten notes spread in an artistic disorder on the dining table, a dark brown velvet chair and the wooden tea table before the sofa, where Joel had stretched his legs on. There was a bow window overlooking the street, enabling the sunlight to take the dark away from the little kitchenette at the back end of the living room. An old TV and a crappy stereo system completed the furniture.

"They took good photos of her. She's cute though. Is she good in bed?" Joel asked

Alex was reading the *Evening Standard*, and Joel's question annoyed him. "It's none of your business!"

"Calm down, Mate, just curious. You can get to know so much about a woman when you are in bed with her, whether she is emotional, if she is selfish or rather ambitious…yes, ambitious. I bet she is when I think about what she is achieving…"

"She is not that kind of girl," Alex said in Lisa's defence. "She has much more style than you think. Now give it a rest."

Joel threw the magazine up in the air, stood up, and came to stand right behind the chair Alex was sitting in.

"To be in love is to be in the weakest possible position," Joel chided his friend. "You go to war but you already know you will lose."

Alex hesitated, and his rage gave way to his sweetness. "I just love her."

It was so clear, even the walls around the table understood it.

"To be in love is beautiful," Joel said, smiling, "yet it is dangerous, because its fulfillment depends on the feelings of the object of one's attention."

"Since when do you understand about feelings, Joel?"

"I have emotions too. I know full well that sex and love are two different things. That is why I try not to get too involved and try to spread my attention between several women. If it goes wrong with one, I always have a chance with the others. Let's say that I don't put all my eggs in one basket."

He was such a narcissist, what Alex had always wanted to be but never had the courage.

"Hence," Joel continued, "I believe that your disappointment stems from the idea of love you built around her. Who knows what thoughts she might be having behind her beautiful eyes? Just to reassure you, I believe that behind her eyes there is absolute emptiness."

"Wrong," Alex said.

A broken heart, Joel thought.

"She's so sweet, the most sensitive girl I have ever met."

"Sensitive?" Joel stepped back. "Has she called you since she signed the contract?"

Alex looked down. "No."

"She is a bitch! She slept with you, and the day after, not only did she run away, she also signed the contract that should have been yours. So much for sensitivity!"

Alex did not reply.

"Want to go for a walk?" Joel asked. "It seems nice outside."

With their conversation on hold, they left the apartment and stepped out into a gloriously clear day.

They went to South Bank, a place that had long inspired writers, painters, lonely people, or people who just wanted to be alone.

"I always thought that this place would inspire me sooner or later," said Alex.

"What do you mean?" Joel asked, looking around at their surroundings.

"One can see so many things here, things that just seem to be and things that just are."

They stood before the railing along the river. Joel took his block notes and began to draw something.

"Working?" Alex asked him.

"Fantasising," Joel said.

He drew a bench, and on the bench he drew a man. Alex looked past him and saw the bench that Joel had just drawn. There was a man on the bench, but in Joel's sketch he looked different, as if he were smiling.

"Why is he laughing?" Alex asked, seeing how Joel had drawn the man.

"Because this is a comic and comics aren't real. This is a happy tramp, and his name is Sip. He gets drunk and enjoys his life like crazy."

Alex turned and motioned with his eyebrows for Joel to look towards the real bench.

"What are you thinking?" Joel asked.

"He doesn't look like a tramp. Put him under a shower, shave him, and dress him up. He could easily look like an intellectual."

Alex was right. The tramp had a dignity and looked like a good person. Joel looked at Alex and then made a move away from him.

"Where are you going?" Alex asked.

"I want to talk to my comic."

Alex stood still, watching Joel walk towards the bench. Joel stopped, sat down, and began to talk to the man. Then he turned and invited Alex to join them.

"His name is Travis," Joel told Alex.

"Nice to meet you, Travis. My name is Alex."

Travis was surprised. Not because Joel was speaking to him, but because he was smiling while doing it.

"Hi, Alex, your friend is a cartoonist?"

Alex had never spent more than a second with someone like Travis in his life, simply because he had never felt he wanted to. But this man was different. He did not seem to be from the street.

"I am a theatre actor," Alex said.

Alex looked at Joel. It should have been a brief, funny interlude and short break, but they were still talking to Travis.

"There are so many people around here. I see them walking every day but no one seems to be happy," Travis observed, nodding towards passers-by.

Alex hesitated and then sat next to the tramp.

"What happens today, happens tomorrow, and you don't remember anything of what's passed, until you wake up one day, you look at what you have achieved, and think about your past."

Joel and Alex exchanged glances. Travis did not sound drunk. Maybe he was crazy.

* * *

His nightmares made a never-ending night unbearable. Alex could not sleep. Lisa was in everything he thought about, in everything he looked at. She was just everywhere, like a nightmare of unreturned love. There was nothing worse than thinking so late at night: a tramp, a bench, Joel and his sketches—and that tramp, again. He got out of bed and went to the window and was met with wind and rain: a perfect scene in which to grow his anguish, but luckily he was at home. Poor Travis, it would have been terrible to be spending such a night on a bench.

Then, as if by magic, inspiration struck. He turned on his computer and wrote for hours, without taking a break, until dawn broke and he fell asleep at his desk. When he woke up, his first thought was of Travis, who had just become the inspiration for his next drama.

Later, he went to South Bank, and he saw the old man again, sitting on the same bench, with his arms crossed as he gazed out at the river.

"Hi, Travis."

Travis turned towards him. He was around sixty years old and, if he were dressed decently, Alex thought, he could have looked younger.

"Who are you?"

"Don't you remember? I was here with Joel yesterday. Joel, the guy who draws comics."

Travis's emotionless face made him feel uncomfortable.

"Comics? What comics?"

Alex remained silent, bewildered. "You tell me."

Travis didn't seem to be paying attention.

But then came a spark of curiosity. "Why did you come here?"

"I wanted to see you," Alex replied.

"What can a young guy like you have in common with an old man like me?"

"Just want to talk."

Travis looked at Alex. "I don't think there is much for us to talk about."

Both of them wanted to talk to each other, however. Alex was curious;

the old man was lonely.

"What would you like to talk about?" Travis asked.

"About anything you like. I don't know what I am doing here."

"Sometimes there is no reason for what happens in life. It just happens," Travis said.

Travis inspected the pocket of his coat, pulled out half a cigarette, and lit it. "Look at the bridge," Travis said, after taking a couple of puffs.

Alex turned towards Waterloo.

"It always seems the same, right?" Travis said, when he saw that Alex was looking towards the bridge. "The water has been flowing beneath it for ages. Tomorrow will be the same, as will all the other tomorrows that follow."

His intensity was almost shocking, and Alex could not stop staring at the old man's eyes.

"What's so special about that bridge that excites your imagination this way?" Alex asked tenuously.

"When I look at that bridge, I see the life that flows, slips through your fingers, making you believe that all you see will remain the same forever, like the water in the river. But life is not like that. Things change and to see is not enough to allow one to understand."

The butt of the cigarette almost burnt Travis's lips. Alex took it out of his mouth, retrieved a new packet of cigarettes from his pocket and handed it over to Travis.

"For whenever you feel like smoking," Alex said, offering the packet. "Just twenty, so I hope you will make them last until the next time we meet."

Travis looked at the packet and his eyes shone.

"How long have you been living like this?" Alex asked.

Tears filled Travis's eyes. It was the first time that someone had engaged him in conversation for the sheer pleasure of it. His wall of loneliness disappeared and he began to cry.

* * *

The snow fell and smothered everything it touched with its heavy white flakes. With a slight shake, the man let the snow fall off his body, stood up from the bench, and took off the plastic bag that enfolded him. The features of his face were broken by furrows of weariness, while his eyes, dark and intense, betrayed resignation mixed with anger. He lit up the remains of a cigar and a sweetish smell rose quickly in the air. He puffed intensely, and a suffering cough broke the silence of the white day.

Sixty years. A long time had passed, and he could not even remember the last time he celebrated his birthday. From time to time a newspaper forgotten somewhere by someone caught his eye in South Bank, and then his memory returned to the past. He stood up and tried to move, but his muscles were locked, pain exploded in the middle of his chest, and his breath was laboured. He knelt down, suffering, while the cold of the morning penetrated his bones. Death could not hurt him more than the miserable life he was now living. He had his head down and his hands in the snow, when a remote buzz from somewhere behind him made him turn. Two children were playing. He too had children, but Destiny had taken them away from him.

Travis Sinclair lived with his loneliness, with the remnants of his life stuck to him. Memories were all he had left, and he was surviving those—a wife he thought he knew, two children he loved more than life itself, and who, instead of loving him back, had grown to be bastards. There was enough to forget. The two children were playing, and Travis could hear their laughter, sculptured in the white silence. How could he have destroyed his life and the life of his family for his damn ambition? He turned and looked at the Thames. The water was flowing, and it seemed like a grey wound in the white dress of the city. He walked towards the bridge and thought, *why me?* He had reached heaven, but all it had brought him was misery.

The cold became unbearable, and the wind grew stronger. Travis fixed the papers under his coat and looked at the bridge, hoping that one day Destiny would give him the strength to cross it again. He sat under the bridge, waiting for the umpteenth night, without sense, of his sad existence. And the night came. Travis was sleeping when the noise of an approaching car brought him back to reality.

"Hey you!

They were three young men. The first was tall and slim and wore a hat pulled down on his forehead that hid his eyes. The second was short, a skinhead wearing a leather jacket. The third must have been the last to join the gang. Insecure, he was hiding behind the first two.

"Hey you, old man!"

Travis could see them all. He was sitting on the ground with his back against the wall, and he was staring at them with an expressionless face.

"What the fuck are you doing you old piece of shit?"

Travis did not react. He was looking at the lights of the building on the other side of the river.

"He's talking to you!"

It was the second who spoke, the skinhead.

"Why don't you answer?"

The skinhead was moving nervously, shaking his arms and staring at the first guy, waiting for a signal. The first guy nodded, and the skinhead kicked Travis's leg with an incredible violence. Travis did not react, just kept staring at the lights that were coming from the other side of the river. The three men looked at each other and then the tall one came closer to him and kicked his leg again. Travis still did not react.

"He's dead!"

"Come on! Kick him, kick him!"

"Let's kill him!" This time it was the third young man who spoke, the one who was hiding behind his two mates.

What could his life be worth to those three men? That was what Travis thought about in that very moment. He turned and read the fear in their eyes. It seemed to be rage, but it would soon have shown itself for what it actually was. The insecure one, who was always hiding, stepped back. So did the second, the skin head.

"You are not even able to kill an old man," Travis said, not really taunting them, but stating a curious fact.

There was only one answer available to the three men.

The tallest guy turned towards the other two. "Let's throw him into the river!"

What an amazing idea. They were so excited they did not realize that Travis was standing.

"Go back to your mother," Travis said, not with guile but resignation.

His words were directed at the third guy, who was still hiding behind the other two and who was now desperately looking at the tallest one, not knowing what to say.

"Do you have a family, kid?" Travis asked.

He called him kid! What an unbearable offence! The tallest came closer and gave him a push. "Shut up you son of a bitch!"

The excitement was back, but only for a moment. Travis was staring at them and a fierce coldness radiated from his eyes. The skinhead guy tried to kick him again, but Travis locked his leg, grabbed his arm and tore it of its socket.

"I am fucking hungry, boy, much more than you can imagine."

He was old and slim, but in that very moment he looked like a wolf. The insecure guy ran back to the car.

"What do you want from me, kids?"

The other two were bewildered, both standing before him. The tall guy was looking at Travis who was almost breaking his friend's arm.

"Help me! Help me!"

But his friend did not make a move. Travis eased his grip and simply stared at them, until they all left. He remained still, until the night swallowed the lights of the car. He looked between the pillars, from where the light emanated. It was intense, and the cloudy sky reflected it like a light on a stage.

"Why me?" he asked aloud, this time.

The loneliness kept him company. The bitterness made him feel alone.

SIX

The sun was shining, and the cold of that Sunday morning made it seem soulless, like an image on a postcard. As Alex lifted the collar of his coat, a sheet of paper, carried by the wind, rose up from the street into the air. There had been no one on the street that morning.

He arrived at a crossroad and waited for the traffic light to change. Instinctively, he looked to his right, and a woman who was at that moment turning his back to him caught his attention. He could see her ash-blonde hair, which tumbled from beneath her hat. In the next moment, the traffic light changed. The woman crossed the street and walked in the opposite direction before stopping in front of a shop window. Her profile reminded him of Lisa. Alex shook his head and tried to ignore this fantasy.

He walked along a street that seemed to go on forever and entered a bar, hungry and exhausted from the cold. He ordered a coffee and sat at a table next to the window overlooking the street. Same scene, same people, and a traffic light that would soon change colour again. A woman turned towards him and what he imagined he saw and what he actually saw were one and the same.

He left the cup on the table and almost ran out of the bar, trying to reach the woman before it was too late. He turned to his right, then to his left, hoping to find the portrait his fantasy had drawn, but he did not see her. Again, he shook his head and tried not to pay attention to what his imagination had told him. He reached Piccadilly and stopped next to the stairs at the feet of the statue of Eros. Then reality dawned on him. People were walking everywhere, and the traffic lights were not one, but two, three, five times as many as those he had counted while having his coffee at the bar. She could have gone anywhere, since Piccadilly was the intersection of many different streets for many different people. She could have disappeared among the shops and the crowds of Soho or the elegant boutiques of Regent Street. Then, among the crowd, a woman with the same hat and hair the colour of ash turned towards him. Alex walked and then ran trying to reach her, but the woman vanished again into masses of people. He stopped, bent double, breathing heavily from the effort of his pursuit. He shook his head and gave up.

He felt desperate, pathetic. Lisa had gone, but he kept seeing her everywhere. He loved her with his heart and soul, but the story was over. Like many beautiful things in life, things that are born grow stronger, give one the illusion that they are part of one's life, and then, when one finally believes they have become part of one's world, they disappear. And he felt bad, because Lisa was the most beautiful thing to have ever entered his life.

* * *

The following day he was glad to see how fast the restructuring work was proceeding at Joe's theatre. The main hall was larger, and the office had been refurbished to a much higher standard, with a modern desk in glass and aluminium frame, steel lacquered shelves plugged into a niche in the wall, a very simple, but elegant, black leathered sofa, and two minimalist chairs on the other side of Joe's desk. There were no more fluorescent lights but two stylish lamps at the corners of the room giving a much warmer light. On the other hand, Joe felt he deserved a nice office after the forty seats of the theatre had more than doubled.

"Alex, we need to talk. Let's go to my office," Joe said when he saw Alex. The pitch of Joe's voice betrayed his tension. And a few moments later, they were sitting in Joe's office. Joe was behind his new desk, while Alex sat in a comfortable chair across from him.

"As you know, the theatre now has a new investor," Joe said.

Alex nodded.

"And, unfortunately, when new investors enter the business things often change."

Alex was caught by surprise, but Joe kept going.

"Personally, I would never have accepted other investors, if I hadn't needed the funds to enlarge the theatre. I did this for that reason, and I did it for you. I expected at least a little help from you to make my life easier. How's the new project going?"

"It will take some time. I have an idea, but I have to think it through properly. When is the deadline?" Alex asked, feeling his stomach sink with anticipation.

"In two weeks."

"I'll do what I can. And what about the rights?" Alex asked, having learned his lesson from *The Black and the White*.

"We're going to refer to the existing agreement."

"I don't remember signing an agreement," Alex said.

"One year. Everything you write during the next year will belong to the theatre. Have you already forgotten that you received an advance payment?"

"But I signed that piece of paper because I had no choice! You know that, Joe! I needed the money to fix my apartment and pay my bills!"

He did not have the courage to look Alex in the eye. "Yes, I know, but the new owner wants the pre-existing agreements to be fulfilled."

At that very moment, the friendship between Alex and Joe faltered.

"I had to accept, Alex. I did it for the theatre. I am really sorry."

"Two weeks, you said?" Alex pressed.

"Yes. That's the deadline they gave me."

Alex left the theatre depressed. Two weeks were enough if he had a plot, but two weeks were not sufficient for someone who had no story line.

He quickly organized a meeting with Judie and Scott at his own place.

"Joe is so stressed that he behaves the same with me," Scott added, having noted something different in Joe as of late that he did not like. "I can't understand why this is happening. We put the show together. It wasn't their idea."

"What do you think you will do, Judie?" Alex asked, turning from Scott to Judie.

"If I can find a job, I'll quit, considering what he pays me," Judie said.

"Have you heard from Lisa?" Alex asked, almost shyly, afraid of his friends' reactions.

"I lost touch with her completely," Judie admitted.

"So what next?" Scott asked, nodding at both Judie and Alex.

"We are on our own," Alex said. "I can't do anything, since I am bound by a contract that ties me to the theatre for the next twelve months. I don't have any choice but to finish my work as soon as I can."

"Can't you just quit?" Scott asked.

"I can't," Alex answered. "I've accepted an advance payment for all the work I'll produce this year, and I have spent it all to fix my crappy flat and pay my bills. I don't have a pound left in my pocket to give him back. So I will be working for him."

Judie was clearly afraid. "I don't want to lose my job," she said. "Going door to door looking for work is something I have had to do in the past. I can't do it again. I won't do it again. I think I'll have a chat with Joe, since I am not writing any play but just acting."

So the three of them ended the meeting and, true to her intentions, Judie went to find Joe.

It took less than half an hour. Joe made the reality clear: it was all in Alex's hands. If Alex delivered his work on schedule, they would be paid. Otherwise, they had better not knock on his door.

Judie then went back to Scott and Alex, heavy hearted and full of anticipation. This time they met in the pub.

* * *

Two days later, Alex went to see Joe at the theatre. He was ready to face some resistance from his end to his idea of a more sophisticated show rather than the usual commercial production that Joe was hoping to get from him.

"A monologue?" Joe asked. He was again meeting with Alex in his new office, and Alex had just pitched his idea about the play being a monologue.

"Yes, Joe, the only idea that came to me."

"What is it about?" Joe asked, and from his tone, Alex could tell he was sceptical.

"Life in general," Alex said. I am planning to use an extended metaphor."

"What's its running time?"

"One hour."

Joe wasn't happy. He handed Alex some faxes.

"This is the group we are thinking of signing. Read it. You'll find everything there. Perhaps you already know them." Then he looked at Alex with sincerity. "I want to give you a chance, but I need you to help me to give it to you. If you don't deliver a credible piece of work, I know they will not accept it."

"Fair enough, but I guarantee you that the monologue is worth the price of the ticket. It is intense, vibrant. Trust me."

"Have you already written something?"

"Tomorrow, on the stage."

"Fine."

* * *

Alex arrived at the theatre exactly on time, aiming to convince Joe to accept his idea.

"Lights please," Alex said. He was on the stage, in a tight, pitch-black T-shirt, like the background of the scene. "Perfect, now narrow and zoom in. Not that strong! You will make me blind!"

"Is it that ok?"

"Perfect. Joe, now relax and enjoy."

Joe nodded. He was alone in the gallery. Alex focused, breathed deeply, and was ready to go.

"Like a light I remember you, indistinct,
one that has turned dark, that doesn't shine.
You are a phantom, but I keep thinking we are together.
It's a crazy dream, without reason,
one that makes me aim, makes me want
what I know I'll never get.
It's my emotion, if I see colours that don't shine.
It's in the emotion…that I am lost.
I want you, I hate you. The more I try to run away,
the more I miss you.
Can you hear my heart? It beats because of love.
This was my gift for you.
But you decided and never said;
you decided and ran away after stealing all my light
and absorbing it into yours.
You wanted to take it all and
you left nothing in my hands.
What remains is faded memory;
it's a glow that slowly dies; it's the twilight of my love…"

Alex went on until the end, without ever stopping, with an intensity that any audience would have loved. Joe knew it well as he perceived, as a spectator, the passion accompanying Alex's words when he talked about the woman who deceived him, about the old tramp and his miserable life under a bridge and about the secret hidden in the drops of the Thames. But he also felt terribly sorry, as he feared there was not much he could do to change Conrad's mind.

"Stop!"

"So?" Alex asked.

"I need to think about it. It wasn't bad, but not exactly what I was expecting to get from you," Joe said.

Judie and Scott had entered without Alex or Joe noticing their presence.

"It was amazing, Joe! What the hell you do have to think about?" Judie said. She stood and began to clap. She ran towards Alex with a smile that spoke more eloquently than any words she could have said.

"I want a copy!"

Alex smiled at her. "I haven't written anything yet."

SEVEN

"Klaus, I'm scared!" Lisa said.

"Don't you like it? Dead or alive!" Klaus replied, appearing to be enjoying himself.

"Slow down, please…slow down!" Lisa insisted.

Klaus did not listen. He was full of coke and Lisa's fear excited him.

"Stop this fucking car!" Lisa demanded.

Klaus slowed down, parked on the side of the street, and turned off the engine. The lights were still on, and the silhouettes of Hampstead Heath were clearly visible beyond the windshield. Klaus had made a crazy run, with the alcohol flowing thicker in his veins than his blood. He wiped his forehead, while his shirt also drenched with sweat stuck to his skin.

Lisa burst out crying with her face in her hands. "You are mad…" she said and opened the door and walked away. She did not know where she was, but she just wanted to get away. Klaus sat in his seat watching her running away. Then he burst out laughing, but a moment before she disappeared into the darkness he turned on the engine and drove towards her.

"Get in."

"Go away!"

"Don't be childish!" Klaus teased.

The car was right next to her, proceeding slowly. Lisa did not turn and kept walking until she broke down and began to run and cry out loud. Klaus accelerated and stopped the car a few metres ahead. He got out and walked towards her.

"Calm down now." He grabbed her arms and held her tightly.

"You're hurting me!"

"Calm down!"

Lisa stopped screaming. The tears ran down her cheeks, and her terror showed in her eyes. "You scared me..." She said this tenderly, almost whispering, while she tried to control herself.

"You have to trust me, Lisa. You know I'd never hurt you."

Then he purposefully moved towards the car.

"Where are we going now?" she asked.

"Home."

"I want to go to my place!"

He drove for half an hour then turned onto Bishop's Avenue. Lisa lowered her head and remained silent. Six months had gone by since they first met. At the beginning, she had felt as if she was living in a romance novel, then things began to change, and time transformed her dream into a perverse relationship with no escape.

Klaus didn't take her home but took her to his place, and at the moment, there was nothing that Lisa could do.

As soon as they were indoors, Klaus headed for the liquor cabinet. "I am going to pour myself a drink. Would you like to join me?" he asked her.

"No, thanks."

Klaus lay down on the sofa. Lisa took off her coat and let it fall near the table in the middle of the room.

"I am going to take a bath," she said.

Klaus put on some music and lit a fire. He wanted atmosphere. Then he grabbed the phone.

"At my place," Lisa heard him say as she left the room. "Bring something and don't come alone."

Half an hour later someone knocked at the door. Klaus let his guests in and took them to the living room.

"Where is she?" Eduard asked.

"She's taking a bath," Klaus answered.

"Tell me she doesn't know anything!" Eduard continued.

Klaus gave him a threatening look. "She doesn't know anything."

After a while, Lisa returned wearing a silky pink dressing gown with her hair wrapped in a towel, looking gorgeous even without makeup.

"Lisa, have you already met Eduard?"

"I think so."

"These are Eddy's friends," Klaus added.

"I figured," Lisa said.

Eddy's friends were two young girls, elegantly dressed, with a kind of stuck-up bitch style. Inga was Swedish, a hard body, enhanced breasts, and deep, horny black eyes. Inna was skinnier but taller than Inga. She had pronounced cheekbones, and her smaller breasts were compensated by long and incredibly sexy legs. They were both Eddy's friends and both were keen to embrace Klaus's friendship as well.

"We thought we could spend some time together. Will you join us?" Eddy asked Lisa.

Lisa shrugged and took a seat on the chair next to the sofa. Klaus left the cigar box open on the table. Eddy stood up and poured everybody something to drink.

"What would you like?" he asked Lisa.

"Martini, thanks."

"These two beautiful girls are actresses, did you know that Klaus?" Eduard said.

"I didn't, what kind of movies do they act in?"

"A serial."

The girls smiled and looked at Klaus.

"You're not jealous, are you darling?" Klaus said, looking over at Lisa in her chair.

"I am not, Klaus. I am not jealous at all." Lisa crossed her legs, uncovering what the dressing gown had hidden. Eddy's attention wandered from the glasses on the table as he stared at Lisa's legs.

"Eddy, could you please hand us a drink? We need something strong," Inga said.

He got off the sofa. The two girls were pretty, but their beauty paled beside Lisa's.

"Here we are," Eddy said, returning to the sofa with drinks for the girls.

Klaus handed the box to his guests and everybody took out cigars.

"Careful you don't smoke out the whole room," Lisa said.

Eddy handed her the Martini. When she took the glass, her dressing gown slipped off one shoulder, revealing a breast for just an instant, but long enough to excite Eddy.

"Don't you smoke?" he asked her.

"I prefer this," Lisa said, tapping on a packet of *Marlboros*.

She was tired. The stress of that night had taken its toll on her, and it was still visible in the tension in her face. She lit up a cigarette, stood up, and went towards the stairs.

"Where are you going?" Klaus asked.

"To my room." She said nothing else.

"Where did she go?" Eddy asked, distracted by Inga and Inna's jokes.

"To bed, Eddy. Lisa goes to sleep early at night, like all good girls do."

Eddy looked at the girls then turned to Klaus.

"What are we going to do now?" Inna asked.

"We'll have a party!" Eddy said and took out a little plastic bag, deposited the coke on the table and, after preparing a line, snorted some.

"Your turn, girls."

Inna moved closer and knelt down beside the table. Eddy stood behind her, enjoying the view of her beautiful neckline.

"And you? Not joining the party?" Eddy asked Inga.

Inga was still sitting, but as soon as Eddy spoke, she moved across to her girlfriend. She hugged her from behind and kissed her neck. Klaus looked at the scene, expressionless, while both Inga and Inna turned towards him. They smiled. It was the first of many such smiles that night.

* * *

"It should open next fall. He's a rising star, and I should get the screenplay by the end of this week." Angela was giving Lisa information about an upcoming screenplay, talking about another rising star of 'Planet Rubinstein'.

Lisa and Angela had decided to meet for a coffee at the *Starbucks* in Motcomb Street, in the heart of Belgravia, one of the most exclusive and expensive areas of London.

"It's a drama," Angela said. "They like your look. I sent them your pictures and they liked them, but I can't promise anything right now."

"I am not so sure I want to say goodbye to the theatre. I love being on the stage so much," Lisa said. She wasn't all that enticed into the dream of being in film that Angela seemed to be creating for her.

"It will only be for a couple of months," Angela said, "but it depends on you. I would recommend you take a look at the screenplay. People who have read it say good things about it."

Angela put the papers back together. Lisa looked tired and troubled. "How is it going with Klaus?"

"Is it that obvious?" Lisa said, feeling exactly as tired and troubled as Angela indicated.

"I'd say so. Would you like to catch up later?"

"I'd love to," Lisa said. "I need to talk to someone."

Each woman went her own way for the duration of the morning.

Then they met later for lunch at *Scalini*, a refined old styled Italian restaurant in Walton Street, in the heart of Chelsea, five minutes walking distance from Harrods, five minutes from South Kensington, and five minutes, in general, from a lot of nice places. Walton Street was a trendy spot among the many of London, with a series of bars and restaurants framed in little townhouses that didn't exceed the two-floor height. With all the buzz at the weekend, if it wasn't for the presence of tall and sexy eastern European girls or young Middle Eastern guys driving their Lambos up and down the road for hours and hours, Walton Street could almost resemble, with a touch of imagination, a kind of light version of Miami South Beach without the beach, especially during a sunny day of summer. They had just been seated when Lisa's phone rang.

Lisa held the phone to her ear and looked away from Angela. "Alright, in half an hour…with Angela…okay."

"Work?" Angela asked, when Lisa had ended the call.

"Klaus. He's joining us."

Angela fixed her hair with her hand, took a little mirror from her purse, and checked to see that her lipstick was in order.

"He is not coming here for you, Angela," Lisa observed dryly.

Angela ignored Lisa's remark. She was just focused on her makeup. "I am not doing it for him, darling. I am doing it for myself. In this world appearances are everything."

They saw Klaus smiling, as he always did in front of beautiful girls. "Good afternoon, princesses."

Klaus bowed before Angela, took her hand, and touched it to his lips. Then he kissed Lisa on her cheek. "A beautiful day made even nicer by the pleasure I have seeing you."

Angela seemed to be walking on a wire between two clouds. She would have loved to throw herself into his arms but tried to restrain herself for the sake of her dignity and her relationship with Lisa.

"We were discussing work," Angela said as Klaus took a seat at the table.

"Anything new on the horizon?" he asked.

"Yes, that new director," Angela said.

"Greg you mean. He's really, really good," Klaus observed.

"Lisa is thinking about it, but she would prefer not to leave her career at the theatre," Angela said.

"I can understand that. Theatre is her passion, but there is more money in the movies. Don't you agree, sweetheart?" Klaus said, still addressing Angela.

Angela smiled. "How did it go last night?"

Lisa blushed and looked down. Klaus smiled at Angela. "Well, really well. We gave a little party at my place. You should come next time."

Angela was embarrassed. Lisa poured herself some wine and seemed distracted.

"How long have you two been dating?" Angela asked.

"Six months, more or less," Lisa said. "But I don't understand why you ask. You should know."

Angela suddenly blushed.

"Are you alright?" Lisa asked her.

Klaus was sitting next to Angela, but his hand was beneath the table and right between Angela's legs.

"Just a little distracted," Angela said, looking more than a little distracted.

"I'll be back in a minute," Lisa said.

Angela and Klaus remained still, while Lisa stood up and then left.

"I can't, Klaus, I can't," Angela said in response to Klaus.

"At eight. At my place," Klaus insisted.

* * *

Angela saw the gate on the right side of the street. She was fifteen minutes away from her rendezvous with madness. She took a tiny bottle of perfume and dabbed a few drops on her neck and between her breasts.

"You can't, Angela, you can't do this…but you want it, right?" She spoke aloud. Whatever she decided would change her relationship with Lisa. She thought about Klaus, and she felt the warmth of his hand between her legs. She closed her eyes and her heartbeat accelerated.

"Once, just once…"

She knew she was lying to herself; as soon as she had crossed the gate, there was no going back. Klaus opened the door with a smile, took her coat, and hung it on a chair near the entrance. Then taking her hand, he led her to the living room.

"I am delighted to see you. It makes me feel honoured to have you here with me tonight."

As he lowered the main lights, music filled the room, creating a much more intimate atmosphere. It was the same old routine.

"Glad to know you as Lisa's agent. You girls are both classy ladies. Something to drink?"

"Martini, thanks."

Martini…just like Lisa. This would be easy.

"To this beautiful night, to our date, to a moment I hope you won't forget," Klaus said as he came to the sofa with their drinks. He sat on the sofa next to Angela and turned his upper body to face her fully.

They touched their two glasses, and Klaus looked at Angela. She was a beautiful woman, so different from Lisa. Those few extra years made her appear more interesting than Lisa. He started to flirt, touching her hand, massaging her fingers while sipping his drink. Angela was tense and waiting for the inevitable to happen. And she wanted it to happen. Klaus left the glass on the table, parted her hair, and kissed her neck.

"I want to fly with you tonight," Klaus whispered, while his lips touched her neck.

She closed her eyes, and said nothing. Anything Klaus decided to do was fine with her.

* * *

It was two in the morning when Angela got out of the bed, collecting her clothes, which were spread all over the floor. She had not had a night of sex like that in ages. She felt guilty, dirty. She had just violated the intimacy of her friend Lisa. Then she turned, looked at Klaus's bare and sculptured back and felt shivers along her spine. She wanted more, she needed him to touch her legs again, kiss her breasts again, fuck her again. She felt she could not live without it. But in the end, the remains of her dignity won the battle with her physical desire and drove her to leave. She was in her car when her mobile rang.

"Angela, it's Lisa."

She almost had a heart attack at the sound of Lisa's voice.

"I need to talk to you…where are you?" Lisa said.

"I'm driving," Angela said, withholding any further information.

"Do you want to come over?"

"I'm really tired tonight, Lisa. Can we make it tomorrow?"

"Sure, I was just troubled, sorry. I'll see you tomorrow. Good night."

* * *

Lisa was waiting for her, while sipping her Martini with her eyes restless. Angela arrived at *Patara* a moment later. *Patara* was a pleasant and understated Thai restaurant in Greek Street, in the middle of Soho, just few metres away from Soho Square, and a couple of hundred metres south of the busy Oxford Street.

"What does the chef recommend?"

Lisa smiled, without answering Angela's question. "You look great today," she said, instead. "Big night last night?"

"I can't complain," Angela said with a bit of reticence.

"Forgive me for calling you so late," Lisa said, taking another sip of her Martini. "I couldn't sleep at all."

"A sleepless night can happen to anyone," Angela said, still evasive. She tried to look as casual as possible, but deep inside she felt the weight of her miserable lie.

"It just happened, all of a sudden," Lisa burst out. "Klaus's crazy behaviour while driving his car that night was the last straw." Lisa closed her eyes, put her hands to her face, and breathed deeply. "I have known him for six months."

Angela looked down. She had known him for just one night, but she probably already knew him much better than Lisa. "What's wrong?" Angela said, trying to work up some required empathy.

Lisa looked sad. "I can't understand. Sometimes he is so nice, but sometimes he's so irrational. Do you have any idea why he behaves like that?"

Angela took Lisa's hand and caressed it tenderly. She showed the sweet expression of a compassionate friend. She was acting, much better than Lisa ever had. "Perhaps it's more about you. You don't look relaxed, but I can't understand why. Your job is going well, I assume, or is there something else you would like to talk about?"

Angela never imagined she could speak in such an enchanting voice. On the other hand, this had happened to her before. How many times had her girlfriends taken away the men she liked? Now it was her turn to take away the man her girlfriend liked.

"I thought I could handle things better," Lisa said. "I never expected to lose control like this."

"Do you think Klaus is seeing someone?" Angela asked, knowing full well the answer.

"Someone else?" Lisa looked thoughtful. "I really can't say if it's just one, many, or a man!"

"I remember I once destroyed a relationship just because of a nervous breakdown," Angela said. "Why don't you have a blood test?"

"Blood test…please, don't be ridiculous." A tear ran down Lisa's cheek and fell to her lips, while Angela continued to tenderly caress her hand.

"Let yourself go," Angela said. "Crying can make you feel better."

"Don't know…but maybe, he's not in love with me anymore."

EIGHT

"There are naked scenes!" Lisa almost shouted, surprised at Angela's news.

"Don't be so dramatic," Angela said, keeping her voice calm. "That's one of the reasons we cast you. Surely you understand that?"

"But it's not a role! I'm only on for a few seconds. I pop up here and there and have to act, ass up in the air for most of it. I don't like it! I don't think this role suits me!"

"Thirty thousand pounds, Lisa. That's what you will be paid for the ass-up-in-the-air scene."

Angela was sitting at her desk, staring at Lisa. For that amount of money she could have found not just one, but a hundred Lisas ready to act that part. But Rubinstein wanted this girl. Lisa took the screenplay and quickly flicked through it.

"When do I start?" Lisa said a little less dramatically, somewhat astounded at the amount of money she would make.

"Time to sign," Angela said with a wry smile, pushing the paperwork towards Lisa.

* * *

"Scene Seven, second. Action!" Greg, the director, shouted abruptly.

Lisa was at the hotel, standing, wearing a black, elegant dress, staring angrily at the leading man. David was in tuxedo with his back to her as he poured himself a drink.

"Think of us, what we have together," David said, delivering his lines. He turned and walked towards her. Lisa unclasped her hair, emphasising her sensual beauty. "I would die for you, you know that?" David continued. He hugged her tight.

"You are always telling me that," Lisa's character said, likewise delivering her lines. "I've heard all this before. It doesn't change anything."

"I don't think I will ever find anyone else like you," David said.

He tried to kiss her, but she rejected him. She did not want this.

"I am sorry, but you don't deserve me," Lisa said in a scathing voice.

David took her hands and invited her to sit on the bed. "I have been an idiot. Forgive me if you can."

He stroked her hair and looked at her passionately. He brushed his hand across her face, then her neck, and finally kissed her shoulder, and then her cheeks, her lips, her mouth, the passion driving their movements faster. They were on the bed, in the middle of a love scene, when he slowly took off her dress.

"Passion! I want to see more passion!" Greg cut in.

David increased his rhythm. Lisa tried to get closer to him, moving in time with him, caressing him. Her breasts were naked and she felt uneasy. She felt as if the fiction had suddenly become reality. She could feel the excitement of her partner, the pressure of his hands on her body, his desire to kiss her for real…She never thought it would be like this. She tried to concentrate and thought about the money she would receive, the things that she would buy, the dresses, the jewels…and the uncomfortable feeling vanished. Her movements dramatically changed, turning into perfect harmony, and she was ready to be kissed as if for real.

"Perfect! Well done, really well done!" Greg cut in again.

It was a wonderful love scene. Greg could not have wished for better.

"You learn quickly how to do a love scene. You have to close your eyes, hold your breath, and move as fast as you can while being careful not to make anyone pregnant."

David was funny. Lisa had met him just a couple of days before shooting the love scene. He was a kind of confident guy, more than six feet tall, with longish blond hair, green eyes, a shade of beard on his face, and a body showing his passion for workout.

"When I saw you," Lisa said, "I immediately thought about what it would be like to do a love scene with you. I have never done it before, and I was afraid I wouldn't be able to go through with it."

"There are four more," David said. "I am sure that with a bit of practice we will be perfect."

Lisa looked at him amused. "Do you have a girlfriend?"

"Nothing serious. What about you?"

"I am seeing Klaus, Rubinstein's assistant," Lisa said.

David knew he did not have a chance, but he kept flirting, thinking about the scene they had filmed that day. He still felt her body beneath his hands, her perfume, her lips…it would have been difficult to walk away.

Lisa left the Studios. She thought about calling a friend, but then she decided to go for a walk on her own. It was a beautiful day, so she went into town and, without realizing it, she found herself in the middle of Mayfair, in Bond Street, admiring the shops and the beautiful buildings.

The area had belonged to the *Grosvenors* since the end of the seventeenth century and was named after the *'May Fair'*, the event that took place between Curzon and Shepherd Market twice a month. However, the tradition had ended a few hundred years later, when the aristocrats of the area claimed that the Fair of May was seriously threatening the elegance of the area. Mayfair was indeed the epitome of London elegance, and it was bordered by Oxford Street, Regent Street, Piccadilly, and Park Lane, in an almost perfect square that included the most elegant shops, restaurants, clubs, and hotels in the city, such as the *Dorchester*, *the Connaught*, and the *Claridge's*.

Lisa passed by Sotheby's, entered a coffee shop, and realized something for the very first time. The desire in the eyes of those who were looking at her reached her skin and made her feel like a woman, in the purest sense of the word. She could have played, betrayed, and run the game the way she wanted to play it, for as long as she wanted to play it. A simple glance and the recipient would have flown to her table to talk to her. The control of her posture, the confidence of her body language, and her eyes would have enchanted anyone. She thought about Klaus, David, and the people she had worked with over the past few days. They all wanted her.

She went home late when the stars were in the sky. The air was fresh, and she felt the approaching spring. She undressed and went into the bathroom to take a warm shower. She emerged some time later, with her hair wet and pulled back, and the mirror, hidden by the steam of the shower, reflected her pleasantly unfocused image. She smoothed her hair once, twice, and suddenly stopped. She looked at her reflection and realized that there was nothing left of the shy Lisa, the one who had been in love with Alex. There was nothing in the woman she saw that even vaguely resembled her former self.

* * *

She spread her dresses on the bed and selected a black one. She put it to one side and took some sexy silk lingerie out of a drawer. She splashed on a dash of the perfume that Angela had bought her, retouched her wonderful eyelashes, and put on some lipstick. She appeared dark and sober, perfect for that evening. She felt confident, with no anxiety, and her thoughts returned to the people who looked at her when she walked down on the street, when she was at the bar or at work. The doorbell rang. It was Klaus, and she pleasantly noticed he was holding a beautiful bouquet of flowers.

"These are for you," he said, also admiring what he saw.

She kissed him on the cheek as she let him in.

"They told me about your performance this afternoon."

"I have David to thank for it," Lisa said, being somewhat demure.

It was as if Klaus had already lost his charms. He was disarmed. It was her turn, and she wanted to play.

"We have ten minutes for a cigarette," Klaus said.

"Would you be mad at me if I say that I would prefer to stay in?" Lisa asked.

He was not expecting this. They had plans.

"Anything wrong?" he asked her.

"No, darling, I'm fine."

She called him darling, Klaus noted. She never had before.

"It would be nice if we could stay home," Lisa continued. "If you like, of course—"

"Sure, Lisa, anything you want. Do you want me to order something to eat?"

"Let's think about that later. Some music?" she asked.

"Why not?" Klaus said.

She had an unusual smile on her face, a mix of surprise and amusement. Lisa was her usual self.

"May I smoke?" Lisa asked.

"This is your place," he said, somewhat amused. "You look so different tonight."

Lisa smiled again. She was enjoying playing the game. "Really?"

"Definitely."

"And how would you define different?"

"Like someone else. And your hair…" Klaus trailed off.

"What's wrong with my hair?"

"You pulled it back."

"Thanks for noticing."

"And your makeup…it's different too," Klaus continued.

"Would you give me a massage?" Lisa asked, breaking Klaus's series of ecstatic compliments.

"Now?"

"Yes, right here on my neck."

Klaus expression looked like that of someone watching a movie without understanding it.

"What are you waiting for?" Lisa insisted.

He came closer but was so clumsy he looked like a beginner. "How is this?"

"A bit more effort would be nice."

He caressed her, continuing to massage her neck, and memories of the Lisa he was sure he knew until the door opened that night came back to him. He went back over the time they had spent together, to the nights that he wished would never end, and he remembered Lisa as she was then. He kissed her neck, but then, suddenly, stepped back.

"What's wrong now?" Lisa asked.

"You changed your perfume." His voice was tinged with something approaching rage.

"Yes, I did. What of it?"

It was the same perfume Angela had worn the night she and Klaus had sex and, for a moment, her face seemed to flicker across Lisa's. He tried to calm himself down and kept massaging her neck. But his touch was insecure.

"Why don't you sit next to me?" Lisa said.

Klaus smiled, as he thought she had not noticed anything.

"Why are you staring at me like that?" Lisa asked.

"You are beautiful like an angel," he said, trying to calm his uneasiness.

She wasn't going to fall for Klaus's cheesy line tonight. "That's a childish thing to say tonight."

Seducing a woman was like an art. Klaus could have slept with all the women he wanted, but he could never have seduced one.

"You have an immense amount of class," he said, trying to gain Lisa's attention, again, but things were going from bad to worse.

"I think I will change with you, dear Klaus," Lisa said.

He felt completely thrown off track. He did not understand what Lisa had in mind.

"Hug me."

He kissed her with passion this time. He began to touch her and Lisa reciprocated. She unbuttoned his shirt and let her hand slip through. She could feel his muscles, his tension, and she loved it. Then she took his belt off and started to caress him. She was playing as she never had before, and she was enjoying herself. Klaus kept touching her, kissing her, without knowing what was about to happen. Lisa kept her eyes open, detached from the scene. She looked at him, while he breathed and grunted like a pig, and realized the man kneeling in front of her was a nothing, a loser, unworthy of her.

"No!" She pushed him away.

"What, Lisa?" Klaus said, confused.

"You heard me, Klaus. We are finished."

"But Lisa…"

"Put your clothes on and go."

He looked at her bewildered. No woman had ever dared to talk to him like that. "What the fuck is going on in your mind tonight?" he said.

"That's the door," Lisa said, indicating it dramatically, with an outstretched arm and a pointing finger.

He stood rooted to the spot with his mouth wide open. He was standing, half naked, with his trousers around his ankles. He could never have anticipated something like this. He got dressed, deeply humiliated, but a moment before he left, Lisa said, "When you see Angela, tell her that I really enjoyed spending the night with you."

Klaus did not reply. He just didn't have any words to say, he just felt bewildered after Lisa had rejected the beauty of his body, the only source of confidence he had. He put on his trousers, walked towards the exit, and left, slamming the door behind him in a mix of impotence and frustration.

NINE

"Lisa is here for you, Mr Rubinstein," his secretary said from the inter-office intercom.

Rubinstein pressed the button on his intercom set. "Let her in."

Lisa was wearing a flowery dress that gave her a very girly look. The secretary looked at her with a hint of envy and let her in. Rubinstein sat at the back of the room, behind his desk.

"Good morning, Lisa."

"Good morning, Mr Rubinstein."

"This is the first time that I'm meeting someone without an appointment," Rubinstein said, as if to clearly delineate that this was an exception he was not used to making. He was very serious.

"I was passing by, and I thought I'd come and say hello," Lisa said. "I hope I'm not disturbing you."

Rubinstein's mind was immersed somewhere else, and she felt as if she was intruding. So she decided to get to the point. "You have always intrigued me, Mr Rubinstein."

What a bad start, she thought. Had she wanted to make it any worse, it would have been impossible.

"Intrigued? Strange expression," he said sarcastically.

"I've always wondered how you spent your days."

"Like any other producer. I have a meeting in a moment, so if you don't have any other questions…"

"I wanted to talk to you about the film," Lisa said, firmly.

"Is there something wrong?" Rubinstein said, looking somewhat startled.

She had played the right card and she got his attention. "First, I wanted to thank you for the opportunity that you have given me and just to let you know that I am available for any other project that you think might be suitable for me. Maybe we could even discuss this in a relaxed way over dinner?"

She was direct in a way that Rubinstein would never have imagined. A simple try, but effective, that seemed to hit right at the centre of Rubinstein thoughts.

"Okay, let's say Saturday night at my place."

* * *

Lisa had just shut the door behind her when she saw Klaus speaking with the secretary.

"He is busy right now with Lisa."

The click of the door made him turn round, and he saw her come out of Rubinstein's office.

"And so just like that you're now entertaining yourself with 'Yaron'." His tone was nasty.

"If I entertained myself with you, then I can entertain myself with anybody."

He came towards her, grabbed her arm, and pulled it.

"I decide what goes on here; don't forget it."

"Take your filthy hand off my arm," Lisa snapped.

Klaus got nervous and pushed her. "You're playing with fire," he said, once again thrown off by this new and different Lisa.

"Absolutely, Klaus, I will try to be careful." She walked away calmly, but inside she was trembling. She turned around and once more caught Klaus's eye. He smiled at her sarcastically as he stood in front of Rubinstein's office.

* * *

"Good morning, Mr Rubinstein," Klaus said, when he entered Yaron's office.

"I have just finished talking with Lisa," Mr Rubenstein said, looking up at Klaus.

"I know. I ran into her outside."

"It seems that she enjoyed the cinematographic experience. I was thinking of giving her a part in the next film. What do you think?"

Rubinstein's question demanded an answer that he would like. Klaus needed to be careful, but as difficult as it might have been, he would do anything to get what he wanted. He lowered his gaze and sighed, hoping Rubinstein was hooked.

"Did you want to tell me something?" Yaron said.

He was hooked.

"It's about Lisa," Klaus said, feeling hesitant and nervous.

"Come to the point," Yaron said, his voice rising with impatience.

"I've spoken with Angela. It seems that Lisa has asked her to find a way to break the contract with us. Maybe she is working with someone else now."

"But she only just told me that she wanted to work on other films!"

Klaus blushed. "I think she only did it to increase her salary."

"Goddamn bitch!" Rubenstein burst out.

This was amazing. It couldn't have gone better.

"How much of what you say is true?" Rubinstein pressed.

"One hundred percent," Klaus said. "Angela is another on my list."

There was maliciousness on Klaus's face and Rubinstein put some papers on the desk.

"What was that beautiful Italian girl called? Stefania?" Rubinstein asked.

"Exactly," Klaus said, feeling his hope rise. "Were you thinking of something in particular for her?"

"She would be perfect to take Lisa's place," Rubinstein said.

"Yes, she's perfect, Mr Rubinstein. Really perfect."

Lisa couldn't have known, nor ever have imagined that Klaus's influence on Rubinstein could be quite so strong. She arrived at his place on Saturday evening, well aware that pulling back at that moment in time was basically out of the question. She knocked on the door, slightly late. The butler opened the door and showed her into the sitting room. Rubinstein was sitting on the sofa with his back turned to her.

"Make yourself at home," he said.

She sat down in the armchair opposite. The opening of the silk skirt showed her legs.

"Have you been at the sea?" he asked her.

"No," she said, "just a few hours spent in the park."

Rubinstein liked women, but Lisa had never noticed any particular interest from him in relation to her. The butler entered the room and put down a tray with some glasses.

"It's called Secrets," Rubinstein said, referring to the drinks. I actually invented this cocktail."

Lisa took a glass expecting him to do the same. "What are we toasting?" she asked.

"Don't you think you should be the one proposing the toast?"

Rubinstein said, rather mysteriously.

The question was said in such a way that it was impossible for Lisa not to understand something was up.

"Let's see…to how lucky I am to be sitting here with such an interesting person. Yes, I think I could say that. Interesting definitely seems the appropriate word in this case."

"How long have you been in the show business, Lisa?" Rubinstein asked, still somewhat opaque as to his intentions.

"For about a year, or maybe less, and you?" Lisa said.

"Thirty-two years, Lisa." He sipped his cocktail and continued. "I started when I was young, and now I am reaping the rewards from what I've sown."

"With success, I would say."

Flattery was something Rubinstein was no longer taken in by, not for a long time. He had come from nothing and had met countless girls like Lisa in his time. He was now oblivious.

"Sure, Lisa, but success comes with sacrifice, not with words. I've seen many people in my time thinking that by hitting on this or that producer they will make their career, but nobody has ever really made it unless they actually had talent. If you're lacking in talent you're out of the running in a moment."

The allusion was perfectly clear and Lisa felt all control slipping away from her. She wasn't sure about Rubinstein because she was no longer sure of herself. "I started as a supermarket cashier, and then, after two years, I found work in a jeweler's shop. She looked up shyly and Rubinstein's attention gave her the courage to continue on.

"Did you go to college?" he asked.

"For only a year. I was studying art. I really liked painting, but I had to leave."

"You couldn't afford it?" Rubinstein asked, urging her onward.

"I wasn't able to look after my brother. He was too young to work."

"Tell me about your parents."

This time there was no need to even pretend.

"My parents died when I was a child."

"I'm sorry."

"A little girl immediately became my brother's mother," Lisa said.

"And where does your brother live?"

"With his grandparents. It doesn't seem the time for him to follow me in this adventure. It's only right that everyone should grow up without rushing the time."

"I agree," Rubinstein added, "inexperience can bring one to cross difficult roads, and when you find yourself in such situations, it is almost impossible to turn back."

"I know. It's why I wanted to speak with you. I don't want to rush the time."

This last sentence made him forget all what Klaus had said about her. He saw her as young, beautiful, and defenceless, and all suspicion of her faded away.

"I am surprised, even one might say intrigued, as you would say, my dear. What exactly do you want to talk about?"

"About my work, Mr Rubinstein."

"Are you talking about the last scenes you shot with Greg?"

"No, not those. I am talking more about the problem that a girl has to contend with living alone when someone is saying awful things about her behind her back."

Rubinstein was watching her, trying to understand if Lisa was incredibly stupid or incredibly sharp.

"For example?" he asked her.

She took a moment, needing to think of the right answer that would give her advantage in the situation over Klaus.

"When I agreed to work for you, my life had been turned upside down. I lost my boyfriend, left my friends behind, and found myself alone in a reality that I found hard to keep up with in terms of pace. That was when the problems started. I made many mistakes and decisions without any prior thought that now could ruin my future."

"That depends on the type of mistakes you've made," Rubinstein said, still uncommitted to making a conclusion about her.

"I caved in a moment of loneliness," she said, shutting her eyes and taking a deep breath. "I had an affair with Klaus."

Crazy, Lisa! Did you really think you could win over that shark of Rubinstein with such a revelation? She thought. He wasn't in fact at all surprised. One might say he had even taken it for granted.

"Klaus likes lots of beautiful girls, and you are by no means the first. You should have expected such a thing."

"He blackmailed me," Lisa said. She took a gamble and there was no way back.

Rubinstein's expression changed dramatically and became dark.

"Blackmail you? That is a strong word, and you should think twice before you make such accusations."

Lisa was trapped. It was quite clear that it would be impossible to outdo Klaus when it came to Rubinstein's loyalties.

"He is not the person I imagined. We broke up, and he continued to call me saying that if I didn't want to see him then that would be the end of my work with you."

Lisa was neither stupid nor sharp. She was just incredibly naive.

"Klaus has been my assistant for a very long time, and if what you have just told me is true it would mean that I am not capable of choosing the right people. I will not accept any more insinuations." As far as he was concerned the conversation was over.

"I hope you don't think badly of me," Lisa said.

Rubinstein's phone rang before he had a chance to answer.

"No, I'm not busy..." he said into the phone. "In a minute or so, I will be free to speak...I'll call you back." He looked at Lisa and smiled. "Do you mind leaving me now? I have some work to do."

* * *

Stefania was beautifully and typically Latin. She had dark eyes, curly, black hair, and a warm and contagious smile; she was the complete opposite of Lisa.

"This is Greg and these are the boys that will be taking care of you," Klaus said. Klaus was calm, much more relaxed than the week before. He had cut it off with Lisa and was now waiting for Stefania. It would be impossible to do better than that.

"I imagine that you already know something about this," Greg said to her. "Your role is different, much more direct and intense, without the physical aspect being involved. That was Lisa's role. Yours instead represents the mental challenge, the woman that excites David, but the one that will never give in."

"I'm just going to say hi to someone," Klaus said.

Lisa was in the studio. She was not meant to be there that day. He approached her in his arrogant manner, just like always. "You have a new companion," he said, turning towards Stefania. "Cute, don't you think?"

"Yes, very cute," Lisa said, trying to hide her surprise. As much as she tried to be natural she was sure that everyone present could see through it. To see Stefania speaking with Greg and with the other assistants was a nasty shock for her.

"Come. I'll introduce you," Klaus said, taking Lisa by the elbow, a controlling gesture. "She may need some advice from you now that she has taken your place."

A moment later, Lisa was standing before Stefania, struggling to keep her composure in face of the shock that had just been delivered. "Hi, Stefania," she said. "Klaus has been saying great things about you."

Stefania looked at her, not unkindly, and even perhaps ignorant as to what Lisa's role would be in relation to Klaus. "Thanks," Stefania said. "I know that this is also your first time, so I am sure we will get on very well."

"Yes," replied Lisa, "I am sure of it."

She moved away because she desperately needed to call Angela.

A few minutes later, Lisa had Angela on the phone. "Did you know?" Lisa asked her.

"I had discussed it with Klaus," Angela said. "Did you meet her?"

"She's here in the studios, and I don't like the way they are talking to her. It feels like there is only her here."

"I don't know what gave you that impression," Angela said. "It is only that she has been good at seizing the occasion."

"Liar!" Lisa burst out. "I can't understand why you insist on defending Klaus! I know very well that he was behind all of this."

Angela didn't reply.

"I don't care if you are fucking Klaus," Lisa continued, "but I can assure you that he will do with you exactly what he did with me."

"Calm down, your hysteria is exhausting," Angela replied unkindly.

"I am fed up!" Lisa said. "Fed up with you, with Klaus, with films… everything!"

Angela didn't have time to reply. Lisa had already hung up.

TEN

It was two in the morning and Lisa could not sleep. Her outburst from the day before had revealed her psychological weakness to Angela. *How stupid!* Lisa thought. With her silly behaviour, the already bitter relationship with Klaus would have been even more difficult to recover. She could just not allow herself to be so emotional when dealing with sharks like Rubinstein and Klaus, or a bitch like Angela. Lisa had to be careful as she was perfectly aware that any further signs of weakness would have led towards her professional suicide. She got out of the bed and went to the kitchen, without knowing what she was looking for, and went back to bed knowing she would not have any chance of falling asleep due to her nervousness. She went back and forth between the bedroom and the kitchen five times in just a few minutes, to then end up crying with her face drawn into the pillow, victim of a panic attack in desperate need of advice. Eventually, tiredness won over anxiety and she fell asleep for a few hours just before dawn; enough though to give her some rest after a night full of bad thought. As she woke up, she called Beverley, the only person she thought could have helped her. Beverley was a lawyer, much older, much wiser and much smarter than Lisa. They had met a few years back when Lisa was seeking advice on copyright issues at the beginning of her acting career. Beverley quickly recognised her and this was enough to put Lisa at ease.

"Don't be naive. I can understand the emotional side of things, but to ask for compensation would be counterproductive and lead your career towards an instant self-destruction. You haven't the faintest chance of winning, trust me. Keep waiting and don't make the first move," Beverley wisely said. "Either Klaus or Rubinstein will tell you what to do."

***

The wait didn't last long. A couple of days later, Angela told Lisa that she needed to speak to her, and it wasn't difficult for Lisa to imagine why. They met at *Aubaine* in Old Brompton road for lunch, a place with a pleasant and light French-Mediterranean feel, not far from Walton Street, where they had had lunch the day that Klaus insinuated himself and had flirted with Angela in front of Lisa.

"Hi, Angela," Lisa said as she came to the table.

"Good morning to you, Lisa," Angela said and waited for Lisa to sit down. "I don't want to waste your time or to sit here wasting mine. I spoke with Rubinstein about your situation, and there are two possible outcomes: either you accept a minor part or they can ask for the breach of the contract for non-compliance of your obligations."

Lisa swallowed bitterly. "It was Klaus, isn't that right?"

"Is this a question, a declaration, or something else?" Angela snapped.

"Leave it."

Lisa left, without even for a second worrying about inventing some excuse.

"Good luck facing the real world, sweetheart," Angela muttered.

She had watched many young actors meet the same end as Lisa. In one moment, they were stars, and the day after that, nobody even remembered who they were.

After she left *Aubaine*, Lisa called Beverley and filled her in on their proposal. Beverly told her exactly the same as before—to stay calm and wait.

"There is only one thing I don't understand," Beverley said, "if they decided to kick you out, why do they want to give you an alternative? It is almost as if they wanted to get rid of you but at the same time they don't want to let you go."

"I would love so much to understand it myself," Lisa said.

Later, when Lisa walked in to the studio, the shooting had already started. The script had a small variation and it had been adapted to let Stefania step up. Klaus was involved in a quiet discussion with Greg.

"Hi, Klaus," Lisa said.

He was taken aback by the peaceful tone of Lisa's greeting.

"How come you're still here?" Klaus asked.

He was short, even if she had been friendly with him, because he simply did not want to know anything more of her.

"I wanted to see Stefania at work," Lisa said.

"She's great, very expressive I would say. She got into the part immediately."

And she surely got rid of her knickers immediately, too, you goddamn pig! Lisa thought. She found it hard not to tell Stefania, but, at the same time, she kept it diplomatic. "You're right, she's not bad."

The scene ended, and Stefania smiled when her eyes caught those of Klaus's. "How did I do?"

"I think you were great, but it is up to Greg to decide," Klaus said.

"Great, I second that," Lisa said.

Her compliments surprised everyone.

"Really?" Stefania asked, looking more closely at Lisa, smiling readily.

"Yes, I also said it to Klaus."

Stefania looked at Klaus with the innocence of a teenager. "I am really happy, but if you have some advice to give me, then it is very welcome."

"Of course, Stefania, now that we're working together, I will have a number of suggestions to give you," Lisa said, and just to make sure there was no misunderstanding, she gave Klaus another smile.

It was almost seven in the evening when Greg decided it was enough for the day. Lisa had stayed calm and kept flicking through the script. Every so often, her eyes strayed from the pages, and she looked up on set, where Greg was chatting with Klaus, whilst Stefania repeated the lines of the film. She stared at both men for a moment and she caught a glimpse of perversion between the two of them while they looked at Stefania. She quickly dismissed what her instinct seemed to pitch in her mind and thought back to her encounter with Rubinstein, reproaching herself for her stupidity. She had been playing with fire. Then she looked at Greg, now smiling at Stefania, and realized that she couldn't go back into that game. One sneeze from Rubinstein would be enough, or one of Klaus's looks would make it difficult to keep the game under control. She was left with two options: to make friends with Stefania or to try and make things up with Klaus. The first option meant she could just try and hope for the best, whilst the second meant she simply needed to have a stomach that was harder than his. Either way, neither of the roads would guarantee her the outcome she wanted.

"Okay, guys, see you tomorrow at eight," Greg said.

The lights went out. Lisa stopped flicking through the script and got up to leave. Klaus was a few steps in front of her with Stefania right next to him. The two stopped and Lisa passed them by, keeping enough distance so as to not feel obliged to stop and talk with them. She had just got to her car, when the sound of high heels made her turn round.

"I have a problem with my car," Stefania said "would you mind giving me a lift into town?"

"No problem. I'm going there anyway," Lisa responded.

Stefania smiled, because she loved to smile. As soon as Lisa turned on the engine it began to rain.

"Shit no!" Lisa said. "Every time one looks forward to enjoying the evening, there's always something that goes wrong."

"It's always like that," Stefania agreed, "almost as if they do it on purpose or something. The secret is to take no notice and to pull out straight into your road."

"Do you feel like coming over to my place?" Lisa asked, suddenly, without thinking. "We could order sushi and wait for it to stop raining."

"You're a genius!" Stefania said.

They left the restaurant and got home loaded with packages and packets. Lisa's place was a very nice and neat flat in a modern block close to Battersea Square on the southern side of the Thames. It was decorated in a simple but pleasant way, with attention to the smallest details. There were flowers and candles on the table, modern spotlights in the ceilings, a brand new audio/video system, a couple of *Lalique* crystals and a cute teddy bear sitting on the sofa. That was the only memory left of the old, sweet Lisa. She went about making something to drink, whilst Stefania sorted out food. When they were satisfied, they started with the cans of beer.

"I never imagined that this could be happening right now, you know? If I think that just a few months ago I argued with my agent and almost decided to quit and go travelling in Europe, I get shivers just thinking about it."

"Where did you meet Klaus?" Lisa asked her.

"At a party. A friend of your agent introduced me."

"Angela?"

"Yes, exactly."

Her Latin spirit came out with each sip of the beer. She was already tipsy and she needed just a small nudge from Lisa and she would be talking about everything. It did not take long to Lisa.

"Wonderful example of a human being. Have you been seeing each other for long?" Lisa asked.

Stefania stopped drinking her beer and burst out laughing.

"Typical example of a stallion for reproduction, you mean. One would need to hibernate his sperm the day he decides to leave us and die. If I think of the nights that we have spent together, I'm sure I could have an orgasm right now. Anyway, it's been more or less a year now."

"A year?" Lisa asked.

"Yes, a year, maybe a month more, or a month less."

Lisa felt like a blade had been punched into the middle of her chest. She was beside herself, just like an elementary student can get lost in the middle of a lesson at the university. Her experiences came to nothing, and that wasn't even counting her inability to see people for what they really were. She really had believed she had been the only one for Klaus, but Stefania's words challenged the limit of her imagination.

"What do you mean being together?" Lisa asked, trying to regain her composure.

Stefania had just opened her second can and was looking at her sweetly. "That one fucks, Lisa, and you cannot imagine how beautiful it is having sex with Klaus."

"I can imagine."

"Why are you looking at me like that?"

"Because you seemed really in love with him in the Studio."

"It's true, Lisa, I am…crazily in love with Klaus."

Clearly she was joking but Lisa didn't catch on.

"In love with a guy like that? With someone who goes with so many other women at the same time?"

"How naive you are," Stefania said. "What does it matter sharing a guy with others when you can have him any time you want? I think it is the most obtainable of any relationship."

Lisa nodded, took a beer and opened it. Maybe if she let herself go a bit, she would have actually enjoyed a nice evening.

"I wish I could think like that," Lisa said, but she wondered if she really meant it.

"It's never too late to start."

* * *

It seemed a good idea to Stefania to get Lisa involved, to return the favour. They agreed to meet in the evening around ten and went together to Dan's party, which was at *Novikov*, a nice fusion between the atmosphere of an Italian and Asian restaurant and a touch of Russian party vibes in Berkeley Street, in the heart of Mayfair.

"We're going to have so much fun!" Stefania said.

"I've never been to a party like this," Lisa said.

"You've never been to *Novikov*?" Stefania asked, surprised.

"No," Lisa said.

"You've never been to one of Dan's nights out?"

"Never," Lisa said.

Stefania looked at Lisa, clearly taken aback. "But can one ask where exactly you have been till today?"

Lisa started to say, "No," again, when they entered the restaurant, and Stefania spoke to the host. "Hey, Sasha, there are two of us. This is Lisa."

Sasha greeted her warmly and gave a kiss to both of them.

"Don't freak out, little one," Stefania said. "This is only the beginning."

Stefania took Lisa by the hand and dragged her along behind her. Dan had got the nicest table at the back of the lounge bar downstairs, and the tables were already set up with the bottles of wine and liquor they would be drinking.

"It's deafening!" Lisa shouted.

"Have faith!" Stefania shouted back. "In a bit you won't hear anything."

They sat down in the corner. Dan was sitting between Sadie and Porsha, two incredibly beautiful Somalia twin sisters, with big black eyes, wonderfully full, dark-red lips, amber complexion, killer smiles, and near to perfection, although with very slim figures.

"Stef, my love," Dan said. He got up and signaled to free up a space next to him.

Stefania introduced Lisa to Dan.

"Hey, Dan, nice to meet you," Lisa said.

Dan nodded and then signaled to one of the girls to leave to let Lisa sit down.

"I really wanted you to meet her," Stefania said, when she sat down. "She is new to the scene."

Dan smiled. "I promise I will do everything I can to make sure she is okay. Guys!" he said, turning to the others that were sitting around him. "Lisa wants to have fun. Make sure that happens…understood?"

"Hey, Lisa, I'm Patrick," one of the guys said. "I hope I am up to the task."

What a gorgeous guy! Lisa thought, studying Patrick surreptitiously. Dark, tall, and athletic. Stefania's friends definitely weren't bad at all. The party began to kick off. Lisa lost control when it came to the vodka, and the music that seemed so loud at the beginning was now just barely audible.

Stefania leaned in close to Lisa. "Patrick is dying for you," she said in a quiet voice.

"I have no intention to let somebody die for me," Lisa said quickly, but in the meantime she was looking at Patrick. "He's cute though."

"What were you expecting?" Stefania asked. She filled her vodka glass and moved forward to say something to Patrick. He looked at Lisa, and she returned the look with a smile, then he got up and sat down near her.

"Do you want to dance?" he asked, right away.

Drop-dead gorgeous, Lisa thought. He had the deepest blue eyes she had ever seen with sensuality emanating from his body at his every move.

"I'd prefer to stay seated for a while, if you don't mind," Lisa said.

"As you wish." Patrick took a last sip from his glass and jumped into the crowd.

"Why didn't you go with him?" Stefania asked.

"I don't feel like it," Lisa said, regretting that Patrick had left. "It doesn't seem the right time to me and, anyway, I don't want to."

"Okay, now, I will think about it," Stefania said and got up from the sofa and took Lisa by the hand. Lisa tried to resist, but gave in.

"We've ended up near him," Lisa shouted into Stefania's ear.

"Let's have fun, then." Stefania placed herself between Patrick and the girl he was dancing with near the table for more space. Then she grabbed Lisa and, in a moment, Lisa was dancing with them. Lisa began to enjoy it and the more she danced, the more her eyes betrayed her attraction to Patrick. When the DJ moved onto a new tune, Lisa glanced towards the entrance. She was tipsy. Stefania was no longer with her but sitting on the sofa, engaged with Dan. Klaus had just arrived and was moving towards them. Lisa wanted him to see her.

"I'll be back in a second," Lisa said. "Wait here."

Patrick let her go, but his heart went broken.

"Hey, Klaus," Lisa said, coming up to Klaus, "I didn't know you were coming."

"The surprise is mutual," Klaus said with distaste evident in his expression.

Stefania and Dan were kissing. She was tipsy, too, and beginning to feel tired.

"Your new flame seems to be having a lot of fun with Dan," Lisa said, indicating the two with a nod of her head.

"Stefania is a friend, and I give a lot to my friends. Who is the guy you were dancing with?" Klaus asked.

"Patrick. Cute name, don't you think?"

"Perfect for a gay guy. Are you drinking anything?"

"I'm completely drunk," Lisa said. "I think I should go home."

Klaus began to be excited. The more he watched Lisa, the bigger he saw his chance to spend the night with her.

"I need to talk to Stefania," Lisa said, suddenly, moving away from Klaus.

Klaus looked at her maliciously. Stefania smiled, kissed Dan, and went to rescue her girlfriend.

"Did we pass the limit honey?" Stefania said to Lisa.

Lisa struggled to open her eyes, and Stefania turned towards Klaus.

"Take her home, Klaus. I'll stay here with Dan, but do not even try to be the usual bastard with her."

Klaus helped Lisa stand on her feet and went towards the exit.

It was a strange feeling being alone with Lisa again. She was sitting next to him, in the car, half asleep and so defenceless. Once they arrived at his house, he opened the car door to let her out. She was sleeping, with a dreamy expression painted on her face, and Klaus had no other choice than to take her in his arms.

He took her shoes off and lay her down on the bed. Her body moved nervously, as if she was about to awaken, but then she fell again in the world of dreams. Klaus pulled the blanket over her and went to his room. He left his clothes on the floor and jumped into the shower. His thoughts went back to the beautiful nights spent with Lisa, and his obsession returned. He clinched his teeth and violently punched the wall.

"Bitch! Bitch, bitch, bitch!"

He felt nervous. She had humiliated him, challenged him, and now she was in his bed, wonderfully defenceless. He calmed down, dried off, and went back to her room. Her arms were behind her head, and her hair was spread on her face. Klaus's excitement changed and turned into animal instinct. He got closer and began to caress her, grazing her nose, then her lips, and then her shoulders. He stayed still, to admire her, hating her and loving her. He remembered the last time he had had sex with her, and the pleasure of that memory became frustration. He kissed her, and Lisa moved on her side, turning her back to him. Klaus stayed still, doubtful, but then, again, got closer. He caressed her, and Lisa did not move this time, making him feel more confident. He then lifted her shirt and touched her breasts. Lisa moved slowly this time, then faster and faster, until Klaus lay on top of her. Lisa did not offer any resistance and let him do anything he wished.

"Take me, Klaus."

"Why, Lisa, why?" she whispered almost inaudibly, and she felt ashamed of her own words. Klaus took her with force, giving space to his instincts and exploded, without realizing. Then, tired, he turned on his side, sure in his heart to have cancelled the memory of that humiliation forever.

* * *

The lights of dawn discretely entered the room. Lisa was awake; Klaus was sleeping naked, with no shame. She stood up, entered the bathroom, and closed the door behind her. She looked at herself in the mirror and what she saw made her feel bad. She felt dirty, miserable, with no dignity at all. A ray of sun in the darkness of her soul brought back a different Lisa. The shy and sweet Lisa, the Lisa in love with Alex. How far gone was that time? She switched off the light and went back to bed, aware that she would never dare to challenge him again.

ELEVEN

Five kilos lost in a month obliged Lisa to renew in part her wardrobe. Since that night with Klaus, she did not have the courage to look at herself in the mirror again, such was the shame she felt for herself.

She stopped to say hello to a friend and drove towards Hampstead. The lights at Klaus's house were on, and she recognized Eddy's car. She opened the door, passed by the living room, careful not to generate noise, and then she heard indistinguishable laughter, a typical thing at one of Klaus's happy parties.

She entered the room nervously. She was slim and pale, with her face barely hiding her anxiety. She closed the door behind her and hoped that the gesture could, in a way, leave the bad thoughts behind her as well. She leaned with her back against the wall and slowly let herself slip down on the floor. She wanted to cancel what was left of her conscience; she wanted to be like one of the whores who were celebrating and laughing downstairs but, instead, she began to cry, feeling worse than them. She entered the bathroom, took off her clothes, swallowed a couple of sleeping pills, made her way to bed, and fell asleep.

Downstairs, Klaus and Eddy were intent on executing their ritual once again. The coke was on the table, and the two girls lay, completely trashed, on the sofa. One of them was sick, but it did not represent an issue for the party that night. Klaus opened his eyes in the middle of the night, stood up staggering, and went closer to Eddy.

"I'll fuck Kate, you fuck the other one."

Eddy smelled so bad that, for a moment, Klaus felt like throwing up. Kate was sleeping, lying on the sofa in an unusual position for a normal person. She mumbled something, but at the end, she stood up under Klaus's persistence. They were totally trashed and they went up the stairs hand in hand, to avoid losing each other. He opened the door and dragged her into the room.

"We've got to find the switcher."

"I don't give a shit about it."

"Here's the bed. You lay down, and I'll go to the bathroom."

He turned on the light and did not like what he saw. His shirt was dirty from the blood flowing out of his nose, while the mirror reflected the lunar pallor of his face.

"There's someone in the bed!" Kate said in a loud, alarmed voice.

Kate was got lost in the darkness, where Lisa was sleeping, and could not manage to calm down.

"It must be Lisa," Klaus said from the bathroom, as if having Lisa and Kate in the same bed was something absolutely normal.

"I am not going to sleep with her!"

Her voice came to his ears with the same effect of fingernails on a blackboard. Klaus found it amusing and began to laugh, then he heard the noise of high heels, and this too seemed something definitely worth a laugh.

"Decide: me or the little sleeping whore!"

He did not reply, and Kate entered the bathroom. She saw him laughing, bent on his knees with toothpaste flowing out of his mouth. Kate got closer, until her legs touched his head. She looked at him, vexed, with hands on her hips, while the worn out makeup around her lips made her look like a clown. Klaus tried to behave, but could not hold back, making Kate fly into a rage. She kicked him with all the energy she had. Her foot hit his stomach, and the toothpaste went down the wrong way. Klaus began coughing, instinctively stretching his hand looking for help.

"You don't make me laugh," Kate said. She thought about the usual scene, but Klaus was about to drown.

"Stop it, I don't buy it," Kate said of Klaus's choking act.

Klaus could not answer. He was turning purple and could not feel his legs any longer. Desperately, he grabbed her skirt holding it tight. Kate could not hold back and, laughing like a perfect idiot, in an attempt to get rid of his hold on her, she lost her balance, falling on him.

Unknowingly, she gave him the help he desperately needed. The blow saved him, and his face slowly went back to its natural colour. He stood up, kicking her over and breathing rapidly. He calmed down a few minutes afterwards, and when the fear gave way to relief, he turned towards her. She was intent on adjusting her stockings, completely unaware of the tragedy she could have caused.

"Look at what you've done! You snagged my stockings!"

He could not stand it. He hit her so hard that she fell on the floor.

She began to cry and then picked up the contents of her purse that had been knocked onto the floor and went away.

The noises from the bathroom woke Lisa up. There was little the sleeping pills could do. She saw the scene in the bathroom and pretended to be asleep when Klaus flopped down half-naked in bed. She waited for him to be asleep, and then she went down to the living room. The scene there was revolting: the girl was lying on the floor and Eddy was snoring next to her feet, without a shirt. There were alcohol stains on the sofa and traces of coke on the table. She could not figure how Klaus could be Rubinstein's assistant, because he was completely out of control.

* * *

The following day, Klaus was not in the bed next to her. Intrigued, she went downstairs and looked outside through a window, where a car she did not remember was parked. She heard noises coming out of the studio, and she stopped about a metre from the door. Klaus was on the phone; he was pale, with shadows under his eyes. She got closer and tried to listen at the door.

"Tomorrow…yes. I have Tanya…no mess…she's here with me now. He will give it to you, Mr. Rubinstein."

He hung up and rubbed his temples.

"Done! You'll have it tonight," Klaus said to someone in the room with him.

"Fine, at seven, but try to be on time," the other person said.

It wasn't Klaus's voice, but it sounded familiar.

"Who was here yesterday?" the familiar voice asked.

"Kate."

"I think we agreed on Rachel."

"Yes, you're right. I was completely out of control. I'll make up for it as soon as I can," Klaus said.

"Hurry up, then. Rubinstein doesn't like to wait," the other voice said.

As hard as she tried, she could not remember whose voice that was. A mobile phone rang.

"Who does the car outside belong to?" the voice asked.

"To Lisa," Klaus said. "She was here with me last night."

"She would be a great blow," the man said. "She's at the top of the list; strange you did not think about it."

Klaus hesitated. "Give me two weeks."

"I would like to think you would be up to it."

"I am always up to it," Klaus said, with an edge of irritation in his voice.

The conversation ended. They stood up and walked towards the door. Lisa stepped back and entered another room a second before being noticed.

"And what's it about?" The man asked indicating a DVD on the table.

"Stefania. Do you want me to put it on your bill?"

"No, it's not worth much, but I suggest you to watch out where you leave your things. See you later tonight and try not to get me in trouble. Solving your messes is the last thing I want to do."

Lisa left the door ajar to be able to see them. She saw Klaus, and then she saw the other man. He was wearing a light blazer, and he had a distinguished bearing. Then the man turned and Lisa almost fainted when she saw his face. It was Greg, the art director.

* * *

A wrong day could happen to anyone, especially to someone who was in a rush during rush hour. Lisa did not like to drive, and more than once, she felt tempted to get out of the car and leave it in the middle of the traffic. It had been quite some time since she had heard from Klaus and, after that strange conversation she had heard at his place, he had literally disappeared, making her happy to be alone. She had spent some time getting to know Stefania and now they were good friends. In fact, she was fighting through the rush hour traffic of New Oxford Street to get to the *Mitre*, a pub-brasserie in Notting Hill on the corner of Holland Park Avenue and Ladbroke Grove, where she was to meet Stefania, and she was at least using her time in the traffic jam to think about Klaus, his odd behaviour, and other issues that had come up in the months that she had known him.

Finally, after almost an hour, Lisa made her way to her destination. She was frazzled at the rush-hour traffic, and when she saw Stefania already there, she was relieved. As soon as she was able, Lisa ordered a glass of Sauvignon Blanc.

"You know what?" Lisa said, when she finally settled back and took a sip of the wine. "I never understood what Klaus really does. He said he's Rubinstein assistant, but I never saw him working."

"He does everything," Stefania said, also settling back in the chair, turning her body to face Lisa. "He follows the contracts, coordinates the production phases, and then I guess Rubinstein keeps him around because they have known each other for quite a long time. I think that Klaus never worked for anyone else in his life but him."

"And what about Rubinstein?" Lisa asked. "What do you know about him?

"He does his own businesses, he's married to a stunning woman who looks like a marble statue, and he's a workaholic. We never said more than good morning to each other."

"Klaus and Rubinstein are so bloody different," Lisa said. "I can't really understand how they can work together."

"Maybe they are gays?" Stefania said, laughing.

"Ruled out," Lisa said only slightly smiling at Stefania's humour. "And even if they are, I guess Rubinstein is much too clever a person to go to bed with him. Are you still dating Klaus?"

"Once in a while," Stefania said. "I go out with Dan now. You saw the way we were at Dan's party."

"He looks normal at least," Lisa said.

"Are you seeing anyone?" Stefania asked.

"Nope," Lisa said, but it was silly of her to say that.

"People saw you quite often with Klaus."

Lisa blushed. "I am trying to learn from you. Klaus has a great body, there are no strings attached, and then he's a good fuck."

"Welcome to the club!" Stefania said. Stefania enjoyed talking to Lisa. "Wasn't I right? Isn't it beautiful to be free and in love at the same time?"

Lisa nodded.

Stefania set her empty wine glass on the table between them. "Listen, I have an idea. Why don't you come over for dinner tonight? We'll watch a movie and have a drink on the terrace. So?"

"It sounds good. Should we order some Sushi at *Itsu*?" Lisa asked. "Or will we have something different?"

* * *

Stefania lived in Stanhope Gardens in South Kensington not that far from the Museum of National History and Kensington Gardens. The flat was a small one bedroom, neat and clean, with plenty of flowers in every corner and a series of beautiful pictures hanging on one of the walls of the living room that Stefania took when she went to the Continent. She picked a CD and sat on the sofa.

"You like Jazz?" Lisa asked.

"I love it. It relaxes me."

"You are so much different than what I thought."

"Really?" Stefania asked.

"Really. I remember when I saw you on stage. I thought about many things," Lisa said, "but I never thought that we could end up being friends."

"It's been surprising for me, too," Stefania said. "You also gave me the wrong impression. You looked so dark and the typical girl who doesn't trust anything and anyone. Then I changed my mind. Some wine?"

Lisa nodded.

"You looked so delicate, and your face…" Lisa said then trailed off.

"What about my face?"

"I am a hopeless romantic. My heart got broken when I thought about how Klaus could play you along," Lisa said.

"Won't you tell me you are jealous?" Stefania asked.

"Jealous of Klaus? Please…" Lisa said, dismissively.

"No, I didn't mean that…" Stefania said, "jealous that I took your role in the movie actually."

Her words annoyed Lisa. "You mean…you knew it?" Lisa asked.

Stefania smiled and handed her a glass of wine. "Not really knowing it, I perceived it, and when I saw you, I put it together."

"Did Klaus tell you that?"

"A bit came from him, and a bit came from Angela."

"Did they tell you anything about me?"

"I already knew who was in the cast. However, Angela mentioned something about your experience at the theatre," Stefania explained. "It should have been amazing."

"Yes," said Lisa, "it was a beautiful time. The first and likely the last that I have done, I suppose."

She glanced down.

"Did I say anything bad?" Stefania asked.

"I'm alright, don't worry. I have my moments sometimes."

"Would you like to talk about it?" Stefania asked.

Lisa told her about the acting troupe. "We were a great gang. Two guys and two girls. We did not have a penny, and we made do with what we had. I will never forget the spirit with which we faced the messes that were raining down on us. It always seemed as if each day we were living was the most important life of all, and we got down on it like crazy. And those guys were fantastic, united, terribly united."

"Was there anyone in particular?" Stefania asked.

"The guy at the pub. I can't avoid thinking about him any time I drink something," Lisa said.

Her eyes glowed and Stefania noticed it. She only nodded.

"But it's over now," Lisa said. "Maybe it never started. All beautiful things end Stef; I believe that is written somewhere in the universe. Silly me not to do anything to let it last as long as I could."

"We better enjoy things while we can," Stefania said.

* * *

Klaus called Lisa a week later. He was away for business, at least that was what he told her, and he absolutely wanted to see her. Lisa hesitated to agree. She did not want things to go back to the way they were in the past, but as long as she repelled Klaus, her obsession took the upper hand. She would do just that movie, and then she would leave, change agents, and try to find a job somewhere else. Klaus came to pick her up at about eight.

"I'm surprised," she said. "I can't believe you persisted for me to come. I am so pleased about it."

"We just reviewed our production plans," Klaus said. "There could be a part for you."

Rubinstein had invited some people, and Lisa was the kind of woman that could boost his image. He was waiting for them in the drawing room for a toast and to introduce them to his guests.

"This is Lisa," Rubinstein said, "one of the most beautiful faces of our family. She is getting experience with Greg, but in a bit she will be an absolute star."

There were six guests, and apparently all had known one another for a long time. Among them there was Greg, the art director.

"Yaron told us so many things about you, Lisa…it's a pleasure to finally meet you…You are really beautiful…Call me if you want to come to Bermuda…I'm flying to Mexico this weekend."

It was embarrassing. The guests did not stop for a second and overwhelmed her with compliments. It was as if Rubinstein had organized that night just to let those hunters jump on their prey. She was the only woman that night, and the wine helped her to relax.

"I am twenty nine. I will be thirty in May." That was one of the last things Lisa said. The dinner ended shortly thereafter; the guests stood up and went back to the drawing room. Klaus looked after Lisa, after ignoring her almost all night, and Rubinstein remained engaged in conversation with his friends.

"Well done, Yaron, she is stunning," Richard, one of the guests, said. "I will eagerly look forward to hearing from you."

"Everything should be ready this week."

Richard felt a pinch of envy. "All I ask from you is a perfect job. As usual, you set the price."

Greg went over to Klaus and exchanged a few words with him. It was obvious that they were both close to Yaron, and Lisa was still wondering why Greg would be at Klaus's house the day after that foolish party.

The night ended. Rubinstein looked after Lisa, reassuring her about her bright future and showed his guests to the door. Then he spent a few moments talking to Greg without anyone around.

"Klaus must do it tonight. You've got to find the way," an impatient Yaron Rubinstein said.

Lisa wasn't that far away, just next to the door talking to one of the other guests. Greg, who was engaged in a conversation with Rubinstein a moment earlier made a sign, and Klaus went over to him. He exchanged a few words, and then he went back to Lisa.

"It wasn't pleasant to be the only woman here tonight."

"It was Rubinstein's fault," Klaus said. "He spoke so well about you."

Klaus took her hand and Lisa let him do. If Rubinstein invited her to his party, there was little doubt they decided to invest in her. She remembered his words well: she was one of the most beautiful faces of the big family. Maybe Destiny was planning something nice for her. She closed her eyes and woke up in front of Klaus' house.

"Would you like to stay over tonight?"

She did not have any choice, but she was pleased he asked her.

"As you wish."

He was different and very caring that night and his eyes were sweet. He made her feel at home. He put on some music and poured her a drink. They were sitting next to each other and toasted the beginning of a new relationship.

"I'm glad you enjoyed yourself tonight," Klaus said.

"I'm glad, too," Lisa said. "I could stay on this sofa all my life."

Klaus took the glass from her hand and caressed her hair. "You are so beautiful."

He kissed her and Lisa froze, but then she got carried away by his kindness and retuned the kiss with passion. She was no longer used to those attentions, since Klaus was being sweet, completely different from what she had expected. He looked at her intensely, caressed her tenderly, and hugged her passionately. No words were needed. This was a never-ending night. Klaus tried to make her happy rather than satisfy his instincts. She followed her dreams with the enthusiasm of an adolescent, feeling free from her anxiety, her worries, her obligations to do something in the name of an obsession. She felt loved, because that night Klaus loved her.

Lisa was sleeping. Klaus was standing next to the bed staring at her. She was lying naked, with her back turned towards him, and he could see the silhouette of the nose and the lips of the most beautiful woman he had ever had. He entered his studio, closed the door behind him, and opened the door of his hidden room. The monitors showed the bathtub and the bedroom. Lisa was hugging the pillow, and he spent a few moments looking at her. It was the only time when he truly felt something for her. Then he ejected the DVD and grabbed the phone.

* * *

Yaron Rubinstein had just received the confirmation that it was done. He could finally call his friends.

"Good morning Richard," Rubinstein said. "I have the DVD you were looking for."

"Same procedure?"

"No, this time things change, the price quadruples. It's about Lisa, not about just any woman."

"Enjoinment granted?"

"Two hour movie. Klaus did a very good job and Greg added its touch of class to the final editing."

TWELVE

Alex and Joel met at the York Gate, the main entrance of Regent's Park south. They crossed the York Bridge, walked through the Inner Circle, and decided to sit on a bench overlooking the Boating Lake.

"Close your eyes and relax," Joel said.

"Done."

"Now concentrate. You should be able to distinguish the different noises. The wind, the guys playing football, people talking…can you?"

"I don't hear people talking," Alex said.

"Don't worry. Focus on what relaxes you the most."

"The noise of the leaves moved by the wind."

"Perfect. Now breathe deeply, without opening your mouth. You must feel the air within your throat, not as it passes through your nose," Joel said again.

"How long am I supposed to breathe like that?"

"There is no limit. A minute every hour for me is fine."

"What can I think about?" Alex asked.

"Anything you like."

Alex remained still, rolling his head, breathing deeply, and his tension disappeared.

* * *

Loving or hating Sunday usually depended on how the day started. Spring was just on the doorstep, and to be at the park was definitely a beautiful beginning. People were running and puffing, others were walking their dogs, some were reading, and still other people were just strolling. Alex was sitting next to Joel on a bench in the shade of a tree. They both had block notes. Joel used his to sketch in; Alex used his to write down his thoughts.

"If you could fly, what would you draw looking at the park from high in the sky?" Alex asked.

"A flower bed. There are many colours of many different tones: the green of the park, the darker green of the trees, the blue of the sky, and that of the lake. Why do you ask?"

"I was thinking about the parachutists I watch on TV. I always like to see them. As soon as you jump off the plane, you have the impression that the earth is running towards you while you have the sensation to be able to hug it. Then, the more you go down in free fall, the smaller you become, and you can't see where the world starts or where it ends. I wanted to know what you thought about it."

"I prefer to draw while sitting on a bench," Joel said. "It would be difficult up in the air."

"I would love to jump out of a plane, and if I could be born again, I would like to be a cloud forever. I could travel the world in an instant and tell thousands of different stories. Just imagine the places that you could visit."

"I hope you never have to face a hurricane. If it catches you, it makes your head spin and it smashes you against the sharp-pointed branches of a tree from three thousand metres high," Joel said.

"And you? What would you like to be?" Alex asked.

Joel put down the sheets on his lap and thought. "Let's see…what I could be…yes," he said confidently, "a tanning lotion."

"What the hell kind of answer—"

"Imagine the number of women I could touch!" Joel said.

Right, he could never choose a better reincarnation. He took back the sheets and began to draw.

"I want to create a character, but I want him to be clumsy, nice, and forgetful."

"Forgetful…forget…*getful*…call him Getty!" Joel said, his sense of humour coming through.

"It sounds like a gangster!" Alex said, laughing.

"It's the only name that came to mind. It's not that easy to give a name to a comic," Joel said. "The risk of becoming dull is very high."

"I have the same problem when I have to give a title to my plays," Alex said.

"How's your job going?" Joel asked abruptly.

Alex made a face. "I'd like more time, but they backed me against a wall."

"And what about the guys?"

"They're all great. Scott is waiting to hear from Joe. Judie maybe found something to do."

"And you? What are you thinking about doing?" Joel asked.

"I would like to submit the idea to him anyway. Should I not make it on time, I could say that I made an effort, anyway, and wrote something."

"Are you still planning to carry on with the story about the old man?"

"Yes. I would like very much to complete it."

"Have you had a chance to see him again?"

"No, I haven't," Alex said. "The last time I was there I didn't see him."

"Who knows what became of him."

Alex shrugged and Joel went back to his comic.

* * *

Nothing was worse than groping in the darkness. Sometimes Alex felt he was running behind his fantasies without knowing whether he could get something out of it but, at the same time, he did not care. He met up with Scott at *Costa Coffee* in Baker Street, not far from Regent's Park; they never lost contact during those weeks. Scott put pressure on Alex, telling him to follow Joe's advice and produce something quickly.

"If I could do anything they asked me to, I would end up doing a painful job like any bank employee does."

"But do you ever think about money?" Scott asked.

"I do, but I am also sure that money comes when you do things right. There is a huge difference between feeling obliged to do something under requirements and doing what you want to do. I call it passion."

"Judie will start next week. She's going to film a commercial for toothpaste. I wonder where she will find the energy to smile," Scott ironically said.

"I'm happy for her."

Unlike Alex, Scott was down to earth, and if it depended on him, he would do anything Joe asked him to do. "Do you think you'll make it?" Scott asked.

"I am doing everything I can."

"If you need any help…" Scott said, his implication clear.

"Sure, I'll call you."

Alex remained alone, while Scott went to another audition hoping to get a role. Alex took back his notes and read the draft again. It wasn't bad; he had mixed the monologue with a small drama, but he had to work here and there, make it a bit lighter and, above all, easier to comprehend for the audience. But he needed time.

Later, when Alex handed him the script, Joe did not make any comments or give appreciation on the work already done, but just a further confirmation of the hurry he was in. His only concern was to complete and deliver the play by the deadline. It was the only way for Joe to sponsor Alex and try to find a space for him in the program. A week later, he was back at the theatre.

* * *

"I have prepared two variants," Alex said as soon as they met. "The first is completely dedicated to the monologue, while the second evolves into a drama."

Joe knew well that if Alex decided to give him those sheets, it meant that the work was well done. So he would have done all his best to convince them to put it on stage.

"I can't promise, but I'll do my best for your work to be read by tomorrow."

"I'll rely on it."

He took Alex to the door and went back to his desk. He quickly flicked through the sheets and picked up the phone.

"I just sent it to you. I strongly recommend you read it as soon as you can."

Twenty-four hours later, Joe received the confirmation. They wanted to be present at the rehearsal before making any decision about it.

* * *

Joe and Conrad sat on two chairs at the very far end of the hall. A blade of light came out of the base of the stage, so that everything stayed in the dim light. Alex entered the hall, and Joe got worked up. He was in the middle of the stage, trying to set the main light. He stayed still for a moment and then he began to act.

The verses came from deep down in his heart, because he had written them for Lisa. He spoke with his soul, and every word, even the simple ones, was full of emotion. The illusion became reality, as if all those months without her had never passed, and he saw her eyes, touched her lips, felt the love again. So much sweetness lost. Then sadness entered his dream, and it took hold of his memories. It upset his dreams, painted them with another colour, and made them terribly darker, and the light that shined from his eyes, faded.

Alex listened to her voice again, but this time it was cold, far from him, since she was about to deceive him. Sadness left and turned into pain.

Then the tone of those verses changed; his rage exploded and became almost fury, but the image of Lisa who was running away, stealing his heart, made him feel weak, and his words lost their impetuosity, until they got lost in the silence.

He breathed again, but this time as a wounded man. His heart gave way to his reason, and he calmed down. That old man, on the bench, a joy forgotten forever and lost in the river, ran away from himself, from a memory that his heart tried to change into a dream, for his eyes could not look back to that sad past. He did not want to live but to sleep forever, swamped by the darkness, and avoid the light that eventually deceived him.

The storm went by. A shy ray of light cleared the darkness of his solitude and gave him strength, and he ended up thinking about his past. Life could still be different and let a dream come true. He gained confidence, and his eyes shined again.

Alex was happy, as he ended the monologue. Joe stared at him, holding his breath. Alex came down from the stage and walked towards him. Conrad stood up, shook his hand, and introduced himself.

"Conrad Fleming."

Just a name, but said with so much arrogance, Alex thought. Conrad looked at Joe, since this was a sign that he wanted to talk to him in private. They said goodbye to Alex and entered the office.

"So?" Joe asked him.

"Not bad," Conrad said noncommittally.

"Will you give him a chance?"

"I've got to think about it. The calendar is full. Is he still under contract?"

"Yes," Joe said.

"I want to talk to him."

Joe called Alex and he let him know of Conrad's comments, and the three of them met in Joe's office.

"Did you really like it?" Alex asked.

"I already told Joe what I thought about it."

"Alex, why don't you make Conrad aware of the other variant?" Joe said.

"I am shaping a drama around the monologue. It might be original to put them on stage together."

"It could make sense," Conrad said.

Joe nodded, happy for Alex.

"I would need more time though," Alex said.

Conrad turned towards Joe. "I thought the drama was ready."

"I'm still writing it," Alex said.

"Then things change. I can't put it in the calendar. I'm tied up with the schedule."

"Why don't you consider the monologue?" Joe said, turning to Alex.

"To split the two things apart would be a pity," Alex said, "and then the monologue has a sense only if it is linked to the drama. It's a show where emotions come to life. It's the most beautiful thing I have written."

"Do you have a draft?"

"Sure, but I wouldn't want to give it to you until it's completed."

"How long do you need?" Conrad asked.

"A month."

"Too long," Conrad countered.

"You asked me for the drama."

"Show me what you have written so far," Conrad insisted.

"Better not, Conrad," Joe interjected. "Alex has never delivered something half finished."

Conrad lost his patience. "Joe, I am here because you told me to come over today. You asked me to come and meet Alex and to consider this monologue. And now that I am telling you that I could consider the hypothesis to put it on stage in spite of a calendar completely full, someone demands to tell me what I can and what I can't read in my theatre." Then, turning towards Alex, he raised his voice. "You know what? We'll put the monologue on stage on its own."

"Forget it," Alex replied with the same arrogance as Conrad. This was his work and the monologue, without the drama to follow, would have prevented him from realizing his dream.

"Who runs things here?" Conrad said. It was a rhetorical question.

"You, Conrad," Joe said.

"Fine. I expect confirmation by tomorrow that the monologue will go on stage. With or without the person who wrote it."

He left the office, leaving a speechless Joe, together with Alex.

"Why did you reply like that?" Joe chided Alex.

"Because that's my work, and he is an arsehole!"

Joe had to stay calm. As humble as he was, Alex was not used to silently accepting one's arrogance, let alone Conrad's brand of arrogance. But if Conrad said that he would have put the monologue in the calendar, Alex should have given it to him. He was under contract and anything he wrote belonged to the theatre.

"You should be more diplomatic. I am no longer running this place, son."

"That's my work," Alex retorted, "and I am not interested in putting it on stage just half done."

"You are still under contract, and if Conrad wants that monologue, he has all the rights in the world to get it."

"Fine. I will put it on hold and sell it to somebody else when the contract expires."

Joe got closer to him and looked at him with a fatherly attitude.

"Are my eyes lying to you?"

"Please, Joe, don't preach."

"We'll tell Conrad that you agree with him."

"I'm sorry, I can't accept that! I don't agree with him or have any intention of giving him my monologue just because you ask me to. I am the writer, and I am the one who decides when something is finished."

"But you were aware of the deadline, and you knew the time wasn't much," Joe pressed him.

"Exactly, you said that I had little time to complete it. That's why I asked for one more month."

Joe sighed. How difficult it was to teach Alex.

"I am sorry, but I think we don't have any other choice than to give him the monologue. I would be devastated should I see you again at the bar in the pub."

"If you do that...we fall out."

He left with jitters stuck to his skin. A day totally lost to a fight with Joe at his office. But at least he had the confirmation that they liked his idea.

He spent his time walking and thinking over what had happened, and his thoughts began to fight with each other. Maybe he was wrong. He had come to Joe with hope, and Joe had worked hard to give him a chance. It was all thanks to him, and he should have given him his monologue. Yes, he should have, but if he had done so, he would have never put the part he loved the most on stage, and if he wasn't hanging in there with Conrad, they would have never understood the beauty of what he was writing.

When he arrived at his house door, he was fully convinced he had done the right thing. An artist should protect his creation. He took the draft and laid out the sheets on the desk. He wanted to read it, and he knew deep down that sooner or later he would have found the inspiration to write again.

    Words easily flew out of his mind, and the idea had begun to take shape, but then he suddenly stopped. The story frightened him. It seemed impossible, but his instinct told him that what he was writing was leading him towards his destiny.

THIRTEEN

The kid stopped a metre away from the old man. He lay motionless on the bench, supine, with his legs crossed, the coat wide open and the newspaper wrapped all around him. His face was pale, almost greenish, and he stared, with expressionless eyes, at the sky. The kid never thought death could have that old man's face. His mother was far away and she was getting smaller and smaller each second that passed. He butted against a stone that scurried away a few metres ahead. He reached it, picked it up, and held it tight. Then he took aim and threw it. The stone hit the hip of the old man and bounced off the ground to the side. The old man did not react, and the kid ran away panicking.

"Mum! Mum! I've seen a dead man!"

The woman turned and saw her child. He was slightly older than six, and he was pointing at something. He was excited, and she went towards him.

"No, sweetie, he's just sleeping. Let's leave him in peace."

"I told you he's dead! I threw a stone at him, and he didn't even move!"

The woman caressed his hair, kissed his forehead, and glanced at the bench. A street lamp obstructed her sight, but she managed to see the scene. Her girlfriend stood still a few metres ahead waiting for her.

"Someone feels bad!"

Her girlfriend took the kid's hand and walked away. "He's drunk," she said. "We better go. We have plenty of things to do."

She gave a last glance at the old man and agreed. Her girlfriend was right; they had better go.

* * *

The pain in his chest was so terrible that Travis could not feel his legs.

The sky looked at him and he started to count the clouds and to listen to the music he used to when he had a house. He thought about his life, the time lost and the minutes still left for him to live. Then the pain strangled him and the sounds disappeared. He was dying, and he would eventually find out what was beyond the clouds.

"Travis! Hey Travis! Wake up!"

The images blurred and drowned into the fog. There was a shade, floating above him and calling out his name. He was already in the next world and that was why the voice told him to wake up.

"Is everything really over?"

Alex bent over him and delicately tried to help him stand up. He could feel his legs, skinny and without muscles, while the bones were so visible that he thought the old man could break into a thousand little pieces. He laid him down on the bench and fixed the unstitched sweater, folding the old newspaper. People passed by, looked at the scene, intrigued, and then walked away.

"Is it better like that?"

He had his head turned down, as if he still was lost in the world of dreams. Then his eyes opened, his breath became deeper, and his heart beat faster. He turned his head, slowly, as if the effort could break his neck any moment.

"Who are you?" the old man asked.

His voice sounded like a death rattle. He tried to look at Alex and put his hand on his arm.

"I'm Alex. Don't you remember me?" He looked at the old man with tenderness.

"Who are you?" he said again.

He took out a packet of cigarettes, lit one, and put the packet back in Travis's coat.

"Do you remember now?"

The old man's lips barely moved. "Alex."

"Yes, Travis, I am Alex."

He came out of his trance and it seemed that Alex's face took him out of his dream.

"The actor…"

"I promised you."

"Why?"

His every word was such an effort that his body barely stood.

"I'm free to decide how to spend my time, and today I wanted to come and see you."

Travis turned towards the river.

"I saw broken crystals among the flowers."

He was delirious. Alex stayed quiet and listened.

"My eyes entered the body of those who were looking at me. I counted the clouds and realized that the blue can sometimes be black."

Those were his emotions, more than Alex could ever think he could say. Travis began trembling, lifting his hands to his temples.

"I don't feel well."

"Travis! Travis!"

His face was pale, and he breathed with difficulty. Alex tried to help him, shaking him in the hope of letting him recover, but Travis was becoming weaker and weaker. Alex stood up, paralyzed, looking at Travis lying lifeless on the bench. He felt like an intruder into a world that did not belong to him. How did he dare draw on someone who was about to die? He was running into the darkness, and he still could not see the light at the end of the tunnel. He calmed down and tried to do something. Travis collapsed. He laid him properly, lifted his legs, and Travis slowly recovered.

"Stay here."

He entered the bar that was nearby. He ordered sandwiches, bought some biscuits, and anything else he thought might be useful in such a moment. Travis was on the bench, trembling, striving to stand erect on his back. He was weak, without strength, and if Alex had been just a second late, he would have fallen to the ground. He went closer and helped him out. Then he opened the bag and took out the food.

"You've got to put something in your stomach."

Travis brought the sandwich towards his mouth, but he could not remember the taste. He took a bite, and he felt pain. He tried again, slowly, and he felt his pain fading.

"You saved my life."

Those few words were as heavy as a gravestone. He had saved the life of a man with a sandwich, and he felt miserable. Life was unfair, just as it was unfair to take advantage of a man who nearly died to write a drama.

"Do you mind if I eat something with you?"

Travis turned towards him and looked at him tenderly. "It's not nice to eat alone."

Alex smiled and Travis's words swept away his sense of guilt.

"Where do you sleep at night?"

Travis took a bag from under the bench with a blanket and a paper box. "In here."

He did not feel ashamed. Alex took the paper boxes, pictured the old man in his mind and felt torn.

It was dark. Alex had spent the afternoon with Travis and left him with the promise of coming back the next day. He arrived home without realizing it. His mind was all thoughts, and the image of Travis was engraved in his mind. What courage he had. He was sure Travis's was an incredible story. He hadn't been born a tramp; that was clear. Alex just needed to talk to him, but he had to hurry up, realizing Travis could have died had he come just an hour later. He thought about the theatre, about his friends, about Lisa, the woman he had given his heart to, and about Destiny who turned his back on him running away with Lisa. Who knew where she was, whom she was with, and whether she ever thought about him. Too many thoughts. It was a mistake to think about the past. He had to move on and think about his future, about himself. And in that moment, his future wore the mask of Travis, a man he and Joel had met by accident, looking more like a madman than a real tramp.

He did not feel like reading the draft anymore. He wanted to collapse in his bed and sleep and forget about Joe, Conrad, Lisa, and all the rest. Minutes went by, maybe hours, and the list of Alex's thoughts ended. And what about Joel? What became of him? For sure he was not the kind of person who could spend a night to think. He was about to call him, but then he gave up. And what if he had called Lisa? Another foolish act. He turned over nervously. He wanted to do something but, at the same time, he did not feel like doing it. In the end, he made up his mind, grabbed the phone, and dialled her number.

"The number you have called is no longer in use—"

"What an idiot!" Go figure that Lisa would keep the same number. One chance in a million. It was raining outside, and the intensity was growing stronger. He stayed still in his bed looking at the window, as if he could almost touch and feel the cold outside. A life was worth a few sandwiches. He turned over again, anxiously, and did some accounts: with six sandwiches he could save two Travises, with thirty at least ten. Had he been a baker he could save all the Travises who lived in London. What a fucking life! It always discriminated, and many times it was wrong. There were those who lived in buildings overlooking the bridge, and those who lived in the cold under the bridge looking at the buildings. If Destiny dealt two cards to anyone, it was clear that he cheated sometimes.

He could not sleep, because the night enjoyed tormenting his mind. He went to the window, put his hands on the glass, and breathed. The steam stuck to it in a second and did not let him see through. He drew eyes, a nose, and a mouth and put his face on it to look outside. A building, then another building and a cold, grey street.

Where was Travis? Likely under a bridge, to count the drops of the river or trying to run behind them. He got dressed in a hurry with an anxiety he had never felt before.

There was no sign of a taxi on the street, not even if he had paid ten times as much to get one, but only the underground. He waited and caught the last train of the night, got off at Waterloo station, and walked towards South Bank. It was pouring rain and the benches on the riverside were empty. Only a madman could stay there with that weather, and only a madman could be there walking under a bridge, without knowing what bridge to walk under. He went right, towards Waterloo Bridge.

No one was there, and he did not feel like searching around. He stood still, looking around, hesitating. Then he walked back towards Hungerford Bridge. Where could a tramp sleep that night in South Bank? There was a niche under the bridge, or something like that, but he couldn't see. So he went down the stairs, and he caught a glimpse of a silhouette. He came nearer and stepped on the stairs. Alex was tired and the cold was terrible. He was acting without wanting, without knowing what he was really looking for or, maybe, he just wanted to go back home and sleep without remorse. There was someone wrapped in paper boxes. He knelt down and tried to move them.

"Travis?"

That someone moved.

"Travis, it's Alex!"

It must have been him. The hands came out, but Alex could not see, then the head and the chest became more visible.

"Who the fuck is Travis?"

Alex stepped back, but then he mustered up the courage.

"I am looking for the old man who comes to sleep here every night."

"Arsehole! This is not a hotel, and if you don't have any spare change you better get out of here!"

He got discouraged, and the rain was getting stronger every minute. He didn't know what to do or where else to look, and he wondered if he should look under another bridge or go back home and forget that night. And then, he thought again. There were many places where a tramp could hide on such a rainy night, but he wasn't a tramp, and he couldn't think with Travis's mind. He forgot and tried to take courage, since there was nothing else to do but pray that Travis overcame that moment.

The tube was closed, and the only way to go back home was to catch a taxi. A car passed by and splattered him with water, but he couldn't care less. He walked on Sutton, where the darkness was broken by the streetlights along the road when, suddenly, a silhouette hidden by the raindrops and the shadows, kept his hope alive.

"Travis! Travis!"

His voice was far away, covered by the rain pouring down, but it eventually reached him. The silhouette stopped and Alex took heart. It could be Travis; he wanted it to be Travis. He didn't count the puddles or worry about the rain. The silhouette held a bag, and Alex was convinced. He was confident the man walking alone was Travis. Alex was just a few metres away from him.

"Travis!" Alex shouted.

The silhouette turned, and Alex recognized the man he had saved from a certain death. He hesitated at first, but then he moved with joy in his heart, and finally hugged Travis.

"Why are you not under a bridge?" Alex asked.

He was touched and the pouring rain hid his tears. "A man took my place, and I didn't know where else to sleep."

Travis was wrapped in a black garbage bag.

"Where is the cardboard?"

"They took them away from me."

Alex looked at Travis with tenderness. With the empathy pulsing in his heart, Alex took the bag away from Travis's hands. There was just a cloth, and nothing was left from the food he had bought.

"Where are you thinking to go now?" Alex asked.

Travis didn't answer, since there was no answer to such a question. He restricted himself to looking at Alex. Alex made up his mind; he stopped the first taxi he saw and let Travis get in.

"Camden," Alex said. He couldn't think of a different place. Travis would have to stay at his flat.

* * *

Once they had arrived at Alex's flat and Alex opened the door, he said, "You better take off your clothes. I'll give you something fresh."

Travis nodded. The walls, the paintings that hung on them and the frames with the photos…he has a house as well. The memories attacked him again, but Alex's words brought him back to reality.

"Take a shower and put on this pyjama."

Travis stood up, nervously, with the water dropping out of his clothes.

"You don't need to carry the bag with you."

He turned towards Alex and placed his belongings on the floor, then entered the shower and stared at the tap without thinking. Alex was waiting for him in the drawing room and Travis felt ashamed.

"I'll be here just for tonight."

He started coughing and Alex looked at him with affection. A night in a warm place wasn't enough. Travis needed a miracle.

"Fine, but go to bed now. We'll think about the rest tomorrow."

He slipped under the blanket and fell asleep when Alex switched off the lights. Travis was breathing with difficulty, and Alex was sure he could have died had he spent that night in South Bank. Alex lay down on the bed and read the draft of his new show. His excitement grew stronger. He no longer needed to imagine how to finish his work. He only had to enter the drawing room and look at the old man.

The light barely seeped through the curtains. Alex sat on the chair next to the sofa where Travis was sleeping and stared silently at him. His hair was grey, like his beard, and his thin cheeks highlighted his cheekbones. His wrinkles looked like trucks all over his face that witnessed the cold of the nights spent under the bridge in Southbank. Then, he could not distinguish anything anymore. He was falling asleep, but the thought of having Travis stay at his place that night kept him awake.

"Why don't you go to bed?" Travis asked. He was awake.

"I don't feel like it," Alex said.

Travis pushed himself up and rested against the back of the sofa and sat face to face with Alex.

"I couldn't sleep either. Without noises and the cold out there, everything becomes difficult."

"Yes." Alex said, smiling, "I can understand. How long have you been awake?"

"Before dawn. I heard you coming in."

"Why didn't you tell me? We could have talked."

"I wasn't sure you wanted to."

"Why would you think that?"

"For what you've done for me tonight. You came to me without me asking you. You listened to your heart. You listened to me too."

He coughed again, trying to calm the spasm, putting his hands on his chest.

"Do you want to eat something?"

Travis looked at him embarrassed.

"Why do you do it, Alex? Why are you looking after me so much?"

Alex opened the fridge and took out some milk. "Someone told me that there is not always a reason for the things to happen. Sometimes they just happen."

Travis smiled. "You learn quickly."

"Do you want me to put some coffee in it?"

He was happy and trembling; he didn't ask for anything, except to forget what had happened. It was as if life was deceiving him again, and he was afraid to suddenly wake up under a bridge.

"I don't have anything to repay your kindness."

"Yes," said Alex, "there is something you can do."

Travis nodded.

"You will stay here until you get better," Alex said.

He was confused. What had he done to get Alex's affection?

"You have your life, Alex, and I will never forget what you have done for me, but I can't stay here. I've been living on the street for too long, and that's the only place I know."

"You don't even have your boxes anymore. And if it starts raining again?"

"I'll find a place for sure."

What a stubborn old man, Alex thought. "Someone already took your place. I don't think it will be easy to get it back. How much sugar?"

Talking was like a game for Alex, answering was like a drama for Travis.

"I will take you to my doctor tomorrow. We need to do something."

* * *

"You are putting yourself in trouble," Joel said. This time they were at the pub where Alex worked.

Joel had just listened to Alex's story. In his view, the old man could easily be a madman.

"Find a way to get rid of him," Joel warned him.

"Why don't you come over and talk to him, Joel? He's not dangerous as you think."

"Did you leave him alone?" Joel asked, still a bit alarmed.

"I did. He's still in bed. The doctor told me he needs rest. I can't send him away right now."

"You keep making your life difficult, and I can't understand why. But why did you just have to host an old man in your place? And what if he gets comfortable with it? Didn't you think that it would be more and more difficult? Sooner or later you will be tired of him, and you can't keep deceiving him. You will just hurt him."

Joel's words made him think.

"What would you do in my place?" Alex asked. He really wanted to know.

"I could definitely not get rid of him after what you said. Just wait for him to feel a bit better, and then let him understand that you are not living alone, that you have a partner. In short, make up a story."

He left Joel at the entrance of Camden tube station. They would have to meet up later. Alex turned and walked along the road, and while walking he felt alone. He stopped at the pharmacy, ordered what the doctor had prescribed for Travis and went home. Joel was right. He could not keep deceiving Travis, and it would be terrible to send him on the street again. He opened the door and saw that the sofa was in order and the tray was in its place.

"Everything alright?" Alex called out.

He leaned against the door of the bathroom and realized it wasn't shut. He grabbed the phone and called Joel.

"He left."

"Are you sure he won't come back?"

"I don't see his black plastic bag."

"It's for the best. You got what you wanted without the problem of telling him to go. Relax, Alex. Travis belongs to the street."

FOURTEEN

Joe was at his office, staring at the soulless phone that was lying on the desk. He had to make the phone call, but he had to be sure about the right words to say and the right pitch to use before approaching Conrad. It would not be an easy one to make. He closed his eyes and thought about Alex and his emotional reaction driven by pride, then about Conrad, his cold voice and his arrogance driven by money. Then, at last, he thought about himself, the theatre and the sacrifices he had made. He swallowed his doubts, grabbed the phone and dialed Conrad's phone number, hoping to put together two people who could not be more different from each other.

Conrad's voice came through loud and clear on the phone: "I am not going to wait. Contracts are done to be respected and he's already been paid to produce. I want the monologue to be completed by the deadline, or he will be out of work for the next twelve months."

"Let's wait a little bit longer, Conrad," Joe urged, "just a few more days. I am sure Alex will do as you wish."

"Tomorrow. Not later."

There was not that much that Joe could do. Conrad hung up on him, and it wasn't wise for him to call him back. He did not have any choice, but he didn't want to clash with Alex, either. So he decided to take him out for dinner at *Zilli*, on Brewer Street, in the heart of Soho.

* * *

"I wasn't expecting you to ask me out for dinner," Alex said as they entered the building.

The restaurant was nice, and the table where the waiter seated them was next to the window that overlooked the alley. The interior was bluish like the colour of the sea, because in that place the seafood was great.

Alex and Joe chatted while waiting for their orders. Joe was in no rush to bring up the subject of the monologue. "If I could eat here every night, it would be the end for me. This sauce is excellent."

"I agree," Alex said.

"How's your love life going?"

Alex was hesitant to answer. He would have much preferred to avoid the issue. "I don't think that much about it."

"You need a holiday, just get away for a few days," Joe suggested.

"I can't, I have too much mess in my head," Alex said.

"You're still in touch with the guys?"

"On and off. I've heard that Judie's back in business."

"I've heard that as well. I am happy for her."

Joe waved, and the waiter brought another bottle of wine.

"What are you thinking about?" Joe asked, when the waiter had come and gone.

"Usual stuff," Alex said. "Sometimes I wonder where Destiny is taking me."

"I would wait a bit longer before asking myself that question."

"But if I keep waiting, I'll be old without realizing what I have done with my life."

Alex grabbed the bottle and was about to top up the glass when Joe stopped him.

"You've had enough, Alex."

"Please, don't preach," Alex said. It seemed that of late many of their conversations involved Alex's objections to Joe's preaching.

"Okay, but wine has to be tasted slowly and drunk differently than water."

Alex smiled, put the bottle back on the table, and focused on his spaghetti.

"Have you ever felt so close to getting something that you know you will never have again?"

"I wish I had a child," Joe said. "The only regret of my life."

"That's why your eyes are glowing?" Alex observed.

"I am not joking, Alex, I miss it, but I had to think about it a long time ago."

Joe looked at the glass and touched it slightly with his hand. He wanted to talk; he needed to. "It would be nice to have a child. Your life changes so much. Time flies so quickly, but you are happy to get old as you want to see your child growing older and to spend your time waiting for this to happen. And all you do, you do it for him. Have I ever told you the story of my father?"

Alex nodded.

"My father began working with his dad when he was twelve, then he ran away from home. He was a rebel. My mother met him when he was just a teenager, and it was love at first sight. They ended up together, and after a year my brother was born. What a crazy family. They acted on the street, with my brother still in the baby-buggy. My father was in love with his job; he felt it deeply, down to his soul. But the problems began when he decided to buy the theatre. He got into debt just because he hoped my brother would become an actor, but when he realized that he wasn't able, he thought about me and decided not to chuck in."

"And did you like it?" Alex asked.

"I was a total failure at acting, but I like to manage things. I handled the children's shows, while my dad looked after those in the evening. But when he passed away, I had to be involved body and soul in the theatre."

"And what about your brother? Do you still hear from him?" Alex asked.

"Once in a while. Mostly during Christmas."

"Not an easy life."

"Not easy at all," Joe said. "That's why I told you it's important to have an heir. Because you know that even though your job drains you, you keep going with the dream to see your child harvest what you sowed. Sometimes I wonder whether there is really a reason for me to dedicate all my time to the theatre, but that's the only way I have to keep dreaming. Who knows, maybe I'll have a child when I am seventy, and one day he will get it all."

"You didn't answer my question," said Alex. "You didn't tell me yet why you didn't think about it."

Joe made a face. His smile slowly died, and his lips formed and arch of melancholy.

"I didn't answer your question because I don't have an answer to give you. I didn't think about it, Alex. That's the truth. I didn't listen to my heart. I always stopped a second before taking the chance. Be different from me, because at the end, the risk you take is to regret all the things you didn't do when you could."

"Foregone words. Do you remember the sentence I always talked to you about?"

"The important moments?" Joe asked.

"Yes, right. The person who wrote it thought just like you, and after blowing his chance, he tried to justify his mistakes by saying that the event that changes your life is difficult to catch or, rather, impossible. And as it usually happens, he who gives advise is not able to solve his messes." Alex filled the glass with wine, and this time Joe did not interfere.

"Teaching is different from compelling," Joe offered, "because he who listens can decide. The only thing I feel like telling you is that sometimes there is no reason for the things that happen."

"Right, they just happen," Alex said.

"So, I would like to go backwards," Joe continued, "when things were real, genuine, when we used to take turns working until late to prepare the show. I don't like it now. We were a family at that time."

"Do you really think so?" Alex asked.

Joe nodded.

"So then tell me, Joe, why did that family flake off when you sold a stake in the theatre? Perhaps it wasn't a family, or perhaps someone did not behave like a father. Think about Judie, Scott…if I'm not wrong, they both came to you, and look what happened to them. They both disappeared. Or think about what you are attempting to do to me because Conrad wants to put the monologue on stage…if you say we were a family, one thing is for sure…you were not our father."

Once Alex had spoken those words, the situation plunged.

"I expressed myself improperly," Joe said. "There are things that go beyond what you see. That theatre is still there because of the memory of my father. I promised him to follow his path, and the only way to do that was to sell a stake to Conrad. It would be so easy to sell everything and change life. I would love to tell you about the son I wish I had, but I can't do it, because I want to keep my promise. Feel free to decide what to do."

What he said was in part true, but he succeeded in answering Alex in a convincing manner. He challenged Alex on the values he cared about the most: family and friendship.

"I didn't want to reach this stage, Joe. I wanted you to stand up for the integrity of the artist."

"Forget it."

"Did you sell it all?"

"No, I didn't. I still own thirty percent, but I can't make any decision."

Alex cared a lot about Joe's friendship, and if he dogged Joe's heels on, it was just because he couldn't stand Conrad's arrogance.

"Why can't you wait one more month?"

"Conrad wants to go on stage with your monologue. He found it interesting, and he still has some room for his program. It's a matter of timing, and I have no doubt that he would give you the time you need if he had the chance."

"He's arrogant, and I can't stand that."

"Nobody's perfect, Alex, not even you, but I love you. As you see, there aren't problems that can't be solved."

That was the only time Alex smiled that night. He appreciated Joe's words.

"Okay, let's assume I trust you for an act of faith. But supposing I'd like to start with the monologue, will I have any chance to bring it on stage with the drama if I deliver by the deadline?"

"I think so. I don't see any reason why it shouldn't be possible."

Joe poured some wine into Alex's glass and didn't pay any more attention to him.

"To the monologue?" Joe said and raised his glass.

Alex hesitated for a while, but Joe's smile convinced him. "To the monologue."

Joe left, but Alex didn't feel like going home. He was more tipsy than sober, and he got angry with the crowd and the cars circulating around him. No one wanted to be his friend: Joe, Conrad, Travis, and not even the monologue. It was all fault of *The Black and the White*. If he hadn't presented it, Judie wouldn't have lost her job, and Lisa wouldn't have run away. It was his fault, and now life bonded him to the theatre for a legal clause. *Fucking Destiny!* It entered his house without being invited to decide what to do with his life. It was true: there were no reasons for the things to happen.

Alex staggered along the street, bumping into a street lamp with his knee. Intolerance turned into rage and exploded. He kicked a trashcan and anything else he found along his way.

It was two o'clock of a drunken night, but he liked walking around at that time. Walking on the street in the middle of the night was like watching a movie from a different angle; one could fear what he usually liked and find nice what usually scared him. People avoided him, because Alex looked like a madman that night. Then, finally, the hangover went away, and the images flowed regularly. He ended up being tired and alone, lying down on the street, near a trashcan that he had previously kicked and let fall on the ground.

The tiredness made him feel weaker, and in the weakness the anxiety grew stronger. Alex was alone in the world, after losing his family in a car accident when he was only a five-year-old kid. He escaped death by a miracle and was adopted and raised by an old couple who looked at him more as entertainment in their boring existence than a child in need of love. It had been a long time since the accident, but he well remembered his mother's looks. She was beautiful and caring…and a tender smile appeared on his face. But it didn't last long as the smell of whiskey evaporating from a broken bottle on the sidewalk reminded him of his father. It was because his father was driving drunk that his mother died. What a cruel destiny for such a young kid and what a cruel life for such a young man. Alex was approaching thirty and had never had a father to confide his secrets to or a girlfriend to share love with. He thought about his life, and the bitter taste of his loneliness hit him so violently that he cried. He was desperately looking for love, but he was too proud to admit it to himself. He had his dreams to escape a reality that often gave him the illusion of love. This time around, the illusion was in Lisa's eyes.

With thought after thought Alex ended up in Berwick Street, the dirtiest area of Soho, a place that smelled of leftover vegetables and fish that were sold at the market during the day. But at night, the smell of dirt didn't come from the stalls in the middle of the street but from the signs that invited one to have sex with 'Beautiful blonde models' who worked there. Alex stood up with difficulty and his glance fell on the line of fluorescent signs full of *'Eros', 'Sex',* and *'Pole Dancing'* of Walker's Court, while on the windowsills of the sleazy houses, the writhing *'Models'* shaped by red fluorescent pipes, towered up on the street, in front of heavy purple curtains, which did not allow one to see through them.

A whore came out on the street. She wore a dark coat and white boots and quickly noticed Alex. Their glances touched. She hesitated then went closer. It happened suddenly. He saw the scar on her face, heard the footsteps of someone coming from behind, and then came the pain in the back, a blow to his leg, and the cold of the street knocked against his face.

He woke up at the first light of dawn, among some broken garbage bags. People who passed by pretended not to look at him. He tried to turn and felt cold on his feet; he wasn't wearing any shoes. Then he tried to take a look at the time, but his wristwatch was gone. He had been robbed and left in an alley. If he wished to live as a tramp, there was no better way than that morning to start.

The days passed by, but Alex remembered the night he lived as a tramp after spending the evening like a king. He opened his wardrobe, took out some old woollen clothes, and put them on, looking quite like a tramp. He moved mechanically and heard the door closing behind him. He took the tube and arrived at South Bank.

The sky reflected the lights of the city, giving the impression of a show organized in a colossal theatre, where for once, actors were not human beings but were the wind, the rain, and the sadness of people who walked by the river so late on their own.

The rain became stronger, but he never thought to go back home, not even for a second. He was lost in a tunnel, where the light he could see at the end was the light of his own madness. He arrived distraught at the Oxo Gallery, trying to find shelter between the floor and a shop window. He crashed and fell into the world of dreams.

It was his mother's birthday. He was four, and he was playing with her on the sofa.

"Let's see if you guess…how many are the seven dwarfs?"

His mum was sweet. She had delicate features and a beautiful smile.

"Seven?"

"How clever, my boy! Now your mummy will give you a beautiful slice of cake."

"Can I ride on your shoulders?"

"The knight and his horse are going to the kitchen to eat a beautiful cake!"

He was so happy. He could see the world from the top, as if he were on the moon. His mother loved him and she was so different from his father who came in and left the house without saying hello to anyone. The door slammed. His father was back. His mother put him down on the floor, and the smile died on her face. No one wanted to play anymore.

"Hi, Dad."

His father turned. He was tall, huge, and almost bald, and Alex never remembered him smiling.

"Go to your room."

He glanced down and did as he was told. He was lying on his bed, when heard his mum screaming. There was a noise, something broke, and many other noises he had never heard before. He put his head under the pillow, frightened. Four years of life were little time for hating, but enough time to understand.

He slowly opened the door, trying to avoid any noise, and saw his father at the table with a bottle in his hand. He wasn't able to read, yet he remembered the name he yelled anytime he was home: Whiskey. His mother stepped in, looked at her man and got scared.

* * *

Alex never saw him. The man came closer, wanting to know who had taken his place. He held a black plastic bag in his hand, and the glimmer of light that came from behind made his silhouette look like a ghost. He came closer, and his memory recalled the only person who had treated him like a human being in those six long years. He knelt down, pulled out the paper boxes and put them around the boy with care. Then he sat in the corner and collapsed, while Alex's dream continued.

* * *

The wind hit his face, moved his hair, and forced him to shut his eyes. So much time had passed. He was now almost thirty. The pilot made a sign, and he jumped out of the plane happily, as he always liked to see the earth running towards the sky. Joel was on a cloud, and he said hello when Alex fell by. Then he saw the city, his friends, and even Joe standing on the roof of the theatre, while making gestures to him. From above, the river looked like a wire and then he remembered his mother's words.

"When the river breaks the city in two; I will sew it with a fantasy wire."

His mother could do anything, even sewing the city with a wire of fantasy.

"It is too late, Alex, and I can't sew any longer," his mother said in the dream.

The river listened to those words and took the place of the wire. Clouds looked like faces, and one hid, laughing, between the other clouds, with Conrad's arrogance and his father's evil. The river was just a few steps away and was quickly running towards the sky. He pulled the cord, but nothing happened, and a cloud laughed at him with insolence. It was the cloud with Lisa's face, and it was playing with his parachute.

Alex woke up with sweat and raindrops drenching his body, while his madness put roots in his soul. Better stop playing, if he didn't want someone to write about the death of a young man on a rainy night in South Bank. He stood up and got rid of the paper boxes. His thoughts crashed, while he stared, void of emotions, at the scene.

Tears flooded his eyes, and he pitied that old man. He felt so ashamed that he wished he could drown in the river. How could he take advantage of that poor man and his drama? Travis's life was far worse than the worst of his nightmares. There was nothing to write or to think about. He knelt down and caressed Travis's hair. His nose and his temples were blue, and it was as if life and death decided to fight against each other.

He rushed on the street crying aloud for help, but no one paid attention to his despair. Then, suddenly, a noise brought him back to reality. It was a car. He saw its headlights. He ran fast, then faster, without feeling the puddles, his legs becoming heavy and the fire burning his lungs. The car was about to turn. He cried aloud and tears blurred his sight. He threw himself onto the street without thinking and the impact was inevitable.

"My God…what have I done? Please, please…don't die…you hear me? Please say something…please …"

The driver held Alex's head in his hands, desperate, trying to resuscitate him.

"It hurts…"

Alex started to breathe, and the man sighed with relief. "Praised be the Lord! Where does it hurt? Can you tell?"

"Here…in my chest…Travis …I have to go to Travis…"

He tried to stand up, but he couldn't. He coughed and blood came out of his mouth.

"Don't move…I'll call an ambulance."

"Travis…"

FIFTEEN

Travis was teaching his philosophy class at the university. "Motionless things do not change," he said. "It is your perception that makes them different from what they are in their own essence."

"Equality is what separates us," one of the students said.

"Exactly! It's just like that," Travis agreed. "Another example, guys… Chris, what do you associate with red?"

"Rage."

"And you, Francis?"

"Passion."

"And you, Daphne?"

"A bad feeling."

Travis looked at his guys. Some were silent and waiting for him to talk, others were sceptical, as it usually happened during his classes. He took a red card and showed it to the class.

"Equality and diversity. Same colour but different emotional states."

"Like your birth. We all are the same at the beginning, then some become rich and others end up poor."

Travis stopped, lowered his arms, and left the red card on the desk. He came closer to Jamie and looked at him tenderly. The world was not against him.

"What your life obliges you to do, or enables you to be is not like a colour painted on paper, Jamie, but it is what you can get out of what your existence offers."

Jamie lowered his eyes.

"See you tomorrow."

Lucy was waiting for him with the children outside, a boy and a girl, both with typical problems of their age. Nicholas, the oldest, was in his last year of college, while Beth was about to become a freshman the year afterwards. He was crazy in love with his son, just like his wife worshiped her daughter. It was Nicholas's birthday and they were about to have lunch to celebrate.

Nicholas was strong, black headed, and dark, with intense brown eyes. He liked to wear jeans and crumpled sweaters, holding a grudge against everything and everyone. Beth, on the other hand, was the spitting image of her mother when she was younger. She was beautiful, blonde, and delicate, with immense blue eyes. They were two different siblings, always fighting, like many other siblings.

Travis's wife Lucy looked like a woman who had been tired since the day she was born, although she had just turned forty-seven. She decided to marry Travis and ran away with the idea of changing him, as she could not stand to see her husband wasting his time with thoughts that did not lead to anything real. She had calmed down with time and took comfort in listing the boats that had sailed without her. "I should have married a different man…I wanted to be a lawyer…I could be living a different life…"

She often used to tell him this, but Travis, instead of resenting her, smiled at her. Then he used to go to his studio and read his books. A perfect husband and an ideal father were all he wanted to be and all he was convinced he could be.

"If you say that anything follows logic but you can't define what logic is, you might as well stop thinking and be set to enjoy the things you see," Nicholas said.

Travis never replied to his son's remarks, sure that time would change his behaviour.

They had just sat at the table in the living room when his mother asked the customary question. "You didn't tell us yet what you wanted for your birthday."

"I have everything, Mum," Nicholas said. "I don't need anything."

"Not even a wish?" Lucy persisted.

"I've already told you, fuck!" Nicholas exploded.

Beth was horrified by her brother's reaction. After all, her mother just tried to be nice to him.

"Forget it," Travis said. "It's his birthday, and he has the right to vent his feelings."

Nicholas looked at Travis with anger. "Fucking dick head…"

"What did you say, Nicholas?"

"Nothing, Dad. Just thinking out loud."

"He said, 'fucking dick head!'" Beth said.

Travis looked at Nicholas. "Did you really say that?"

Nicholas did not reply. He stood up and left. Lucy tried to follow him, but Travis stopped her with a gesture. "Give him time to vent his feelings, and then it will all be easier."

"He needs you, Travis."

* * *

A few hours later, Travis knocked on the door to Nicholas's room.

"Hi, Dad."

His eyes were swollen, and it was clear that he had been crying. Travis closed the door and leaned against the wall without talking. "Can I sit next to you?" he asked, after a few moments.

Nicholas did not reply. It was his way of saying yes. Travis sat on the bedside, and tenderly caressed Nicholas's hair.

"What's going on, Son?"

"My life."

Travis smiled. It was impossible that such a clever and brilliant young man could be so negative about his own existence.

"Could you explain why?"

"I feel bad. I need a doctor," Nicholas said, burying his head in the pillow.

"A doctor? Do you think he will help you feel better?"

"Hopefully he can solve the mess I have in my head."

"I don't think there is a doctor who could understand your problem better than you could. You have to relax. Things always get set right."

Nicholas turned and leaned against the bed to better look at his father.

"And why does it take so long for my things to set right?"

"Because you think too much, and you let your anxiety grow. Just act as if nothing has happened, and I'm sure things will get better."

"I can't, Dad. It seems as if someone is living inside of me and slowly killing me."

"Do you promise not to get mad if I tell you something?"

Nicholas nodded.

"Yours is a growth problem, typical of guys your age, and it's normal to feel inner pressure. You're just growing older."

"That's all?"

Travis smiled. At least he could enjoy Nicholas's attention now.

"Yes, Nicholas, that's it. It is called *'Angst'*. It is the existential crisis, when you have to give answers to the questions your subconscious is asking you."

He caressed his son's hair once again and stood up.

"Well, I'm happy to see you calm. There's a solution to any problem, as you can see."

Nicholas buried his head in the pillow and heard the door closing.

"What the fuck do you know about how I feel?"

* * *

The classroom was full that day. Travis was leaning against the desk with his hands behind him, waiting for his students to be ready.

"Things happen by virtue of a pre-existing cause and perpetuate in an unchanging chain of events, where the latter is subject to the former. *Pre-determinism*. Daphne, help me escape this prison."

Daphne stood up embarrassed. She was affected by Travis's magnetism and hoped that none of her classmates noticed. She focused and tried to reply. "*Free Will*. It could be a way."

"Not bad. But now explain to your classmates how you would define '*Free Will*' if you relate it to a system that perpetuates itself throughout a chain of events that cannot be separated one from another."

"If we think of *Free Will*," Daphne said, "we have to necessarily plug it into our universe. A universe where the chain of inseparable events is altered and influenced by our social environment."

Travis began to pace up and down the class, thoughtful.

"Thank you, Daphne. Let's focus, guys. Daphne told us about *pre-determinism* as a series of events, where the former generates the latter. Then she spoke about *Free Will*. Is there anyone who can tell me how to let two completely different concepts coincide?"

Nicholas raised his hand, surprising Travis. His son was not one of his students, and it was unthinkable to see him here.

"Yes, Nicholas, go ahead."

"Our existence," Nicholas said.

"Why do you say so?"

"*Free Will* without our existence would not be possible. As such, every single choice we make in turn generates other choices that, at the end, outline our path."

"Hence you would see a multiplicity of events as one bigger event that regroups them all!"

"Just like that."

"Interesting, Nicholas, really interesting theory. I hence deduce what follows: every choice made by an individual in the space of his own existence is a little step of a long walk. Consequently, an emotional state, for example, depression," Travis added, to make his speech lighter, "has a meaning in the fraction of time when it actually shows, without playing a relevant role in our final emotional state. But if so, we have a contradiction."

"And that would be?" asked Nicholas.

"We shouldn't be worried about our intermediate emotional states, but just about our final one: will we end our life happy or sad about our own existence? You, Nicholas, how do you feel now?"

Nicholas tottered. It was clear that those words referred to the talk they'd had in his room the night before.

"What can I say? You just said it all, Dad."

The guys turned. No one knew that Nicholas was their professor's son. Nicholas stood up and walked towards the door.

"Don't you wish to stay until the end of our class?"

"No."

The door closed and the students looked at Travis.

"Nicholas is my son, and last night we had a long talk. Today through our thoughts, I was hoping to go deep at the heart of his problem and find the solution. But as you saw, I was only able to create friction that I could have happily avoided."

"What a guy, though!"

"I am sorry, Daphne?"

"Great personality your son. He's not short on dialectics, and then not everyone would be able to hold such a conversation trying to overturn the points of view of most of the audience."

"Why, Daphne, wouldn't you be able to do the same?"

* * *

He went home a bit later than usual, after he stopped by the library to pick up some books that could help him develop his theory. Travis was drained, and he just wanted to go to bed and wake up a year later. He parked the car and opened the door of the house. Beth wasn't in, but he recognized Lucy's voice coming out of the kitchen; she was on the phone. He couldn't think about anything but Nicholas. Travis entered Nicholas's room and saw his sneakers near the bed and his jeans on the floor. Typical traces of someone in a hurry.

"Have you seen Nicholas?"

Lucy shrugged while smoking her cigarette, as if speaking on the phone with her girlfriend was the only thing in the world she cared about.

"Could you please answer, at least?"

She looked annoyed. She put her hand on the receiver and took the cigarette from her lips.

"Can't you see I am on the phone?"

"Yes, I can," Travis said, exasperated. "You are always on the phone, but Nicholas's room is empty. Do you have any idea where he might have gone?"

"No, I don't, and at this very moment I am caught by much more important things than tracing your son!"

To let rip wouldn't have helped. He tried to contact Beth again.

"Sweetheart, do you have any idea where Nicholas could be?"

"What, Dad? I can't hear you! There's a party going on here and the music is so loud!"

"I asked you where Nicholas is."

"Nicholas? No, he's not here with me. Did you try his mobile?"

"Yes, Beth, I did."

"Bye, Dad. I'll see you later."

Sure, later, he thought. Anytime he waited for her to come back home she didn't. How difficult was the job of being a father? Nicholas was supposed to be home, since Travis had planned his class for him, to let Nicholas feel Travis was close to him and that the bad moments could be ridden out by confronting each other.

He thought about his son and saw himself when he was young. How differently he had faced problems. He had never suffered the events. On the contrary, he dominated them through knowledge, through relentless and consistent research of a different world, of a perfect world, since he never felt like facing the real one.

'By three methods we may learn wisdom: first, by reflection, which is noblest; second, by imitation, which is the easiest; and third, by experience, which is the bitterest.' Travis thought *Confucius* was right.

It was true, experience hurt. There was no more bitter a thing than experience in the world, and that was why he chose to become a philosopher. Reflection was the noblest: it took you away from your world, it made you dream the perfect beauty, and then it introduced the harmony of the universe. But it was just an illusion, like a game done on purpose to hurt you. Sooner or later, the flight ended and the fall was unmerciful. There was no need for one to reflect, if one lived in a world that didn't know what to do with what one reflected about.

It had to be three in the morning. Travis was in bed and anxious about Nicholas. He turned aside and saw Lucy's silhouette. Lucky her… she was calmly sleeping; she had long since found the solution to the problem; she blamed Destiny, so she didn't have anything to reproach herself for, for the rest of her life.

He heard the lock release on the front door. It had to be Nicholas, and he suddenly felt nervous. The feeling of the father at unease with his son, the failure of a method of paternal advise…but then his thoughts vanished, as he was a perfect father. If Nicholas was having his trouble, it was because he refused to follow the logic. *Everything starts and everything ends*, he thought, *the good as well as the evil.*

He wore his nightgown and got off the bed carefully to avoid waking Lucy. As he came out of his room, the sweetish smell of the pot Nicholas was smoking filled his nostrils. He pushed the door open to Nicholas's room and entered. Nicholas was in the bathroom and from the noises he heard, Nicholas was taking a shower.

"Nicholas?"

His son didn't answer. He armed himself with patience and waited. He sat on a chair and glanced over his son's notes. Some messed-up papers and a couple books abandoned probably halfway through, while a pile of fitness magazines lay on the desk, a clear sign of Nicholas's mastery of the subject.

"Why are you looking at my things?" Nicholas said.

Travis did not realize his son was standing just behind him.

"I was waiting for you."

"You shouldn't put your hands in someone else's stuff before asking for permission!"

Travis nodded. "You are perfectly right, Nick. I shouldn't. I just wanted to know if you have anything else to tell me."

"What the hell are you doing in my bedroom so late at night?" Nicholas said, without responding to his father's question.

"I wanted to talk to you."

"I'm tired. I just want to go to bed."

Travis stood up. Impoliteness was something he had never taught his children. "I've been waiting for you since dinner."

"I had something to do."

"I was hurt. I was expecting a different reaction after today's class."

"Different? But what are you thinking about when you speak? Do you think you're the Messiah who brings the Word to the world? Or do you like to make fun of people who confide in you?"

"No, Nick, I was just hoping to help you."

"Not at all, Dad, all you do is kill my soul, make me anxious, and torture my mind. That's what you do every day. There can't be a different world than yours, right? Do you think you were smart today to use your words that way with me? Why do you lead your speeches just the fucking way you like to? It's not the way to help me overcome my troubles!" Nicholas threw himself on the bed and stared at the ceiling, the only thing he loved to do when he wanted to be detached from the world.

Travis would have liked to caress him, hug him, and make Nicholas feel he was close to him, but he did not do anything. Was he to blame for telling his child to stay calm and reflect?

"Get out of here!" Nicholas said. "I can't stand looking at you!"

Travis noted the shadows under his eyes.

"You smoked pot again?"

"Yes, I did. I wanted to smoke my fucking pot! It makes me feel good."

"I am sorry, Nick, really." Travis turned and left the room.

"No, Dad, you don't give a fuck about who is around you. You just want to show people how good you are with your words, but you never make an effort to understand why your son doesn't talk to you!"

Travis turned towards the door, and this time he paid attention to the words and not to his child's plea, and doubts began to creep into his beliefs.

SIXTEEN

"Should I wear the black or red one?" Beth asked, pulling two different tops out of the wardrobe.

"Black is sexier," Monica answered.

Beth was very cute and Monica was her best friend. They were both around twenty.

"Is Jamie coming tonight?" Monica asked.

"They told me he should go to Lexie's party. Please, Monica, let him go to the party!"

"What will you give me if I focus and let him go?"

"I'll give him up to you after my first love night."

"Deal done! Now focus…Jamie, go to the party…Jamie, go to the party…"

"Don't be silly," Beth said. "If you want him you have to put a bit more effort into it. Call Lexie; she knows him much better than you."

Monica grabbed the phone and dialled.

"Hi, Lexie, we are two losers looking for love."

"Hi, Monica," Lexie said. "How's the other loser?"

"In front of the mirror busy with her makeup. She still believes in miracles."

"Bitch!" Beth said from the bathroom.

"The loser would like to meet with Jamie, for a hot and spicy night… is he going to your party?"

"Just spoke with him. He's not sure yet, but Matt and Gary will be here."

"Beth?" Monica called. "Lexie is not sure Jamie will go, but she said that Matt and Gary will."

Beth turned. She was struggling with her makeup, then looked at Monica and shrugged.

"She doesn't seem to be too interested. She's focused on Jamie."
"I can give you his number."
"Okay."
"I'll be waiting for you around eight."
"Should we call him?" Monica asked after hanging up with Lexie.
"Sure."
She smiled mischievously and dialled the number.
"Jamie?"
"Yes, this is he. Who's this?"
"A gorgeous looking girl, who would love to meet you at Lexie's party."
"Tell me more!"
"If you want to know more, just go to the party tonight."
"Have we met before?" Jamie asked.
"I don't think so. Had we met, you wouldn't forget."
"Hmmm...I'm starting to like this conversation!" Jamie's tone quickly changed.
"Getting hot, honey?" Monica teased. "Just think about what will happen when we meet."
"Okay, let's meet tonight, but I want to know your name."
"You will know it at the right time."
"Perfect! Just give me a hint. How will I know who you are?"
"Easy, Jamie, I'll be wearing a red top...no, sorry, a black one. You just need to look around. I feel you'll be able to recognize the desire in a woman's eyes. Won't you?"
"You bet!"
Monica hung up. She was radiant. "Mission accomplished!"
"The desire in a woman's eyes?" Beth asked, laughing. "How could you make up such bullshit?"
"*The end justifies the means*," Monica said. "He accepted. That's what counts the most."

* * *

It was seven and Beth had been ready for quite some time. She didn't want to be late, and she didn't want to meet her father before the party, either. Monica was lying on the bed reading a fashion magazine.
"Do you think Jamie will like me?" she asked.
"Men just need to see a pair of legs underneath a skirt to get wet."
"Stop it, Monica! I'm serious. How do I look?"
"Bloody gorgeous...If I were Jamie I would jump you straight away."
Monica lit up a couple of cigarettes, handing one to Beth, and after a

few moments, the room looked like the inside of a chimney flue.

"I have to tell my mum that I won't be home for dinner tonight," Beth said.

"Doesn't she know we're going to the party?"

"Not yet. I preferred not to tell her. It's a stormy atmosphere at home."

"Wise decision, then."

Beth left the room, fixed her hair, and went downstairs into the drawing room.

"Mum, I'm going out with Monica. We'll have dinner somewhere."

"You're not going to wait for Dad?"

"Come on, Mum, Monica came here just to see me. I can't tell her to have dinner at our house."

The ploy worked with Beth's mother, and so they were on the road at a quarter to eight in the evening. Monica and Beth walked together. They looked like two people who were ready to bite the world before kicking it. Beth's body was so tight on her hips that she often slipped her hand between her breasts to feel more comfortable, while she drowned her features in makeup that didn't do her justice. She looked like a girl disguised as a woman. She was just too fake to look real.

Monica was more experienced and quite comfortable with those kinds of games. She had dressed up as a woman since she was fourteen; the result was that she had enjoyed little of her adolescence. They both had one thing on their minds: fly high, be crazy, take risks, and feel shivers all over their spine.

A girl opened the door when they arrived at Lexie's. The girl was drunk, but she could allow herself to be, since her parents didn't live there. She wore a black dress and a piercing in her lower lip. She greeted them without telling them her name and left the door open.

"Hold on tight. We'll get down tonight," Monica said, as they entered the house.

They caught a glimpse of Lexie. She was chatting with two guys a few years older than she was.

"Hi, Lexie," Monica said.

"It's a great start girls!" Lexie replied.

"I see," Monica said, observing the men with Lexie. One of the two guys stared deeply at Monica, and it was clear that he wouldn't be happy just talking to her. The other didn't seem to be much interested in Lexie.

"Brad, José, these two beautiful women are Monica and Beth."

They spent some time talking to one another, but none of them succeeded in getting the girls' attention. Beth was there for Jamie, and Monica was there for no one; but she was confident she would find a reason to enjoy the party.

"Vodka or beer?" Lexie asked.

"Let's take it easy, Monica," Beth said. "A beer will be enough for now."

"Let's skip the queue," Monica said.

There was a bunch of people at the table where the drinks were being served. Monica was in front of Beth, trying to fill their glasses, so Beth looked around. She didn't recognise a lot of faces, yet she liked a lot of them. She was so happy to be at the party that the excitement shone through her makeup.

"I hope your body belongs to the person I talked to tonight," the boy said. Beth knew he was Jamie.

He looked at her deeply, and she blushed, embarrassed. "Shame, my search continues, then," Jamie said, taking Beth's embarrassment to mean no.

Beth almost fainted with nerves. She couldn't let him get away. "Hi, Jamie," she said quickly.

"I received a strange phone call today, and for a moment, I thought the voice belonged to you, since you are the only girl wearing a black top tonight."

Beth turned and blushed like fire. Luckily her makeup hid it.

"I don't understand what you mean," Beth said.

He stared at her and did his best to make her feel uncomfortable. There was malice in his eyes and Beth felt caught. "It doesn't matter," he said, stroking his beard, pretending to be distracted. "What's your name? Susie? Claire?"

If he wanted to kill her dream he was succeeding perfectly.

"Beth! My name is Beth!"

She turned and walked towards Monica with a terrible void in her soul.

"Beth! You look terrible," Monica said. "We're here for a party, and you look like you're having a horrible time." Monica burst out laughing. She didn't even ask Beth what had happened.

"Stop laughing, bitch! He could at least have remembered my name."

"Excuse me one sec, Val," Monica said, her look turning to concern for her friend.

She hooked Beth through her arm and walked her away, looking for a place where to talk.

"He didn't even recognize you?"

Beth glanced down and hit the bottle of beer.

"Barely. I don't know what he thought. He just said that he hoped it was me who called him."

"Then why are you so troubled? Beth, that's what you wanted. He just tried to pick you up!"

Beth looked at her thoughtfully. "Are you sure?"

"Of course! He hoped it was you. It seems logical."

Beth turned and tried to catch Jamie's eyes. He was standing right in front of her, talking, drinking, and smoking. Then, suddenly, he looked at her intently for just a moment, to let her understand, and then he turned back to his friends.

"He looked at me, I swear! I can die if I lie. He looked at me!"

"I told you, Beth. Now relax, and if he looks at you again, smile but don't encourage him too much, so he won't feel cocky. Men are a bunch of idiots. I bet he'll come back to you when he thinks you blew him off."

Monica was right. Men were the stupidest animals on the face of the earth, especially those at Lexie's party. The front door opened and Nicholas entered.

"Shit! That pain in the ass of my brother is here!" Beth said.

Monica turned. Nicholas was with other guys older than he, and she didn't find him at all a pain in the ass. On the contrary, she smiled at him when she saw him.

"Shit! My sister is here tonight!" Nicholas said.

Brother and sister looked at each other like two dogs defending their territory. Beth couldn't stand the fact that Nicholas could say something about her behaviour. Beth went closer to her brother, determined to face him.

"I come in peace, Nick. I solemnly promise not to say a word about what you'll do tonight. Do whatever you like, but let me do the same."

He let her talk. "It seems a fair deal," he said.

They turned and went back to their friends.

"What did you tell him, Beth?"

"Everybody minds his own business tonight. Why are you staring at him?"

Monica couldn't take her eyes off Nicholas; she had found a reason to enjoy the party. And she was right. In just a few moments, she was in his arms ready to explore his lips.

"Come on, Monica, stop it," Nicholas said. "People are looking at us!"

She didn't pay attention and began to unbutton his shirt.

Look at that bitch! Beth thought watching the scene from the other side of the room, while smoking and drowning in the smoke cloud like all the other people. *Want to bet she's trying to squeeze Nick tonight?* she thought again.

But when Beth turned back, she didn't see her girlfriend but Jamie, who was looking at her without arrogance.

"You're beautiful, Beth," Jamie said.

Her heartbeat increased and she shivered with delight.

He touched her chin, lifted her head. "Shall we go upstairs?"

Beth didn't reply, but Jamie took her hand and she let him do it. They went up the stairs, and the music seemed to vanish from her head. She was excited and held Jamie's hand. It was dark in the room, and she barely recognized the silhouettes of two bodies twisted together on the other bed.

"Come here, Beth."

She went closer and felt his hands, but his moves weren't smooth. Beth leaned against the wall, and Jamie lifted her skirt. She opened her eyes and saw the two bodies on the bed. Monica lay supine, with her breasts in the air, while the man was taking her. She felt dizzy, and what she saw was like a soundless movie. She was tired, full of alcohol, and she had smoked, so she let herself be carried away, feeling Jamie's fingers pushing something between her lips.

"No, no Jamie…"

"Swallow."

He kept pushing whatever it was between her lips, holding her tighter and touching her deeply.

"What's that?"

"Don't ask."

Beth opened her lips and swallowed. Jamie entered her, and she could no longer see anything. Then she thought she was dreaming when she saw Nicholas, naked, lying on the bed with Monica.

Nicholas jumped off the bed, trying to cover himself as best he could to escape from Beth's sight. Monica just laughed and looked at her girlfriend. Jamie was focused on Beth, and the sudden noises made him stop. There was no life in Beth's eyes, but that was the last thing he cared about. Jamie turned, speechless, when he recognized the professor's son.

Nicholas opened the door and ran away holding his clothes. Beth stayed still, pale like the moon, wrapped in Jamie's arms, quickly losing consciousness.

"Beth! Beth!"

She fainted. Jamie was smiling. Monica looked at Beth lying on the floor and Jamie with his trousers down to his ankles. She didn't have any scruples. She went closer and kissed his neck.

* * *

Travis heard the door lock release. It was past four when Nicholas came back.

"Where is your sister?"

Travis's voice startled him. He closed the door and didn't answer.

"She didn't come back yet?"

Travis couldn't stand Nicholas's tone and walked towards him in a fury. "I won't allow you to talk to me this way!"

Nicholas didn't lose his composure and looked at him with contempt. "You won't allow? And who are you to say so?"

Travis slapped him so violently he fell. Nicholas was on his knees, he wanted to break the world in two, but he didn't have the courage. He held back his tears and went to his room, slamming the door.

"Open the door, Nicholas! Open this fucking door, damn it!"

Nicholas was on his bed, staring at the ceiling. He could hear his father yelling, but he wouldn't open the door. He hated him and to see him lose his calm gave Nicholas immense pleasure. He was so good about giving advice to calm everyone down, but he couldn't even hold his own temper.

"Nicholas, if don't open this fucking door I will push it down!"

Nicholas still didn't reply and he lit up a joint and kept contemplating the ceiling. In the meantime, Travis continued to shout until he woke up Lucy.

"What's going on?" she said, coming down the hall.

She had never seen her husband in such an angry state.

"Tell your son to open this damned door!"

"Nicholas, it's your mother. Please open the door. Your father wants to talk to you."

Her voice didn't have any strength or authority. She sounded as if she were reading her to-do list.

Travis could see that Lucy had no authority. Lucy was short sighted and, in her rush, she had forgotten her glasses in her bedroom. Her face was pinched looking without her glasses, more like a mouse than a woman, while trying to bring her husband's neurosis into focus. He moved her away roughly and went back to fighting with Nicholas.

"If you don't come out now, you won't come out any more!"

The sound of the key in the front door lock was providential, as Travis left Lucy alone, to run down to the front door. Monica just stepped in with Beth right behind her, clinging to Monica's shoulder, in a semi-unconscious state.

"My God…Beth!" Travis said, running towards her, pushing Monica away. Beth looked terribly pale.

"Has she been drinking?" he asked Monica.

"A bit."

"What else did she take tonight?"

"Nothing special," Monica said, with a shrug in her voice, as if Travis's question was unimportant. "We went to a party, we drank, and we smoked."

"Any drugs?" Travis pressed.

"Absolutely not!"

"Lucy, call a doctor, quickly!" Travis shouted.

"It's five in the morning…" Lucy said.

Travis looked at her, shaking his head. "Forget it. We'll take her to A&E."

"Should I come?" Lucy asked.

Travis didn't reply, but stared at his wife, making her feel worth less than nothing.

"Mrs Lucy! Beth just woke up!"

Travis was in his room, but Monica's voice made him come back to the drawing room. Beth was lying on the sofa and Lucy was close enough to choke her.

"Let her breathe!" Travis said.

Travis made his way between them, knelt down, and caressed his daughter. "Can you hear me sweetheart?"

Beth opened her eyes, recognized him, and smiled.

"Thank the Lord!"

"Shall we go to the emergency?" she asked Travis, but she was becoming sleepier by the minute.

"I don't think we need to. Bring some water and a fresh towel."

Lucy stood up and came back to the sofa after a few moments. Travis passed the tip of the wet towel over Beth's forehead and dampened her lips.

"She's recovering!" Monica said.

"You're right," Lucy said. She was sitting a couple of metres away and couldn't wait to go back to bed.

"Let's go to the bedroom, Beth." He took her in his arms with tenderness and went upstairs. Beth was light and delicate like a flower, but on her face, her innocence had vanished. Travis passed by Nicholas's room with an unpleasant feeling. Travis couldn't or he didn't want to understand, but what he felt was something evil.

"I put Beth to bed. Monica, you can stay here if you wish. I'll talk to your parents."

"Is Nicholas sleeping?" she asked.

"I don't know, but he refuses to open the door. Forget it. I'll talk to him tomorrow. It will be better."

Dawn came. Beth was sleeping, and her parents were too. Monica followed their advice and stayed the night. Nicholas was the only one awake and was busy counting the spots in the ceiling, thinking about his father…the cause of all his neuroses. He didn't know whether to hate him or kick him in front of a doctor. His father had never been able to support him, even though he desperately tried to make him understand. The only thing his father repeated obsessively, until Nicholas was nauseous, was there was always a solution to any problem.

He got off the bed, instinctively, since there was no way for him to fall asleep again. He opened the door, careful not to make noise, and entered the studio. It was a small room where three of the four walls were full of shelves with piles of books. He went closer for a close look at some of them. Some were about philosophy, some about physics, while others contained the biographies of famous characters. He despised these books and, again, thought about his father, in love with things that couldn't exist, with 'truths' that were pursued and would be pursued forever, but they did not exist.

SEVENTEEN

'He was wasting his life with words, pursuing logic and his unreal world'

It was a grey morning and a cold Sunday…two conditions often tied together in winter. Travis didn't like the colours that morning, which matched his disillusionment and discouragement. Grey and cold were perfect topics for a person used to distributing words, but not in that moment. Travis just needed advice.

His father had taught him that the job of a good parent could be judged from many little things. The first was without doubt, seeing his son's smile. If it was bright and mirrored the light of a sunny day, then likely the parenting was good; if, however, it was of the colour of a rainy night, then one could hope it would last only a short time.

Travis couldn't remember Nicholas's smile and, for as long as he loved him, he still didn't understand him. He thought he had given him all that he needed: confidence, love, and calm. All a son could hope to find in his parent, and the best advice on how to face his little crises! *All things met an inevitable end, the good as well as the evil*, he thought again.

His thoughts led him to South Bank, to the little book market. It was a perfect place to find some colour on a dull afternoon. There were piles of books on wooden stalls, and people were looking here and there for something to read or just to kill time. Travis glanced through an old edition of an essay that reminded him of his youth, and smiled. Then he enjoyed touching the back of the books with his fingers, arranged in good order, until, distracted by his thoughts, he bumped into the person next to him. He wanted to apologize but couldn't say anything. The old man looked at him severely, straight in the eyes, and made him feel the weight of the questions his subconscious had asked him long ago, but to which his ego had always denied the answer. And he felt small, and then smaller, until he went back to when he was a young boy, while his life flowed before him like a movie that told a story and revealed its emotions in only a second. He felt overwhelmed. The wave came, and it was like a storm of emotions that hit his chest and threw him violently into the air. He shivered, felt tremors, and felt the fear flowing in his veins. His breath came faster. He closed his eyes, trying to escape an emotional earthquake that didn't have any reason to exist…He focused and asserted himself to stay calm.

He opened his eyes a few moments later, sweaty and nervous. The light of the afternoon seemed to be sharp like a blade. But what had happened? Who was the old man? Where was he? He looked around, bewildered, but there was no sign of his presence. He leaned towards a bookstall and his glance fell on a book, barely kept together by a crumpled binding that revealed the weight of time. Travis opened it with trembling hands, and his eyes focused on the only sentence that sprang out of the yellowish page: *'He was wasting his life with words, pursuing logic and his unreal world…'* Shocked, he closed the book and put it back in its place.

He went beyond Waterloo Bridge, walking towards the Tate Modern. A double row of trees kept him company, silently, forming an alley, and next to each of them was a wooden bench. Travis chose one near the end, near Gabriel's Wharf, where the Riverside Walk ended in a rotunda overlooking the river in an area with plenty of colourful restaurants. He took a seat and let his thoughts carry him away. Who was that old man?

A woman was walking two children holding their hands. One of the children came closer and pulled his coat. Travis turned but didn't smile at him. His face was exhausted and the child retraced his steps.

"Let the gentleman be in peace," the mother said.

The woman took her child away, and Travis stared at them until they both disappeared. The short stop on the bench calmed him down and, for a moment, he swept away the image of the old man who had scared him to death. He stood up, but he could not stop thinking about the old man for the rest of the day.

* * *

Lucy was in the kitchen and didn't hear Travis opening the door. She was preparing something for Beth who was disinterestedly flicking through the pages of a magazine.

"Hey, Dad!" Beth said, apparently glad to see him.

"Hi, Beth," Travis said and took off the coat. He went to his wife. She had her back to him, messing with the cookers. Her hair was pulled back.

"Where's Nicholas?" he asked her.

"He went out with his friends."

"Is he coming back for lunch?" Travis asked.

"I think so. He didn't say anything to let me think he wasn't."

"Lucy, turn around."

When she did, Travis pulled her into his arms and gave her a kiss. He tried hard to remember when they'd last had sex, and he couldn't believe how long it had been.

Beth suddenly stepped in the kitchen, and Lucy instinctively moved Travis away and turned back to the stove.

"I hope you didn't stop because of me!" Beth said.

"No, Beth, your mother hadn't finished cooking yet. Have you seen Nicholas this morning?"

"He must have gone out early. I didn't even hear him waking up. He usually makes a lot of noise."

"Do you mind setting the table in the living room?" Lucy asked.

Beth took some dishes and left the kitchen with Travis. Since that foolish night they hadn't had a chance to talk. Travis looked at his daughter. She was delicate like a flower and one didn't need to do that much to hurt her. And Travis didn't want that to happen.

"I'm glad to see that those shadows under your eyes have gone," he said.

She touched her face. His words brought Jamie back to her mind, Lexie's party, the ecstasy tablet, and her strong discomfort, which made her lose consciousness.

"Thanks, Dad."

Nicholas came in and went straight to his room without saying hello to anyone. In the meantime, Lucy entered the living room and put the food on the table. Everything was ready to start.

"What a nice smell, Mum! It makes me feel so hungry."

Lucy was happy, since Travis's kiss gave her a lift. The noise of Nicholas running down the stairs sounded more like a horse than the footsteps of a human being. He sat on the chair and stretched his arms on the table.

"At least say 'hi.'" Travis said.

"Hi," Nicholas said without feeling and then began stuffing his mouth with food.

Lucy and Beth looked at each other. Lucy seemed not to pay any more attention. Beth's expression, however, was a clear attempt to highlight her brother's bestial behaviour.

"You're a pig!" Beth said.

Nicholas stopped gorging and looked at his sister full of hatred.

"It's better than leaning your face against the wall for Jamie."

Beth's face went red and her embarrassment was so strong she had to leave the table. Travis watched the scene like an unwitting spectator, but Nicholas's pitch made him think of something unpleasant. Lucy stood up and followed her daughter into the bathroom, so that Travis and Nicholas remained by themselves.

"Why is your sister behaving like that?"

"You're the family behaviour specialist…try to use logic."

"I asked you a question, Nicholas!"

Travis summoned all his willpower to stay calm, but it was tough, since Nicholas was trying his best to annoy him.

"That's your problem, Prof," Nicholas said sarcastically while aping his students. "You ask too much. If you'd take the trouble to think more about the answers you already have, you wouldn't waste your time pursuing the stars, and you would not fall in the well."

Travis had never heard his son speaking without arrogance or without any sign of something that was close to a complaint. So he did not remain insensible to Nicholas's words.

"Your words are full of wisdom. I will stop asking questions, and I will seek the answers in what my eyes see."

"You better buy a new pair of glasses then!"

What an insult! Travis thought, taken by surprise.

Nicholas continued eating, but this time he stayed composed, holding back his laughter with difficulty. He had successfully annoyed his mother, his sister, and his father in less than a minute. *Success across the board*, he thought. He could stop acting, since it was useless to continue to behave like a pig.

Lucy and Beth came back to the table. Lucy was hugging her daughter and helped her sit on the chair, but judging from the expression on her face, it was as if a truck had decided to park on her stomach. Beth stared at her plate, and if Lucy did not fill it on time, she would burst out crying. Nicholas immensely enjoyed the scene. He was amused, imagining his mother with her hands on her face, shaking her head, horrified by Beth's story. He was sure that they had talked about her night with Jamie, and for sure Beth didn't have the courage to tell her that he was there in the same room with Monica.

That picture was just the contrary of what the obsessive calm of his father could ever produce. Nicholas wanted *Chaos*, in all senses, a world in which the effects were disproportionate to their causes and where his way of being, which made him look like a geek in other people's eyes, could eventually be accepted.

His way of being annoyed people, hurt them, and caused trouble. He had tried to pay heed to Travis's advice on more than one occasion, but the outcome had been a disaster. Hence, he decided he should be himself. At least he shouldn't pretend and feel frustrated forever. He didn't worry about understanding his father's insane mind; rather, he focused on things he needed to do. He absolutely had to get rid of Beth, and then, he would undermine his father's beliefs, make him suffer, and lead him towards inner purification through pain. And once he put his father on his knees, he would tell him, "Why don't you use logic?" And what about his mother? What would he make of her? She was worth less than zero, a nobody, an appendix, a decorative object in the house. She was just an ornament. He would leave her free to choose her own death. He couldn't stand to live with them anymore. He had to stay calm and wait for the right moment to give them each a final blow. *Right, calm,* he thought. It was the first time that he agreed with his father. A glass fell to the floor and broke in a thousand pieces, putting an end to his mega scenery of action.

"I am pleased to see you finally calm," Travis said to Nicholas.

Beth and his mother watched silently. Nicholas rarely smiled at his father, and this time his smile seemed sincere.

"Are you alright?" Lucy asked.

"Yes, Mum, I was distracted, and I was thinking how much fun we had at Lexie's party…"

"You are such an arsehole!" Beth murmured.

"Nick, Beth told me everything. Maybe she drank too much, but she told me that you both had fun. I know Monica was there, right?" Lucy added.

Childish, futile attempt at intimidation. A classic of two born losers, Nicholas thought.

"A great party? It's true, Mum, we both enjoyed it a lot."

Travis could not imagine, but he immensely and silently enjoyed the apparent familiar harmony. Then, they got hungry, as their thoughts vanished before the beautiful meal. Beth seemed to have recovered, as had Lucy, while Nicholas was happy to have been able to create a big mess.

"Dad, do you have class tomorrow?" Nicholas asked.

"A couple hours, why do you ask?"

"I'd like to come, and I promise I will be quiet and stay until the end this time."

An unexpected wave of joy overwhelmed Travis. It took so little to make his father happy. He filled his glass and kept eating.

The dinner ended in chitchatting, without the horrible tension that had made them so nervous during the last few days. Beth went to her room, Lucy cleared away the dishes, and Travis dedicated himself to reading.

Nicholas was still hungry and ate a slice of bread, while thinking about the day. If anyone had told him that he would be able to create harmony with his presence, he would have thought him mad. But so much so, it went like that. In that very moment, he became the main character of his microcosm. Whether or not he smiled, the other behaved accordingly. However, their reaction was driven by his extraordinary social behaviour that day. Once the family harmony turned into habit everything would have gone back to normal. Lucy would feel tired again, Beth would continue to speak ill of him before his parents, and his father would try to indoctrinate him with his sacred idiocies.

"I'm going to my room," Nicholas announced.

"Bye bye," Lucy said. She was doing dishes.

What an awful woman, Nicholas thought. Had she been his wife, he would have committed suicide just a second after the wedding. Then he changed his mind and decided that he would rather kill her. He locked the door, took off his shoes, and threw himself on the bed. He turned on the radio and lit up a cigarette. After only a few seconds, he grabbed the phone.

"Monica," he said, as soon as he heard her voice.

"Nicholas," Monica said, and he realized she had quickly recognized his voice, as well. "I didn't expect your call," she said.

"I was thinking about Lexie's party."

Monica remained quiet for a moment, apparently considering what he had said. "It was beautiful."

"I want to make it again."

"When?" Monica asked.

"Now."

"I want it, too," Monica said, with a breathless tone in her voice. "Are you alone?"

"I am not," Nicholas said. "The three dick heads are still around."

"Do you want to come over?"

"Now?" Nicholas asked.

"In half an hour. My parents are leaving, and I'll be alone."

"Then it's time to go out," he said. He hung up, lit up another cigarette, and stayed on the bed staring at the ceiling.

* * *

Monica lived close to Notting Hill tube station, and he arrived there after a short walk.

"Come in, Nicholas," Monica said, greeting him at the door.

He crossed the doorstep mechanically, managing only a cold hello. He looked around, sulky. To Monica he looked different since the last time she had seen him.

"What's wrong?"

"Is there anything to drink?" Nicholas said.

Monica was wearing jeans and a light sweater. She had expected a much warmer greeting. "Would you like some wine?"

"Beer, please."

He lay down on the sofa without waiting for her to invite him. There was little difference from how he was behaving now and how he behaved when he was at his parents' place.

"How's Beth?" Monica asked, trying to break the coldness.

"She whines and annoys me all the time. Other than that, she's fine."

Monica tried to smile as she left the room. He was talking about her best girlfriend. She came back to the drawing room with a glass of wine and a cold beer and sat next to him. Nicholas swallowed half his beer in one shot.

"You drank half of that in two seconds!" Monica observed, stating the obvious.

Nicholas smiled. "I beat my record then."

Monica took his hand and kissed his fingers. "Do you feel like…?"

"I do."

"I would suggest doing it after we smoke some pot. Let's go to my room."

She let Nicholas lay down on the bed while she took some hash from a little bag. Nicholas helped her roll it.

"Good stuff," he said.

"Thanks."

"It makes my head spin like crazy."

Nicholas was lying supine, with open arms, while Monica leaned her head against his shoulder. Then she turned and began to kiss his neck while she lifted his sweater. They could feel their heartbeats getting faster, while the drug quickly made them lose their inhibitions.

Nicholas closed his eyes and enjoyed the pleasure of smoking. Monica had already unfastened his belt, when Nicholas, caught in a fit of madness, turned her supine, and went astride on her.

"I like it so much more, this way," he said.

He unbuttoned his trousers, and she slipped her hand under his sweater. Nicholas, in a total daze, put his hand on her neck.

"Do you like it?"

"I love it."

Nicholas held her tighter.

"And now?"

"I am getting wet."

She began to move her legs and breathed deeper. Nicholas puffed the rest of the joint and closed his eyes. He could feel Monica's skin, and he liked to hold her neck tight. It was so thin and fragile that he could break it, holding just a little bit tighter.

"You're hurting me…" Monica struggled to say, choking on her words.

Nicholas didn't pay attention and held her neck tighter, until the pleasure of what was supposed to be a sensual game slowly turned into pain. Monica opened her eyes and looked at Nicholas. He was shaking his head unnaturally, as if he was moving jerkily, while she started to breathe with difficulty.

"Nicholas please…stop it!"

He did not loosen up. Monica put her hands on his trying to get rid of his grasp, but he held even tighter.

"Nicholas…"

He opened his eyes and saw Monica's face becoming purple. He tried to give the impulse to his hand and ease off, but he couldn't. He had never felt like that. The trip was lasting too long and it could end up in a drama.

"Forgive me, Monica. I don't know what happened to me."

Monica coughed and stared at him. He looked like a madman. Exhausted, completely at the mercy of the events, with the effect of the smoke and alcohol showing in his eyes. He was so sensual. She felt like having sex with him and took her clothes off.

Nicholas went down on her and caressed her, stricken with an excitement that drove him crazy. Her skin was milky, and the nipples were hard, on top of round, firm breasts. Monica held his buttocks and pulled him towards her. They were dying to possess each other, two volcanoes about to erupt.

At the peak of their excitement, Nicholas lay down on a side, but kept touching Monica with his fingers until she came. Her excitement grew stronger, while his slowly faded. Looking at Monica jerking and moaning was more exciting than to physically possess her. He could dictate her starts, decide where and when to touch her, to increase or interrupt her orgasm. He felt like the master of the game, but he wished it was different. It had to be pure, sweet, without the impetuosity to guide him and tell him how to make love. And his mood changed. He got off the bed and put his clothes on.

"You are a fucking whore!" he screamed at her.

Monica didn't pay attention. She saw blurred silhouettes, heard his voice, like an echo from afar, and her lust overshadowed her mind. The door slammed and jolted her back to reality. Nicholas wasn't there. He had gone and left her with a desire she could not fulfill.

* * *

His legs hurt and his head was still spinning. If he could have, he would have kicked everything around him. He burst out crying for no reason, and his father's voice echoed in his head. He hated him, with his whole being. It was because of him that he was walking alone on the street, risking falling on the ground at any second or ran down by a car. It was because of his father's fucking speeches, his lousy egotism, and that fucking calm!

Nicholas was desperate. He felt alone, without the strength to live serenely in the world, because there was always something or someone that conspired against him. The world was rotten, and he wanted to change it by any means he could. He would try hard to identify his fellows, the minds that were still pure, and he would teach them how to use logic. His logic, however, was very different from his father's logic.

"We are all queuing up," a man said to Nicholas.

Nicholas didn't even turn to see who had spoken. Then the man hit his shoulder.

"I'm talking to you, arsehole. There is a queue, and I got here first."

Nicholas realized he was in front of a ticket counter at the tube station of Notting Hill Gate, but he barely remembered how he had ended up there. The guy behind him was taller and a few years older than he. He wore a dark suit and conveyed the typical arrogance of those who believe that the world would stop without them. Nicholas stepped back and let the man pass, but he didn't stop staring at him.

"Do you have a problem?"

Nicholas didn't reply. The train was about to approach. There were a lot of people waiting, and he would likely have to wait for the next train to get on. So he killed the time looking around, and he recognized the guy who was in the queue behind him. *The presumption in people*. He also thought about putting him in a cage.

"Queue up!"

Nicholas remembered his words and the arrogance of yet another person who tried to step into his life. He felt his anger grow stronger. The train exited the tunnel, and Nicholas went closer to the man. Nobody could have noticed. He was standing less than a metre away, and he only had to put his hand on the man's shoulder and push him and let him fall on the rails. The headlights were visible and so close. People crowded. He closed his eyes and didn't think.

EIGHTEEN

"Someone got killed at the Notting Hill station last night," Beth said to Nicholas, when they were sitting in the kitchen the next morning.

"It was me," Nicholas said. "I did it."

Beth looked at him hopelessly.

"Maybe Monica was there when it happened."

"Yes, and they will call her to give an identikit of the murderer."

Beth left the newspaper on the table.

"I can't understand how you can say so many idiotic things. If you keep going like this, there will come a day when someone will throw you under a train, for real."

"Beth, stop it! It makes no sense to fight about a newspaper article!" Lucy said.

"Someone has been killed, Mum!"

"These things happen, unfortunately. Learn the lesson from it. At least you will remember to be careful when you're waiting to catch the train next time," Lucy said.

"The yellow line…don't ever cross it. That's the limit between life… and death," Nicholas said.

Lucy looked at Nicholas, the TV was on, and there was breaking news.

"…the police have no evidence, but two witnesses confirmed seeing a guy push the man a few moments before the train approached…"

Nicholas changed the channel. It was a normal chronicle, an accident that didn't deserve too much attention.

"I'm going to my room," he said, getting up from the sofa.

"Will you be here for dinner tonight?" asked Lucy.

"Don't know."

Her watch said six in the afternoon. Travis was supposed to be home at any moment from one of those nonsensical conferences, where he tried to explain his theory about social mechanisms. Lucy poured herself a cup of tea and poured one for Beth as well.

"Did you notice how weird Nicholas was today?" Beth said, sipping her tea.

Lucy seemed to be busier sipping from her cup than listening to her daughter's question.

"Why do you think so, sweetheart?"

"It was as if he wasn't there, as if he was thinking about completely different things."

"He's always like that," Lucy said, without looking up from her tea.

"If you say so…"

With his eyes closed and hands on his chest, Nicholas was desperately trying to calm his breathing. Anxiety attacked him, when he was confident he had overcome the latest crisis. He wiped the sweat from his forehead and kept smoking.

Damn lights! If it was just a bit darker, no one could see him. He wanted to celebrate for having set his instinct free from that mental cage, but two witnesses had seen a guy. They saw a guy doing what? Nicholas didn't even remember. He just remembered the pleasure he felt in seeing the shaken body, but feeling pleasure that way…was he crazy? Yes, maybe he was, because he was able to always find the easiest and fastest solution to everything. People called it *madness*; he thought of it as intelligence in the purest state, with no bonds or social imposition on his actions. The paradigm of Nicholas's world was the paradigm of the world of madmen.

He finished smoking and went into the bathroom. He looked at himself in the mirror and didn't see a wrinkle or anything that showed uneasiness, but his eyes reflected a sick light. He tried to read it, hoping to find the essence of his whole world, when someone knocked at the door.

"Nicholas?" It was his father.

"I'm busy!"

He didn't feel like talking to the old fogey. He changed his shirt while his father was waiting.

"Can I get in Nicholas?" his father asked, and Nicholas could hear a slight tremor of frustration in his voice.

"I don't think I've invited you in, Dad."

Travis went back to the drawing room. Nicholas inspected the package of cigarettes on the desk, took one, and lit it. He loved smoking, and he felt like the living prototype of a purifier. The smoke went down to his lungs, collected the wastes his brain expelled after burning the oxygen, and spit them into the world he hated. He wished it could spit it on his father's face. He stood before the mirror.

"Dear professor, you are talking nonsense. The void fills up your brain, creating a huge decompression that causes a unidirectional air flux, and lets your words come out of your mouth. Your son will demonstrate during the class the uselessness of your theories. Professor Nicholas, please make yourself comfortable and take the role of the gaga." Nicholas spoke to the image in the mirror.

The words came naturally out of his mind, as he thought out loud. He put on his jacket and went downstairs.

"Don't wait for me. I'll see you tomorrow."

"Nicholas, come here, please."

He fumed and walked towards his father.

"What's up now?"

"I would like to talk to you."

"I am about to go out, can't you see?"

"If you don't have anything that cannot be postponed until tomorrow, I would like you to stay here tonight."

"I have something to do."

He walked towards the door and muttered something offensive about Travis.

"One last thing…"

He opened the front door but Travis's voice reached him before he could close it.

"…the nothing can't fill up the brain: subject and predicate negate each other a priori. Yours is a senseless sentence. I would warmly recommend you put an effort into preserving your brain, as I wouldn't like the little you have to get lost in the air with your words."

Nicholas slammed the door, but this time Travis did not pay attention to his gesture. Lucy remained silent, Beth, on the other hand, was incredulous. They had never heard Travis talking to his son like that.

* * *

He was supposed to meet with Jamie. He managed to get his numbers and was waiting for him in a pub not far from his place. He saw him entering with a friend, and he nodded for Jamie to come closer.

"What a surprise to hear from you," Nicholas said.

"I bet it was. It doesn't happen that often to have the son of your professor as an orgy mate."

Nicholas was in a very good mood, and Jamie instantly liked his attitude.

"This is Adel," Jamie said.

They shook hands.

"What would you like to drink? Nicholas asked Adel.

"A beer for me," Adel said.

"Are you Jamie's classmate?" Nicholas asked.

Adel was touchy, and Nicholas's questions made him feel uncomfortable.

"Adel just moved to London," Jamie said, "and he's looking around for a job."

"What do you do?" Nicholas asked.

"Wines. I am trying to make the right contacts."

Jamie could see that Nicholas's questions annoyed Adel, so he thought it best to change subject. "You know I couldn't believe my eyes when I saw you in the bedroom?"

"Agreed. It was so absurd that I struggle even now to believe it is true."

"We just met then, right?" Jamie said.

Nicholas nodded. He liked Jamie; there was definitely something perverted about him. There was little doubt they could become friends.

"How do you like the fuddy-duddy lectures?" Nicholas asked.

What a hell of a question, Jamie thought. Of course he couldn't say he found them boring. "They're…interesting," he said, instead.

"I am sure you can be more explicit," Nicholas prodded. He said it with a smile on his face, and Jamie immediately felt comfortable.

"Ok, then the lectures are weird, stressful, but not the usual stuff, and it always depends on the way you look at them. You've got to use your brain but no doubt you could even find them exciting. Let's say that I am convincing myself I like them so far."

Adel grabbed his beer and moved next to a couple of blondes sitting at the bar on their own.

"He doesn't waste any time…where is he from?" Nicholas asked, glancing at Adel and the two women.

"Algeria." Jamie noticed Nicholas grimace. "Anything wrong?"

"Not at all, but he clearly feels uncomfortable. I wonder why you let him come with you."

"He's staying at my place, so I thought it was impolite not to invite him to go out."

"He's not really into wines, is he?"

Jamie remained expressionless. Then Nicholas's smile made him feel relaxed.

"He says he is."

"I would love to taste one of his wines, then," Nicholas said, raising his eyebrows.

Jamie burst out laughing at the gesture.

"Pity we couldn't get any at Lexie's," Nicholas said.

"You can't complain," Jamie said.

"I know I can't."

"Who was the cutie you were shagging?" Jamie asked.

"Monica. One of Lexis's girlfriends."

"She's not bad. And it wasn't bad the one I was having sex with, either."

"Beth?"

"Do you know her?" Jamie asked.

"Of course I do. She's the daughter of your professor."

The news came as a shock to Jamie. It couldn't be true. Nicholas was talking about Beth as if she was one of the little bitches one could have a one-night stand with. But at the end, considering Beth's performance, she didn't differ that much from a bitch.

"Fuck! Not even at the lottery can you can get this kind of jackpot. Adel, want to have some fun?" Jamie said.

He was so involved in picking up the two blondes that he didn't even turn at Jamie's words.

"What an arsehole!" Jamie said of Adel's behaviour.

"He's your friend, Jamie. You chose him."

Jamie turned to Nicholas. "It's weird for me to ask…but what did you think when you saw your sister making out with me?"

Yes, Jamie was a pervert. No doubt. "That she would have probably stopped pissing me off."

Adel was on another planet, busy kissing one of the girl's hands. Jamie and Nicholas didn't talk any more about Lexie's party, as they had fine-tuned in on a much higher frequency with each other. There was a strange feeling between the two, a kind of mutual respect, based on the idea they had about each other.

"Will you come back to one of our lectures?" Jamie asked.

"I think so, even though it will be tough to tolerate my dad talking."

"Do you like our debates? I mean the way the lessons are carried out."

"I like the relationship you guys have with the subject. In search of the truth, an attempt to criticize and develop pre-existing philosophies, and adapt them to our existence," Nicholas said, impressed with his own instant analysis.

"I guess your father is pretty good at that."

Nicholas closed his eyes and sighed, feeling annoyed. "He's old…and he thinks that wisdom comes with age. He doesn't understand a fucking thing! Instead, he lives a dull, emotionless life, and he wants to draw me into his world! You better not listen to him, Jamie. He's trying to stop time and progress and stay alive in his uselessness. He's the enemy of our minds' freedom. He's a danger that we should avoid."

Jamie tried to justify Nicholas's words with the fourth beer he was drinking. Nicholas's eyes were different; they sparkled with a strange glare that Jamie found fascinating.

"We need a superior mind, one that could establish times and parameters for our catharsis, avoiding people who have failed in their lives. They could still have the power to influence the social dictates in society, in the name of 'truths' that no longer have any reason to exist."

Jamie stopped drinking. "How are things between the two of you?" he asked, aware that they couldn't be very good at all.

Oddly, Nicholas smiled at Jamie's question. "We both want to possess the truth, but in a different way. He persists in something that never gave the results he wanted, and he is making a pathetic attempt to hand down to future generations a method that leaks water from everywhere." Nicholas sipped his beer. "But do you realize the age difference between us? Do you think it's possible that someone who belongs to the past can want you to grow or have your own ideas and to follow a life that can just be yours, with doctrines that belong to another period? He has this freaking fear that someone could overturn his values, which he teaches, and let them disappear into oblivion for good."

"Panta rei," Jamie added.

"That's the problem," Nicholas said, "things change and often for a reason. And the true reason is that the world belongs to those who live and have the courage to change things that don't work. It does not belong to those who lived it in the past like my father, who were not able to improve it and, hence, who merely appear at the window and watch things flow. If you want to win, you have to fight at the fence and not go undercover to see what happens."

"Nicholas, it's a mess in here. Want to come to my place and keep talking there?"

Nicholas nodded, asked for the bill, and then they left together—

neither thought of Adel. He was far from their thoughts.

* * *

The floor creaked, and the moquette was old and dirty. There were no paintings on the walls, and the drawing room was a heap of many different things. A pile of CDs, newspapers, and magazine were amassed together into a basket, and the sofa was the only place where one could sit without disturbing the perfect harmony of that mess.

"Make yourself comfortable. Wine, beer, or…?"

"Beer."

Jamie went to the kitchen and came back after a moment. Nicholas leaned back, resting his head against the back of the sofa, looking at the ceiling. It was old, and it looked as if the paint might fall on him any moment. He glanced at the window and saw that the wooden frames felt the weight of time. There was a picture on the chimney but no books on the shelves that stood next the window.

"Just taken out of the fridge," Jamie said, holding a beer out to Nicholas.

Nicholas stretched his arm and grabbed it. "Where do you keep your books?" he asked.

"In my bedroom."

"Why not on the shelves?"

"I prefer not to. Their sight would put me off, reminding me that I have something I must read."

"My bedroom is empty," said Nicholas.

"If you like it so…"

"I will fill it with books one day, but now I just have to use my time to think."

"How's it going with your parents?"

"It's a dead relationship," Nicholas said, taking a long pull from the beer.

"You better leave them, then," Jamie said, likewise tilting his beer to his lips and drinking.

"Not now. I want to lock in my memory the last images of a place I know I won't see again."

"It usually happens when I go on holiday."

"Hence, there is no need for me to add anything."

"I can't understand you," Jamie said.

Nicholas stopped staring at the ceiling and placed the bottle on the floor. "The swan song. My father is planning something, and I intend to understand what he's aiming at, then I'll attack him at the crucial moment, destroying his fucking certainties bit by bit."

Jamie was older than Nicholas, but Nicholas's words came out with such energy they would subdue anyone. Jamie thought that Nicholas had the same mind of his father but with a fierce determination. He was the spitting image of a madman.

"What did you study?" Jamie asked, out of context to his thoughts.

"Math."

"It's a family fight then," Jamie asked.

"Indeed, but maybe I'm wrong. I better become a philosopher. You don't do fucking anything from day to night."

"It's never too late. If you wish, I can help you prepare for the exams." Jamie wanted to joke, but Nicholas's mind was somewhere else.

"I don't give a damn about the courses!" Nicholas said. "A book doesn't make a philosopher of you! I want to find the squaring of the circle and destroy that way of thinking forever. I can't stand it. I can't stand that those who think they bring certainty to the world through dialectic would be allowed to do it in the future! Do you understand, Jamie? Do you understand the importance of creating a new and different way to face problems?"

Jamie was thinking about totally different things. He was thinking about Beth's legs, Monica's boobs, and about the guy who was sitting in front of him, and speaking as if he was possessed. The jigsaw puzzle was weird, and he wasn't sure he had the key to understand it.

"Just tell me what you think you will be able to bring to the system to make it change," Jamie said.

"Facts against words. I will let people like my father understand that to find the solution to problems they should stop analysing things from the outside, and have the balls to face the problems directly."

"*Empiricism?*"

"No, Jamie, it doesn't have anything to do with that. I want to go to the root of the cause, because my inner suffering doesn't depend on something I've done but on something that has been created around me since I was born—a fucking cage that harnesses those gifted with capabilities above the average and labels them as madmen. Have you ever asked yourself why history has always been written by those who have won? In your opinion, why do you think that the books you study are full of famous words that were left for you to learn until you are sick of it, words that work perfectly to isolate you in a world that has nothing to do with the real one? They are indoctrinating you, Jamie! Even the famous *Free Will* is a terrible swindle! There is no *Free Will* in the world we live in, but just a box where there is a bit of room for you to move and gives you the illusion that you walk on your legs. Society created the box, and you have to do all that you can to shatter it, if you want to get out of the cage they have locked you in. You've got to do so many more things than those you think you should do. Don't think, Jamie, but just follow your instinct and what it tells you. This is the only way to have justice."

"Holy shit, Nicholas!"

"So, what do you think?" Nicholas asked.

"That when I listen to you I realize I'm blindfold," Jamie said, exasperated. "But then, your words just sound like those I've heard so many times in the past. I see it's difficult, really. I've been fascinated by your thoughts, but I can't see how they could breach the system. How can you overturn a lifestyle centuries old and have it adopted by anyone?"

"Anything that led to progress seemed absurd and difficult to comprehend before it was adopted. Then when it worked, it became normal and part of your life, while the old habits were removed in an instant. The founders of the principles on which world is based, will defend what they believe in until they die. They fear changes, and that is why they will never allow you to think in a different way. Those who make history are few, while those who speak about how things should be are those who run away first, even if changes take a minimum of effort," Nicholas explained.

"So, you don't want to create another model of social behaviour, but just demonstrate that the current one is a fake!"

"Exactly!"

"Then that's different."

"Completely different."

Jamie stayed silent, waiting for an answer that didn't come, as Nicholas already seemed to have decided that he had said enough for that day.

* * *

Nicholas had a bite to eat on the way back home, but he wasn't hungry. He just didn't want to go back and meet his father. The more he talked to people keen to listen to what he had to say, the more he compared Travis's talks to a prison. He stayed out, until he got lost between the pubs and the folklore of Coven Garden Square.

'Convent Garden was what it was called in the past because of the kitchen garden of the Abbey of Saint Paul, located there to supply the products to Westminster. There

was a clear influence of Italian architecture, the Palladian and its Neo-classicism, precisely because the Curator of the Works of the King, who was awarded the job by the Earl of Bedford II, chose it as reference the city of Livorno.'

The light in the drawing room was on, but the TV wasn't. That meant that his father was locked in his studio. He went closer to the door without making any noise and saw his father busy scribbling on his papers. He went upstairs and lay down in bed, without falling asleep, but waiting to hear the usual footsteps in the house. Then he would go downstairs again. However, he thought that Monica's butt was a good way to kill time. He grabbed the phone and called her.

"Monica," Nicholas said when Monica answered.

"Why did you call me?" she asked.

"I was thinking of you."

"It's a bit too late, don't you think?"

"Sorry."

"You're an arsehole!"

Nicholas pushed back the phone. "Can you hear me now?" he asked.

"You sound distant," she said.

"I am distant, Monica, so calm down. Otherwise my voice will go away forever."

Monica waited, while Nicholas brought the phone closer to his mouth. He could hear her breathing. "I was spaced out. My brain exploded, and I just didn't realize what I was doing."

"It doesn't justify your behaviour."

"I just said I'm sorry."

"And what do you expect, Nicholas? That I stay here waiting for you to come back?"

"No, I just want to talk to you."

"You could have called me earlier if that's all you wanted to get from me."

"Why the hell do you have to behave like that? Why don't you accept things when they come naturally? Would you prefer me to call you every day to ask you how things are and similar bullshit? I called you because I wanted to hear your voice; I wanted to hear you talking, without the need to act in a role that I couldn't care less about! I just wanted to follow my instinct, Monica. Is there anything more beautiful than being spontaneous?"

"I've thought about you so much."

She was sincere, and Nicholas grinned. "I am happy to hear that, if it's true," he said.

"I've being thinking of you since you left, and I still can't understand why you behaved so badly."

Nicholas unbuttoned his shirt and put his hand on his chest. There was sweetness in Monica's voice, and this calmed him down. He had thought about her too, but, likely, in a different way.

"Did you miss me?" he asked her.

"I did."

"Do you want to see me?"

"I do."

"When?"

"Now."

Nicholas got excited. The firm conviction shining through Monica's voice washed away his doubts and brought his mind back to her body. "Are you excited?" he asked.

"I am."

"What would you do for me?" he asked.

"Anything you want."

"Would you kill for me?"

Monica didn't reply. The night was messing it all up and the emotions got mixed into each other living on the physical tiredness, while the mind found rich soil to start again with its perverse games.

"I would," she said, finally.

"You must show me, then."

"How?"

There was surprise in her voice, and Nicholas wanted to see if she meant what she said. "Go to the tube and push anyone under the first train that approaches."

"Like at Notting Hill?" she asked.

"Yes."

"Where were you when it happened?" she asked him.

"At the station."

"It must have been horrible."

"No," said Nicholas, "it was pleasant."

"Did you kill him, then? That was you?"

He hesitated before answering. "Do you see me capable of doing such a thing?"

"Did you kill him?" she insisted.

"You know me, Monica, and you have all the possible elements to guess."

Monica felt reassured by his pitch. "You freaked me out! For a moment I thought it could have been you!"

"It's so easy with you…a word to throw you into the panic and two words to calm you down."

"It is not like that, I swear. It's just that…you scare me sometimes."

"Are you talking about the last time at your place?"

"No, I just read your eyes."

"What's wrong with my eyes?"

"They shine with a strange light."

He started to like it. "The eyes of a madman?" he asked.

"No, Nicholas, they are just different eyes. I can't explain."

His father's footsteps brought his attention to the bedroom door. The door was ajar, and Travis had apparently caught a glimpse of light.

"I didn't hear you come back. Who are you talking to?" Travis asked him.

"A friend."

"Don't you think it's a bit too late to be on the phone?" Travis asked.

Nicholas was just too tired to fight again, at least not at the moment. It wasn't worth it, because to fight with his father when he was tired couldn't give him any satisfaction.

"I'll hang up in two seconds."

Travis closed the door, but he re-opened it an instant later.

"Are you alright? Do you want to have a chat with me?"

He was so sweet, maybe he was learning to behave like a father.

"See you tomorrow," Nicholas said, cutting the conversation short.

"Monica?" he said into the phone.

"Yes, I am here."

"I have to leave you."

"It's fine."

Nicholas hung up. He remained motionless with the phone on his chest waiting to be sure everyone was asleep. He just didn't want his father to see him going downstairs, because he would have asked those hateful questions and wanted an explanation for his behaviour.

It was dark in the aisle. Nicholas closed the door and went down the stairs. Travis had left the door of the studio open. Nicholas stepped in and switched on the light.

The desk was full of papers, something unusual for a person like his father. There were books left open, lots of notes here and there. The typical symptoms of an embryonic concept. He tried to understand, but then he was deeply touched by the words he read in a sheet.

I love you, Nicholas

NINETEEN

One day I will understand the underlying causes of the events, I will be able to see them untied from each other and, in a future not far off, I will maybe dominate them...stop it, Travis, now breathe, relax, and think.

Travis was in South Bank, sitting on a bench while looking at the other side of the river. He did not have class that day. He just wanted to sit and think.

You have to find the solution...Now stop thinking in third person. I have to find the solution...You must talk to yourself as you, to feel the responsibility of your acts on yourself. Nicholas...why does he behave like that? Am I perhaps losing something I won't be able to get back? I don't have to be distracted. I have to put a brake on my ambition to have a clear picture of what happens in the world. Which world? The one I want to live in or the one I really feel? My family, my job, my friends. Yes, that's the right order. Nicholas...I miss you Nicholas, I love you Nicholas, more than my life, but I need you to help me understand you. Maybe, if I could detach, I could evaluate things differently.

It was a beautiful sunny day, and the river was flowing. Billions and billions and billions of water drops were just flowing by, and he wouldn't see them again. They flowed past, imperturbable, without distractions, but they all listened to the thoughts of people like Travis.

I want to enter the water, count the drops, put them on line and unveil their secrets. So what, Travis? Did you find the answer to your question? I did. Things happen in only one way because...because humankind was born from a microorganism and from an endless coincidence of events. A one-time joint, a whirlwind that enters a room and messing it all up creates the perfect mechanism. Well done, I feel you are on the right track. My universe is Nicholas, Beth, and Lucy. All that revolves around my world represents its own limit. I can't go any farther, but I want control. Okay, I stop feeling emotions and everything changes. Nicholas is suffering? I try not to give him any advice, but I wait for things to happen. Entropy: things left on their own find their own balance. I never left Nicholas free to decide. I made a mistake. I can't see things only through my eyes. I have to learn to wait and see how the events evolve around his Free Will. But then…how can I manage them? I must consider my universe as many drops that make a river…Nicholas, Beth, and Lucy…they are the drops of my micro-universe, the boundary beyond which the effects cannot coincide. This is represented by the bend of a river. If I remain on the bench of my detachment, I'll be able to observe and comprehend them, but I have to refrain from touching the water, as I could pollute it with my emotions. The cold, the warmth…they don't have to exist. Fine, I am getting at it. So…things must flow and happen according to their own free choice. If I could let them happen within their universe I could maybe control them. Yes, Travis, it's just like that. Well done! Now keep going…But when is the moment when everything coincides? Free Will, events' causality…if I can find that point, no, if I can understand when they cross…then the problem is solved. Try hard, think, come on, Travis, you are making it! Just one point, to reproduce the status of perfect balance: Nicholas's Free Will, my Free Will…they cross within our universe and coincide. Fate, my thoughts finally get along well with his. But what about Destiny? How should I place it in the scheme of things? It's the final stage, it's the sea, where the river drowns and terminates. It becomes part of the whole, of the cosmos, where everything coincides, where time stops, where there are no more choices to make but just harmony. Yes, I found the answer, perhaps I understood. What coincides in a fraction of time, when more events cross is just one point of my own universe, where it has a better chance of happening…but then? How can I understand when all points coincide? How can I know exactly when each other universe overlaps? How can I foresee the expectations and wishes of anyone? I will probably not be able to do it, because in the same moment when all coincides, all breaks apart, all is destined to change, to split anyone's life into two different stories. Don't think about it, Travis. No, I won't. It doesn't matter, because in that moment, if all coincides, you and I, Nicholas, will be happy.

A ray of sunshine rebounded on the railing before him, hitting Travis in his eyes, and put an end to his reflections. A perfect coincidence, and in that very moment, Travis stopped conceiving thoughts.

* * *

The following day Travis prepared the topics he wished to discuss with the students and was anxious to analyse their reactions. He remained in his office all day and came out only when he felt completely satisfied. Nicholas and Beth sat at the table. She and her angel face, he and his unmistakable grouch face.

"Would you like to come to class tomorrow? I am inviting you this time."

"To leave the classroom again?" Nicholas replied.

His answer didn't bother Travis. On the contrary, it made him smile. "I hope you won't. I need your feedback."

"Fine, I'll try to come."

It was just a random answer, without interest, one that wouldn't increase the level of tension before going to bed.

* * *

The classroom was full. A few minutes were left before class started, and Travis was waiting anxiously for the moment to talk. His curiosity about how the class would react was almost palpable, but he had little doubt about how the lesson was going to develop; it would be another marathon of dialectics. Nicholas sat at a desk in the next to the last row, next to Jamie, and their eyes met for an instant. Then they both went back to their own thoughts. Travis was standing and soon began acting, according to his customary habits. He walked slowly back and forth in the class, with his hands crossed behind his back, elaborating sensations.

"*Free Will, Predeterminism, Chaos, and Sociological model.* Who's able to open the debate?"

Chris raised his hand. "The world is ruled by mechanical laws. As such, any event has its prior cause."

"How would you relate your assumption to society?" Travis asked.

"Emotional states?" Chris asked.

"The comparison doesn't hold," Travis said.

"Why not?" Chris asked.

"Social behaviour is not predictable."

Travis looked at his students and felt their interest about the topic.

"It is not possible to apply the principles of classic mechanics to the social universe for one reason: it is not possible to quantify all the forces that come into play. So? Who is able to continue my lecture? Chris?"

Chris lowered his head. Then Daphne raised her hand and Travis nodded.

"*Quantum mechanics?*" she asked.

"Why, Daphne?"

"Probabilistic forecast of an effect, given its cause."

"Could you please translate that into understandable words, Daphne?"

"In a sub-universe, in such case we could compare it to the social universe, some causes generate behaviours that are not perfectly predictable beforehand. There are variables that cannot be included in a linear model of cause and effect."

"Fine, Daphne, could you make it clearer for your classmates?"

"If we want to relate to the social, we should talk about *Free Will*. As such, a free choice, in this case the cause, could originate an effect not perfectly dependent on what one has chosen to do. Thus, on the basis of our studies about social behaviour, we can only forecast, with a some degree of probability, a specific future event."

Travis was proud. The students were responding well to his encouragement. Suddenly, the students turned towards the next to the last row. Nicholas had just raised his hand. Travis noticed him and held back his joy with difficulty.

"Tell us, Nicholas."

"There is a clear contradiction in Daphne's explanation."

"Why?"

"*Free Will* can't solve the problem at its roots, since we don't even know whether there is something that could be defined as *Free Will*. If there is, we should be able to quantify it just as we do anything else that exists."

It was a superb speech.

"You are not altogether wrong, and I agree in part with what you say. But then, if *Free Will*, in the sense of free choice, can't be quantified, what makes the social universe unpredictable or probabilistic?"

Nicholas felt uncomfortable, and he could feel the pressure of Travis's questions, but this time he managed to control himself and the whole exploded into a continuous tension of his muscles. Travis kept going.

"What we cannot foresee in any way, is the causality factor which remains unknown. As such, we can think of ourselves as individuals who act according to their *Free Will*, independently from a mechanical model that would reduce our capability of thinking and, as such, our being human. But now, we face another dilemma. Chris?"

He didn't reply.

"Daphne?"

She wasn't able to reply either. Nicholas raised his hand but then, slowly, lowered it again.

"To have with a good approximation the correspondence between the cause and its likely effect in the social universe, we should study the choices that are made without the effect to be immediately visible: I am enrolling at the University of another city. How will my life change? Would it be possible to bring it back to a plausible forecast or will it remain shrouded in mystery? The answers would seem obvious: we examine the record of occurrences of the people who made a similar choice and we relate the effect to the sub-universe of the individual who is making the choice. This is a probabilistic approximation of the future evolution of the society."

Nicholas raised his hand. "I don't agree. If the explanation holds it would almost seem that we should be able to foresee the future."

"It is incorrect to talk about forecast of the future, Nicholas. It is all about probabilistic approximation of an event. More or less this would be equal to, say, if we know the cause, we will likely have this kind of effect. But there is something else I would like to talk about, guys. In your opinion, would it be possible to foresee the moment in which an event could change someone's life?"

"Prof, are you referring to Destiny?" Chris asked.

Travis thought about it. He leaned against the desk and looked at the floor. It was just his way of finding the most proper words.

"Destiny…I could define as such the sole and unrepeatable coincidence that changes our lives. Chris, imagine for a moment that you write a love letter, the primal cause, to seduce a beautiful girl, the effect you want to generate. Imagine then to appear at the window and to look at two girls who are waiting to read what you have written. You let your wonderful love letter flutter through the air, until it lands thirty centimetres from the girl you are in love with. Next to her, is the girl you can't stand, who is part of your social sub-universe, namely one of the people with whom you could potentially get in contact and who, if she read what you wrote, would stick to you like a fly to honey…which girl would you prefer to read your letter?"

"The good looking one!"

The guys laughed.

"Good choice. I see you have fine tastes for women…so I was saying, thirty centimetres, then twenty, then ten, then two…Chris, your new girlfriend is about to grab the letter and make your dream come true, when a passing car generates a gust of wind that pushes the letter into the hands of the girl you don't like…and you will likely end up getting married and live together with her for the rest of your life. That's Destiny. A light, imperceptible gust of wind generated by a sum of coincidences, the letter that flutters in front of the two girls, and the car that passes by in that very moment, which changes your life forever."

"Casualty!"

"No," said Travis, "Destiny."

"Sorry, Prof, what's the difference between coincidence and Destiny?"

"Destiny is the coincidence that cannot repeat in the same identical way and, as such, changes your life the moment it happens. You won't write a letter for that woman again; you married the other one, and she ran away disappointed."

"Sure, but I can always bump into the girl I really like again."

Travis was expecting to hear that.

"You are right. If that woman ran away from my world, for example in Australia, the probability that I would see her again is practically non-existent, but if she stays in contact with me, then things change."

"Why?" Daphne asked.

"Because I could recreate the conditions for my choice and let them work for the gust of wind to be favourable to me this time. I could recreate the conditions knowing the time and the space in which the cause and the effect are linked to each other. In other words, recreating the same chain of events, I could reasonably think to change Destiny."

"No one can change Destiny!" Nicholas said.

Father and son looked at each other intensely, as if the class didn't exist. Nicholas had perceived perfectly that Travis was trying to manoeuvre him into one conclusion, as if everything could banally be led to the relation between cause and effect.

"I am not trying to foresee it, Nicholas, I am just trying to say that if I know everything about someone and see him acting within a micro-universe, which is perfectly known to me, I can reasonably assume that if I recreate the basic conditions, this someone could go towards a destiny that I had in some way foreseen."

TWENTY

"What is your instinct telling you?" Jamie asked. He and Nicholas were in Jamie's flat.

"That my father hates me."

"That's excessive," Jamie said. "Parents don't hate their children. At worst, they break their balls."

Jamie was lying on the sofa, while Nicholas was flicking through the CDs.

"What about some jazz?"

"No way!"

"Then put on what you like."

Nicholas went closer to the base of the sofa, where a light, coming from a lamp placed on the floor, lit up the room. The joint was ready, and they would share it.

"Take it," Nicholas said, holding out the joint.

Jamie grabbed it and puffed. "Good stuff."

"How was class today?"

"Your father was not in the schedule. Better like this, the last time my brain was smoking."

"I'm happy for you," Nicholas said.

"My head still hurts, though," Jamie said.

"Smoke and you will heal."

"Should I trust you?" Jamie asked.

"I would if I were you." Nicholas stood up and got two more beers.

"I could spend a year lying on the sofa. Joint, beer…I just need a woman."

"Call that bitch of Beth."

"She's your sister! How can you say something like that?"

"If she was not my sister," Nicholas said, "I wouldn't even be interested in getting to know her. I can't see what you find so exciting about her."

Jamie puffed again, this time filling his lungs. Then he gave the joint back to Nicholas. In his entire life, it had never happened that he was fucking his professor's daughter and openly discussing it with her brother. But Nicholas was everything but normal.

"Monica's ass excites me more," Jamie said.

"She's a bitch as well," Nicholas countered.

"Gorgeous though. Bitch, but gorgeous. Which is fine with me."

"If you look at her from a different angle," Nicholas said.

"Is your old man aware of Beth and me?" Jamie asked.

"You mean what happened at Lexie's?"

Jamie nodded.

"No, otherwise he would bury her alive and probably shoot me. My mother knows, though."

"And what does she think about it?"

"What a fucking stupid question, Jamie! But what would you expect her to say? That she gives a party for Beth and her girlfriends? I thought you were clever!"

They smoked and talked, while the topics they discussed just filled the air with noise.

"I think I'm clever," Jamie said.

"Lucky you, if you believe it. However, I will put you to the test."

"I'm ready."

"Call Beth and ask her to come over."

"Now?"

"Now."

Jamie grabbed the phone. "Hi, Beth," he said, as soon as she answered the phone.

"Jamie?"

"Yeah, it's me. Was wondering how you're doing."

Nicholas gave him a thumb up. Jamie's pitch was right.

"I wasn't expecting your call."

"Surprises have a different flavour." He could hear Beth's giggle.

"What are you doing?" she asked him.

"I am reflecting upon the mysteries of the world."

He put his hand on his mouth to suffocate his laughter.

"It must really be an important thing. I guess you've spent the whole day reflecting upon it."

Beth was coping well.

"And you? How do you spend your time while I am reflecting?" Jamie asked.

"I'm having a drink."

"By yourself?"

"No, with a girlfriend," Beth said.

"Interesting."

"Why?"

"Among the things I was reflecting upon, I thought that I'd like to see you," Jamie said.

"Where?" she asked.

"My house."

"And what about my girlfriend?"

"Tell her to come over. There's company for her as well."

"I'll talk to her and let you know. What's your address?"

Jamie told her and Beth hung up.

"How did it go?" Nicholas asked.

"What do you think?"

"Easy bet. Ten against one she will not resist."

"Easy win, she's coming over. And she's not alone," Jamie said, smugly.

"Who's with her?"

"I don't have a clue. Maybe it'll be a nice surprise."

"Do you have a video camera?" Nicholas asked.

"Why?"

"Don't answer a question with another question! Do you have it or not?"

"It's in there in the drawer." Jamie pointed to a chest of drawers next to the fireplace.

"I want to film while you're having sex."

Nicholas's perversion was running faster than he thought. Jamie felt uncomfortable. "You're joking, I suppose."

"I'm not. I want to film you and Beth while you're fucking."

Nicholas already had the video camera in his hands. He was checking to see that it was set to start, and he had a serious expression on his face. "Can I use the DVD in here?" he asked.

Jamie nodded.

"When Beth arrives, don't tell her I'm here, but tell her girlfriend to go into the bathroom, since you wish to stay alone with Beth."

"Okay."

"Leave the light on. I need it for the camera. Then I'll step in and film you. It shouldn't take more than a couple of minutes."

"And what if she realizes you're here?"

"I have already seen her fucking. It shouldn't be a problem for her."

"You are crazy!"

He left the camera on the floor and went closer to the sofa. "Don't ever, ever say that again. Never!"

They heard the entry phone buzzing. Jamie stood up and answered. "Third floor."

Jamie remained with his arms against the wall. He was nervous because of Nick. He went back to the drawing room and tried to face him.

"I don't know, but this doesn't seem like a great idea to me. Why do you want to film your sister while she fucks?"

"You would never understand it, because you don't have a father like mine."

The doorbell rang, and Jamie let Beth and her girlfriend come in. The girlfriend was pretty much her age. Beth was happy to see Jamie again, but it was as if Jamie wasn't there. He was tired, spaced out, and nervous.

Beth's girlfriend didn't say a word. She was looking around, and then, she introduced herself. "I'm Claire."

Jamie looked at her with a grimace and invited them to follow him to the drawing room. To Jamie, it looked like a slow-motion scene, made on purpose for Jamie who was carrying himself and his discomfort with difficulty.

"Are you alright?" Beth asked.

Jamie puffed the last bit of his joint, and blew smoke into Beth and Claire's faces.

"You want a beer?"

It was a terrible effort to ask that question. Jaime was tired, and Nicholas's perversion made him wish the game would stop.

"Claire," Jamie said, leaning his arm on the wall, "I have a surprise for you."

Claire turned towards Beth and looked at her and shrugged.

"And what would that be?" Claire asked.

"My friend is waiting for you in the bathroom. Beth and I have many things to talk about. Isn't that right, Beth?"

He caressed her back and Beth came closer to him and smiled.

"Beth? So...should I go to the bathroom?" Claire asked, uncertain.

Beth nodded and sat on the sofa with Jamie. The flat was small. Claire was alone and heard Beth talking about Jamie almost every day, but that night something excited her. It was dark all around, and a few metres ahead a blade of light, coming out of the bathroom, showed her the way. She pushed the door ajar and saw Nicholas sitting down on the floor, smoking. He was in the middle of two cans of beer, looking at the ceiling, expressionless. She wore a skirt with a leather jacket, and looked very, very pretty to Nicholas.

Nicholas turned towards Claire and gestured for her to sit down next to him. Ten minutes went by, just the time it took to finish the cigarette and totally relax. The only words that broke the silence came from the music that Jamie had put on. Without saying a word, Nicholas slipped his hand between Claire's legs. She didn't reject him; on the contrary, she invited him to push deeper. She was young, a few years younger than he was, and he was excited to see her with her eyes shut while biting her lips trying to hold in her desire. Nicholas was dying to have sex, and the pressure in his head would have made his brain explode had he waited just one more minute. His caress became a grasp, and he began to unbutton her shirt. Claire let him do it, happy to see him do it, since she liked to be caressed by a man who didn't waste any time.

Monica belonged to the past. He felt important for Claire; he felt free. He lifted her skirt and invited her to sit on top of him. Claire moved with an infinite gentleness, disclosing a world he did not think existed until then. He caressed her legs, kissed her breasts with passion, while a river grew inside him.

They looked at each other at the same time, Nicholas's dark, intense eyes and Claire's green, elusive eyes. They remained still, for a moment to feel their bodies meld into each other, until they could not resist any longer, and exploded. There was no more Jamie, Monica, Beth, or his father. The explosion washed his problems away, emptying him out and making his eyelids heavy. Claire was on top of him, kissing his neck. It was passion, the most beautiful thing he had ever tried.

They calmed down. Claire slipped onto her side and began to smoke again. Nicholas needed to stand up and feel the icy-cold water flowing all over his skin. The video camera was in the corner on the other side of the bathroom, and he picked it up.

Claire saw him going out and accompanied him with a smile. It was dark outside the bathroom, and the notes of the music took him into the drawing room where Jamie had left the light on. He could see them.

Jamie was sitting on the sofa while Beth was moving on top of him completely naked. Nicholas started shooting the scene, without emotion. Beth ran the game, while Jamie lay, looking lifeless, like a piece of meat between her legs.

"Beth!"

She opened her eyes, turned, and looked at her brother. Her expression was distorted, paralyzed, and the panic quickly spread on her face. She looked at him, desperate, in tears, trying to cover her breasts and get off the sofa. The incredulity of that moment surpassed the power of her imagination. Her brother had planned everything with the only intent to ruin her life forever. *Fucking bastard!* She felt trapped, panic-stricken, and conscious that a person who embodied hell had twisted her.

Nicholas stopped shooting after the house door slammed. He saw Jamie, naked and spaced out, looking at him, scared by the sick smile on Nicholas's face.

* * *

Never before like that night had going home looked so different to Nicholas. Something had definitely been broken. The TV was on and he saw the back of his father's head above the back of the sofa. Nicholas pitied him. His father was still convinced he could dominate the events, but the events were there, with Nicholas about to destroy him.

He walked up the stairs mechanically. His father's hello sounded like a very far echo, and every stair step was another step towards total detachment. Beth's room was empty, and he felt something for her, a sense of guilt. But it lasted no more than a second. Then he entered his room, went to the PC and connected the video camera.

The images on the screen flowed in slow motion, in an agonizing silence. Beth was looking at him with desperation in her eyes, as if he was evil. Jamie was lying on the sofa, with his head pulled back and his eyes looking at the ceiling, with an expressionless face, just like a puppet. Nicholas locked the image on Beth's eyes and zoomed in until they filled the screen. He lay down on the bed, with Claire's face overlapping Beth's in his imagination, and the sense of emptiness gave space to the pleasure he felt in having sex with her.

Travis switched off the TV. Beth wasn't home yet, and Nicholas had just come in, passing behind him and not saying hello. He had bought Nicholas a gift that day and wanted to give it to him right then. His instinct told him it was the best moment to do it. Lucy was sleeping. She could fall asleep anywhere after eleven. He caressed her and took the glasses to the kitchen. Nicholas was in his room with Travis standing still, just outside. He wanted to open the door, hug his child, and give him the gift, but this child was Nicholas, not just any boy, and that impulse had to be controlled. He knocked lightly on the door.

Nicholas was lying on the bed, with his arms crossed under his head, with his eyes on the PC and Beth's desperation. He knew his father was behind the door. He was waiting for him to make a gesture and encourage him to enter, and Nicholas was excited, equally split between the lives of two different people—a person that he had irreparably destroyed and a person that he would destroy in the next five minutes.

"Come in, Dad." It was his death sentence.

Nicholas's calm voice gave him hope, and he entered barely hiding his joy.

"Hi, Nick."

Nicholas eyes were absent and belonged to a young man who had lost all his innocence in only two minutes. Travis felt uncomfortable.

"How did it go tonight?" Travis asked him.

Nicholas looked at him coldly and didn't answer.

"I hope you'll like this."

Travis handed the bag to his son and held his breath, hoping to have a hug from him. Nicholas took out the jogging suit and the sneakers. They were beautiful. He could see the effort Travis had made in choosing them. It could really be a pleasant gift between a different father and son. He laid them down on the bed and stared at Travis intensely. He could see his hope, the hope of a father who was trying to win the love of his son, but Nicholas wanted a different gift, he wanted a Beth-like look, one that was desperate. And he wanted pain, much pain, the kind of suffering that enters the soul, puts it down on its knees and gives it a different life. That was the perfect gift he aimed to receive from his father.

"Thanks, it's really cool."

Travis felt his heart beating faster. It was a terrific effort from him to get closer to Nicholas and abandon the principles on which he based his existence. He wanted to hug him, but he was waiting for his son to move first. He was on the bed, expressionless and terrifyingly cold. Travis felt his detachment and decided to go closer to him, sensing his self-control was on the edge of falling apart.

"I just want you help me understand you."

That was the moment. Travis had admitted his mistake and was now defenceless. If Nicholas had hit him in that very moment, it could have been the final blow for him. Nicholas looked at the monitor on his desk and Travis followed his son's eyes until he looked at the screen.

"Is that Beth?" he asked perceiving something evil.

Nicholas didn't answer, but he smiled at Travis. It was not the smile Travis was hoping to see. He went closer to the monitor and what he read in Beth's eyes was fear.

"Where did you take this picture?" Travis asked, his voice sounded choked off.

Nicholas didn't want to reply. Travis turned towards the monitor and felt a strong sense of *Angst*, something very close to physical pain. The video camera was linked to a cable and it was clear that the image was still. His heartbeat grew stronger. Maybe it was because of the dim light of the monitor, the only light in the room. Maybe it was from wanting a hug that didn't happen. Or maybe it was the fear to push that button. He moved his hand, hesitating. The video camera was cold, like Nicholas's heart. Travis unlocked the button and the images began to flow.

What happened was something that Travis didn't even comprehend. In one second, in only one second, his life ran under his eyes. His wife, the day Beth was born, his lectures given in the name of logic. He didn't need any of them. He felt emptied, soulless. Every frame was a blade that entered his chest, pushing stronger and deeper. Pain wasn't enough to describe what he felt. His tears remained trapped in his throat, his chest exploded, and his legs surrendered.

Travis was on his knees, with his hands against the desk, silently crying. Nicholas remained expressionless, witnessing the scene but, strangely, he didn't feel anything. Watching his father collapsing before an image that had just filmed the failure of his whole life, didn't give him any relief. Nicholas wanted more. He felt he deserved more. He and only he had to be the cause of his father's failure, not the image of Beth on the monitor. He felt surpassed in a ranking of merit that only he could see.

He remained standing, behind his father, feeling close to him for the first time in his life, in the name of the pain of a father who wasn't able to let his son love him, and the pain of a son who wasn't able to let his father love him.

Nicholas looked at the monitor. The movie was now at the end. Three minutes of total madness had destroyed a life. His father was crying.

Travis would have liked to stand up, beat his son, or go back on his knees and ask for his mercy. That moment was everything and the contrary of everything.

TWENTY-ONE

"Your son is ill, very ill."

Lucy listened to the doctor in tears. "Is there any hope that he can recover?"

"We should necessarily wait for some time before we can have a reasonable idea as to if and when that will be possible."

"How long?" Lucy asked.

"Two…three years. Maybe longer. We need enough time to evaluate the evolution of his mental state."

The shame was as strong as the pain, if not stronger. A mad son meant the end of her social ambitions. Who knew how her girlfriends would react to the news, who knew if they would still invite her or pretend not to know her. It was Travis's fault; she had been stupid not to notice that in time. She might have been able to avoid that.

"Aren't you going to say anything? It's about your son, damn it!" Lucy said, glaring at Travis.

Travis was lost in thought, lost in the despair of a man who had seen his entire world vanish, his dreams and all that he lived and hoped for die.

"What does my son have?" Travis finally asked.

"A serious mental disorder," the doctor said.

"What does that mean?" Travis asked, going through the motions, but still not connected to the reality before him.

"Nicholas reacts to the external stimulus in an incontrollable and obsessive way," the doctor explained. "He feels that everything around him is against him and, as such, the only way to survive is to identify a guilty person to blame for his failure and to destroy this person by creating a completely opposite personality."

"What is the cause, doctor?" Lucy asked.

"It's hard to say. Probably a trauma, a feeling of abandonment at a previous time, such as childhood or adolescence, that dug deeply and slowly in his psyche until it exploded."

"Is he crazy?" Lucy asked.

"No, Madam, your son is ill."

"Can I see him?" Travis asked.

The doctor stood up and led the way along the corridor with Lucy in tears and not able to stop. They arrived at a door, with a little plastic window, and the doctor invited them to come closer. Nicholas was lying on the bed, with his arms crossed behind his head, staring at the ceiling.

"What is he doing?" Travis asked.

"He is releasing his tension. There is nothing or no one in there who can remind him of a past he has to fight against."

Travis's eyes glittered. Nicholas…the most important part of his world, recovered in there. Tears began flowing down his cheeks.

There was still daylight when they came back home, but it seemed as if the darkness of the night had already fallen. Lucy had not stopped crying since they left the clinic. Travis, instead, walked restlessly back and forth in the studio, from the kitchen and the drawing room. The tragedy was too big to comprehend.

"It's your fault!" Lucy said, her voice high and shrill. "If you had been closer to him he would not be there!"

Travis's frustration peaked. It wasn't enough to have his son in the clinic. There was also a wife who was doing her best to send him there to keep him company.

"I think I have been a good father," Travis said, without emotion, almost whispering, without being convinced, and he felt ashamed.

"I can't believe how I could marry you," Lucy said, taking a different tack. "You are a loser, good for nothing, and my family is ruined and you still dare to say you have been a good father!"

Travis turned and sat at the table behind the sofa. Lucy was inconsolable. Her life, a life that could have been better, was over without leaving her any hope.

"Why? Why did I trust you?" Lucy said.

It was the revenge of the wretched, a poor person who insults another poor person because he is not able to become rich. The show could not have been any better with an actress like Lucy. Travis looked at his wife again. He was not angry at her, or even disappointed, he was just destroyed. He did not have anything anymore; his universe had collapsed, hit at his foundations, and there was no point in replying to her words, as any word could only exalt them. He needed to regain the calm, the same calm that he so much preached to his children; he had to have it himself, but it seemed so damned hard to get it. How different it was to think that way. How difficult it was now that he had to face the problem. Nicholas was right. One needed to see the problem from the inside to solve it, and from what he could see, it seemed an impossible mission.

The notes still lay on his desk in his studio. They were soulless papers. He grabbed the sheets, tore them up, and threw them in the bin.

The days went by slowly, and every gesture or word from Lucy was a challenge to his self-control. She thought often out loud, inveighing against cruel Destiny, concerned about more about her girlfriends' reaction than about Nicholas, while Beth, fallen into a deep dumbness, was trying to avoid meeting her father's eyes. Nothing was left but teaching. The class, the students, the thoughts, his freedom…it was not the same anymore, and he did not have the necessary energy to carry his students away.

* * *

Students stayed still, waiting to hear what he had to say that day, and nobody spoke. Travis was standing in front of the desk, with his arms folded. Jamie was sitting in the next to the last row, and his deep and menacing eyes resembled Nicholas's. Travis should have spoken, as it was proper it happened, but he could not.

"Professor." It was Jamie. Travis looked up and faced him.

"What are we going to talk about today?"

He breathed deeply and stared at the floor. He could not end up being a victim of his own thoughts; he had to react.

"Reality versus appearance. Who would like to kick off?"

Chris raised his hand. "*Plato's 'Theory of Ideas.'* What appears is known to us through sensations and, as such, it represents just an imperfect image of the forms. Only the world of the forms possesses the highest and most fundamental kind of reality."

Travis nodded and put an end to Chris's speech.

"One of the main characterizations of the European philosophy is a continuous recollection of *Plato*, and this is something we already know. I am interested in another aspect: what you feel. Free your thoughts, build your philosophy!"

Here they were again. The interest was alive. He could feel it, see it. The students were on the same wavelength again, accepting his hunger of freedom with no more constrictions, with no more cages that could send other people like his son to the clinic.

"Daphne?"

"My emotions." She said that from the bottom of her heart, hoping Travis could perceive what she felt for him.

"Yes, Daphne, keep going."

"There is no universal reality. The true law that rules the world is the passion of the soul."

"I want more wickedness in your exposition…keep going, damn it!"

It was an outburst. Travis did not realize it, but his frustration was clear to the students and a stroke for Daphne. Jamie stood up, without asking for permission, since there was no need anymore.

"My philosophy? Why, Professor? Do you really believe that in such a world there is someone who might be interested in how I feel? In how I judge the things I see? You want to see more wickedness in our answers, and I'll try to give you all the possible wickedness. I don't even know what my reality is! I am confused, desperate, spaced out. I drink and I go with women whose names I don't even know! Why do I do that? Because that's the way the world appears to me: a huge, enormous market, where I can take what I want with the money I have, but where there is no direction for those who don't know how to shop. That world, Prof, wants to fuck my soul, cheat on me! And who gives a damn if, at the end, I feel bad or I starve, as that market will be crowded forever! It will be full of people like me, who maybe feel bad because no one has told them what the important things in life are and why. Like your damn classes! It is the first time I find them interesting. The first time, in so long, because you, your words, your thoughts always came first. Before me, before us, before you know what I want, with no time to listen to a word from my imagination—before all that—you try to put your words in my head. One, among the words you say, that you always want to hear from those who cannot reply, yet words they have to listen to against their own will. That is how the world appears to me, and I will never know if there is a better one or if what I see is the world that is. The world appears to me as confused, and it appears that reality is made up by words like yours, by the thoughts of those who have power in their hands. It is not necessary to kill to show one's power. Power is the ability to influence people, giving a damn if people can die because of that. What matters is to occupy a space and talk, talk, and talk, labelling those who don't want to listen as asocial. And what about time? Why do you always speak about time and then you box it in an unchangeable and motionless doctrinism? If time leads things to become, why don't you and the people like you ever change? And now you ask me how I see reality? Do you want me to see it the way you want it to appear or the way it is?"

Jamie was done. He had spit all he had inside, with impetuosity, giving a damn for the first time, and he was happy, finally out of the cage. He could now see the world the way he wanted, and he could speak and not just stay quiet and listen.

He stared at Travis, and the whole classroom stared at him. Nicholas was right. The only way to change the world was to give the world to those who could change with it, and not to those who sat, talked, and indoctrinated others. Change came from those who acted, not from those who stayed on a balcony and were happy to see and judge things from above. Daphne stood up.

"Jamie is right. Let's go back to your thesis. I thought about it a lot, and I came to a conclusion. Why do you worry so much about finding a way to understand how Destiny works and pay so little attention to why things happen? It seems like nonsense to me, really; one is burning his brain, fantasizing between philosophy and mathematics without caring about why people feel bad and die. It is because those who feel bad and die do not have the same right to hope for and enjoy a better future? Can you please tell me why, Professor?"

It was Chris's turn now. He was almost afraid to stand, but he joined Jamie and Daphne in chorus.

"*Plato* says that the perfect society is a regulated one, presided over by academics, where philosophers occupy the highest class, since they are the only ones who can see beyond the cave. I wouldn't be surprised to see philosophers confined on a mountain with a flock of sheep in their care. Could you please explain, dear professor, why those who teach do not use words or thoughts to solve the current problems that would let people feel better instead of creating new problems? Today, Jamie and Daphne enlightened me. They taught me not to fear what I would like to say, and so I don't. They gave me the courage to try to open the cage I was in, afraid of a world that made me feel lonely, a world that sucked my energy away without me seeing the light at the end of the tunnel. How I wish, Professor, your words could show me the way, but your words…are without soul and part of a world that I can't understand."

Silence fell over the classroom. Travis's invitation to an open debate triggered a chain reaction that seemed impossible to stop. All the students stared at him, expressionless, but conscious that an irreversible process had begun. A noise came from the last row. Jamie stood up again and was serious, tremendously serious.

"Can you tell us about Nicholas?" Jamie asked.

Jamie's question was a stab in the back. Travis felt a sharp pain in his chest. His muscles got tense and he blushed. Who was that kid who dared to talk to his professor in such an insolent manner?

"Nicholas is not well and he preferred to stay home," Travis said.

Travis suddenly wanted to end the debate and turned towards the papers on his desk. Jamie was still standing, and he did not show any intention of sitting down. Travis turned and looked at him again. He had to behave like a philosopher: calm and reflective.

"Is there anything else you would like to add, Jamie?"

It was a challenging look. Something was about to explode, and Travis quickly realized it.

"If there is nothing else, I'd like to end class for today."

"Why is your son in that fucking clinic?" Jamie said. His words were like bullets aimed at Travis's heart.

Too late. The guys looked at Travis, and he recognized his failure in Jamie's words. He had to resist, but the shame overwhelmed him. How did Jamie know? Who had told him? Then he remembered the movie and the image of an animal taking advantage of Beth.

They all knew. They all knew about his son, his failure, about Beth having sex with one of them, maybe with many of them. They had made fun of him, yes; they had all pretended that morning, and they all took their vengeance on him. He was a failure as a father, as a professor, as a human being. His life ended at that very moment. His daughter, so sweet and innocent, had sex with one of his students, while his son filmed the scene.

Shame Travis, shame! You are the model of the perfect loser. No one could have failed in so many things at the same precise moment. But you did. Was this coincidence or Destiny, perhaps?

Travis was dead, even though his heart was beating, and he was breathing. He could not open his eyes, he did not have the energy or, perhaps, he did not have the courage. He felt as if he were in a cage and he could now touch the bars and hear the murmurs of his students who were attending his slow agonizing death. Jamie was the first to dig his grave. He left the class in a deathly hush. The other students remained still, waiting or hoping for a reaction, but Travis had already directed all of his energy to defend the last bit of his dignity. Another student stood up and followed Jamie out of the classroom, then Chris left, and then all the others left. One by one they passed by him, looked at him and left.

He opened his eyes only when he was sure that none of his students were still in the classroom. The image of the floor was all he could see. He did not have the courage to lift his glance. Daphne was in front of him, tightly holding the notes of the course. She looked at him with tenderness. Maybe she just wanted to thank him for all those beautiful hours. She came closer, touched his shoulder and left, knowing, deep in her heart, that she would never see her professor again.

He walked slowly towards the door, holding his breath and never turning back, for fear he had to destroy the memory that had been placed before him. He often thought about the moment where everything ended, but he had never thought that his end could be so dramatic. He had destroyed his son and buried himself.

He went home late at night, and the walls that had represented his safety for years seemed to revolt against him. He walked up the stairs with difficulty, sure to find Lucy asleep, and he blessed it was like that. At least, this could save him from having a gun against his temple.

The light in the bedroom was off and the bed was untouched. There was no reason in the whole universe not to find his wife home that late at night, and there was no reason not to find his daughter. He entered his bedroom, turned on the lights, and saw a newspaper lying on the bed. It was a copy of the *Evening Standard* and the identikit of two men dominated, disrespectfully, the front cover. He was hit by the headline: *Do you know them?*

One of the two was Nicholas, the identikit of the potential murderer at the Nothing Hill Station. Travis knelt down, and then he let himself fall to the floor. A piece of paper came out of the newspaper. It was Lucy's writing:

Murderer

Travis fainted and hoped to die. Maybe that night it would happen.

TWENTY-TWO

'He was wasting his life with words, pursuing logic and his unreal world…'

A gust of wind came and threw him, irreparably, towards the end. The university asked for and obtained his resignation, while Lucy filed for divorce. Lucy, the apathetic Lucy, so predictable to annoy him, had been seeing someone else for ages without him being the least bit suspicious all those years. And what about that wonderful flower of Beth? She was not even home when he went by to collect his last things: a bag, some money in the bank, and a destroyed life.

He rented a flat and managed to stretch his dignity by a few more months, then the money ran out, and his hope ended with it. He started to drink, to obsessively hang around and to sleep on the street. He was letting himself die; he wanted to die, but he remained attached to life, since death could not give him another chance.

And, in the meantime, his life passed by, and he remained to watch it like an actor who doesn't have any role in the film anymore. He ended up in South Bank; if he had to die he wanted to die where his end had begun.

It had almost been a year, and Travis's home was now along the river. He used to sit on the bench and think. Had he had another chance to hold back the years, who knew if he would have made the same choices, who knew if he would have gotten married and had children. He sighed and, in the meantime, from the bench, he could see the lights of London beyond the Thames, which took the place of the sun, inviting him to move to the other side of the river. They always shined and never turned off.

Travis believed that light was his destiny, and that was why he was so afraid. He knew that the moment he had decided to follow it beyond the bridge, he could have drowned in the darkness again. The light was there, as if it were waiting for him. But for all its intensity, it would have remained forever dark.

TWENTY-THREE

King's Road was the most known street in Chelsea. It extended from Sloane Square to Putney Bridge and left its mark on the twentieth century for two main reasons: first, it was the place where the mini-skirt was born in the early sixties and, second, it became popular for the punk style of the seventies.

The Royal Court Theatre, one of the most famous Fringe Theatres of London, together with Peter Jones's shopping mall, dominated the square. The shops on King's Road were always of lower quality the closer they were to the World's End, the point where the Road turned and the street crossed the Thames.

Lisa rented a flat in Cadogan Gardens, in a wonderful Victorian building, right between King's Road and Sloane Square, the rectangle included between the areas of Knightsbridge and Chelsea. She always dreamt of living there, since that was the place to live for those who were wealthy and those who pretended to be.

"Remember that not taking advantage of people is the biggest mistake you could do in this city. London is full of men who would do anything to go out with a beautiful woman, and we just need to make them feel important. It's so easy, Lisa…"

Stefania said those words over a cup of tea at *Patisserie Valerie* a cosy French Cafe' at the western end of Duke of York Square, two steps south of King's Road and the exclusive department store of Peter Jones. Lisa sat at the other side of the table, indifferent to Stefania's words as she was thinking about something completely different.

"What's wrong with you now?" Stefania asked, seeing that Lisa didn't seem to be paying attention.

"I was just wondering whether the price I pay to take advantage of people is the right one."

"Are you referring to your relationship with Klaus?" Stefania asked.

Lisa nodded.

"It's not worth it to talk about dignity with those who don't have any," Stefania said.

She was right. She was good in understanding the people she dealt with. Unlike Lisa, Stefania was able to compromise without losing her smile. That was the price to pay to obtain something worth so much more.

They talked about that for a while, until they both became bored of something they could no longer gossip about. They finished their tea, paid the bill, and went out on the street.

"Fancy catching up later?" Lisa asked.

"Sure, I'll call you around four."

She waited for Stefania to enter a taxi waiting in Sloane Square and then walked home. The unpacked boxes lay near the wall of the drawing room, since she didn't have any time to unpack. She put on a CD, took off her shoes, and lay down on the sofa. The light of that beautiful sunny afternoon was filtered by the Venetian blinds, lighting the drawing room in many little strips and playing with the reflection of the vanilla coloured moquette. A pair of paintings hung on the wall, and the plants that she had just ordered provided a touch of life to her flat. She was happy to be there. It was the world she wished to live in and the world where a Ferrari would not cause anyone turn his or her head.

A couple of hours later, after reading and re-reading a magazine and putting her thoughts in order, she could not resist the temptation to open a box. It was small and of a different colour from the others, but it contained almost all the pictures she had collected during the course of many years. The first picture she took out was of a little Lisa, at the age of four, maybe five. She put it aside and took a few more pictures out of the box. There was one when she was at school, on holiday, and when she began to look like a little baby woman.

She lightly touched the first letter that a man had written to her, fifteen years before, half of her past life, and the tremor of a bitter smile moved her lips. Maybe she was wasting her life. She glanced at the drawing room, at the paintings she had bought, and she was not frightened by her doubts anymore. Emotions, as beautiful as they were, could never rent a place like that.

Stefania called her at four sharp and picked her up at six, with two new friends. There was an exhibition at the Tate Modern, and Lisa liked the idea very much. She put on a pair of jeans, a white silky shirt, and a light overcoat, since the weather fought with the spring that night. Stefania didn't normally visit art galleries, but she could not reject the invitation from Victor, her new lawyer. Morris, on the other hand, was a slightly introverted guy, and Victor invited him out as well, since he knew Lisa was joining the party.

"I've never seen her. I've just been told that she's gorgeous," Victor told Morris.

Morris saw Lisa and felt happy to be at the Tate. The four of them walked around with Lisa and Stefania in the lead and, a few steps behind them, Victor and Morris.

"What do you think about Victor?" Stefania asked.

Lisa looked at him. He was completely absorbed in admiring a *Kandinsky*.

"A very confident man," she said.

"And what about Morris?"

"Rejected," Lisa replied quickly.

Lisa did not have any interest in him. The only goal she had was to make as much money as possible and get rid of Klaus as soon as she could manage her career without him. Morris seemed to be interested in a painting or, rather, he was just trying to impress Lisa.

"He created the abstract painting. Look at this painting. It seems as if we are standing in front of different pieces of separate images that highlight his inner emptiness."

Lisa went closer, and so did Stefania and Victor.

"Are you an expert of art?" Lisa asked, looking at Morris so intensely that he felt shivers along his spine.

"I liked it very much. Painting is the noblest expression of feelings," he said.

Lisa was next to him and was looking at the painting. And, from what Stefania could tell, Lisa seemed to have changed her mind about him.

"It is beautiful!" Lisa said.

Morris became cockier. Until that point, Lisa did not even realize he existed, but now she was giving him all the attention he hoped for.

"Perfect harmony of forms…pure research of being," Morris stated.

"You are probably confusing it with the production of his second German period." The voice was firm and came from behind them. Morris turned first; then Lisa, Victor and Stefania turned in unison. It was a young man, around thirty, but his intense expression made him look older than he was. He was looking at Morris with the confidence that a professor might have in front of a child.

"The forms are not perfect. *Cossacks* dates back to nineteen ten. That was when *Kandinsky* freed his inner pressure, and satisfied his need to put his emotions on canvas. There was no balance at all, just an explosion of feelings that were visibly magnified by the intensity of the colours he used rather than by the complexity of the forms of the painting."

Morris didn't reply.

"Are you an art critic?" Lisa asked.

The difference of personality between him and Morris was clear, as clear as his confidence when he looked at Lisa straight in the eyes.

"I am just an art lover," the young man said.

He didn't show anything like arrogance. He was simply expressing something he was definitely competent about, and this was enough to knock Morris off his pedestal in front of Lisa.

"The true artist tries to express what he feels on an inner level, ignoring any sensation that comes from external stimulus. This is why *Kandinsky* is known as the pioneer of the *abstract painting*."

The young man's mobile phone rang.

"Would you please excuse me…?"

He listened motionless, then greeted the four of them with a nod and walked towards the exit. Morris remained quiet, limiting himself to listening, as he quickly realized that in only a minute he had lost the attention he had tried to get from Lisa during the whole afternoon.

"How cool…" Lisa said.

"And he's cute too!" Stefania echoed.

Lisa tried to follow him with her glance while she could, but he soon disappeared among the crowd. They spent the rest of the evening admiring the masterpieces spread throughout the gallery. Victor went back to Stefania, while Morris followed Lisa like a shadow, without saying a word. They took Lisa home around ten.

"Are you sure you don't want to join us for dinner?" Stefania asked.

"Thanks, Stef, but I have to wake up early tomorrow."

Morris wanted to be the last one to say goodbye, so he waited for her to get out of the car and accompanied her to the house.

"Can I call you?" he asked her.

Lisa barely raised a smile. She was tired.

"Let's get in touch through Stefania. Thanks, Morris, and good night."

It was just a polite way to get rid of someone. She closed the door behind her and closed the door on that evening.

* * *

Klaus didn't call her, and she didn't look for him. *Better*, Lisa thought. Things are beautiful if done with pleasure. She took off her trousers and the silky shirt and wore a jogging suit to feel more comfortable. She wasn't hungry, but a snack would have killed that little appetite she had. The music filled the flat, and she decided to take a shower. She dried and stood still before the mirror to look at herself. Her hair was straight, covering part of her face, while the light tan she had got in the sun that day made the intense green of her eyes even more vivid.

The noise of the cars that passed didn't enable anyone to sleep, but she managed to do that during the time when everyone else remained awake, and she woke up when everyone else fell asleep. It was dawn. She kicked the blanket and remained sitting on the bedside, with her elbows on her legs and her hands holding her face. There was nothing to worry about, so she could not explain the grip on her stomach.

She went down to the drawing room and turned on the light. The box was still on the sofa, and the pictures were spread all around it. She picked them up and looked at them. She flicked through her memories, and each was tied up to an image: a little flower, then the stem grows longer, the petals blossom, and the beauty floods. If she had stopped time, she would have made an effort to picture the important moments. She didn't have many and she could count them on only one hand. If she was lucky, she could use a couple of fingers of her other hand, too. That was not much for her first thirty years. But thanks goodness she didn't go out with Klaus; otherwise, she would have other things to remember, such as the violence she suffered, the repressed frustration, or the terror that flowed in the veins instead of blood. Wonderful moments, she could not complain at all; and then, had she not met him, she wouldn't have been able to rent the beautiful flat, buy the jewels, let alone enjoy Rubinstein's parties with all those millionaires on holiday. *Beautiful life, really a beautiful one.*

The grip on her stomach became stronger; maybe she had made a mistake in picking her memories, since they were not those that could make her smile come back, so she put more effort in thinking of the right ones. She thought of herself when she was a child, but she couldn't recall more than three events. She tried to include the memories of when she was an adult, too, but the number didn't grow either. She moved slightly, and one picture of Alex fell from the sofa to the floor. They had taken it at the theatre, and Alex was there, on the stage, looking happy. She looked at her hand and she started to count again, then she put the pictures back in the box and went back to her room. There was the first light of dawn, but she could have cared less. She went to bed and smiled. Maybe the anxiety would leave time for her to sleep.

* * *

Klaus called Lisa in the middle of the week and invited her for dinner at his place. He was waiting for her that night, along with a few more friends, to organize a small party.

"Eddy is coming with a couple more guys. We start at nine."

The discouragement helped her to hang up. For the first time, going to Klaus's seemed to be gruelling. She wearily chose something to wear and picked a pair of black trousers, purposely not tight, trying to look as sober as possible.

When she arrived at the dinner, she recognized the car. It was Eddy's and she grimaced. She could not think of anything worse than the time she had met him at Klaus's. He was sitting on a chair smoking a cigar, with a bottle of cognac on the table next to him, and not that far from a girl, definitely one of his circle. There were seven people in all. Five girls and two men. Klaus was standing, next to the bar.

"Lisa!"

He was waiting for her to come over and hug him, but that simple gesture felt like an incredible effort. Klaus shirt was unbuttoned to the middle of his chest just to show off the tan he had gotten in the Caribbean. He had gone there to better cope with the stress.

"Hi, Klaus," Lisa said.

It didn't sound like the happiest hello.

"Don't you say hi to my friend?"

The pig laughed, with the cigar clinched in his teeth, while winking at one of the girls. It was monotonous scene, like being at a slaughter, where the girls were cows that would soon be eviscerated.

"How are you Eddy?" Lisa asked, with even less enthusiasm.

He seemed to be having a good time and no one could stop his mood.

"Great, honey! These young ladies are Gisele, Kim, Stacey, and Jana."

"Nice to meet you. I'm Lisa," she replied with a forced smile.

"What would you like to drink, sweetheart?"

"I'm fine, Klaus, thanks."

"I'll pour you a Cosmopolitan then."

"If I really have to..." she said, without conviction. She sat on a chair and looked at the four girls quacking with Eddy. Who knew what he thought about her. She felt Klaus hugging her from behind, kissing her neck, and soon realized he was much more relaxed than the last time they met. Likely thanks to the prostitutes he had time to enjoy. He was sitting on the armrest, with his hand on her shoulder while chatting with Eddy, his best mate.

"Have you ever gone to the Tate?" Lisa asked.

"Why do you ask me something like that?" Klaus asked.

"Have you been there or not?" Lisa said, slightly raising her voice.

"Of course I have been there, darling. Why?"

"I was there last Saturday. It was crowded."

"I'm not surprised. There are always plenty of people there. One more cognac, Eddy?"

Klaus dispensed with the subject of the Tate in less than a minute. The doorbell rang and Klaus went to open the door.

"Hi, Gil, come in," Klaus said. "We have been waiting for you."

Gil looked normal, completely different from Eddy and Klaus. Lisa managed to look at him for more than five seconds without feeling sick, as he seemed clean, like a flower in a pigsty. Klaus sat back next to her and the party began. The girls, who had never been at Klaus's before that night, seemed the only ones to show a fresh enthusiasm. Eddy, on the other hand, seemed already tired, but managed to smile anyway, while Gil started to warm up and to be the only one Lisa ended up talking to, the one who annoyed her the least. Klaus nodded, Gil stood up and swapped seats with him. He now sat next to Lisa while Eddy looked at him and laughed. Gil was uncomfortable, while Klaus was flirting with two of the available girls. He never had behaved like that with Lisa, in front of his friends. She felt bad vibes all around her, insecure, empty, and anything but beautiful. Those two bitches were all over Klaus, playing with him. Her head was spinning, and she could not see Eddy or Klaus very well, or the two bitches, and she didn't even see Gil. She felt unusually warm, a humid sensation, right on her shoulder. She turned her head with effort and recognized Gil. She tried to get rid of him, but she didn't have the strength.

"Be good," he said.

His voice was so confident and so close to her ears that she could feel the warmth of his breath. Then his arm moved and began to go down on her back. Her head was spinning so much that she could not even hear Eddy's laughter, and he was sitting just in front of her. The contact became stronger, but the more she moved in an attempt to get rid of him, the more Gil got excited.

Then she suddenly felt cold. Her shirt was wide open, and the pressure of Gil's hand became stronger. He knelt down, almost falling on the floor, with his head between her legs. Klaus was fucking, Eddy was doing the same, and the two remaining girls were having sex with each other. She was in the full swing of an orgy and felt like garbage.

"Let me go…" Lisa said.

Gil was desperately trying to lower her pants.

"Let me go, you fucking bastard!" Lisa screamed.

The strength left her, and she could not escape his grip.

She was crying, but no one gave a damn about her. She didn't want to stay there, she didn't want to stay with Klaus, see Eddy having sex, or feel Gil's tongue on her skin. She just wanted to get out of there. Gil looked up, spaced out more than she was, desperately trying to tear off her pants. Desperation was the only thing that would save her. She tried to stand up, but she could not get rid of Gil, who was drowning between her legs. She felt a retching, then a strong stomach spasm. She begged forgiveness for all the sins she had committed and swore to herself that she would change, if she had the energy to come out of the spiral she was in. Gil looked at her and the light she saw in his eyes told her that he would have done anything to have sex with her. He was also losing his strength and, in that precise moment, she felt her legs again.

She kicked him right in his face. Gil reeled violently, knocking his head against the table, and a blood puddle quickly filled the floor. Lisa managed to stand up, staggering, holding the trousers that Gil had unzipped, while Eddy would have likely ended up dying if he had have kept on fucking that bitch. Then she slowly turned towards Klaus. The second bitch was riding him and no one seemed keen on slowing down. She didn't hear anything, and everything seemed to move slowly. Then, in the orgasm, Klaus' eyes met hers. It was the last time.

She left the house and walked desperately in the middle of the street, until someone, moved to pity, picked her up and took her home. She wanted to die. She ran to the bathroom and vomited, crying, while the remorse exploded. She had trod on her dignity, put it on sale, and gave it to someone who didn't even know what dignity was, for a bunch of pounds and her flat. Shame squeezed her to the floor, even lower than the level where Klaus had squeezed her. That was the bottom, and it was far lower than she could even remotely imagine. She stood up and, timorous, went closer to the mirror to look at her image. The tears had upset her image, and her eyes had drowned in the makeup. There was nothing of the Lisa she was proud of, who worked at Joe's theatre. There was just a body without a soul, an image that made her feel ashamed to exist. She touched her neck, then her heart and closed her eyes to feel her heartbeat.

The scissors were next to the mirror. She grabbed them and brought the tips near her veins, pushing harder and harder, until blood came out. She wanted to die, but she didn't have the courage. She looked at herself again and began to cut her hair neurotically. The wisps fell in the sink and, in her impetuosity, she broke the mirror to pieces.

TWENTY-FOUR

It was a different awakening. She wanted to get up, enter the bathroom, and admire herself in what was left of the mirror. She kept caressing her hair, looking at the daylight filtering through the curtains, when the noise of the cars that passed by on the street broke her dream and forced her out of the bed. She was barefoot, and the floor in the bathroom was cold. For a moment she pretended with herself not to be interested, but then she could not resist the temptation.

Her face was bizarrely framed by many rebel wisps, and her hair fell down all around her shoulder in different lengths. She touched her head, trying to give herself a more decent look, and a smile appeared on her face. She looked so much younger.

She went out at lunchtime, wearing a sweater, marine-like trousers, and a pair of sneakers. She felt good wearing sunglasses, as she did with the baseball cap that covered her forehead entirely. It would have been difficult for anyone to recognize her.

Hyde Park was not far, so she bought an orange juice and walked. A couple sat on a bench, completely involved in their cuddling, so her mind began recalling memories, pushing her back in time, when she was at the theatre, as if these last terrible months had never happened. There was Joe smoking, Judie arriving always before Scott, and then there was Alex, who served the beer behind the bar. Thoughts let her fly again. She remembered the night she had spent with him, intense and sweet, and shivers went down her spine. She sat on a bench, grabbed a stone and, with anger, threw it far into the lake.

She got up after drinking her juice, happy to spend some time walking around on her own. Her conscience was discreet that day, as it put her remorse aside and let the rest of the day pass quietly.

As soon as she got home and closed the door, an annoying beep broke her dreams. There were four messages on her answering machine, and the fear of hearing Klaus's voice again forced her to relive the nightmare of the night before. She turned on the stereo, lay down on the sofa, and closed her eyes. Just half an hour went by, and then someone was knocking at the door, adding to the annoying beep from the answering machine.

"Where have you been…what did you do to your hair? My God… you ruined yourself!"

She didn't want to see Stefania or to hear her stupid voice. She lowered her eyes and went back to the drawing room leaving the door ajar.

"Why did you cut it?" Stefania asked, still surprised. "I've been calling you continuously since this morning, but your phone was disconnected."

That's why I switched it off, Lisa thought. But she replied more diplomatically. "I didn't have time to charge it."

Stefania entered the living room, dropped her bag on the chair and went to the sofa.

"Can I touch it?" Stefania asked. She didn't even wait for a reply and passed her hand through Lisa's hair.

"Does this have anything to do with Klaus?"

Lisa shook her head.

"Then why? It will take forever for it to grow long again."

"I don't give a damn," Lisa said.

Stefania grimaced, got up, and went to the kitchen.

"Did you finish the coffee?"

"I stopped drinking it," Lisa said.

She was pissed not to be alone, and she couldn't wait for Stefania to leave.

"I received a phone call from Klaus, but he didn't even mention what you did to your hair."

Hearing that name again made Lisa feel sick, and she cursed the moment she had opened the door.

"I'm tired, Stef, I think I'll go upstairs to take a nap."

"He wanted to see me tonight," Stefania said. "Don't you think that's a bit weird?" She said it jokingly, but Lisa didn't feel like laughing. She got off the sofa and went upstairs.

"I give him to you. There won't be a next time. We broke up. Please pull the door shut well when you leave. There's a problem with the lock."

Stefania saw her going up the stairs without even turning. She grabbed her purse and left. Lisa heard the door slam and went back to the drawing room to check her messages.

"I really don't know where you are. I'll be in your area today, and I might pass by your flat…"

"Just got some new proposals, and I would like to discuss them with you. Call me as soon as you hear this message…"

"Funny last night…don't you think? Pity for Gil…you left him so sad…"

"Fucking bastard!" Lisa said. She slammed the phone on the floor, but she didn't allow the anxiety to devour her this time. She grabbed her jacket and went to a hairdresser.

* * *

"I need you to fix my hair."

"Sorry, Miss, but we don't accept clients without appointments."

"But look at me! Do you think I can walk around London like this?" She was hysterical and that was enough to convince the girl.

"Let's see…maybe we can do something. In an hour? Is that fine for you?"

"Perfect! I will be back in an hour, sharp."

The guy did a good job. He gave her a jaunty look that made her feel happy.

* * *

The next day she went to Soho, to Angela's office.

"Good morning, Lisa. Take a seat," Angela said when Lisa entered her office.

"Since when are we so formal?" she asked, but notwithstanding her tentative joke, Angela's face didn't change at all.

"Klaus just called me."

Lisa lowered her eyes and the anxiety found rich soil. She made an effort not to betray her emotions but that was not enough to deceive Angela.

"You don't need to control yourself. Did anything happen between you two guys?"

"What did he tell you?" she asked.

Angela grabbed the email and handed it over to Lisa.

"What's this?"

"Read it."

She gave it a quick glance and returned it to Angela. "What does it mean?"

"The party is over, money lacks, and your series goes to hell."

"But I have a confirmed contract!"

Angela stood up and went to the classifier. "This is your file. You find the contractual conditions under point four."

She spent a few minutes to evaluate things and then looked at her agent again.

"Fine, I can also be like that. But if they decide to stop the series, why should they consider my contract void?"

"No audience, no money. No money, no contracts. That's show business. I am sorry, honey, the party is over for me as well."

"And what about the proposals you mentioned over the phone?"

Angela shrugged. "With your hair like that, I don't think I will be able to place you anywhere. Let's talk about it in a few months, assuming your hair will enable us to do so."

"Did you have any chance to talk to Rubinstein?"

"Absolutely not, and it would be useless anyway. He fully confides in Klaus."

"Shit!" Lisa said, feeling everything give way.

"You can well say that."

"When did you receive the email?" Lisa asked.

"This morning."

"But how could it happen so quickly?"

Angela shrugged, then she drew an imaginary arc up in the air. "The faster you rise, the faster you fall."

Lisa snorted, as she saw the money flying out of the window.

"And what now?"

"You have to stay calm and patient. I will let you know as soon as there is any news."

"All over?" Lisa asked, tentatively.

"Yes, all over for now."

"But don't you have another option, a minor role, or commercials? And what about theatre? Could I go back there?"

Angela quickly flicked through the papers. "Liverpool, Manchester…"

Lisa sank in the chair. "I want to stay in London."

"So, you better wait. We are too much into the season now. We could try to find something as soon as the next one begins."

There was really not much more that could be done, and it was useless to continue talking to Angela.

"How much do I have to cash in?"

"Peanuts."

The phone rang.

"Yes, this is she…I'll be free in five minutes…I'll be waiting for you." She hung up, stood up, and went back to the classifier. But the file she pulled out wasn't related to Lisa. "Let's touch base next week, okay?"

* * *

Walking in Soho without a job was a sign that her life had to change. The underground station wasn't far, so she walked to Leicester Square and, on impulse, she caught the Northern line. She arrived in Camden after a few stops, and she couldn't resist to the temptation to go back to *The Oxford Arms*. She walked all the way up on Chalk Farm Road and remained outside, undecided, to look through the windows of the pub. She then opened the outer door and went up the stairs, hoping to read the names of her old friends on the posters hanging on the walls. It would have been nice to have a chat with Joe.

She almost bumped into him, as he was walking towards the stairs, but she came short of courage. So she turned and went down on the street. She waited a few more minutes and entered the building only when she saw him going away with someone.

A girl who was handling a series of brochures soon noticed her.

"Can I help you?"

"I was just looking around. I see the theatre's been refurbished."

The girl smiled proudly. "Yes, it's been almost a month now. It is so much larger."

"Do you mind if I take a look around?"

"Not at all."

The girl went back to her brochures. Lisa kept staring at her and, in the meantime, tried to find evidence that could remind her of her old friends. She didn't see anything, so she asked again.

"Miss?"

The girl smiled at her.

"Is Alex working here?"

"Alex? I don't know who you are talking about."

"When did you start working here?"

"About a month ago."

"I see." The curiosity led her in there and, maybe, not just her curiosity. "Thanks anyway."

She closed the door and kept walking along the road. It took a while before she arrived in Piccadilly, and she continued towards Knightsbridge, following the South side of Hyde Park, and entered Harrods where she stopped and did some shopping. She arrived home crunching an apple and was surprised to hear the beep again. Not many people knew her phone number.

"There is always a way to get back in the loop…"

It was Klaus's voice. She screamed as panic attacked, when she thought she had calmed down again. She huddled on the sofa, shuddering in fear and trembling. She knew that it was difficult to get rid of Klaus so quickly. She needed to do something. She could not continue in starts and stops, ending up a victim of her neurosis whenever she heard his voice. Her mobile phone in the kitchen rang, scaring her again and making her think her phone was possessed. She stood up, exhausted, entered the kitchen, and switched it off, but when she was back on her sofa, the doorbell rang. She was living a horror movie.

She started trembling. She didn't want to answer the door; she wanted to run away, but she didn't know any safer place. The house phone stopped ringing moments before the answering machine came on. Then it rang again, this time louder and louder.

"That's enough! Enough! Enough!"

She stood up neurotically and grabbed the phone.

"Stop! Stop! Stop!"

She screamed as loudly as she could, not realizing that the caller had already hung up. Her head was spinning, her legs hurt, and she burst out crying. She couldn't wait to run away, but she was afraid to end up in the middle of the street. After a good ten minutes of panic, the tension took her energy away, and it was a good thing, and she quickly fell asleep.

Klaus was outside walking around the building, casting sidelong glances at the flat, when he recognized Lisa cuddled up on the sofa. He went closer to the building and started tapping on the ground floor window. He continued for a few seconds and only stopped when Lisa moved. Then she turned and Klaus tapped again. He was deliberately not letting her fall asleep, and when she was waking up he suddenly stopped bothering her. He kept going with his perverse game for a few more minutes, until he thought there was a better way to drive her crazy. He grabbed his mobile phone and dialled her number.

She was dreaming. It was the only way to escape a cage that was shrinking with each breath. She was asleep, and the phone's trill was like a gun poised to shoot. Then her headache became stronger, and the images of the living room took the place of her dream. She massaged her head, while the sound grew stronger, as if it was willing her to get off the sofa. She stretched her arm to unplug the cable when the phone stopped ringing.

Klaus was enjoying the scene. Lisa was lying still on the sofa, moving her head, like in a nightmare. He dialled the number again, making the phone ring. Lisa stood up with difficulty and grabbed the phone, but she didn't hear anyone speaking. She unplugged the cables with anger and went back to the sofa, covering her head with a pillow. Klaus grimaced, but he didn't give up. He went to the house door and rang the bell.

"Enough!"

The phone, the phone, the phone and now the doorbell! She'd had enough. One more ring and her head would have exploded. She was barefoot and went towards the door, ready to attack whoever was trying to torture her.

"Surprise, surprise!" Klaus said when she opened the door.

She felt the earth move under her feet and her stomach went upside down. Klaus was standing right in front of her with a bunch of flowers. He was smiling at her, as if nothing had happened between them. And now he was standing there, a few centimetres from her, waiting for her to let him in. Lisa stayed still, petrified to look at that monster. That was enough for Klaus to consider it as a welcome.

"Nice nest. It seems as if you started to enjoy life." Then the kindness in his voice disappeared and he became harsh. "Why did you unplug the phone?"

He was furious and Lisa was afraid.

"It's over." She almost whispered. Klaus moved up next to her and looked down at her from his height. There was only evil in his eyes, nothing else. He grabbed her arm and held it tight.

"I say when it's over."

"You're hurting me!" Lisa said, trying to free her arm.

"We have a couple of things pending," Klaus said and pushed her away from the living room, towards the stairs.

"Where do you want to go?"

"Upstairs, sweetheart."

"Let me go, Klaus. I beg you, let me go…"

She burst out crying and the fear overwhelmed her. Klaus dragged her to the stairs, while Lisa desperately tried to cling to the living room door, fighting Klaus's grip. Then he lifted her and went up the stairs. Lisa struggled, cried, and screamed, but she could not win against him.

He threw her on the bed, closed the door, and straddled her, immobilizing her. She had never seen him like that. If he used drugs, she couldn't remotely imagine which ones he got.

"Now, my dear, we swallow a candy."

He pulled out a little box and opened it. Death disguised itself as Klaus, and Lisa screamed with all the breath she had. He couldn't have cared less. He gripped her neck, pulled out the pill, and plugged it into her mouth, holding her jowl tight until she swallowed it.

Lisa had lost her strength, so he could loosen his grip. He got off the bed, adjusted the lights, and took the video camera he carried with him. He placed it on a shelf on the opposite wall and turned it on. The shot was perfect. He took off his jacket, lay down on the bed and stared at the lens.

"First scene: undressing Lisa. Action!"

Lisa heard his words like a far away echo, but she could do nothing, since she didn't feel her body. She tried to move her arms, her legs, but all she managed was a sound that came out of her mouth like a plea. Klaus took off her jeans, and then he concentrated on her shirt. He unbuttoned it slowly, remaining on the opposite side of the camera to not obstruct that crazy movie, and he spoke, saying words that Lisa could not understand.

She lay motionless, just wearing her panties and bra. Klaus took them both off and began to gently play with her nipples. He caressed her legs, and she seemed to enjoy his attentions. Then he began to kiss her everywhere, with more passion, until she started to moan with pleasure. That was the moment. He got off the bed, took the video camera, and filmed her in a close-up. She was touching herself, and her weakness made her appear even more beautiful. Her breath accelerated, and she was about to explode. Klaus stood up, placed the camera on the shelf, and went back to her, slave of his perversion.

"Second scene: seducing Lisa. Action!"

He took off his shirt, keeping his trousers on. He lay down on the bed, and this time he went down on her. He kissed her lips, and she kissed him back disclosing all the passion she had.

But he kept playing, exciting her, taking her to the limit, but he never gave her satisfaction. He went down and kissed her stomach. She grabbed his hair. She wanted him, Klaus knew it, but he would take her later. For now, he had to think about the show that the clients wanted to watch, and then he could concentrate on satisfying his beastly needs. He moved his lips down along her legs, closer to Lisa's passion, and his kisses became more and more intense.

"I can't...I can't..."

But she could...It would be a success. It was enough. Lisa was ready to be taken, and he felt his desire pushing inside. He emerged from between her legs and stared at the camera, eventually pronouncing the words that excited him the most.

"Third scene: raping Lisa. Action!"

Lisa was lying supine, posed between pleasure and suffering. Klaus looked at her, but in his eyes there was no tenderness. He touched her again, but without gentleness this time, as his play wanted him to be harsh and treat her like a prostitute. Lisa was under the effect of drugs, but she noticed his sudden change without understanding why. Klaus's hands touched her hips, forcing her to turn, and then Klaus took her, letting her feel all the power of his body. She wanted to scream but, once again, she couldn't do anything. She just felt pain, and the despair into which she fell drowned the silence of her bitter tears.

He had finished. He got off the bed and went to the wall, where the camera was. He framed Lisa and filmed her a last time. She was lying motionless, giving her back to the ceiling, in a lake of tears.

"Fourth scene: once upon a time there was Lisa..."

He was in his car, with the video camera placed in the front seat next to him. He grabbed the phone and called Rubinstein.

"I have the movie you wanted."

TWENTY-FIVE

She moved out of her flat, changed banks, friends, and mobile phone number. She threw away all the memories of her first thirty years and moved to the other side of the river.

She rented a one-bedroom flat in Southwark, with kitchen annexed to the living room, just the basics to live. She changed habits, from the wake-up call to hours she slept, until nothing remained of her previous life. She didn't use makeup, not even the minimum that a woman would have to feel like a female and spent days and days listening to her music and looking at the photos she had collected during the course of her life. It was terror, total paranoia, but she didn't feel sad to give up a lifestyle that had overwhelmed her. She found a job as a waitress at *The Wharf*, a little restaurant in Gabriel's Wharf, in South Bank, along the Thames.

It was three o'clock one afternoon. She had an hour off work, and she thought that it was a nice idea to take a look at the book market under Bridge. There were plenty of people. There were those who went to the bar under the bridge for a coffee and those who took advantage of those moments to try to build a culture at a cheap price. Lisa was not part of either world; she just desperately needed a dream and that quaint book market, for as little as it was, attracted her. She glanced around, bought a couple of books about Shakespeare, and sat on a bench not far from the market.

She read the first part of a tragedy as though she were ravished and, even though she had lived enough to make up a story of her own, she would not be able to write down two lines of such beautiful poetry and prose. She looked up and observed the people who strolled past, until an old man who sat on another bench a dozen metres from her, caught her attention. A moment later, a young man passed by, slightly touching her, and she saw him sitting next to the tramp, opening a bag and taking out a sandwich. He had to have a very sweet soul.

She kept walking, and this time she went towards Blackfriars, until she reached the Tate Modern. She enjoyed contemplating the *Dalis*, the *Picassos*, and the *Andy Warhols*, but a *Vassily Kandinsky* painting caught her attention, the same one she had admired with Morris.

"*Cossacks*. The prelude to the *Composition IV*." She turned and recognized that face. "I see you like Kandinsky."

It was the same young man who had given an art lesson to Morris, and she was surprised he remembered her.

"So you remember me?" she asked.

"The arts lovers always meet again," he said.

He didn't say any more but he turned and kept walking, directing his attention to other paintings.

After about an hour spent trying to escape the mental labyrinth of a *Mondrian* or a *Malevich*, Lisa thought it was worth taking a break to drink something. So she decided to go to the bar at the floor and ordered a coffee. There was a long queue, but it lasted less than she thought. She went out to the balcony and leaned against the railing to observe people coming and going, to view the Thames and Saint Paul's Cathedral on the other side of the river.

While sipping her coffee, she caught a glimpse of the young man intent on taking notes. She felt intrigued, and she would have enjoyed a chat with him. But she remained, hesitating between the balcony and the gallery floor, limiting herself to observing him. A noise that came from behind her broke the spell, so she decided to go home, leaving her hesitation and doubt at the Tate.

* * *

"To be or not to be…"

She would have given her soul to act in a theatre.

What a beautiful sentence, she thought. "To be or not to be…Lisa. That's my problem!"

Since she had decided to leave her previous life on the other side of the Thames, she enjoyed looking at the photos and recalling her memories. Now, pictures apart, she had two more things to think about: the joy of a simple life and the man who always talked about *Vassily Kandinsky*. Two memories in only one month. Perhaps her life was really beginning to change.

The alarm rang at six sharp. She lay around for a few more minutes, and then she jumped out of the bed and took a shower. A pair of jeans and a light t-shirt under the jacket was enough. There was still half an hour left, and Jean and Matt, the other two people she worked with, were already at the restaurant.

"Hi, Lisa."

"Hi, guys."

She went to change and put on her uniform.

"Number Five is uncovered. Will you look after it?"

"I already have Two, Four, and Eight…" Then she hesitated a second. "That's fine, I'll take Five as well."

At seven, sharp, Jean opened the door and the first clients came to the bar.

"Cappuccino, and two muffins."

"Four pounds seventy."

"What would you like to have, Sir?"

"Just coffee, thanks."

They went on like this until ten, without stopping a second. Then the crowd diminished, and the flow normalized around eleven.

"A coffee and a slice of apple pie."

"Sure, Sir."

Lisa moved away from the bar and listened without even looking at the client. Jean prepared the coffee, and then Lisa saw the client. She felt as though she might faint, as the client was the same person who loved *Kandinsky*.

"Three pounds fifty."

He left the money at the bar and took a place at a table near the entrance. Lisa saw him pulling some papers and sketching something while sipping his coffee. She couldn't stop staring at him, but she didn't have the courage to go closer. She didn't want him to see her working there. He seemed to live in a perfect harmony with a wonderful inner balance. Another client came in and took a place at the table next to her.

"Coffee, please."

She had just turned to go to the bar, when she saw the '*Kandinsky man*' going out. The new client became unpleasant, and she felt tired of smiling at him.

She stopped working around three with nothing else to do but walk along the Thames. So she walked towards the Tate, cast her glance towards the bench where she usually sat, and recognized the same old man she had seen before. There was always a young man with him, with his back turned. She dismissed them from her mind, as she entered the Tate and went to the floor where she had first met the young man. She looked emotionlessly at the paintings hanging on the walls, until she focused on another *Kandinsky*. If there was a way to meet that man again, waiting in front of that painting was definitely the best one.

She heard footsteps behind her and held her breath, hoping it was him. She turned, but she was disappointed, and the smile on her face faded. Clearly, that afternoon was not going well. She only hoped to meet that young man, again; she didn't know why. She got tired of waiting and went to the bookstore with the intention of buying something. "I would like something about *Vassily Kandinsky*," she told the clerk.

"There are a few books down there, under 'abstract painting,'" the clerk said.

Lisa took a couple of the books and went happily to the cashier. Now she had one more thing to fill her empty days. She could study, as well as visit the gallery. On her way home, she started to feel different. She had just bought two books, and she felt excited, feeling the same shivers she used to feel when she was a teenager. There was no simpler life than the one she had decided to live. No glamour dresses to wear at night, no dates to put on the agenda, no one to tell her what she could and could not think about. Hers would be a life simple and straight, like the lines she saw in *Mondrian*'s paintings exhibited at the Tate. Her life was a painting, too, a jam of figures with no head or tail and with a mix of colours that blended into each other. She walked for ten minutes without even realizing where she put her feet. Once home, she turned on the radio and lay down on the sofa, with the two books on her legs.

She stopped reading a few hours later without regretting a minute of the time she had spent. What a genius *Kandinsky* was! Two degrees thrown in the garbage to pursue his dream and become a painter. She had also thrown something away, but it had not been a degree. She had thrown away the only person who might ever have loved her. She placed the books on the floor and picked up Alex's picture, which she studied only for a little while. Would it be one of the things from her past that she would regret?

Finally, feeling tired, she went to bed and thought of all the things she did not think about during the day. She was thirty, she didn't have a friend, she was living a miserable life, and she had thrown her career away. She couldn't do any worse, even if she tried, and in the meantime, she was alone, employed as a waitress in a bar with the strange idea to go to the Tate hoping to meet someone that she had barely seen a couple of times. No, her destiny couldn't be like that.

The sweat emerged on her forehead, and the spasms came back. She wasn't in her beautiful flat anymore; she was living in a modest place, on the other side of the river, and she had said goodbye to that world forever. She was in bed holding the picture of Alex and a couple of books about a painter she had begun to love. There was nothing that could hurt her but her dreams. She felt relieved and the nightmare ended.

The alarm rang at six the next morning and at six in the morning after that. Her new existence was two months old, and the enthusiasm for her new life left room for the dullness to creep in, and a few things began to annoy her, like Matt's harsh voice or Jean's moods. Lisa wanted to change, again. There was no point in continuing to live like this.

She always ended at three in the afternoon, so the people who came to the bar were all of little interest. They offered her the night shift, but she always declined, since it would have been hard for her to have at least a bit of life for herself. And, in the meantime, the phone calls increased. A mate of Jean's, a friend of Matt's…all people who just wanted to take her to bed.

It started to rain one Sunday, and she didn't have to work. But she went out anyway and couldn't give up stopping by *The Wharf* to have a coffee and say hi to the guys, since she didn't know anyone besides them.

She sat at a table next to the window that overlooked the river. She was reading a newspaper and didn't pay much attention to the people who came in and out of the place. While flicking through the pages of the newspaper, she had time to observe the person who was sitting in front of her. She was quite sure she had seen that old man sitting somewhere on a bench outside, and she was surprised to see him in there. He looked like a tramp, but he was dressed too decently to be one. Then, studying him in detail, she thought he looked like a normal person, even though the clothes he was wearing looked miserable. She could not understand. He was sixty-ish, with intense eyes and a sort of charisma that she could not explain. It wasn't common to bump into such people. She drank her coffee, said goodbye to the guys, and went out, glancing one more time at the old man.

And there she was again, with a lot of free time and nobody to enjoy it with. She would have loved to remember and live as many moments as possible, but perhaps it was not so important to have someone close to her. The sky was grey, rain fell on her face, but the noise of the people hanging around kept her company during her stroll. She leaned against the railing that overlooked the river, the Thames, another side of London, and her loneliness. She felt she wouldn't be able to stand it much longer; she wanted to live. She turned and thought about the Tate Gallery, the only thing she had to do.

Two minutes later she was standing before the *Kandinsky* painting and felt that in front of that painting, her life would change. She saw people passing by, and the same people saw her standing there, while time went by. An hour passed, then two, without anything happening. Her legs hurt, and it was difficult to keep standing, so she sat on a chair in the middle of the floor. She was tired, confused, disappointed. The impulse that guided her there had lost its momentum and had turned into discouragement. She thought it would have been so much easier had she not met that man at the Tate. She stood up and decided to leave, but the gallery was just a few metres away, and it would be a pity if she had not waited five minutes longer. She decided to take one last chance, since Destiny could be strange, the way it surprised people. And in fact, Destiny decided to help her.

The man was standing in front of the painting, absorbed in his own thoughts. Lisa felt her heart beat faster and her life sparkle, as it never had in the last few months. She slowly went closer, trying to avoid him seeing her. She just wanted it to be a casual encounter, as casual as the day they met.

"Art lovers always meet, again," she said.

The man turned. Lisa was smiling and looking at him with her amazing green eyes.

"It really seems that this is the only painting we love in the whole gallery," she said.

"Right."

So much time had gone since she felt interested in a man. "*Kandinsky* is the painter I like the most."

"I like him a lot too," the young man said.

She was making all possible efforts, but the conversation hadn't taken off yet, and the chitchat still revolved around the painting.

"Are you writing something?" she asked him.

He opened the book of notes and flicked through the pages.

"Yes. I come here on different days, look at the paintings, and register my emotions."

"And do they change often?"

"It basically depends on the day."

"You mean that they depend on the way you wake up?"

He smiled this time. Lisa's questions were spontaneous.

"Not really. I like to see each painting more than once, so that my emotional state can suggest something that, in different moments, I could never perceive."

His hair was black and short, but Lisa fell in love with his eyes.

"I'm Lisa."

Such a beautiful girl who was desperately trying to get his attention. He was surprised. "I am Nicholas."

They looked in each other eyes for a few seconds without saying a word.

"I bought some books about *Kandinsky*."

"The further you go in the reading, the more *Kandinsky* will become fascinating."

"Are you a painter?" Lisa asked.

"No," he replied. "I teach math to children."

She liked his voice.

"I work in a restaurant nearby."

"And do you like that job?"

"Not really, but I need it."

They stopped at the bar, not the best possible place, but definitely the nearest place to sit. They both wanted to talk to each other. Nicholas ordered the coffees. She was happy, as it had been more than two months since she had spent time with a normal person, and those ten minutes were a breath of fresh air in her isolation. She saw him coming back with a tray and the same expression he had since they met.

"Here we go." He placed the cups on the table and handed one to Lisa.

"Do you ever smile?" Lisa asked.

"Do you fancy people who always smile?" He was quick to reply and Lisa hesitated.

"In small doses," she said.

He seemed to lighten up a bit, but his shady expression returned quickly.

"It's the first time I've talked to someone at the Tate," Lisa admitted.

"It's the first time for me, too," he said.

"Do you come here often?" Lisa answered.

"A couple of times a week."

"It is strange to see a math teacher who loves paintings so much."

Nicholas sipped his coffee. "It can happen, you know? A lot of people have hidden passions. What about you?"

"Theatre."

"That's art anyway."

"Just another way of expression."

"Can I ask you a question?" Nicholas asked.

"Sure," Lisa said.

"Was your hair longer at one time?"

Lisa smiled and caressed her hair. "I wanted to call it a day. In all senses."

"It had to be difficult. Women love their hair, especially if it is beautiful like yours."

There was no malice in his compliment. Lisa knew it, but it was clear how that appreciation let her expression change. Nicholas realized it and tried to change the subject. "Which other painters do you like?"

Right, that was a question to ask while sipping a coffee at the Tate.

"*Picasso* and *Matisse*, but I am not as familiar with them as you are with *Kandinsky*," Lisa admitted.

"Great choice, though. They were two great artists in clear competition with each other. There was an exhibition in here, have you seen it?"

"Unfortunately not, but should it happen again, I won't miss it," Lisa said.

"Do you live nearby?"

"In Southwark."

"I live in Bermondsey."

"It's not that far."

Nicholas nodded. "Just two stops."

They kept going for half an hour, and then they both thought it was time to think about their own stuff. They left the gallery and ended up walking on the riverside.

"I go that way," Lisa said.

"I can accompany you if you wish."

"Thanks, but I prefer to walk on my own."

"So…are we meeting again?" Nicholas asked.

"You bet. Arts lovers always meet again."

They held each other's hand and neither seemed willing to leave.

"That's fine. To the next time then."

He went closer and gave her a kiss on her cheek. He remained still watching her leave, then he walked towards Waterloo Bridge and ten minutes later he was home. His was a small flat, with furniture worn out by time and a room dedicated to his great passion. He washed his hands and felt ready to dream. He grabbed the brush and began to paint Lisa.

* * *

When they saw her coming in it was clear that something had happened.

"Hi, Lisa," they said in unison.

"Hi, guys, all fine today?" Lisa's face shone with a different light.

"All normal here, and you?"

"Me?" She had been lucky to meet a man after such a long time. Matt nodded and Jean did the same, and Lisa knew they could see something different about her. "It's maybe the spring effect," she said lamely. She closed the issue with those words, but she looked at them, barely holding her smile. She was standing behind the bar, when she saw the old man coming in.

"Good morning, dear sir, what can I offer you today?"

The guys never saw Lisa so happy.

"Just a coffee."

"One pound forty."

The old man grabbed the cup and sat at the table at the bottom. Matt came up to her.

"Then you tell us what's going on."

She smiled and her eyes shone, just as they once had.

"Is it about a man?" Jean asked, who had also come up to the counter.

Lisa nodded.

"Something serious then!"

She shrugged and prepared the cappuccino a client had asked for. She cashed in and checked if the old man was still sitting at the table. He was there, flicking through the pages of a magazine. She still had a minute free, so she grabbed a muffin and gave it to him.

"With our compliments."

He smiled with immense tenderness, his only way to thank her, and enjoyed the cake.

* * *

It was finally three. Lisa changed and left the restaurant. As she walked, she felt like breathing deeply. She was enthusiastic, and perhaps not only for Nicholas. She eventually understood that her life could start again, with the enthusiasm of her youth, and all of a sudden, those fateful thirty years seemed just above the age of a child. Then she thought about what she would like to ask for in her life, and she didn't have any doubt. She would ask for love.

She passed the Tate Modern and the Millennium Bridge that linked it to the other side of the river towards Saint Paul, and arrived, after a few minutes at the Shakespeare Globe. The guide welcomed her and ten other people and began to tell the story…

It was fifteen ninety-eight when 'The Theatre', the oldest auditorium in London, due to the expiration of the rental agreement with the landlord, was dismantled and moved from the north of the city to Southwark, beyond the Thames. It was then assembled and adorned with a Globe and the writing 'totus mundi agit historionem', 'the whole world is a theatre', without the stage to be covered by a roof, but surrounded by three galleries one on top of the other with the highest gallery protected by a thatched roof. A year later, William Shakespeare and four other actors of the Chamberlein's Men, put on the first show on the stage. But in sixteen thirteen, a cannon used for the drama Henry VIII shot in the air and set fire to the thatch destroying the structure. The theatre was rebuilt, but then, ultimately, destroyed by the Puritans, thirty years later.

It was thanks to Sam Wanamaker, around the late eighties of the twentieth century, that the theatre was rebuilt next to the place where it was first erected and was an almost identical copy of the original, even with the same thatched roof, banned in sixteen sixty-six after the Great Fire of London. And since that time, the theatre was known as the 'Shakespeare Globe'.

* * *

After half an hour and a story told with great passion, Lisa imagined herself as an actress of the seventeenth century. She felt overwhelmed by history, and the desire to act on that stage became irresistible.

She was glad to be there, and a couple of hours later, she felt completely exhausted. She was not used to being happy anymore and, while she walked back home, she thought of Nicholas. She didn't realize yet what she felt, but she loved the calm and the energy he was able to transmit to her. So she dreamt of seeing him again, maybe in front of a *Kandinsky*, and of them talking about art and having dinner and then… and then Lisa stopped dreaming. That was just a reaction to the experience she'd had with Klaus. She didn't feel anything for Nicholas; he was just the first normal man she had met at the end of the tunnel. Had she waited and evaluated what seemed likely to happen to her, she would have stopped spinning like a top and likely fallen in love with the right person. She put Nicholas aside and thought to remember the beautiful moments again. Alex came quickly to her mind, and she felt like a coward. How could she forget about him for someone she had just met? The euphoria went to her head, and she swore to herself that she would never betray him for Nicholas. But in the meantime, those dark, intense eyes were digging into her thoughts.

She spent the last hours of that day reading the books of Shakespeare, and any time, at any passage, she stared at a point in the air and thought about being on the stage of that wonderful theatre. She hoped Destiny would give her some help. She went to bed and thought about Nicholas again.

TWENTY-SIX

"How is he?" Alex asked.

The doctor grimaced. "Pneumonia, with the beginnings of frostbite."

"Will he recover?"

"Let's hope and pray," the doctor said.

Travis was in a hospital room, and his breath sounded like a death rattle. Alex stopped by the door and prayed to God to save him.

It was night when the phone rang. For a moment, he didn't have the energy to get off the bed and answer it, but when he heard the message from the hospital, he got up and called the doctor. Travis was still unconscious, but the situation was under control. If he had survived that day, he could begin to hope. He hung up and sighed, relieved, as he felt affection for that old man. He pushed the button and listened to the other messages.

"You should come to the theatre as soon as you can. I had another conversation with Conrad. The sooner you move the better…"

There were no more messages, since not many people called Alex. He first went to the A&E, spoke with the doctor, and said hello to Travis, trying to cheer him up. He would call later and maybe come by again. Joe, in the meantime, was waiting for him at the pub.

* * *

"Hi, Alex," Joe said, when he saw him fighting his way through the crowd.

"Hi, Joe," Alex said. "Sorry I'm late. I had some problems."

"What a blow you've got!" Joe said, looking at the purple wound on Alex's temple.

"That's nothing. A friend got much worse than that, unfortunately," Alex said, lightly touching his temple.

"Nothing serious I hope," Joe said, studying his friend's face.

"He's at the hospital. I just hope he makes it."

The emotion overwhelmed him, and Joe hugged him tight. "I am sorry, Alex."

"I've listened to the message today. How did it go with Conrad?"

Joe's expression changed, but his seriousness didn't indicate anything new. "It's getting more and more difficult to talk to him. He reminded me more than once about the contract you signed."

"One year," Alex said, "I remember well. There's no need to remind me."

"He wants the monologue."

He didn't waste any time; he was straightforward. He was clearly under pressure.

"Why?"

"Maybe he likes it, don't you think so?"

Alex thought about the monologue when he first spoke about it with Joe at the theatre, about the argument he'd had with Conrad, and about Travis, who lay in bed with his life hanging by a thread. It seemed absurd to keep arguing for something that had no importance for him anymore. It seemed absurd to call such a situation a problem, when someone was fighting for his life at the hospital. It seemed absurd that Joe was worried about Conrad.

"I will bring it over to you tomorrow."

Joe relaxed.

"Under one condition, though," Alex said.

"That would be?"

"That this monologue will be signed in the name of the person who made it possible for me to write it."

It was a strange request he didn't have any answer for.

"I have to talk to Conrad about it. I don't know whether it will be a problem or not. Anything else?"

"I want to call it a day, Joe."

Joe pushed himself towards the back of the chair, worried. "Anything wrong?"

"You dare to ask me that?"

Joe nodded. "Would you like to talk to Conrad?"

"And tell him what? That I have the balls full of arseholes like him? I never liked that man, and I don't like you that much right now."

He had lost touch with Alex. He stared at his eyes, but he saw a different person, who spoke with emotions that were leading him out of control.

"Relax, Alex. You are the actor. Conrad runs the theatre, but that's it. No one should dare to tell you how to write your things, nor should you dare to tell him how to run the theatre."

Alex looked at Joe up and down in contempt. "Whose side are you on?"

He felt embarrassed, but the decision had been made. Alex was a friend, but the theatre was a piece of his life.

"I will let you know about the signature. That's all I can tell you tonight."

He didn't need to hear anything else. The message was clear.

"It doesn't matter. Conrad will never get my monologue whether signed by me or by anyone else."

He stood up and left, and Joe didn't even try to stop him. He saw him going out of the pub, nervously. He had lost face but, more importantly, he had lost a friend.

Alex called Joel. "Come with me to the hospital."

"What's wrong with you?"

"Not with me…with Travis."

"Alex, please, don't tell me you are back in that mess!"

"Stop it, Joel. He's a human being! So, are you coming with me or not?"

He didn't have any choice. "Give me ten minutes."

He was quick. The ten minutes hadn't even passed before he was there.

"What a bad blow you've got. Are you sure it's about the old man?"

Alex nodded and stopped the first taxi that passed by.

"Sorry if I have been an arsehole. It's just that when you see the things from outside, you feel everything differently. Did you hear anything?"

"I did not, Joel, I just hope things aren't getting any worse."

The taxi took them to the entry of the hospital. Alex got out, and his anxiety was clearly visible. Luckily, he bumped into the doctor.

"Doctor, we met this afternoon early."

"Yes, I remember," the doctor said.

"How is he?"

"Stable I would say."

Alex wanted to know more. Joel was standing by his side, powerless.

"That's a good sign, isn't it? Stable means it's going well, right?"

"Yes, stable is a good sign, but let's not try to make hurried prognoses. Let's say that it's not going that badly. If he doesn't get any worse tonight, his clinical case could positively evolve."

Alex was emotional and Joel was touched.

"Can we see him?" Joel asked.

The doctor turned towards him.

"Sorry, guys. He's in intensive care."

Joel looked at Alex. He was trying to find an answer.

"What should we do now?" Joel asked.

"I'll stay here," Alex said.

The doctor patted his shoulder.

"You better go home. Should anything change I'll call you."

He was a good man and was nice to Alex. He handed his mobile phone over to the doctor on call that night.

* * *

Three weeks went by before there was some visible improvement, but Travis was saved by his desperation to stay alive. He fought against death and won. They discharged him in a wheelchair, and Alex and Joel came to pick him up.

"Travis." Alex hugged him and burst out crying. The nurse was touched, and Joel felt something as well.

"Do you remember Joel?" Alex asked, drying his eyes.

"The comics drawer?"

Alex turned towards Joel. He went closer and caressed Travis.

"Hi Travis, you're right. I'm the crazy comics drawer. Happy to see you again."

Those were true words, and Travis gave him a tender smile, as he felt loved, eventually out of a tunnel, and with an explosion of emotions inside. There was no need for Joel to learn more about Travis through Alex; he had also begun to hang out with them more and more often. So Travis soon had two new friends, two guys who slowly revived a flame that seemed to have gone out forever.

"We have to tidy up the room. I think I will buy a desk and a couple of posters."

Travis was sitting on a chair, sipping his chamomile tea and looking at his two new friends who cared about him so much.

"What about this box?" Joel asked.

"In my room, under the window, otherwise let's leave it next to the front door."

After about an hour of chat, Alex's studio became Travis's room. Joel helped him stand up and took him in there.

"What do you think?"

Slightly more than two metres by two, a window that overlooked the building on the other side of the mews, a bed that looked more like a camp bed, with a chair at one end, and a hook to hang his clothes. But it was all for him. It was the room that Destiny booked for his new existence.

"It's wonderful."

The walls were white and a bit dirty, but to Travis they seemed full of life. For someone who used to find reasons for things to happen, there was no explanation for what was happening now. It seemed as if Destiny was enjoying having fun with him, but the flat, the guys, Joel's grimaces as he was moving furniture or Alex's intense glance were real.

"Can I sit?" he asked Alex indicating the bed.

"You don't need to ask for anything from anyone in here."

The movie began to flow before his eyes. The bridge, the street, that bench that represented his only chance to understand Destiny passed by and gave space to the faces of these guys, to these four walls and to the daylight. Travis felt emotional and his eyes shone.

"Come on Travis, life is a wheel. Sometimes it can spin in the right direction as well."

Alex left him alone. Travis took off his shoes, lay down on the bed, and crossed his hands under his head. He stared at the ceiling and noticed it was of a different colour than the grey of the bridge. He felt at peace and closed his eyes and fell asleep. Joel was with Alex, and he finished making jokes about Travis after living his drama in first person.

"I would like to apologize about being such an arsehole with Travis."

"It doesn't matter. You're always an arsehole," Alex said, smiling. "I need a beer. Want one?"

Joel nodded and Alex stood up.

"Life is a matter of luck. Just think for a second if I were in Travis's shoes."

It was rare to hear Joel speaking so intensely.

"You would already be dead," Alex said bluntly.

"So you think I'm that pathetic?"

"It's not about that, Joel. You need luck and enormous courage."

"You're right."

"He's been living like a tramp for who knows how long. Do you think it's easy to open your eyes, realize you're under a bridge, without anyone who treats you like a human being?"

Alex handed Joel the beer and sat at the other end of the sofa.

"It's not the best life you can live," Joel agreed.

"That's for sure."

"Did he tell you anything about himself?"

"Sorry?"

"About his past, his family, his loves," Joel said, "his job…something about his life."

"I haven't had the chance to talk about all that so far."

"Strange," Joel said. "I was sure he'd already told you a lot."

"We have all the time we want."

Joel placed the can on the table and seemed thoughtful.

"Something wrong?"

"It's a complex case, anyway."

"What do you mean?"

"Travis is a stranger," Joel said.

"I already know that. So what?"

"You are making a serious commitment."

"I am perfectly aware of that, but it's not a problem at all."

"I would like to know what you think about this story. I'm just curious, nothing more than that."

"And you, Joel, what do you think about it?" Alex asked.

"Difficult situation, complex evolution."

Alex nodded. "Solutions?"

"Only one: adoption."

"I can't be his child for sure!" Alex said.

"I wasn't speaking about you. I was speaking about him. You adopt him, and he becomes your father."

It wasn't a bad idea. "You're right. I could kill two birds with one stone. I get rid of a problem, and I give him back some dignity."

"What do you think about it?" Joel asked.

"Great idea. I would get rid of my inner conflicts." Alex stood up and went to Travis room.

"What do you want to do?" Joel asked.

Alex waived his hand without turning towards him. Joel had to stay there and wait.

"May I come in?" Alex asked knocking on the door; it was slightly ajar.

Travis lay on his side and seemed to be sleeping. Alex went closer and stopped behind Travis's shoulder. He waited a few seconds for a reaction and then went back to the living room, where Joel sat. Travis followed him with his eyes and had listened to every word they had said since he lay down on the bed. One of the few advantages he got from

I, Destiny

living on the street—to sleep and listen at the same time.

"Dad is sleeping?" he just wanted to joke with him and Alex didn't take it personally this time.

"And if we called him grandfather?"

Joel had excluded that hypothesis. "It makes him old."

"Right," Alex said.

"How do you see him?"

"Father figure, looking for love."

"Did we exclude Dad, right?"

Alex nodded. "Uncle?"

"Dull. Let's call him Travis."

"Perfect! I like it."

Travis smiled. He held the pillow tight between his arms and smelled the perfume of the sheets and the freshness of the cotton on his face. He dreamt and heard, again, the noises and the voices under the bridge, but he didn't feel abandoned.

"So?" Joel asked.

"He's sleeping."

"He needs it. Let him recover, even though I think that this big change for him is like a trauma."

"From the street to a home…can you imagine the emotional storm he's dealing with now?"

"We don't have to deceive him, Alex. The moment he begins to feel used to your company and to the warmth of this place, sending him back to the street would mean sending him to die."

Alex was standing next to the table, gathering his notes. "These sheets are his job." He handed the notes to Joel and waited for his comment.

"Did he write this?" Joel asked.

"He didn't, but I could only write it because of him."

He flicked through the pages. "Beautiful and intense, I would say. Does it have anything to do with your next show?"

Alex took the pages back. It was clear that Joel's question made him anxious.

"I am at a crossroads."

"Life is all a matter of crossroads," Joel replied.

"Did you start addressing Destiny directly?"

Joel lit up a cigarette, took off his shoes, and stretched his legs on the table.

"How can I know? I'm lucky to wake up every day. We'll find an agreement about the rest."

"Minimalist," Alex said.

"Are you still in contact with Joe and the guys?" Joel asked, relaxing into the sofa.

"Scott is out. Judie just found another job, and I don't want to have anything to do with Joe again."

"Nice picture. I need a screenwriter for my comics. Maybe I'll hire you."

Alex smiled. Joel was serious though. "Why did you break up with Joe? I thought it was true friendship between the two of you."

"It's not his fault. It's because of the guy who is running things. A certain Conrad Fleming, such an arrogant bastard."

"From the way you're talking about it, it's hard to believe you guys got along well."

"I can't stand him. He's the kind of guy who causes trouble. It's because of him that Joe and I broke up."

Joel was paying attention to Alex's words and, at the same time, he was producing smoke rings in the air.

"And what can you tell about yourself? Are you sure you didn't do anything to let things go bust?"

"Joel, please."

"That's your problem, Alex. You've always been screwed by your temper. I can understand it from the pitch of your answer. You are touchy; that's why you haven't got what you deserve yet."

Alex didn't even try to reply. Joel was the only one from whom he would have accepted such criticism. "Help me understand."

That was a huge effort of humility. Joel extinguished the cigarette and focused on him. "You have to stay calm and not think that when people talk to you in a way you don't like, they just do it because they don't get along well with you. What's the name of the boss of the theatre?"

"Conrad."

"Perfect, just think of Conrad as if he had to deal with people even more difficult than he is, who are putting him under terrible pressure. Do you think he would be happy to deal with people who lose their temper for nothing, like you?"

"Am I really like you're saying?"

"You're not bad. You just find it difficult to deal with people who think differently than you."

Alex found it tough to accept. He couldn't stand the idea of Joel blaming him without being perfectly aware of what really happened before judging his behaviour, right or wrong. He tried to point it out.

"Did you like the monologue?" Alex asked.

"It seems really good, from the little time I've spent on it."

"That's just the first part of the show that I'd like to produce."

"And what about the rest?"

"I'll need some more time, but Joe couldn't give it to me, since Conrad objected. So they offered me to do just the first part of the scene."

"It doesn't sound like a bad idea."

"I told Joe that I could accept it if the monologue is signed by Travis, and only if we breach the agreement that still binds me to the theatre."

"And what did he say?"

"Concerning the potential signature that would attribute the copyrights, he has to talk with Conrad first. In case I decide unilaterally to terminate the contract, I wouldn't be able to write anything for anyone else until the contract I have with the theatre legally expires."

"Is that all? I thought it could have been much worse."

Alex was clearly waiting for his advice, and it didn't take long for Joel to reply. "You should resign, close an agreement with someone you trust, and send Conrad to hell."

Alex didn't say anything and Joel seemed to meditate.

"Or maybe the truth is something else?" Joel asked.

Emotions, emotions and, again, emotions…Alex's joy and pain.

"That theatre is part of my life, that's the truth. I'm tied to the memories and to Joe."

Joel didn't buy it. He knew Alex better than anyone else.

"Why that sad look? Is there anything else I don't know that I should?"

Alex looked at the notes on the desk.

"Or are you still thinking about the bitch?"

Alex looked up and that was his answer. Yes, he was still thinking about her.

"You should stop being a dreamer, because you will never get anything from life. You have to get rid of her once and for all, otherwise you will stop living!"

Alex swallowed.

"And Joe, what about him?" Joel continued. "Did he treat you the way you wanted to be treated? Who did he choose, you or Conrad?"

"Conrad."

"You are not stupid, Alex. If you think, you can find the answer yourself. Move your ass and organize your life!"

Alex put his notes back into the folder. In the meantime, Joel looked at him.

"I can't understand you. You had the courage to adopt a tramp and give him back a life, but you can't make up your mind for a bunch of bullshitters?"

Joel was right. He could cope with the situation and take advantage of it.

"And what about the theatre? Who tells me that it will be easy to find anyone who could produce the show?"

Joel's sigh was so intense that, for a moment, Alex was afraid Travis could hear it as well. "You just have to decide which path to walk on. You've been able to create a show about Destiny, and you cannot even make a choice?"

Alex felt enlightened. "You're right. I'll resign. I'll call the guys, I'll produce the show, and I'll look for a theatre to perform it in!"

"Yes, Alex! That's what I like!" Joel had given Alex back some confidence.

* * *

Alex didn't waste any time and thought about how to take on his next challenge. He wanted to mend the relationship with Joe, but he thought he could sort this out later. On the other hand, he owed Joe an answer after Joe spoke with Conrad. He worked hard, got back in touch with the guys, and decided to meet up with Scott at *Caffe' Nero* in Jamestown Road, a few steps away from Camden High Street and not far from where he lived. Scott was already at the table, flicking through the pages of the latest *Time Out* edition.

"Alex!" he said when he saw him. "Long time no see. Fancy a cup of coffee?"

"Cappuccino for me."

It was eleven in the morning and they did not remember the last time they both met.

"So glad to see you," Alex said.

"I was surprised to hear from you. You look great!"

"I haven't gone to war yet," he said with a smile. "Let's talk about you, though. Are you working at anything? Tell me everything. I'm curious."

"A couple of little things…peanuts I would say. A theatre down in South Bank and little things here and there."

"And Joe? Have you seen him?"

"No, I haven't," Scott said. "I left him my new number, but he never called back."

"And what about Judie? How's she doing?"

"I saw her last week. I guess she's fine. She's seeing someone and keeps going with her job. She's happy, I guess."

"That's great news. I'll go get something to eat."

Scott was part of his deepest memories, part of that wonderful group of people that had changed his life. He went back to the table and put a cake on his plate.

"And what about you? It's been quite a long time since I've heard from you," Scott said.

"I'm working on a project, but I think it will take another month to complete it."

"What's it about?"

"It's all about reality. How it looks and how much truth there is in what you see."

"Sounds like a *The Black and the White* style."

Alex hesitated and looked through the window. "It's something different this time. It starts with a monologue and ends with a drama. It's deeper because the story's real."

Scott loved Alex's style, and also because Alex meant work for him.

"I like it, but I would like to take a look at the play. Would it be possible?"

"The monologue is done. I should start with the drama in the next few days. Would you like to work on it?"

"Anytime, anyhow. I can't wait!"

So Alex had made the first step. Next, he had to talk to Judie. *"You've been able to create a show about Destiny and you are not even able to make a choice?"* Joel's words echoed in his head. In a way, he had already challenged Destiny and if he did it once, he could do it again.

So, a few hours later, Alex called Judie. "It's Alex, how are you?" Rather than meeting Judie someplace, he had tried her old cell number and was delighted when she picked up right away.

"What a nice surprise!" Judie said. I'm fine, and yourself?"

"Just finished having a chat with Scott."

"I met up with him last week," Judie said.

"I know, he told me so much about you. How is your love life going?"

"What can I say my love…time will tell."

"I wish you the best, Judie. But, now, I want to talk to you about a certain project…"

So, now he had taken the second step by calling Judie, and they agreed to meet over lunch at *The Westbourne*, a popular gastropub in Notting Hill. When he saw her walk into the pub, he felt the same emotions again. Judie was happy to meet him, and she gave him a very warm smile. Alex realized how much she had changed and found her to be much more intriguing since the last time he had seen her. He answered all of her questions with enthusiasm. Judie agreed on the terms and the time of the project. The circle was slowly closing, bringing back all the things he had dealt with since the story had begun; Travis, Joel, Scott, and Judie were all on his side now. Only Lisa was missing, but it wasn't a surprise anymore. She would not be part of his life again.

There were still a few details to sort, like the theatre, but he would think about that later.

TWENTY-SEVEN

"Alex should be here any minute," Joe said. Conrad was with Joe at the office, impatiently waiting for Alex. He decided to face him directly and discuss his requests, since it was clear that Joe was no longer able to deal with the case. The tension was tangible, and it was his intention to put an end to a story that was slowly evolving.

"That's a great start," Conrad said, "if you recognize the morning from the dawn, then it's pitch black."

Joe was even more nervous, since he'd had a chance to experience Conrad's resolution at his own expense during those past months. With an on-going legal commitment, there was no excuse; he would have never allowed Alex to fool him, at the cost of destroying his career. Alex eventually came. Joe sighed with relief and walked towards him and shook his hand. Conrad, on the other hand, did not even stand up or look at him.

"Lesson number one: never be late at a business meeting," Conrad said.

"There was a delay at the tube station that cost me a lot of time," Alex said.

"Lesson number two: never try to justify your delay." Conrad said.

Alex couldn't expect to face such contentiousness from Conrad and felt uncomfortable. He turned to Joe, expecting to be backed up, but nothing happened.

"Listen to me, boy…I've already wasted time with you. You have a contract and contracts have to be honoured. The conversation is over."

Conrad didn't stand up and didn't even wait for Alex to sit. He just attacked him. Joe had to do something, otherwise the meeting would end before it started, but he didn't find the courage to say anything.

"I already spoke with Joe." Alex was keen to call it an end as well.

"Joe?" Conrad said.

He was involved as well. It was a very bad day. He stood up and threw himself into the fray. "Alex is ready to give us his monologue, but he has a few conditions."

Conrad smiled sarcastically. "Congratulations on your mediation skills…So, what conditions is the boy talking about?"

'Boy'…again. There was no escape. "I won't be signing the monologue, but someone else will. Second, I want out of the one-year contract."

Conrad turned to Joe. He was not aware of the second request. "What is this farce?"

"I told you, Conrad, Alex had a few points to discuss."

Conrad stood up. He couldn't stand it any longer. "That's too much! No monologue. I am no longer interested! As far as I am concerned, boy, your position will be a subject for my lawyers and should there be a chance for me to lose even a cent, I will let you live the rest of your days in the middle of the street."

He grabbed his briefcase and walked to the door. Then he turned and stood firm. He faced Joe. "Tomorrow, eight sharp. We need to talk."

"Fuck!" he said when Conrad slammed the door. "It's turning bad, my boy."

"I'm sorry," Alex said.

There was no need to add anything else. Joe was broken and, considering Conrad's reputation, it would have been impossible to put the pieces together again. Alex didn't know what to say; he just felt guilty but then dismissed the thought from his mind. His life was at stake; no one could tell him what to do with it. And he strongly believed that he had done the right thing not to give in to Conrad's threats. He felt stronger and hugged Joe.

"Life is a wheel and will start spinning again in our favour, sooner or later. One way or another."

He left the office, but a second before closing the door on his past, he looked at Joe one more time. Joe was sitting at his desk, with his face in his hands and maybe crying. The theatre was his whole life, and Conrad had just kicked it.

Alex was free. No matter what Conrad threatened to do, there was little his lawyers could do if Travis signed his work. He still had to give back to Conrad the money he had got from Joe beforehand, but that was nothing compared to the value of freedom. He smiled and felt cynical, just like Conrad, and he had come to enjoy it.

"Free!" he said aloud.

Travis opened the door when he saw the happiness on Alex's face.

"Did you have a nice day?" Alex asked.

"Wonderful!" Travis said. He wore one of Alex's sweatshirts that made him look so much younger than he was.

"What did you do?"

"I thought your place needed to be cleaned." He said the words with pride, as if the gesture helped him claim back some of his dignity.

"It's been great having you with me," Alex said.

"But you didn't tell me yet how it went."

"I'm finally free to do whatever I want."

"I am happy you feel like that." Travis stared at a point in the air and seemed to be absorbed by a thousand different thoughts.

"What are you staring at?"

Travis shrugged. "Nothing special."

"I have an idea. How about we go for a walk?"

"Yes, I'd like to," Travis said.

There was no need for Travis to add anything else, since his eyes said it for him. He missed the view of the Thames, the bench that signalled the beginning and end of a dream, the people coming and going, wondering who that old man was who was always alone. Alex walked next to him, watching him.

How strange, Alex thought. Travis had returned to the place where he had almost died, but despite that, he managed to feel powerful emotions.

"Let's go over there," Travis said. He pointed at the bench, but he didn't wait for any answer. He was the king of that place. He was touched and walked impatiently, hoping deep inside that no one would sit there before they made it. Travis remained silent, and Alex limited himself to sitting next to him. Travis was restless and moved as if he could not find the right position anymore after sleeping in a bed for a month. He eventually relaxed and began to look at the Thames.

"Everything started from this bench," Travis said, looking straight ahead at the water.

Here it was. That was the moment Alex had been waiting for. He didn't have to do anything but listen.

"Six years. That's how long I was here. One day I sat on this bench, I looked at the Thames, and I started to think."

His eyes stopped glowing. They were full of melancholy.

"I thought I could stop time, change Destiny…Can you believe it,

Alex? Just because one day I came here and looked at the Thames."

Travis turned towards Alex, inviting him to enter his thoughts, and Alex moved closer.

"What do you see in that river?" Alex asked.

"The point where my presumption was born."

Alex would have paid to live that moment, but now he just wanted to enjoy it; listening to those words was like imagining six years of loneliness spent thinking on a bench. That was Travis's secret.

"I should have stopped and not dared to defy something bigger than me. Can you see the Thames?"

Alex nodded.

"One drop cannot change the river's flow."

His eyes were full of tears. Alex didn't understand.

"I would trade what's left of my life with just one more day with my son Nicholas." He turned to Alex. "You're about my son's age. When you will become a father, you will understand."

They did not pay attention to time. They stood up and entered the bar a few metres from the bench. Travis liked that place.

"It's nice here," he said. "I think that I'll stop here anytime I miss my bench."

Alex noticed a girl opening a little door just behind the bar. She was tall, blonde, with short hair. He could barely see her. She had to be beautiful.

They were both happy to be there. They both ordered coffee. It was just a little thing, but it made their lives look nicer. They eventually left, and Travis asked Alex to remain alone for a moment. He needed some time on his own to feel emotions that only he could feel.

"Don't worry, Travis."

Travis needed time to cry out the bitterness that had almost killed him, when he was alone and rotting under a bridge.

* * *

"Who wants to be the first to read?" Alex asked.

The troupe were at Alex's place, and Judie and Scott had already read the script. They were enthusiastic about it, and Alex decided to proceed differently by involving them from the very beginning.

"The monologue itself won't be able to hold up the whole show, so I think the drama should develop in a lighter way; otherwise, it'll make it a heavy night."

Alex took note of Judie's comment and pointed at Scott.

"I guess we should decide about the duration of the play," Scott said, "and then try to split the time between the monologue and the drama in a more logical way. I would make the monologue shorter."

Alex nodded. Scott's criticism made sense, or else the show could lose its rhythm and reduce the tension.

"We're back to old times! Do you remember, guys?"

Alex was tired, so he changed the subject. They all needed a break. He prepared tea and filled a bowl with biscuits that he placed at the centre of the table. Judie was sitting on the chair with her legs on the armrest. Scott sat properly, like a student in the middle of the class.

"When are you going to introduce him to us?" Judie asked.

"In a bit. He's taking a walk in South Bank."

"The call of his past life," Scott said.

"It would be the same thing for anyone. He spent six years over there."

"That's crazy! I wouldn't even last six hours," Judie said.

Alex poured the tea and served Scott on the sofa and Judie on the chair.

"Watch out!" he said to her.

"It's hot, I know…"

"You'd ruin my chair if you let it fall."

"Funny."

Alex went back to the table.

"How did you guys meet?" Judie asked.

"Joel met him first. We were there, and he started talking to him."

"When you go out with Joel, you never know what will happen," Scott said.

"He's just an extroverted person," Alex said.

"Is he still working for the comics company?" Judie asked. She had turned in the chair and was sitting up, sipping her tea.

Alex nodded.

"I saw his sketches," Scott said. "They're amazing."

"He's talented," Alex agreed.

"Genius and dissipation, just like you." Judie was smiling at him. She had that little something for Alex and he could feel it.

"Judie is right, you have an incredible talent, too," Scott said.

"I pass, then," Alex said. He had the face of a happy child. He made a tremendous effort to look serious, but at the end, his face blossomed into a wonderful smile. The only thing he really loved was to be loved by those he really loved. The doorbell rang.

"I think it's him," Alex said.

He opened the door, took Travis by the arm, and led him into the living room.

"Guys, this is Travis."

Judie and Scott stood up. This was an important event.

"Hi Travis, I am Judie."

"And I am Scott."

They were hypnotised and they could not realize how a person, whose life was literally in the middle of a street, could end up at Alex's place. It would have been an amazing character for a movie, but now that he was standing before them, they didn't know what to say. Travis took care to alleviate their embarrassment. "Alex told me a lot about the two of you. I know you are the reason for his enthusiasm, and it's a beautiful thing to see you reunited again."

"We're working on a project, even though we don't have a theatre to stage it yet."

Judie was excited and was amused by the idea of Travis being there. She would have done what she could to make him feel comfortable.

"Have you ever had the chance to read the script of *The Black and the White*?" Scott asked.

They overwhelmed Travis with questions, and Travis felt delighted by all the attention he received.

"No, I haven't had a chance yet, but I'll be glad to take a look at it, if Alex wishes."

Alex went to his room and came back with a file. "Here's the script. These guys acted with me."

Travis took the script. He couldn't wait to read it because he felt like a professor again for the first time in six years.

They were all looking at him, wondering just for a moment what sense it made to put a script in the hands of a tramp. Then, the thought left their minds at the same speed it had entered. They were all focused on Alex's project.

"Don't pay too much attention to my presence," Travis said. "Act as if I'm not here."

They hadn't even remotely thought about that. Travis, in that room, was like a drop of water in the river Thames.

"Do you plan to base it on the style of *The Black and the White*?" Scott asked.

"I don't think so. The monologue should be enough. I would like it to be Shakespearean in style, with real characters, no more Souls or Imaginations."

"I agree that's a much better change, but the structure should remain pretty much similar," Judie added.

"Which would mean…?"

"You talk about a 'dark light', then about her, which I assume to be her, and then you talk about secrets hidden in water drops and about an old man. Travis, isn't it?"

Alex nodded.

"It's not an easy thing to pitch, and the risk of trivialising it is huge," Scott said.

"What do you think about it, guys?" Alex asked.

"Should be the same style of *The Black and the White*. Too difficult to stage it otherwise."

"And what do you think?" he asked Judie.

"We should put in writing the various passages and then see if it's worth choosing something abstract or real, as you're planning to do."

"Makes sense. Thanks, Judie."

"So? Should we start?" Scott asked.

"I will try to send you something next week and then hope to get your constructive feedback."

"That's fine."

It was late and almost dinnertime. Judie complained that she was starving and showed the first signs of tiredness. Scott said he'd keep going until the morning after, but he wasn't too excited to spend the rest of the night between Alex and Travis. So they both said goodbye and left. Travis, in the meantime, had put the pages of the play back together. From time to time he shook his head, as if he could not believe what he had just read, completely unaware that Alex was looking at him.

"So?"

"It's wonderful, vibrant, intense. I don't have anything else to say."

"Really?"

"Yes."

"I am glad you liked it. Did you find anything difficult to understand?"

Alex could hardly believe Travis was able to make any comments. After all, he was just a tramp.

"The most beautiful thing is to imagine stopping Time to let Destiny die. It is the first time that the imagination takes such an important feature in an existential dilemma."

Alex stopped, bemused. Travis was a tramp…how the hell could he speak like that?

"I beg your pardon?"

"Imagination is an unconscious defence mechanism that unloads the psychic pressure. It's a relief valve: to imagine equals escape."

The play was the sparkle that heated his old passions, and Alex continued to not believe what he had just heard. Travis's confidence in expressing his thoughts was indeed a surprise.

"Where did you learn to talk like this?"

Travis couldn't hold it in any longer. His arms and his legs trembled, and he felt the pressure of his own emotion. He couldn't believe it either that he was still able to 'speak like that', but at least those long six years had not deprived him of his power of thought.

"I taught at university."

The revelation was strong, and Alex kept staring at Travis like a character that came out of a dream.

"So you can easily follow the plot?"

Travis smiled, just for the happiness in saying yes…he could follow the plot.

"Yes, Alex, I can follow the plot."

His answer, said with no hesitation, dramatically changed Alex's opinion of Travis. He grabbed his notes and handed them to Travis.

"Then, do you mind taking a look at this? I'm curious to know what you think about it, as well."

It was the monologue. If he was able to write something like that, he had to say thanks to the man who was standing before him. He remained seated on the chair, next to the sofa, and patiently waited for Travis's comments.

Travis felt the tension growing stronger, but he wouldn't give up. He wanted to help Alex, but the doubts returned, knowing that if he failed, he wouldn't get another chance. He put the sheets on the sofa and closed his eyes to better concentrate. Alex quickly noticed that Travis really loved him and the suffering that he saw in Travis's wish to help him made him feel even closer. He sat next to Travis and tried to summarize.

"It is not that easy to go back to work after six years of holidays. That's enough for today, so take the notes, read them whenever you feel like it and don't talk about it until you want to. When you feel that you would like to have a chat with me, just let me know, and I'll be happy to discuss it with you."

He couldn't have picked better words, since Travis took the papers and smiled. He would read it, but without the pressure to show something at all costs; in that way he would be able to help him. The evening passed into the night. Travis went to his room, while Alex remained in the drawing room to work on his project. The computer was on and he kept scrolling down the screen on the pages he had written, until he realized that his concentration had waned. The story seemed to be enthralling, but it still missed the link between his thoughts and the characters he was trying to shape. He had to translate what he thought into a life-like drama, or leave everything in a timeless dimension, just like *The Black and the White*. The difference this time, though, was that he could rely on Travis's story, so he focused on the project again.

A man sits on a bench and starts to think. Fine, that could be a beginning, but then? Could he represent the water drops? And the river? He was tired, and he decided to postpone the work to the following day. Too many thoughts so late at night would run the risk of laying out the work in the wrong way. He crossed his arms on the table and let his head fall on them. Maybe he fell asleep, as he completely lost the sense of time. He opened his eyes with a big yawn and looked at his watch. Four o'clock. The night had already passed by and somebody else was sitting at the table.

Travis was writing something on a blank sheet of paper. He locked eyes with Alex, still sleepy, and he waved him to stay upright. He looked serious, like a teacher preaching to his students.

TWENTY-EIGHT

"It's amazing, Judie, really. It's something you must definitely see. I'll call Scott."

And so Alex invited Scott to come over to his flat around six.

He hung up enthusiastically. Travis had shown him things from a different angle, which if he followed his advice, the effect would be even better. They were all at his place. Joel had been there since that afternoon and had already had a chance to talk to Travis, but Judie and Scott had no idea what they had discussed. They arrived together, at six sharp. Joel went to open the door while Alex and Travis kept working in the living room, trying to set things properly for the meeting. Alex invited them to come in as soon as he saw them. He kissed Judie's cheek and shook hands with Scott.

"We're on the right path, guys. I had a long conversation with Travis about our project, and I have to admit that the result is outstanding."

Scott looked at Judie, perplexed. He didn't know anything about Travis. He had just met him. So, to hear Alex introducing him as a sort of partner in the project was strange to Scott. Judie, on the other hand, was intrigued by Travis and how he had appeared out of the blue in Alex's life. But if Alex seemed to be happy to have him around, there had to be a reason. They just took seats and Alex handed them a sheet.

"I've highlighted the points we'll discuss today, which are the results of the exchange of ideas between Travis and me about the project. First of all, we have refined the monologue and have drawn on the same monologue as the basis for developing the drama."

"Same style as *The Black and the White*?" Scott asked.

Alex waved him to wait while waiting for Travis to nod.

"Okay, the issue is simple. Travis took a look at *The Black and the White* play and came back with very interesting points. The first comment is that we should and could have given more depth to the characters. The second refers to the monologue itself which, even though pleasant to listen to, remains superficial. As such, we should work on its intensity, in case we plan to tie the content to the characters of the drama.

"Which would mean…?" Judie asked.

They still couldn't get the message. Alex took the sheets and began to read.

"For example, take a look at the first part. Scott, read the highlights."

Scott took the sheet.

"Like a light I remember you, indistinct, one that has turned dark, that doesn't shine. You are a phantom but keep thinking we are together. It's a crazy dream without a reason that makes me aim, makes me want what I know I'll never get."

He put the sheet on the table and looked at Alex.

"That's how the show begins. How would you see the first scene?"

"A light?" Judie guessed.

"Scott, would you please answer Judie?" Alex asked.

"I'm fine with what Judie said."

"Travis?"

"A light and a phantom…the illusion that dies into the shade…feeling something for someone you know nothing about anymore…the anxiety turns into *Angst*."

"Please, Judie, would you mind continuing?"

"I want you. I hate you. The more I try to run away, the more I miss you… What remains is faded memory; it's a glow that slowly dies…"

"Any comment?"

She shrugged.

"Travis?"

He felt the importance of the moment and the expectations of the audience.

"The point at issue is to accept or not accept love in your own reality… essence against existence…to be able to think of ourselves as we do of someone else…to be able to detach from someone who made us suffer. We create our moral revenge to regain our own dignity, while pushing that of the other into the darkness."

Judie and Scott were speechless at Travis's ability. They were still thinking of Travis as 'just a tramp' with no real idea where he had come from.

"Keep going," Alex said to Judie.

"I think of you…and the memory remains of a ghost that hides again, for not returning what it stole…I hope that one day you will stop, think, and return what you took away from me. But let it happen soon; otherwise, I'll turn my back on you, and I will run away forever…"

"Come on, Judie, concentrate and imagine. You must feel these words and think you are on the stage. What do you see?"

"It's tough. The verses you have highlighted are so powerful they could become scenes themselves."

"No, Judie. That's where you're wrong. These are not scenes but emotions. Let's forget for a moment about seeing things for what they appear to be, but let's try to put on the stage what we feel deep inside. What could the last verses you read make you imagine?"

Judie found it difficult to reply. It was the first time that someone had asked her to transform verses into a scene. She was holding the sheet but could not imagine anything different from what she had read.

"The defeat, Judie. The defeat! Blaming someone we are no longer able to face, as we feel betrayed, deprives us of our purest sentiment of love. Can't you see the desperate attempt to overturn a situation, where we are hammered from the very first moment? Can't you see the hidden threat, where it says, *'But let it happen soon; otherwise, I'll turn my back on you, and I'll run away forever…'* Can't you see the despair, the drama of this person, who can just menace without addressing, without seeing, without knowing, yet hoping unavailingly that his words will one day be heard by the one who stole his feelings? It's the revenge, Judie. All these words are said to threaten and not hurt, hoping someone will come back. The instinct of survival is wishing for what we can't see, hoping not to drown in the darkness."

Judie remained silent. Alex's words echoed intensely and eventually made her 'feel' the scene.

"I think I understand now. It is not a matter of the character I see in the play; it is his emotional state. So we could stage something that would let me feel the same emotions and not necessarily the same characters that I see described in the monologue."

"You got it!" said Alex slapping the table. At the end they all started to understand. "Keep going, Travis."

"That's life. It can be nice, it can be sad. It might empower you with love…deceive you and look at you with its detachment…hunt you while you run and try to hide. What are you expecting when you stop and think about it? That life comes back to you and asks to be forgiven? That night I slept beside the river…I listened to the

silence, I talked…and I asked it why it never spoke with me before…And the voice of silence began to whisper…I heard sounds that could not be…"

"Scott, want to keep going?"

There was no way for him to say no, nor could he have refused. He didn't want to be left behind as the only one who could not understand.

"This is a thought. The person is meditating about his life. I guess that, yes, he is trying to say that one doesn't need to wait for the things to happen but goes and gets them before it is too late."

"Exactly! Perfect!" Alex said, slapping the table again. Elaborate on the last sentence."

It was getting tough, but Scott felt that he was competing with Judie.

"The silence that falls on me…I begin to understand the reality, the things I haven't noticed before."

"Come on, Scott, you are getting close! Don't look at the words anymore, but feel them inside!"

Scott shrugged and gave up.

"Travis?"

"Silence is a metaphor. It represents the abstraction, the effort of the mind to get rid of the daily constraints to achieve the truth. It is a stage of purity where there is no contamination, only thought."

Judie looked at him, ravished, and Joel stopped drawing on his notebook. Alex was happy, as Travis was now his reason for pride.

"Once touched on the perfection, the mind frees from the physical impurities beginning to see the light at the end of the tunnel. The true values resurface, condemning the false one, the one who runs away to the eternal darkness for good," Travis continued.

"Is all that clear, now?"

"Yes," Judie quickly replied, "I would definitely say yes. Can I continue?"

He could not refuse. He saw her involved, identifying herself with the moment of the show's origination, and if she acted with the same passion she was now showing, she would become a star.

"You were a shade with the illusion of a glow…I should have been calm…I should have waited, to understand the things the river tried to say. I would have learned to choose, I could have avoided mistakes…"

"Can you follow?" The question came from Scott. He was almost resigned to just simply showing up in the room. Acting was something natural for him, but feeling with the intensity Alex could…well, that was not him.

"Can I try to explain?" No one objected. Judie was tense, her concentration was at an apex and likely exceeding it. "The illusion, the scarce consideration for the things that really count, to let ourselves be carried away more by what appears than by what actually is…" she paused.

"Perfect, Judie…try to elaborate a bit more now."

"Why, Alex? Am I saying something wrong?"

"Absolutely not, but the last part…"

He laid the sheet on the table and turned to Travis.

"If we could eventually succeed in not being involved in anything that surrounds us, if we could really evaluate an event, not for what it appears to be to us but in isolation, yet within a context where each event of our existence is inevitably connected to another one, we would be able to judge the positives and the drawbacks of any of our actions. It is the detachment I told you about…the ability to let the events surround us without being concerned by our emotions," Travis said.

Alex looked at Judie and Scott. Joel took a chair and sat at the table.

"Let me continue," Alex said and took up a page to read from. *"An old man I will remember…to tell another fairy tale…It was a dark light that made him blind and threw him into his loneliness…The same dark light has now blinded me…"*

Alex was playing with his own creation. Scott raised his hand.

"The contact with reality."

It wasn't enough to impress Alex.

"Last night, Travis gave me his own interpretation. I have to admit that I loved it, and although Scott's answer is not completely wrong, I would like you to listen to the same things he told me." Then he looked at Travis. "The guys are waiting."

Travis took the paper from Alex, and Judie realized his hand was trembling. He tried to stay calm, just as he used to do with his students when he taught.

"This meeting with…an old man like many others…like a drop of that river…is the materialization of something magic. It is an event that just happens once in a lifetime." He paused and breathed deeply, as if he were living what he had just read. "It is the moment when Destiny lets him perceive the last page of the story he wrote for anyone of us…the sad life of the old man. The future we would likely face, should we not decide to stop staring at that light that makes us blind and confused about real values. And I…" he said emotionally, "and I see in these verses another story…my story. I am that old man, the same old man who was made blind and who was forced to live under a bridge for six years, continuing to run behind a dream transformed into an illusion by that light, hiding his blindness in the darkness, the truth he was not able to see…"

Travis couldn't speak any longer. He dried a tear and gave the paper back to Alex. It was Alex's turn to conclude.

"I hope you got the message. What I'm planning to stage is Travis's life."

The investiture. Had he picked a name for the meeting at his place, it couldn't have been any better. He could not read their minds, but he didn't care. Once again, he decided his own way. Travis wasn't aware, as no one was aware that day, the decision was made at that very moment. There couldn't be any better story for his drama than what had inspired the monologue. Travis, and only Travis, could represent the character he was planning to stage.

Judie and Scott turned defensive. The beautiful fairy tale of the old man under a bridge was over. Travis was now an enemy, in all and for all. Judie remained emotionless, dumb, while Scott was bothered by not being able to better interpret the verses. What a bad impression for a graduated in dramatic arts, especially if given in front of a tramp.

"Did you already choose the title?" Joel asked.

"Yes, *The Dark Light*. And I hope that it will shine when we will act on stage."

Although it was a perfect title, it made Judie and Scott's envy surface.

"I bet Travis chose it," Scott said sarcastically.

"Of course he did! I really can't see anyone in here more qualified than he is. The monologue is about his life, not about ours!"

"And what about the play for the show? Who's working on it now?"

"We are," Alex said.

"Understood," said a disconsolate Scott. "I thought I could help."

"Thanks, but that's Travis' story, and no one knows it better than he does."

"I don't want to sound arrogant, but what background does he have to help you out and develop the idea?" Scott asked.

That was the moment of revelation. It was better like that, Alex thought. Everyone had to know it sooner or later.

"He has a Doctorate in Philosophy. Is that enough?"

Joel, Scott, and Judie looked at Travis. He was still, with his usual sweet expression and intent on writing something on the blank sheet before him. Alex's words didn't touch him, since he didn't need anyone to remind him of who he was. He just was.

*　*　*

"Who could have imagined that? A Doctorate in Philosophy," Judie said soon after she and Scott left Alex's place.

"I couldn't," Scott said. "I wouldn't have bet a penny. How could I have imagined something like that when you know that the person who sits before you has spent six years under a bridge?"

"Impossible. We couldn't remotely suppose that he wasn't a tramp six years ago," Judie said.

"Had we known it in time…but it came out of the blue," Scott said.

"But tell me…what do you think about the whole story? Can it be a success?" Judie asked. Scott paused and seemed to meditate.

"It will be Travis' life; that's what Alex said. I just hope it will be interesting enough to justify the effort we're putting into it," Scott said.

Judie smiled. "Stop being so pessimistic, Scott. The fact that he came from under a bridge and into a house is already great material. If you then add a Doctorate in Philosophy, and who knows what else on top of that, I guess we could really be dealing with one of the most original shows in quite some time."

"A monologue and a drama based on a true story. By the way, what do you think?" Scott asked. He was looking at Judie.

"Great. And then, hearing the words from Travis, the one who inspired Alex, has really been something special."

"I agree," Scott said.

They had just arrived at Camden tube station when Scott looked worried.

"What's wrong with you now?" Judie asked him.

"We are all jobless. Alex fell out with Joe, and he doesn't seem that worried that we don't even have a theatre. It will be difficult to produce the show during this season. Perhaps during the next one."

"I agree. Had we had a manager, someone who could find us an open place, at night, under the stars…Can you imagine how beautiful it would be? *The Dark Light* in the moonlight…It would be a perfect slogan!"

Contagious Judie. She succeeded in making Scott smile, and that was all she wanted. A gloomy attitude within a group with no money and no theatre could destroy their dream. And no one could allow that.

"I'm home," Scott announced, as they approached his flat.

"I'll call you tomorrow, then?" Judie said. "The usual coffee?"

"Okay," Scott said. "Give me five."

She opened her hand and slapped her palm against Scott's. That was the way they had to be—one heart and one soul. It was the only way they would have a chance.

* * *

The work, in the meantime, was going ahead as scheduled. Travis began to open up a bit more, to talk about his life, and to continually refer to the illusions that life gave him: deceit, betrayal, and *volte-faces*. His memories were full of bitterness and regrets, but at least there was space for different emotions in his present life. The two months he'd spent with Alex felt like this was just the beginning, when Destiny decided to sort out things and apologize. Travis did not want to think about it. It would be useless and cruel to deceive himself again.

He never mentioned anything about Nicholas, preferring to remain vague. He just told him that he and his wife had two children, but he talked about his students, the debates he had with them when he was teaching, and his eyes shone. They went back to South Bank quite often, as Travis couldn't detach from that bench. It was a piece of his existence, of his desperation and, now, of his new hope.

"I wish you knew how beautiful it is to stay here at night, seated, looking beyond the other side of the river…you can see the city lights that invite you whenever they shine. How I wish you could feel at least a part of the emotions I feel."

Alex could. He could feel them through Travis's words and see them through his eyes. They stood up every now and then, walked along the river and back again to the same bench.

"You seriously can't sit on a different bench?" Alex asked, and then Travis looked at him, smiling, like a father does with his son when he speaks about the things he will learn from life.

"No, Alex, I could never do that. I waited for six years to meet Destiny again, and it met me on this bench. It would be nice to talk a bit about ourselves, about what I wished it hadn't taken away from me and about what it put aside for me, instead."

* * *

The days went by. In the morning, Travis talked and Alex took notes, and in the evening, Alex gave him back the words translated into a play, waiting for his comment. Spring had just arrived and those hateful rainy days began to eventually take longer pauses.

"Why don't you have a girlfriend?" Travis asked him one day.

His question was totally unexpected, when Alex was about to bite into a sandwich.

"I don't think this is the best moment to start thinking about it," Alex said.

He sounded a bit harsh, but Travis didn't seem to be bothered.

"You're probably right. To think and to feel is a very complex thing," Travis said. "One often tends to exclude the other."

His words made sense, and Alex needed to talk. "Do you think I should have a girlfriend?"

"You don't have to, ever. If you don't find the right one for you, you better stay alone."

"I agree."

Alex had found her. Travis didn't know, but Alex had lost her forever. He shrugged and kept enjoying the sandwich. A woman passed by just when Alex bent down to pick up a tissue from the bag left on the floor. He turned and saw her entering *the Wharf*. She had very short hair and a slender figure. The way she moved brought back to his memory the illusion of love while a growing anxiety started to take over his body. He couldn't see her face. His curiosity told him to leave the bench where he sat and follow her to see who she was. His mind told him not to. *You are a hopeless case,* Alex thought of himself.

* * *

A week later, the guys were back at Alex's place. They spent the whole afternoon reviewing the draft together, to make sure the various passages flowed, and to exchange feedback and impressions. They wrapped up a few hours later. Judie was the first to put down the draft on the table.

"So?"

"It takes me. It's exciting!" Judie looked at Travis. "I feel so sorry for what you went through."

"Scott?"

"Great hook with the monologue."

They had just finished reading six years of Travis's life in barely two hours. Travis sat on his chair pretending to be absorbed in reading Alex's draft.

"Destiny realized he was wrong at the end," Joel said.

He was not part of the group, but he had followed the story since the very beginning, and he felt as if he were sharing it as well. Had he not talked to Travis that day, there would have been no show.

"Destiny is like a tailor who doesn't see," Travis said.

"Should we put them in the play, Alex?" Scott asked.

There was no mockery in his words, but Alex got the impression that Scott was playing with Travis's emotions.

"Stop it! It could happen to you one day. I suggest you not make fun of Destiny. Anyway, let's get organized quickly. Scott, I need your help."

"I'm all ears."

"What chance do we have to stage the show down in South Bank?" Alex asked.

"Zero," Scott said.

"Better than I thought, then," Alex replied.

It definitely wasn't the best way to feed their enthusiasm.

"Do you guys know any agent who could let us work before the end of the season?"

"Never used agents. I've always done it by myself," Judie said.

"Joel?"

He also shook his head.

"When do you think it will be ready?" Joel asked.

"Three, four days at the latest. It needs more pace, and I want a few passages to flow better," Alex said.

"Do you miss your son?" It was Judie who spoke. None of them was thinking about the draft. Travis remained silent, almost regretting that he had helped Alex let his memories resurface. Nicholas was his greatest secret, and jealousy rose up in his chest for sharing it with other people.

"It's amazing. I really don't know what else to say." Judie was still holding the draft and her emotion was real.

* * *

The work was ready within Alex's expected deadline. Each of them received a copy and each had the task of talking to theatres to propose the work. They all met ten days later at Alex's place.

"Nothing to do." Scott was the first to talk.

"They guaranteed their interest for the September schedule," Judie said.

"Thanks, but we're not interested. We can find more than one theatre available for September."

"Maybe there is one," Joel said.

Everyone turned his or her attention to him.

"Really?" Alex asked.

"Yes, but we have to give up all our rights and have at least one of their actors on stage."

"I'm not interested," Alex said. "This is our work; giving it to someone else would just throw it away."

"But no one is available to produce it with Travis's signature," Scott said. "He doesn't have any past and, as such, he is not in demand."

"He's right. We better think about a September schedule."

"That's too far away," Alex objected. "We have to put it on stage before the end of the season."

"Sorry, Alex, but that seems impossible. Unless you have an idea," Scott said.

"I can't get over it. If Conrad hadn't persisted in having it that means that we've done something good."

"Are you thinking of calling him?" Judie asked.

Alex looked at Judie, as if she had just stabbed him in the back. "I'd rather give up writing than go to Conrad."

She glanced down and Scott made a brusque movement, almost one of rage. "It hurts. Things have to be so bloody difficult anytime it's about me!"

Scott's reaction was amiss and clearly dictated by desperation.

"It's not about you, Scott," Alex said. "It's about a show we don't have a sponsor for."

He tried hard to stay as calm as possible. Scott and Judie were all he had, and if there were any misunderstanding that overpowered their friendship, they would have also blown his dreams away. Joel and Judie looked at Alex, silently following the scene, and the tension created in that very moment could divide them or unite them forever.

"I need to work!" Scott said.

They all needed to work. Alex knew it and could not take the risk of losing Scott.

"Why don't you go back to Conrad?" Scott said, echoing Judie from a moment earlier. "Maybe if you give him the work he can send us on stage quickly."

"Because this is Travis's story, and it was Destiny who let us know him."

Scott bit his lip and looked around, trying to gain some support. He first looked at Judie, then at Joel, and then at Travis.

"Beautiful words, but things don't change at the end. I have to pay my rent and maintain my younger brother. I'm the only one who works, and if I don't get something in my pocket at the end of the month, I will end up like a tramp in the middle of a street."

Travis glanced down, and Scott realized he had just offended him.

"I am not speaking about you, Travis. I know that no one else knows the sense of what I just said better than you do, but I must think about myself."

The happening is concealed, unobserved, in the perfect harmony of things…'

Destiny whispered those words to Alex. He turned to Scott, without tension, but conscious that it was the moment to behave as a leader.

"We have a chance. Destiny is giving it to us. It doesn't talk, but it presents chances disguised as difficult moments. It's on us to understand when the moment has come, and the moment is now. We all win together, Scott, not on our own, but if we stay united, we will take this chance." Then he put his hands on the table and leaned towards him, not to give him the chance to look somewhere else. "If, within one week, we don't find a theatre, I'll give you my flat. You will never end up in the middle of a street."

Determination. That was what the group still lacked. They all needed to have the same will, the same drive, the same hunger. They needed the hunger that Travis had in making a new life and the drive that Alex had to bring his drama on stage. He never stopped staring at Scott; he wanted to read inside of him and feel the effect of those words in the heart of the weakest ring of the chain.

"Fine, Alex. One week, but I won't wait any longer," Scott said, and it was a challenge.

Alex got what he wanted—more time and more hope.

"We all agree, then?"

Scott nodded and Judie did the same. They were just waiting to receive Alex's instructions.

"We will start tomorrow. We divide the city into three parts, one for each of us."

"What about me?" Joel was looking at Alex.

"Do you want to help?" Alex asked.

"Yes, boss!"

"You start with the theatres."

"But we already tried to approach them," Judie said.

"Sure, I know, but now we'll go there again to knock at their doors, and if they tell us to come by later, we wait outside, until we speak with those who can decide. Only then I will accept the verdict."

That was the way the adventure had to kick off—fearlessly. Alex was acting to appear as strong and confident as he could; he was also feeling tired and perplexed. He had never thought he would have to lead something like this. He thought for a moment of *Don Quixote* against the windmill, but there were enough similarities to let the comparison hold. *The happening is concealed, unobserved, in the perfect harmony of things…* Alex thought, once again, about the sentence he had read in that little old book and the event he had been waiting for since then, and he suddenly realized that, in that moment, Destiny was there, nearby, observing him.

* * *

Alex's enthusiasm let them fly. They walked around London from top to bottom and were not afraid of asking and waiting. They all had the drive Alex wished to see. They met again on the fourth day at Alex's flat, and they all began to tell what they had done. Judie was the first to talk.

"Nine theatres, four of them agreed to meet us again. They would like one of their actors to try the monologue to see the effect on stage. There are three more left."

She thought she had done a good job, and so Alex did.

"Did they schedule a day for us to meet in the diary?"

"I have to call them tomorrow, and if they give us the green light, they'll try it in the afternoon. Fingers crossed."

It was going well, and at least had he failed, he would not have had any remorse. It was his turn to talk, and it was obvious to everyone to expect to hear better news than what they were able to do on their own. But the theatres he had approached had all refused. Too big…too ambitious…too wretched. He didn't have any luck.

"I have two answers. I should go back to them in a couple of days and try the monologue and only one scene. That's all they asked me to do."

It wasn't true, but he felt he had to lie to keep their drive going. If they had perceived his discouragement, they would have all left the field. And this could not happen, since there were still three days left on Scott's deadline.

"That's great," Judie said.

Her eyes were glowing, and the smile on Scott's face now appeared more often. He closed his eyes, and if Destiny existed, that was the moment to show him it did. In the following two days, Judie and Scott ended their theatre hunting. They had gotten a couple of promises, but nothing more, and Scott's enthusiasm quickly lost steam. Judie soon realized that and called Alex.

"He's giving up. He doesn't want to come around anymore. He has his head in the clouds, and I don't know what else to do."

Alex didn't want the dream to end. It would have been wrong to throw in the towel, now that the drama was ready to go. So they all met again the evening of the day before the last of Scott's week to summarize the progress of theatre hunting. Judie put a letter on the table confirming the invitation to go into serious discussion for a scheduled start in September, but Scott continually shook his head. He had stopped believing, and within twenty-four hours he would be able to dedicate himself completely to his own things again. He felt a bit sad about the idea, but there was nothing he could do other than what he had actually done.

"And with this, I am done," Judie said.

They all looked at Alex, but there was no smile or enthusiasm on his face, either. For as long as he tried, he could not make the pretence continue.

"Maybe we have one," he said.

Why not? All in all he still had one more day and it did not make any sense to give up before the end had come.

"Do you have a promise?" Scott asked him.

"They will decide tomorrow. They listened to the monologue and tried one scene."

Joel followed distractedly, but he knew Alex so well to perceive that he didn't know who else to pray to. And his support was all for him.

"We just need to wait for the last few hours," Alex said.

They ended around midnight, but the atmosphere didn't glimmer with any sign of hope. Scott was distractedly chatting with Joel, while the enthusiasm ran out of the window together with the smoke of Judie's cigarette. Alex and Travis were the only ones who still believed in miracles.

The morning after, at around eight, Alex's mobile phone rang.

"Are you still working on your project?"

It was Joe. They met for lunch somewhere in Camden, and as soon as he saw him, Alex quickly understood that something had happened.

"I'll be meeting with the guys tonight. Can you come over?" Alex asked.

* * *

It was eight at night and they all met at Alex's place again. Joe did not show up or give him his news.

"I'm sorry, Alex, but there is nothing to do. No one can help us and, at this stage, we all believe that the only sensible thing to do is to give the monologue to Conrad."

It was the end, because that sentence had just one answer. But strangely, Alex didn't seem to be worried at all.

"It's nice to see you relaxed," Scott added. "The important thing is to know we have done our best."

"Right," Alex said.

And in the meantime, Alex kept on smiling and looking at his notes. It was around nine when the doorbell rang. Alex knew who was about to come in.

When they all saw him, it was like seeing a ghost. Scott and Judie jumped to their feet.

"Joe?" They called his name in unison. It had been ages since they'd heard from him, and the last thing they expected was to see him again that night at Alex's place.

"I guess Joe is here to tell us something," Alex said.

Joe didn't have a nice expression, but then, looking at his guys, he felt the old, great enthusiasm.

"Conrad and I just fell out."

There was a moment of embarrassing silence. Then Scott, the one detached the most, spoke again. "What does this mean?"

"I am out of my own theatre. I sold him all that I had."

He was smiling, though. Unless he had turned into a madman, he had something else to say.

"Why that face?" Joel asked.

Joe turned and looked at Joel with an even bigger smile, while the excitement was quickly regaining life. "The art director of the Regent's Park Theatre is a great friend of mine," he said.

They stood up again and the notes flew all over the place. Judie's cigarette dropped from her lips, and Joel took the chance to grab her chair and sit in her place.

"And it happens that he greatly appreciated the play that he just finished reading tonight."

"So?" Judie could not stand it any longer. One more minute and her anxiety would have exploded.

"The show will be performed next month, but just for one night, out of schedule. This, of course, is if you all agree."

They raised their hands in the air and shouted for joy. Alex looked at them and eventually smiled. Destiny was there, right next to him, and it had listened to his prayer.

TWENTY-NINE

"Just that. Perfect."

He had just started the drawing, but he strove to see its completion ahead of time, since that was the way *Kandinsky* used to do. He spoke out loud and looked at the white canvas before him. Then he grabbed the pencil and began to draw lines. Nicholas didn't remotely know what painting was. He had never taken classes, and didn't have any talent, but he persisted in drawing sketches on canvas, as if he was a great painter. Late at night, the canvas had barely changed colour. It had just become darker, and no one would have understood it was the portrait of a woman. He remained still, standing before his painting, contemplating it with infinite love. A muddle of lines, flavoured here and there by some coloured spots…his masterpiece.

He held his breath and fell on his knees, and the dream became a vortex of indistinct reflexes, of glares undoing each other and of two green fires at the end. It all ended on the canvas, in those sketches passed off as art. Suddenly, he had a sharp headache, a very strong pain.

"Don't let yourself go, Nicholas. You could just hurt yourself," the doctor used to tell him.

He puffed, then the anxiety attacked him, and his veins began to tighten in his temples. He entered the bathroom in a sweat, opened the cabinet, and swallowed the pill.

"Well done, Nicholas. Don't ever forget to take that pill," the doctor used to tell him.

The lights faded and the vortex pushed him back to the surface. The emotion was still on his face, and was reflected in the mirror before him. He leaned against the wall with his hands trying to calm his breath, and the grip that was strangling him finally loosened. He entered the room and contemplated his painting again, the attempt to transform his madness into love for her. He closed his eyes and finally dreamt.

* * *

"It was his return to Russia that converted him to the geometric forms. You can see it well from the painting," Nicholas said to Lisa.

They had met again at the Tate Modern, officially unexpectedly, but in reality with the deepest hope to bump into each other again. Lisa and Nicholas were standing in front of *'Swinging'*, a painting *Kandinsky* had made during his second stay in Germany.

"What does it mean?" she asked him.

"The symbolism of the geometric forms, the calm after the emotional storm when his first years in Germany ended in the explosion of the thousand colours. Look at how clean and balanced the image is."

The more Nicholas talked, the more Lisa felt touched. The passion with which he described his feelings in front of that masterpiece made her fall in love with *Kandinsky* even before understanding his style. Just silence stood between her and the painting.

"It gives me a sense of peace," she said.

He smiled at her. He wanted to listen to her words, look at her eyes, and read the same passion in her. "The perfect balance," he said.

"And the lines?" she asked, trying to follow his explanation.

"Rhythm and dynamic force. They push it high in the sky, towards the universe, beyond anything that exists…like a piece of music. You can only appreciate it if you can feel it inside, deep in your soul."

She listened to his words, delighted. She had never met anyone like him, so distant from all that appeared around him.

"How long have you loved art so much?"

"Just a few years," he said.

"But you sound as if you've been studying art since you were born."

Nicholas was happy. He just wanted to enjoy every single second he spent with her and, in the meantime, he was trying to catch her eye, her gestures, and her expression of joy, which he stored in his soul. He would have freed them later, in front of the canvas, a painting just for her, and he was dreaming, as he had never met a woman like Lisa. He took her hand while going down the stairs, and she looked at him, with her green eyes shining and revealing emotions. They walked outside the Tate, along the Thames, without talking. He was so different from Klaus.

"Here we are," she said as they arrived at *the Wharf*.

"Do you want me to pass by to pick you up when you finish?"

Her smile looked like the sun.

"At eleven, sharp."

"I'll be here then."

He stepped away, not wanting to leave. She remained still, contemplating his tough, carved features and his deep eyes, until her wristwatch told her to go.

Behind the bar, in her working uniform, she lost the sense of time. She just thought of the moment she would see him again, the waiting, and that strange emotion she felt whenever she saw the *Kandinsky*. The first time it had been by chance, and Destiny had dealt two dice on the table and when two similar numbers had come out it was hers and Nicholas's. Crazy player Destiny…it let you start dreaming, then kicked you out of your bed when the night was not over yet, and sent you back to sleep during the daytime. Alex, Klaus, Nicholas were three seasons of a crazy year. She glanced through the window, and she wondered where he would have waited for her. Maybe in the moonlight, on the bank of the river, where he would have kissed her. She no longer remembered a kiss that could taste of love. Silly Lisa, but what she was thinking about? About another illusion, another pain that could leave wounds in her soul, and about a love story that could never be born?

"Lisa! There is plenty to do and you keep daydreaming!"

The clients were waiting, hungry, and she was still lost in her dreams. She worked a bit longer and then she locked herself in the bathroom to get changed. No one was walking outside at that time at night, and she was worried. She turned towards Waterloo Bridge, then towards the Oxo Gallery, and she stopped at the rotunda overlooking the river. She had never paid attention to London at night. Beyond Blackfriars, Saint Paul Cathedral dominated, with its white stone popping out of the darkness of the night. To the left, there was the Savoy. She had already been there with Klaus and the thought made her look in the opposite direction. An old man was sitting on a bench just a few metres from her and she tried to understand who he was. *Oh yes!* It was the old man who used to come to the bar in the morning. How could she not recognize him? She had the idea to sit on the bench near him. She saw him turning, and she was sure that he also understood who she was.

Eleven fifteen. She looked at the restaurant and then all around it, but she did not see Nicholas. The street lamps were on and the old man was still on the bench.

Eleven twenty. No sign of Nicholas. Strange he was late, strange that the only times he was on time was always by chance. The old man sat motionless, looking at Saint Paul.

Eleven thirty. The tension grabbed her hand, but where was Nicholas's hand? Lisa stood up. Her mind was full of thoughts about Nicholas, about her date, and the desire she had to look into his eyes. And in the meantime, the old man had no thoughts, as he didn't have any date at eleven at night.

"Do you mind if I sit next to you?" she asked him.

He turned and she finally looked at him.

She saw him smiling, as he understood who she was. She sat next to him, without bothering him; she just wanted to talk while waiting for Nicholas.

A quarter to midnight. Maybe Nicholas wasn't going to come. The old man and Lisa were sitting together, without talking, but lost in their own thoughts.

"He didn't come?"

"I beg your pardon?"

"He didn't come?"

Sure, it wasn't difficult to figure out what a girl could be doing sitting on a bench at that time in the night.

"It seems so."

And in the meantime, they both looked at the river.

"What drives you to stay here?"

What an indiscreet question! Lisa thought. "I was waiting for a friend," Lisa replied.

"Go home. He will call you."

She looked at him bemused.

"He doesn't even have my number."

You are talking to him! But what are you doing? Are you getting acquainted with a tramp on the river at midnight? Lisa thought.

"If he wants you, he will know where to find you."

His voice was warm, reassuring. She would have wanted to come closer and spend more time with him.

"And you? What are you doing so late on this bench?"

"I look at the Thames, I feel the water that flows underneath, and I count the lights on the other side of the river. I have many things to do, as you can see."

He turned towards Waterloo and then again towards the Tate. It was vain now. The old man sat no farther than a metre from her and spoke with her without looking at her eyes.

"Do you come here every night?" she asked.

He had spent many nights there. Time no longer made any sense to him.

"Hoping it doesn't pour rain," he said.

Lisa smiled. "Don't you have a family?"

She just wanted to talk and not to waste any more time in useless waiting.

"My family is all you can see."

"I am afraid I don't get it."

"The night, the wind caressing my face, the river, the lights, this bench, my loneliness…"

"I meant family, like wife and kids," Lisa said.

He turned towards her.

"Your true family is who shares the bad moments with you, without leaving you alone."

"I'm sorry," Lisa said. "I didn't mean to enter this conversation."

"This family has never let me down," the old man said.

His answer made her think.

"Have you spent many nights like this?"

"Six years."

Lisa looked at the river. It was dark, of the same colour as the night that had just started. How difficult it was to talk now. A failed date, a broken spell, and now the old man. She turned towards him again. Madness, just madness could push her to stay on the bank of the river at that time of the night.

"Are you going to sleep on the bench?"

The inertia of that strange moment led her to ask him that question. Nicholas was out of her mind and, at least in that moment, it wasn't him who filled her thoughts, yet that strange person who loved the night. He nodded. "I would like to. It is a beautiful night to remember."

"Where do you live?"

"At a friend's that Destiny wanted me to meet."

"You had great luck."

"Yes, I am a guest at his place, but tonight I want to stay at mine."

One o'clock in the morning. Late for Lisa, late for everything.

"Are you coming to the bar tomorrow? I'll buy you a coffee. I start at seven."

She could see him well now. His eyes were deep and intense, just like

Nicholas's.

"I'll come by with pleasure."

Lisa stood up. It was time to go.

"My name is Lisa."

"I am Travis."

"I'll see you tomorrow, Travis."

"Yes, Lisa, see you tomorrow."

She disappeared in the night. The same night that had swallowed him for six long years.

He stood up a few minutes after Lisa had left and walked towards Hungerford Bridge. He wanted to see the place again where he had spent his last years. He looked at the river and saw the lights shining; he went down the stairs and arrived under the bridge. Someone was sleeping wrapped in a cloth. Travis went up the steps and went closer. The young man lay on a side and he had to be pretty much Alex's age. Travis turned towards the river and saw the light seep through the pillars lighting up part of the bridge. Another life was going wasted. Emotion made his eyes glow, and he knelt down trying to give the young man all the strength he had.

"Don't give up, son, don't give up."

He turned and went away, drowning in the darkness of the night.

* * *

One hour left before his date, one hour that seemed never to pass. Anytime he thought about her eyes, her smile, he could not keep control. He felt bad, and the pill couldn't help him more than that. He was lovesick. He breathed heavily, with one hand on the easel and the other on his leg. The spots spanned around the floor and he feared going mad. He entered the bathroom, grabbed the bottle, and swallowed one more pill, confident it would be enough. He had to stay calm or otherwise the pressure he had in his soul would explode. He opened his mouth and looked at his throat in the mirror while the pressure was mounting. Where was his painting? Where was that beautiful painting?

"Go, Nicholas, grab the brush and paint," the doctor used to tell him.

What a good doctor. He was always right and knew the world of madmen better than anyone else, and he knew how to make Nicholas feel well. He grabbed the brush and went closer to the canvas. But where was the music? He could not begin without it. He turned on the stereo and he felt happy to listen to it. Yes, now everything was perfect; he could start painting and feel emotions again. He closed his eyes and brought the brush near the canvas.

The shivers inflamed his skin like blasts, as he was creating in that very moment a piece of love, a piece of hate, a piece of light, and a piece of shade. All pieces he had in his soul and all part of a soul that now was in pieces. And the canvas filled up with colours, with no pattern, following the desperation he had in his heart. How could he have destroyed everything, kick his family, and condemn himself to madness? Why had he allowed a sick colour to ruin the beauty of a painting? He hated himself, he hated his body, and he hated the tremendous oppression that had pierced his brain for years. Just the painting was left. Just the music. Just the canvas, a few brushes, and a bunch of colours.

"You are very ill, Nicholas," the doctor used to tell him.

Twisted lines, colours that looked like spots and that made the whole canvas sticky. His madness vomited onto the canvas. He felt sympathy for that painting and felt pity for himself.

"You are ill, Nicholas."

It was his voice this time, and not the one of the good doctor. He let himself down on the floor, with the brushes in his hands and with his hands trying to wipe out his tears. He opened his arms and remained still, staring at his beloved ceiling.

"Ceiling, I beg you, fall down on me and make me die!"

The ceiling was above him and was looking at him. No one had asked it anything similar before.

Ten thirty in the evening. Half an hour away from his date. A panic attack overwhelmed him; he opened his eyes wide, stood back on his feet, and walked back and forth within the little room, smashing his head on the wall. He could not meet her like this, with the remorse feeding his madness. He could not meet her like this, without giving her that painting. He could not meet her, but he desperately wanted to see her.

It was about eleven. Nicholas remained nearby the Oxo Gallery from where he could see the restaurant where she worked. He was nervous, and many times he was on the verge of going back home. If that tension had left him free for a second, he would have maybe found the courage to walk towards her, say hello and look around. He walked two steps backwards and began to walk towards the Tate Modern, but then he stopped. Lisa was waiting for him.

You must go to her, Nicholas.

Yes, he would have gone and told her he was ill. He felt strong, convinced, then came the anxiety again, and his footsteps that were confident became doubtful, then uncertain, and then heavy like the concrete.

The railing, where was the railing? *To your right, Nicholas. It's there, just a metre away.*

He leaned with all his body weight trying to stop the tremor that was shaking his legs. He felt horrible and, in the meantime, Lisa was waiting to see that confident person again, the person who gave her the calm she had always looked for.

"The other one, please, you must be the other one! She doesn't want to see you like that. Damn, Nicholas, she is waiting for you!" He spoke out loud and people avoided him like he had swine flu. Poor Nicholas, he couldn't choose a worse moment to feel so bad.

Eleven thirty. He was there, hidden in the darkness, and did not stop looking at her for a second. He stood up and sat on the bench where an old man was seated.

Did you see? She already betrayed you! She is with someone else, and you were just a half hour late. She doesn't deserve your painting. She doesn't deserve your love! You did well, Nicholas, not to go to her. Well done, I am really happy, now you can go home satisfied!

Yes, he could go, but jealousy kept him there and didn't allow him to go.

Midnight had passed. Lisa and that old man were talking and looked as if they were long-time friends. His legs stopped hurting, and the tension gave him a break. He breathed deeply and felt happy not to feel that darn pressure.

Thanks, Nicholas, thanks for coming back, I really thought to die. Are you ready now? Do you feel comfortable to go to her and apologize? No, come on! Don't be silly, now it's too late! You are an hour late and she is speaking with another person! No, it doesn't seem to be her lover, Nicholas; perhaps he's just someone she already knew. Yes, Nicholas, I am sure about that. Don't worry, you are just running the risk of feeling bad again and let your ill side come back. Just try to think about your painting, the art, Kandinsky who waits for you at the gallery, and about all the beautiful colours you have already put on the canvas.

Lisa stood up, and Nicholas saw them both shaking hands. Yes, they were friends. Otherwise, she would not do that. How beautiful to be back to normal, how beautiful to come back home happy with just a pill!

One o'clock in the morning. It was late for Nicholas, late for Lisa, late for everyone. He left and he thought for a moment to stop her, apologize for the many thoughts and the words never said. She had left and there was nothing to do anymore.

I, Destiny

He found the courage to walk when he saw her disappear. Slowly, step after step, towards that bench. That man was there, and he just wanted to see who he was. It didn't matter whether it was late now, and if he was dying to go sleep. He walked more decisively, hoping to get there before he left, but he saw him stand and leave.

Travis turned around having sensed someone's eyes on him, and then he kept walking firmly towards Hungerford Bridge.

Nicholas had followed him from a good distance. It was impossible for Travis to see him, but he preferred not to take any risks. Nicholas saw him passing under Waterloo Bridge, stopping for a second along the river, and looking towards the lights of London on the other side of the bank. Nicholas did the same moves, and in the meantime, he was so close to him.

Travis stopped before the stairs that led under the bridge. Nicholas was several metres behind. Nicholas saw him turning, but could not recognize him, so he went closer, and his heart began to beat faster. He was afraid and remained nearby the stairs. From there, he could easily see what the man was doing, without being seen. A tramp lay on the floor in a niche that seemed to be like an old main door. The man knelt down and it seemed as if he caressed the tramp.

Nicholas was behind the curtains, looking at the scene. He saw him standing, turning towards the other side of the river and looking through the pillars. He could have been around sixty, with a face aged by the time and with a soul saddened by a life that should have been miserable with him. The lights of those sad street lamps lit up his face and Nicholas could eventually see his eyes.

THIRTY

The sky was grey, and from time to time raindrops fell from above. The guys were completely absorbed by the rehearsal, so Travis thought to stop by her restaurant.

"Good morning, my young friend."

"Good morning, Travis, some coffee?"

He nodded.

"I haven't seen you for a while. Have you been busy?" she asked.

"I am helping out some guys to realize a dream."

She placed the cup on the bar, grabbed a slice of cake, and put it in the plate.

"Just coffee, thanks."

Lisa smiled. "With our compliments."

It was the first time he could observe her during the daylight. She was so beautiful she looked like a painting.

"That's very kind of you."

He took the tray and went back to his usual table. There were no people at that time of the day, and he could not understand why such a girl was working there. She was just too different, and he could read this on her face.

"Did you sleep on that bench at the end?" She was just behind him, cleaning the nearby table.

"I took a walk."

"So you didn't stay there that night."

She was now standing before him, and it was as if she also wanted to look at him in the daylight. Two intense people, who had a lot in common with each other.

"Not during the last months of my life."

"Matt? I am taking my ten minutes break, okay?"

Matt put his thumb up and Lisa went up to Travis.

"May I take seat?"

"Sure."

"I enjoyed last night, you know?"

"I'm glad to hear that."

"I never stayed talking at night along the Thames. It was wonderful to see the lights on the other side of the river. I should have gone there more often."

"One night is different from many. Let it be just one, enjoy the show and leave, thinking that you would like to see it again," Travis said.

His smile faded, and Travis didn't look like the dear old man she had offered the cake to.

"Yes," she said, "you are right. Much better to leave the table a moment before your stomach is full."

He liked those words. He would have answered the same.

"I have a question for you," Travis said.

"Go on."

"Why is a girl like you wasting her time working in a bar?"

"Because this girl needs to pay her bills. Can I ask you a question?"

It was the minimum he could accept from her. "Sure, Lisa."

"Why does a person like you spend his nights on a bench along the Thames?"

They recognized each other. They both understood each other's secret.

"Life is strange, don't you think? Often things don't have a reason."

"I agree." She was thoughtful.

"Did he ever call back?" Travis asked her.

"He doesn't have my phone number."

It was clear she was thinking about him and she answered without even turning. "This is why you are staring at the void?"

Right, that's why.

"Just right," she said.

"Who was the person you were waiting for?" he asked. He said it without invading her space.

"A beautiful person. A special person. Just like you."

"I cannot remind you of anyone," Travis said, "because there is no one who remembers me."

No, this is not true, Lisa thought, *you remind me of Nicholas.*

"If I stared at his eyes, I could find his look in yours…" she said that convincingly and Travis was surprised.

"What's so special about that person that takes so much of your thoughts?"

"His confidence perhaps or his passion for art."

"Are you in love with him?"

She sighed melancholically. "What do you think?" she turned towards him and looked at him.

"Anyone who could get your emotions is someone who has a lot to give."

"Are you married?" she asked.

She was impertinent, but it was the only way to get him to talk.

"Not anymore," he said.

Interesting answer to tease a woman's curiosity.

"I see," she said. "I guess you have a great story to tell, dear Travis."

"We all have something to say. Isn't it the same for you?" she laughed.

"What will you give me if I disclose my secret?" she asked.

"I don't have that much to give you, but I can listen if you wish."

"Tell me about the children you have. I'm sure you have some. You would be a great father."

A game between two people who knew they looked at things the same way. It was Travis's turn to talk.

"A boy and a girl."

"Are you still in touch with them?" she asked.

Travis glanced down, but there was no sadness on his face, just resignation.

"They will be forever a piece of my heart."

"Sorry, I didn't know."

"To tell you the truth, I don't even know where they are."

He never wanted to talk about this with Alex, but now he was ready to do that with Lisa, someone he had met on a bench in the middle of nowhere. From there, out of the blue, something was pushing them to talk for a moment, something that would have ended without even starting or leaving any memory. That was why they were both talking, as they both felt it wouldn't last.

"Life is a wheel that spins and, sooner or later, what you give and what you get balance each other out." She said that to give him a little hope, but Travis let a sarcastic smile appear on his face.

"It's a wheel that spins, that rolls on a street, and goes away from you. That's life."

I, Destiny

She changed expression and thought about Nicholas again, about her date and about the fact that he hadn't come. Then she thought about Alex, about the love she had taken away from him, and she understood the sense of Travis's words: the wheel was spinning and was going away from her.

"Shouldn't I dream anymore?" she asked.

"You dream if you are not strong enough to face reality."

These were words she always thought about, but she felt hurt hearing them from Travis.

"I thought I would find more strength in a person of your age who spent six years I don't know where, and to whom life didn't give much, yet took away a lot." There was no anger in her words, but just disappointment. "How long do you think you are going to live?"

"It depends on the dream I still want to dream about," he answered.

"So, I don't think you have many dreams left," Lisa said.

He didn't seem affected by those words.

"Don't you say anything?" Lisa continued.

"You remind me so much myself when I was younger," Travis said.

She was bewildered. "Are you pulling my leg?"

"No, I was wasting my time behind my dreams, but now I don't have any time for those who cannot become true."

Matt came closer.

"Lisa, it's been more than half an hour."

"I've got to go. I get off at three, and then I think I'll go to the Tate to enjoy a moment."

She kissed him on his cheek and went to Matt at the bar. Travis stood up and left. He could feel the wind, and drops of rain fell on his face. *What a beautiful girl,* he thought. *She would be perfect for Alex.*

* * *

The painting wasn't there anymore. They took it away. Lisa saw one of the employees of the Tate.

"Where is *Swinging*?"

"It's not here, Miss."

"I can see that." She was nervous. "But why?"

"They have probably given it back for an exhibition at another gallery."

"Would it be possible to know when they will bring it back here?"

The man shrugged, then turned and went away.

And now? The only hope to see Nicholas again had disappeared, along with that painting. She fumed, took a look around, and felt the anxiety growing in the middle of her chest. She would have done something, but she didn't know what to do. What else would he like? She saw another Tate employee passing by and she went up to him.

"Could you please tell me the names of some of the artists of *Kandinsky*'s period?"

"Do you mean a contemporary?"

"Something similar."

"Lets see...*Mondrian*, *Marc*, maybe *Lissitzky*. These are the first names that come to mind."

"Where can I find them?"

"On this floor. Straight ahead, in the last room."

She walked fast, her only goal to stand before those paintings, but she didn't like any of those she saw. She turned, without moving away from the wall. There were people coming and going, and she hoped she would see him.

She spent two hours without seeing anyone who reminded her of his eyes. Tired, disappointed, frustrated, she went back to the stairs, passed by the bookstore, but then she gave up. She couldn't find another Nicholas because there wasn't another *Kandinsky*.

She walked along the river, tapping on the railing with her hand. A young couple passed by her hugging each other, while on a bench an old man held the hand of his woman. It was so sad to see love all around and not find it inside. Her smile faded a few metres afterwards. She missed that emotion so much, because there was nothing beyond love that could fill her life. And Nicholas wasn't there that day.

She went home nervous and her life appeared soulless, like the restaurant she was working for during a rainy Monday night. She took the box and pulled out the pictures, looking at them for no longer than a few seconds, when the box fell down on the floor. Just Alex's picture was left in her hands. She looked at it and turned it over and saw Alex's words transformed into emotion for her. It was so beautiful and delicate...

To Lisa...
Intense, delicate, the perfume comes out of the bedroom
The window is open and the fresh breeze of the night
comes easily through
I imagine the moon, I imagine a lake
I imagine myself in its crystal-cold water
like a black and white movie of a century ago

A bit of that perfume and the movie has colour
A bit of emotion and the movie has soul
In the bedroom, the woman is sleeping
My eyes close, I am dreaming with her'

They were words transformed into poem, and the obsession for Nicholas suddenly faded. She fell asleep on the sofa, holding that picture and dreaming of Alex.

* * *

It was a bad surprise not to find *Swinging*. There was nothing on the wall, not even a painting that could fill the empty space left by the lines and the colour of the other one. He saw a staff member and asked him the same question Lisa had asked before, just a couple of hours before.

"When will it be possible to admire that painting again?"

Same question, same answer. The employee, barely twenty years old, remembered that question and Lisa as well.

"The contemporary artists are straight ahead, in the last room."

He had hoped for a different answer.

"It doesn't matter. Thanks anyway."

The guy went back to the chair and Nicholas walked towards the exit. It was the first time since he had been going to the Tate Modern that he wasn't there for a painting. He was there hoping to see Lisa again, since he didn't have the courage to go where she worked to say hello. The tension left him, and the depression made his legs weak. He left the gallery and saw the familiar show that he had learned by rote: the Thames, the same noises, the same people, and his loneliness. It would have been better if they had never met.

He arrived at Waterloo Bridge and saw what was left of the little bookshop market. All the lights were switched off, all was motionless, and so sadly lifeless. Something told him that, without her, it would have been like reading a book without words. *Damned emotions!* He felt bad whenever he felt any. It wasn't worthwhile, better to remain alone and purify his soul through a masterpiece, like the painting he had almost completed. He went beyond those deserted stalls, when he was hit by something inexplicable, something he couldn't hear, see, or touch. He was bewildered and turned, as if he felt a strange presence, something or someone was observing him. Then the discomfort took shape in the face of an old man who was staring at him. Nicholas felt deep fear. He didn't know where that strange person had come from. He had just appeared out of the blue, but through the features of his face, the intensity of his eyes, he saw his wasted years, a part of his life spent hating the world and feeding his madness. He closed his eyes and forced himself not to think about it. Then, as if by magic, the old man was no longer there. He looked around but could not see him anywhere. He breathed deeply and felt a strong desire to go back home and paint.

Back home in the studio he knelt at the feet of his creation. He closed his eyes and let the music enter his soul, and then, with the brush in the hands out of instinct, he drew what he thought his work needed to turn into a masterpiece. He finished after an hour, exhausted, but with a total sense of peace. He smiled, imagining Lisa's joy for his gift.

But then, suddenly, the anxiety and the pain resurfaced, destroying that peaceful moment. The medicine. He had to take the medicine! He ran to the bathroom, grabbed the box, and swallowed the pill, while desperation broke his heart in two.

"Why?" He shouted out loud.

He could not stand it any longer. That tension would quickly kill him. He prayed for the pill to take effect, before the monster came back to run his brain. He had to resist; he could not give up now that he had almost finished his painting.

"Father, help me!"

He had never said that name in those long six years, but desperation forced him to say it out loud. He didn't and he could not go back to the clinic, because he felt that he would never come out of it again. The calm, only the calm could help him. The painting, where was the painting? He desperately needed to see it. He went back to the room and looked at the canvas. The calm was there, in the lines and the colours and all he had to do was to find it. He knelt down, joined his hands and prayed.

"Help me father, I beg you, I don't want to die!"

The canvas listened to his prayer, and the lines and the colours became the eyes of a man he knew well, but one he had never accepted. They were Travis's eyes, and they were looking at him with infinite tenderness. They caressed his soul and made him feel calm. He stopped crying, and the monster eventually stopped pushing from inside his chest. He understood. It was his father the old man who had been speaking with Lisa.

* * *

"See you tomorrow," Lisa said, as she left the restaurant.

Matt and Jean had become her friends. She finished her shift at twenty minutes after three. Twenty minutes more of that miserable life. *Bad sign,* she thought. If she continued like that her existence could become worse than what she had with Klaus. She didn't go to the Tate. It didn't make any sense. Nicholas would not be back because the painting wasn't there. So she decided to go to the little bookshop market looking for something about Shakespeare. She arrived at Waterloo Bridge and cast a glance at the bookstalls. There were so many things she would have happily bought, but she didn't have time, as someone spoke before she could make it.

"Lisa."

Nicholas was standing behind her, and she felt paralyzed by her emotion.

"I would never expect to see you here," was all she managed to say.

"*Kandinsky* wasn't there so I thought I better take a walk."

She liked his voice immensely. It was firm, yet warm. It was deep, yet sweet.

"I know. I was there a few days ago, because I thought it was the only way to see you again."

Nicholas went closer.

"I'm sorry."

She looked at him and his eyes reminded her of Travis's eyes.

"It would have been nice to see you. It was a wonderful night."

"I couldn't make it. I had to work on something."

He handed her the plastic tube.

"What's this?"

She was innocent and romantic, like a girl who receives a gift and like a woman who sees again the person she had looked for, for so long. And then she was happy, because Nicholas had thought about her.

"No, not here," he said, "better on that bench."

They were in front of the National Theatre, on a beautiful, sunny day.

"You can open it now."

She was completely out of control as the emotions overwhelmed her. She held the tube, took off the cap, and pulled out the canvas with gentleness. She put down the tube on the bench and with a shining smile began to unwind it. Nicholas could love her and imagine her forever, as she was touching the canvas that his soul had painted for her. But something didn't go as it had to, and Lisa's smile faded.

"Something's wrong?"

A ten-year-old boy could definitely do better. She couldn't understand or feel anything at all. The lines and the colours entered each other in a neurotic fit. They looked like arrows hitting balls made by many different colours, without the whole to have any sense of drama or harmony. Nicholas was petrified. The tension grew stronger, attacked his muscles, the calm turned into anxiety, and the anxiety turned into fear.

"What's that?" Lisa asked.

It was just an innocent question. But it had the effect of a stab in his chest. He felt pain and shame. He shouldn't have shown her the most beautiful side of himself. He blushed, and the anger made him sweat.

"That is you," he whispered.

"Me?"

She thought she hadn't observed the painting carefully. She examined the canvas with more attention, trying to find something that could justify his words, but there was nothing painted on the canvas that was her.

"These are my emotions for you."

The noise of those words was even worse than his first answer. If those were his emotions, then what he felt for her was clearly a hallucination, a nightmare perhaps. She tried hard to hide what she thought and smiled.

"Do you like it?"

Nicholas had lost all of his confidence. He was timorous and nervous as she had never seen him before.

"It's original. Thank you, Nicholas, you have been very nice."

It was a different smile, with no intensity. Completely different from the smile she had before she looked at the painting. Nicholas felt uncomfortable. She put the canvas back in the tube, and it was as if she had closed Nicholas into a cage. He could stand it no longer. He stood up and walked the metres that separated him from the railing along the riverbank. He leaned against it and stared at a point in the water.

You shouldn't have done it, Nicholas. She is like all the others. I knew it, and she is making fun of you!

It was coming back. His other self was there and pushing from inside his brain. Himself, his worst enemy.

"Nicholas, it is really very beautiful."

She leaned against the railing, just next to him, but the spell was broken. Nicholas wanted to throw himself into the river rather than show her his ill self. She had betrayed him, and now he knew there was no one left he could love. He turned, and his expression suddenly changed.

"You are just like any girl. You women are all alike! I am always right.

It is not worth loving a woman, as they always do the way they want." His eyes were full of anger, and his voice had become screeching and acute. "Please...go away..." he said with his eyes full of tears. He was desperately fighting against the monster inside, but that voice kept growing stronger and more persistent than ever.

You can't push me back into the darkness! I am here, to protect you, and I am the one who is in charge!

Lisa was shocked, incredulous, and remained still, speechless, while Nicholas clung to the railing, desperately fighting against himself.

"Nicholas! Return to your senses, I beg you!"

But Nicholas couldn't listen to her. He was split in two and each half was trying to take the upper hand. Lisa stepped back, hesitating. She wanted to run away, ask for help, hug him, stay, but she cried. And in the meantime, he was looking at her with eyes glowing with a sinister light.

Can't you see? She doesn't have the courage to stay next to you! She is looking at you as if you have the plague! And you even gave her your painting!

He fell to his knees, covered his face with his hands, and burst out in an endless cry.

"Leave me in peace...please..."

He managed to turn and look at her. He was a destroyed man and his hands were holding the railing as if they were holding the bars of the cage in which he had always been locked.

"Lisa...help me..."

* * *

Lisa was waiting near the door. She had never experienced anything like that in all her life, and now she was crying, destroyed by the desperation she had seen in his eyes. Matt and Jean had decided to come and were waiting with her, to give her some consolation. The doctor came out of the room.

"We managed to get in touch with the clinic from the pills we found in his trousers."

"How is he?"

"Under sedation."

"Is he seriously ill?"

She was about to collapse from the tension.

"He spent four years in a psychiatric clinic."

"What does that mean?"

"I just spoke with his doctor. It is quite a complex case. He can stay in control with his pills, but a wrong dose together with significant emotional stress, can lead to situations like the one you experienced today."

"Will they take him back to the clinic?"

The doctor shrugged.

"The specialist will come to see him tomorrow. I can't say anything more."

She thought about him, about his suffering, and she didn't feel like leaving him alone. She went to see him every day. And any time she went, she carried the canvas he had given her with her. She would always carry it with her.

"There is a visitor for you, Nicholas."

She entered the room and saw him lying on the bed. He was wearing a jogging suit and he seemed relaxed.

"Lisa!"

He was happy to see her.

"I spoke with the doctor. You'll be here for a bit, just long enough to make some necessary checks and review the dosage of your medicine." But she said this in a whisper, as if she didn't believe her own words.

Nicholas held her hand tightly.

"Why are you doing all this for me?" he asked.

She tried hard to hold back her tears, and this was enough to let a beautiful smile light up her face.

"This is a part of you, Nicholas…I will keep this canvas forever."

She kissed his cheek and she felt close to him like never before.

"Where are you going?" he asked.

She turned. "I'll be back soon."

She returned after a while, with a box that looked like a gift.

"Is that for me?"

"Why don't you stop asking and open it?" she said.

His smile reminded her of that of a child. The box contained a set of colours and a book about *Vassily Kandinsky*.

"This is the most beautiful gift I have ever received."

Lisa was touched and looked at the man she would have liked to love like a woman, with sadness in her heart.

"Why do you do that?" he asked her again.

"Because you are a special person, who doesn't have anything to demonstrate to anyone, and I love you just the way you are. Don't ever forget it."

She saw him smiling. For the first time ever, happiness was inside of him and not on a mask. He could not stay in bed. He got up and walked to the window to assemble the easel and hang the canvas on it. Lisa looked at him and felt joy in her heart.

*　*　*

They dismissed him two weeks afterwards and he found Lisa waiting for him, happy to see him again but, more important, happy to see him eventually calm.

"Get in the cab, Nicholas. I'll go say goodbye to the doctor."

The doctor was waiting for her near the entrance. He wanted to tell her something.

"Thank you so much," Lisa said.

The doctor shook her hand and held it tightly.

"We should check how he progresses on a regular basis." Then he looked at her and tried to send her a message. "Have faith."

Lisa felt the anxiety pushing the joy out of her heart.

"What do you mean by that?"

"That sometimes there is no reason for the things that happen. They just happen."

She started to tremble and the emotions overwhelmed her again. "I'm afraid I don't understand you, doctor."

"Something that we call exception just happened. The continued tension between two dominant personalities ended up destroying them both. Of fundamental help, though, was the first visit he received from his mother and sister after six years of detachment as we managed to track them down and convinced them that he needed their help. Their forgiveness for his actions was the final blow for the evil side of his personality. He now feels he no longer has enemies."

Lisa remained silent. The sense of those words was not clear to her yet, but the doctor helped her understand.

"We are just at the beginning of the healing process, but I hope his real self will eventually come out."

"Do you mean he will get better?" she asked, almost shaking.

"Hoping doesn't mean we will see what we hope, but from the first exams, it seems there could be the conditions for what we would call a return to normality."

"He will never have those crises again?"

"We need to be patient and, more important, pray. But now you should go and enjoy the miracle of your gift."

She looked so confused.

"A…miracle?"

"Yes. A miracle."

The doctor's smile warmed her like a ray of sunlight. She turned with her heart beating fast and with just one thought. She had to go home, and maybe she would know.

* * *

"It's so cosy in here," he said when she opened the door.

"Thank you."

Lisa left the canvas and the box on the sofa and led Nicholas with his backpack to the room where he would sleep.

"This is your bed. Make yourself comfortable, and don't worry about anything."

He took possession with enthusiasm, just like an innocent child would do. And like any innocent child, Nicholas had not killed anyone six years back. It was the evil Nicholas that made him believe he had. Lisa turned and saw him busy exploring his new world, as if that adventure was the beginning of a beautiful holiday. She went back to the room and remembered the doctor's words. She could not resist. She took off the cap and pulled the canvas out of the tube.

The emotion in the painting was strong, and even though the painting would never find a place on the wall of the Tate, she would spend a whole day to admire it. There were no more faults or muddles of lines, but just the face of an ageless old man, with silver hair and a long, white beard, who seemed to smile at her tenderly. That painting could give peace and harmony to anyone. Just what Nicholas seemed to have eventually found.

She went back to work a week later, happy like never before. Matt and Jean asked her about Nicholas and so did the manager of the restaurant. They were all happy to hear the good news.

"I almost forgot, Lisa. That old man, remember? He just came by."

Lisa nodded. She had completely forgotten about Travis.

"He left this for you."

She took the envelope and opened it.

'My young friend,

It is an immense pleasure for me to invite you to the show that will take place at the Open Air Theatre in Regent's Park next week. I would love you and whoever will have the pleasure to join you, to come.

Looking forward to seeing you

Travis'

THIRTY-ONE

Joe took a peek behind the stage. The guys were quivering and focused on their cues. There was half an hour left and then the show would start. He closed his eyes and breathed deeply.

"What's up, Joe?"

It was Alex. Nothing could ruin that night. Acting was the most natural thing in the world for him. Joe smiled and caressed him.

"Nothing, son, just my years and my memories."

Alex could not stand Joe's melancholy. "Joe, this is a night of joy, and I want to see happy people. Don't even think for a moment of ruining your life with your stupid thoughts! The past is the past, and your life goes on!"

Alex was right. Who knew what would have happened to his old theatre without Alex giving him help. Better not to think about it; it was much wiser to listen to Alex's advice.

"Judie, I want you to be ready in ten minutes," Alex said.

"Okay."

"Scott?"

He was sitting on the steps of a wooden stair and could not hide his tension. "All fine," Scott said.

He didn't deceive Alex. It was clear that the anxiety was burning his energy away.

"You will be a star, and you will be a millionaire in a year's time."

Alex managed to make Scott smile. Judie was ready; he saw her coming. He lifted his thumb and she nodded. He started to count the time separating him from the entrance on stage where he would eventually find relief from his tension. That was the moment he always dreamt about, and he knew he could not fail.

"The theatre is overbooked," Joe said.

"Come on, guys, ten more minutes. Judie?"

The girl turned again towards him. She was tense and afraid she wouldn't make it. Alex noticed that and went closer, looking at her intensely.

"You are too important for all of us."

Then he turned, leaving her alone with the effect of those words.

"Five minutes."

Joe's voice sounded like a punch in the stomach. The adrenaline started to flow, and the tension increased. Judie was walking nervously back and forth nonstop. Scott was punching the wall, while Alex was the only one who was not reviewing his role.

"One minute to go, guys. I'm going on the stage."

Joe was more nervous than anyone else. If he had waited another instant, he would have exploded. Alex thought about his past, the old theatre, the old cues, and the old loves and threw everything behind his shoulders. There was no time left for anything. The moment was there, on the stage, waiting to be caught. His life would either change now or it wouldn't change any more.

The lights faded, and the night and the stars lit up the stage. A last glance, the confidence to make it and the success would come. The lights designed a circle, and Joe entered in it. It was his turn to kick off the show.

"Good evening."

His pace was studied, allowing the audience to enter the dimension of the show.

"A light, by definition, cannot be dark."

That sentence had the desired effect, and the pause that followed was an invention from Joe. The guys were listening and in their minds they were already characters.

"A light, by definition, doesn't hide secrets, yet on the contrary, it is destined to unveil them. The light we will talk about tonight is a different one, a light that makes us blind, but which at the same time, runs away and hides in the darkness. I don't want to add anything else, but just the hope that at the end of this story, something inside all of us will eventually change."

The highest seat was occupied by the sky, and from there the stage seemed to shine like a star. The silence overwhelmed the theatre, and Alex was the first to enter the stage.

He walked confidently, determined, aware that things would go the way he felt, the way he wanted, and the tension slowly lifted. A dim light from the base of the stage barely lit him, and the drama of that moment was all on his face.

"Like a light I remember you, indistinct, one that has turned dark, that doesn't shine…"

He spoke those words in a sort of trance. It wasn't his voice, but they were his thoughts coming through the one who now spoke. He continued, without stopping, alternating pauses and reflections to a continuous crescendo, to allow for peace and joy. Nobody moved, nobody breathed. The beauty of those words hit everyone deeply in their hearts. The dimension of that monologue went beyond reality, beyond a mere play or a title that could never be the same again. It was Alex the beauty. It was Alex the intensity of that monologue. It was himself who was on stage and his thoughts were using his body to be comprehended.

And finally it was over. His face was wet with his tears and the eyes of the audience were all on him. He let the heart of everyone beat to the rhythm of his words. He bowed and thought he heard the applause, but there was just silence around him. No one wanted to wake up; no one wanted the dream to be over. He opened his eyes, and it was as if Time had suddenly stopped. Not a noise, not a breath. An indistinct silhouette stood up from his seat and Alex tried to understand. But he struggled, because the sweat running down his forehead stung his eyes, not letting him see. Suddenly, the reflex of the silver hair faded and then he understood. It was the old man, the same old man he had met once in the little bookshop market, who now was looking at him with a smile. Then came the applause, growing, and growing again, until the audience was on its feet in the final standing ovation.

* * *

Lisa was there, seated with Nicholas, watching the scene. It was a part of her memories to enter the stage. It was a piece of her life that acted. Her heart started to beat when she recognized the actor's face.

She was crying and Nicholas could not understand why. She was listening to those wonderful words, while the tears streamed down her face. The only meaning that mattered was the present and what she felt for him.

She was the dark light Alex was talking about; she understood it now, and she had run away stealing his love. She felt miserable and began to sob.

'You wanted to get it all and you left nothing in my hands…'

Yes, she took everything. She took his heart, his illusion, his life, without leaving him anything. Not even a memory. Not even a piece of herself.

She deserved to end like that. She deserved to meet Klaus, to be treated like a slut, and to fall in love with Nicholas and his madness. She deserved all of it, because she was worth only this.

She tried to regain her composure, while the unreality of what she saw, of Alex, of Joe who were on the stage without even knowing she was there, like any spectator, made her hope she was dreaming.

Alex bowed. He was just now collecting a small part of the applause he deserved from his life. He had never changed. He had always remained simply himself. She clapped, until her hands hurt. Alex would never be hers again.

* * *

The monologue was over. Alex remained on the stage, held his breath, and looked at the audience. Many faces were hidden in the dark recesses of the theatre, many hopes were hidden in those faces, and there was but one destiny for any one of them.

He wore a tight black T-shirt, and the sweat ran down his temples. He knew it, he felt it. He was a great actor. He closed his eyes and bowed again to hear the applauses. He wanted to get them all for himself, and this time he didn't need to imagine. The audience was real, and they seemed to never end.

He went behind the scenes. The emotion had made Joe's face blush, wet Judie's face with tears, and had given back joy to Scott. They didn't tell him anything, but they remained still, waiting for him to speak. He dried his face and his arms and then, eventually, they heard what they were looking for.

"We won't fail, guys. We won't fail."

He limited himself to staring at them and transmitting the determination he had in taking his drama to success. They were ready, and he could see that from the tension he read on their faces. It was their turn, now, and they knew they could not fail.

The show was in full swing. There was no more space left for thought. What counted was the action and anyone who had a fundamental role. Alex was the first to be back on the stage. The makeup now made him look like an old man. A bench, the river, the other side of London. The story of Travis was about to begin.

* * *

Nicholas watched Alex bowing as he was applauded. Lisa was right next to him, but she hadn't spoken since the young actor entered the stage. He really liked the monologue, but he could not stop looking at Lisa. She was tense, nervous, trying hard to suffocate something that would have exploded anyway. And then he saw her tears, the light in her eyes. It was love that he read on her face.

The monologue was original and vibrant. So he concentrated on the story the show now offered. It was just the life of an old man. It couldn't involve much of a surprise. At most, he would just like it.

Scott entered the stage. He was acting in Nicholas's role. It was the classic hate-love relationship between father and son. Then the words began to flow, evoking Nicholas's memories, like the names that were too specific to just be accidental. Travis and Nicholas. Like his father, like himself. And then he remembered Lisa's words.

An old friend gave me two tickets for the show...

The images and the tension that was building inside of him didn't make him feel bad this time. Travis's eyes had already saved him once. Travis was that old man on the stage. And it was Travis who was Lisa's old friend.

The emotion of recognition overwhelmed him. Incredulity, scepticism and, at the end, the love of a son for his father played through Nicholas as the play went on. Yes, Travis had really suffered during those long six years. He had spent his life sleeping under a bridge, thinking about his mistakes, while Destiny took everything away from him. He could not have suffered more.

Nicholas closed his eyes. That moment was his. Lisa had regained her composure and the passion and the support for Alex's drama had overtaken her initial emotion. But the show belonged to his father. Every cue, every thought, and every pause the actor took, felt like the blood in his veins.

Love is suffering. He would have loved to have his brushes and at least one canvas with him to transform in painting the emotions he now felt. It wasn't too late to make up a life again, like the one his father had just started.

He looked around. He would have liked to see him, and every profile, every head with a light touch of grey, made his wish grow stronger. He held Lisa's hand tight, but Lisa could not understand why. They were two perfect strangers, and both were in love with part of the show.

* * *

Alex and the guys gave all they had, and the audience could feel it. Eventually the dark light came, overwhelming the old man and all the love he had for his family. It was a violent light, blinding, yet human in its evil. The light came from the soul. That was why it was dark.

Travis understood and began to cry, to throw six years of pain out of his soul, when a hand, light and warm, caressed his silver hair. Travis looked up and could not say a word. The same old man that he saw once at the bookshop market and who made him feel powerless, was now looking at him. He had an endless tenderness in his eyes, and when he smiled, he made him feel warmth that repaid him for the six years spent in the cold of his loneliness.

* * *

The show ended. Lisa was crying, because the intensity of love she felt for Alex resurfaced. Nicholas was destroyed, because it was he who had condemned his father to spend six years under a bridge. And on the stage, Alex was exhausted. The success was there in that theatre and he had eventually grabbed it.

"Sorry, Nicholas," Lisa said.

She didn't tell him why, but suddenly he saw her standing and running towards the stage. He had also begun to understand, but he didn't have the courage, or the hope, to look for his father. He tried one last time to look among the many heads and find one that time had made to shine like silver, and he found it. It was the old man, the same old man he had painted on his canvas.

He stood up and the instinct, or perhaps Destiny, pushed him to follow the old man outside in the park, nearby the lake, next to a bench, which reminded him of the night he had seen Lisa talking to an old tramp. The moon was high in the sky and caressed the night with its light.

He looked at the other side of the lake and thought about the show at the theatre. And he felt he wanted to live and not die attached to his memories.

* * *

Tears soaked Travis' face. He saw Lisa, his young friend, running, crying, and laughing to the stage where Alex was enjoying the applause of the audience. That was love, and he felt it without even understanding why. It wasn't a story of him. It was the story of Alex. It was the story of Lisa.

He left the theatre trembling, with the emotion that could have broken him in two at any moment. He remained looking at the moon, while the warmth of the hand of the old man led him outside of the theatre.

Alex opened his eyes and saw the spectators standing. They were clapping, emotional about the wonderful end of the play. Among them there were two more pieces of the puzzle Destiny was playing with that night, two pieces unknown to Alex but perfectly known to both Travis and Nicholas: Lucy and Beth, in tears, while holding each other's hand. The spectators all supported him; they were all trying to catch his eyes to give him a smile. His dream could not end any better. He was happy, and the joy lit his face. Free. That's how he felt. The air of that wonderful night caressed him and made him feel part of the sky. He wanted to fly towards the clouds to look for the light that had stopped shining, to let it shine again. But there was no need anymore. The light was now inside of him.

In silence, along the lake, with the melancholy in his soul—that chapter of Travis's life had lasted six years and had just ended on the stage of the Open Air Theatre. Travis felt like throwing himself into the lake and trying to at least follow the drops and discover their secret. He had arrived. The silence had been his best friend since he had left the theatre. He sat on the bench and looked at that old man intensely. He was smiling at him and hadn't stopped since he had taken his hand.

A wonderful moon was shining high in the sky, but there was no more sign of the presence of that old man. A man was standing still, not far from him, with his back turned towards him, hidden in the shade.

* * *

Lisa arrived at the foot of the stage. Alex was just a couple of metres away. She remained still and felt a piercing pain. It was love. Alex looked up, towards the sky. He could see the stars and, maybe, seeing them shining, he thought about the person he wished was with him on the stage that night.

She would have liked to jump up there, hug him, and look into his eyes, but she did not have the courage. For the first time in her life she feared rejection by someone. She thought about Nicholas, about what she saw in his eyes that day and about his desire for life. And then she broke those psychological chains and went towards him.

Alex had just revealed his wish to the stars. He could still see the people. Some of them were still there, while others were leaving the place, happy to have seen such a beautiful show. He would keep that moment with him forever.

Lisa was patiently waiting. She was looking at him with hope in her heart. The event of the play had split his life into two parts: what had happened until that moment and what would happen from that moment—

Lisa!

He saw her, and he saw her eyes, her lips, and her short hair. It couldn't be possible; it couldn't be real! He was petrified, without being able to move, while his heart was beating crazily.

She was looking at him, smiling. She was hoping and moved her lips without saying a word. He thought he was dreaming, because in the words she mouthed but had not spoken, he read what he always wanted to hear. "Alex, I love you…"

* * *

Nicholas knew Travis was behind him. The end of six years in exile from love would happen on a bench. He would have liked to turn, run towards him, hug him, and ask forgiveness, but he did not have the strength. A lump in his throat and his heart overwhelmed by the emotions were a tough hurdle to face. He loved his father with all his heart. That's why he had hated him for six years, because he had never been able to tell him.

Six years. Too much time had gone since that moment, and he didn't want to lose anymore. He turned, hoping not to collapse under the weight of his emotions and waited with hope in his heart.

Travis looked up. Eventually, the young man stopped, standing in front of him, so perhaps he could now enjoy the view of the lake.

The moon was shining and its light was intense. The young man who had been still, suddenly turned towards him, with his arms folded. Travis wanted to know who he was, but the moon was crazy that night. He lifted his hand above his eyes and tried to cover the moonlight with the palm of his hand.

It was like giving a bit of colour to a silhouette that the darkness made black like the night. It was a young man, quite strong, and he was looking at him with a strange persistence. Travis would have liked to stand up, go closer and ask him why, but he was just too tired. Maybe, if he waited, the young man would leave on his own.

Time went by and the young man remained, still looking at him. *Damned moon! It had to shine just that night!* The young man didn't make a move, while Travis was sitting on the bench and thinking. One more night full of thoughts could not hurt him. And so his mind enjoyed taking him back in time. One, two, three years earlier. Then a further jump backward, in a house, in a family, with Lucy, Beth and—

Nicholas!

Six years of emotions exploded in the middle of his chest. If he didn't die now, he could maybe still follow his dream. He was also looking at him now and the tension transmitted between them both. He had to try...he had to say that name. The light had stopped being dark. Destiny could not continue to play with him. No, it could not.

"Nicholas?"

The young man remained still. He covered his eyes with his hand and sighed. And, suddenly, Destiny stopped playing with him. Nicholas nodded, and Travis's tears spilled from his eyes.

* * *

The spectators left the theatre with a smile on their faces. It had been a play to remember, unexpectedly beautiful for a one night show. As the silence swallowed even the smallest noise, a pale light broke the darkness and lit up the stage again.

"Imagination, help me understand...now that everything is back to where I wished it would be many times, can I hope that Time stops and Destiny dies?"

Sweet Soul, he would have given his life to see everyone happy. I went back and I saw him trembling, on his knees, afraid of the answer.

"Destiny is like Time...it will never die."

Soul looked up and, for a moment, he thought it could be about her.

"Is it still you, Imagination?"

There was no answer. A tear ran down on his face and I felt his desperation. No, I couldn't leave him like that.

"It would be nice to dream forever and imagine that Time stops and Destiny dies, but it wouldn't be my story anymore...it would be yours. And this, until I exist, will never happen."

He was confused, almost lost, trying to understand.

"But...who are you?"

"I am Destiny."

The light on the stage of the Open Air Theatre faded and Soul slowly disappeared into the darkness.

* * *

There was nobody in South Bank that night. I walked tired, touched, thinking about my encounter with Soul and didn't realize I had arrived at Waterloo Bridge. I had my book with me. It was old, crumpled, and its pages, of a yellowish colour, revealed the sign of the times.

I held it tightly in my hands, and it was like feeling the hearts of Alex and Travis beating in unison in the last act of the show. I cast a last glance at it, placed it on an empty bookstall, and wrote these words on its cover:

I, Destiny

I turned and walked away, glad to have eventually found the right title for my story.

THE DARK LIGHT

Like a light I remember you, indistinct, one that has turned dark, that doesn't shine.

You are a phantom, but I keep thinking we are together.

It's a crazy dream, without reason, one that makes me aim, makes me want what I know I'll never get.

It's my emotion, if I see colours that don't shine.

It's in the emotion…that I am lost.

I want you, I hate you. The more I try to run away, the more I miss you.

Can you hear my heart? It beats because of love.

This was my gift for you.

But you decided and never said; you decided and ran away after stealing all my light and absorbing it into yours.

You wanted to take it all and you left nothing in my hands.

What remains is faded memory; it's a glow that slowly dies; it's the twilight of my love.

I think of you…and the memory remains of a ghost that hides again for not returning what it stole.

You deceived me and stole my feelings with the illusion of a fire that will never keep me warm.

I hope one day you'll stop, think, and return what you took away from me.

But let it happen soon; otherwise I'll turn my back on you, and I will run away forever.

That's life. It can be nice, it can be sad. It can empower you with love, deceive you and look at you with its detachment, hunt you while you run and try to hide.

What are you expecting when you stop and think about it?

That life comes back to you and asks to be forgiven?

At night, under a bridge, I have dwelt.

I was looking at the sky. I was looking at the stars. There weren't stars up there but lights that through the pillars have always been reflected.

I thought they might be stars, because I wanted to see them shining.

That night I slept beside the river, waiting for the snow to fall and make me dream.

I have stopped my heart, I have stopped thinking.

I have frozen into the cold my deepest thoughts.

I have listened to the silence. I have talked…and I have asked it why it never spoke with me before.

I have waited. I have wished…I have prayed that it could talk.

And the voice of silence began to whisper. It was sweet, and if I had not paid attention, I could have wasted the magic of that night.

I heard sounds that could not be that made me close to all the things it tried to tell me many times.

But anytime it spoke, I wasn't ready for its words. It's the things that you can see, but that don't exist that change the colour of a dark light and make you think that it can shine.

That was the way I thought of you.

You were a shade with the illusion of a glow. You were a dark light and you deceived me.

I should have been calm; I should have waited, to understand the things the river tried to say.

I would have learned to choose. I could have avoided mistakes.

Like the old man on that bench, when the snow began to fall.

An old man I will remember to tell another fairy tale.

It was a dark light that made him blind and threw him into his loneliness.

The same dark light has now blinded me.

Like an old man, under the bridge, I thought they were stars that I could see.

I look at him again.

He has a past that tries to hide within a drop inside the river.

It was so different before, he would have smiled, talked, and more.

But he's weak. He doesn't have the strength at all; he doesn't have a word to say…he doesn't have a place to go.

I do my best, my greatest effort, to recognize the drop that flows and keeps the secret I try to know…

It's the secret of a pain that will never let him rest; it's the secret of a dream that still keeps his hope alive.

I would like to be the silence and speak with him with sounds that can only give him tenderness.

I would like it if for one second he could look into my light.

My light will never hide; my light will always shine.

My light…is made of love.

ABOUT THE AUTHOR

Alessandro Abate devotes his time to his passion in writing and photography. His first novel *BLUE* was published in Italy in 1999, and his website *streetglimpses.com* displays some of his photos taken during his travels. Alessandro holds a Global Executive MBA at the Columbia Business School and London Business School and dreams of writing his third novel on a beautiful island somewhere in the Caribbean. Part of the proceeds of the sale of *I, Destiny* will be used for charity donations.
You can email Alessandro at I_Destiny@rocketmail.com

Printed in Great Britain
by Amazon